# MAVERICK

SANTA FE CHAPTER

GUARDIANS OF MAYHEM MC
BOOK 2

HOPE STONE

# BOOKS BY HOPE STONE

For the best deals on my books, buy AUTHOR-DIRECT on my new online bookstore!

**Guardians Of Mayhem MC Novella Series (Edgewood Chapter)**

Book 1 - Finn

Book 2 - Havoc

Book 3 - Axle

Book 4 - Rush

Book 5 - Red

Book 6 - Shadow

Book 7: Shaggy

**Guardians Of Mayhem MC Series**

**(Santa Fe Chapter)**

Book 1: Hawk

Book 2: Maverick

Book 3: Mustang

Book 4 - Gunner

Book 5 - Stunt

Book 6 - Mickey

Book 7 - Breaker

Book 8 - Rip

Book 9 - Crow

**Outlaw Souls MC Series**

Book 1 - Ryder

Book 2 - Pin

Book 3 - Trainer

Book 4 - Blade

Book 5 - Diego

Book 6 - Colt

Book 7 - Moves

Book 8 - Butch

**Vengeance & Vows Mafia Series**

Book 1 - Ruthless Vengeance

Book 2 - Ruthless Guardian

Book 3 - Ruthless Betrayal

Book 4 - Ruthless Vows

# CHARACTER LIST

## MEET THE MAIN CHARACTERS MENTIONED
## IN PREVIOUS BOOKS

### Guardians of Mayhem MC Members

**Pop** - President
**Red** - Vice President
**Finn** - Sgt. in Arms (son of Founder, Bulldog)
**Axle** - Enforcer
**Hawk** - Road Captain
**Dutch** - Secretary
**Scout** - Member
**Havoc -** Member
**Rush** - Member
**Shadow** - Member
**Funk** - Chaplain
**Quicks** - Prospect
**Shaggy** - Prospect
**Hawk** - Road Captain
**Maverick** - Member
**Mustang** - Member

### The Women of GOM:

**Chloe** – Finn's girl
**Rosemary** - Havoc's girl
**Brody** – Red's girl
**Penn** – Rush's girl
**Dara** – Shaggy's girl
**Bell** – Axle's girl
**Ava** – Shadow's girl
**Tara** - Hawk's girl
**Stephanie** - Maverick's girl
**Melissa** - Mustang's girl

## Former Members:

**Frank "Bulldog" Finley:** Founder (deceased)
**Hogan "Hoagie" Smits:** Secretary (deceased)
**Tony "Fat Tony" Jordan:** Treasurer (deceased)
**Bobby "Funk" Morrow:** Chaplain (deceased)

# 1

## MAVERICK

*Two and a half years ago...*

The room was dark—almost pitch black. I wanted to turn around and walk out of it, but I didn't. I kept walking forward with the same lanky stride that had been with me for a lifetime toward the large oak table. I ran a shaky hand through my sandy blond hair. I didn't know what to expect. I was approaching 40, and didn't need hair plugs, so I considered myself a lucky guy. I was in some place they called the church meeting room. Pop was sitting with a single candle burning in front of him. His arms were crossed over his chest, and he was mean mugging me, hard. I'd been in the spot for meetings before, but this time it was different. I could make out all the shadows of the Guardian members cloaked in the dark. They were all standing with their hands clasped together in front of them around the edges of the table that I was approaching.

The orange glow from the candle highlighted Pop's wrinkled face. It freaked me all the way out, and not too much in life had the capability to do that. There was a rifle sitting on the table in front, and I observed him put his hand over it and tap the metal. *Tip. Tap. Tip. Tap.* I didn't know what to expect from this motorcycle club. It was all a new experience for me. I just knew I had been called in because I was the bomb expert guy. The one that knew how to blow shit up, and I was pretty handy getting out of tight spots too.

Pop blew the candle out, and now the room was completely shrouded in darkness. "Tell me something, Maverick," Pop said in a deep, gravelly voice.

"Yeah, what is it? Whaddya wanna know?" My voice was casual, but the lump lodged in my throat was not. Shit was weird up in there. I'd defused bombs in Afghanistan with no trouble, and now I felt like I was about to shit my army fatigue cargo pants. Pop coughed as he grasped the gun in his hand, and all the members maintained their silence as I scanned their beady eyes in the darkness.

"I wanna know, are you a snitch?" He paused and started up again before I could answer. "Are you a cop?" Pop barked as he slammed his hand down on the table. He was laying it on real thick, and I couldn't take him seriously. I was the furthest thing from a cop that there ever was. I put my hand on my heart and started laughing hysterically. My laughter rang off the timbers of the walls. Nobody was laughing with me. "Well, are you? Answer the question!" he raged.

"Hell no. I'm not a cop." Pop lifted his hand off the gun, and the light flicked on, flooding the church room.

The guys cried out in unison as Pop raised his arms. "Well, welcome to the Guardians. You are officially a patch." He held up my patch, and I took it proudly. I heard the fizzle of beer as it gushed over my head and ran down into my eyes. I spat it out as the cool liquid ran over the top of my head. I was drowning in beer, not a bad way to go. One of the guys shoved one into my hand, and I wrapped my fingers around it. The guys started chanting. *"Protect thine own. Protect thine own."* The club motto was being belted out minus the harmonies. They wanted me to know that this was what I was now. I joined in and pumped my fist hard. "Protect thine own. Protect thine own!" The motto resonated with me, and I felt like I naturally embodied it. I'd served the United States of America for over a decade. That's all I did, protect other people, and I was still doing it. Axle slung his arm around me.

"Welcome to the club, Maverick. How's it feel?" He clamped his thick hand down on my shoulder as Pop came over and hugged me.

"Pretty damn good, man. I'm not going to lie. I feel real good about life in retirement. I have real kinship with you guys here. I love you all. This feels like pure magic to me. I would be fine in California floating around, but this is a better use of my skills. I'm glad I answered the call." I looked at Pop in appreciation.

"You couldn't go back there. You're one of us now. You're part of the brotherhood," Axle confirmed as he chugged down his beer. He was a big, solid dude, and reminded me a lot of Mustang. If you matched the two of them up together it would be tough to tell them apart from the back. Probably the circumference of Axle's arms were a little bigger. I would keep that to myself; I didn't want Mustang getting his little feelings hurt. He could be a little sensitive at times if you were talking about his skills and physical training. He handed another beer to me, and I reveled in receiving the honor of being a patch.

"You're right, I couldn't go back. It's been a sweet ride here, and I wouldn't have it any other way."

Hawk grinned and fist-bumped me, leaning in for the hug. "Hey, brother, you made it. You're one of us now. A

Guardian of Mayhem because that's exactly what we cause."
We clinked beers high in the air.

"I know. I know. I think I need to smoke a joint as part of
the celebration," I said. I had a little weed smoking habit
that I'd collected from the turmoil of the missions I'd taken
on outside of the Guardians, but it wasn't anything for
anyone to be worried about. A joint just helped me chill out
or celebrate—one of the two.

That was the official day I became a Guardian, and it
was a great day.

The club was in full swing. Axle was strolling through the
warehouse whistling with a wrench in his hand. Hawk was
holding maps in one hand and a coffee in the other. He was
wearing army fatigue cargos like I often did, and he smiled
when he saw me coming his way.

"We meeting in the lunchroom?" I asked.

"You know it" was Hawk's chipper reply. He seemed a lot
happier now that Clint was out of the way. He and Tara were
a sweet couple, and I hated that they had this cloud hanging
over their relationship.

I walked into the cool air-conditioned room and saw that
Mustang and Gunner were already in there. I clasped hands
with both my brothers as a greeting. "Hey, whassup, Gunner,
Mustang? You guys are looking good. I haven't seen you in a
few weeks," I said to them. To get from adrenaline-fueled
missions with three other men only to not have anything
going on was unusual for me. I was a dynamic individual, so
the missions fueled me. I was used to the high-octane world
of high pressure with bombs.

"We haven't had any missions on. From having two to

three a day, it feels so strange. I don't know what to do with myself you know," Gunner mentioned as I squeezed his shoulder.

"You rocking up to the gun range to shoot? Keeping that trigger finger happy?" I asked. I worried about Gunner sometimes. He needed a mission to focus on like a junkie needed heroin.

"Every Friday lunchtime if I can fit it in. So far so good. I've still got a pretty high accuracy rate," he stated in a monotone voice. I wanted Gunner to get a girlfriend so he could divert his focus from accuracy rates. That's what seemed to bring a smile to his face, and I thought that might be a little on the sad side.

"I've been looking for more action too, but hey, can't complain that the city is getting cleaned up. That's gotta be a good thing, huh?" I said.

"It is. That's what I wanted to talk to you about. The missions have started to slow down. We've done a great job helping out, and the narcotics unit is calling it a win on the war on drugs for now. We've got a breather. They do want us on deck, but for the moment we are in cruise mode until any others pop up."

"Cool," I said as I grabbed a water bottle out of the fridge.

"Sort of... One problem replaces another. Wildcard is sniffing around the club. He called Pop the other day asking him for $100K. Can you believe the old fucker?" Hawk snorted.

"No way, man! 100K. Why? What is he on? He can barely walk straight, poor old guy. He needs some of that good California weed I got. That will really get him tapped in." I made the motion to my face as if I was sparking a joint up, and the crew laughed.

"Who knows? He's on some sort of rampage. Old beef from back in the day," Hawk said in an off-handed way.

"How does that affect anything? We can't do anything about him," Mustang said in a begrudging tone.

Hawk shrugged his shoulders. "You're right, we can't. He's annoying, and the last time he was here he caused a scene."

"Speaking of scenes, you and your girl all right? Is she back on track?" My eyebrows lowered as I whispered under my breath.

Hawk rubbed the back of his neck. His hair was a little longer these days, so he had to brush it out of his eyes. He blew out an annoyed breath and looked at me. "She is so-so. Most days are pretty good, but those 10 percent she is a little shaky. She has nightmares, sweats and stuff. I've been with her through it all. She's going to be okay in the end. I wish she'd never met him."

"Nah. It's turned out as it should. If she wasn't with Clint, you would never have met her."

"That's true and a good perspective to look at it from." Hawk absorbed what I was saying and sipped more of his coffee in contemplation.

"I'm glad you guys are sticking out together. That's good news. Love. That's the cure for the world," I declared, even though I'd been unlucky in the department. I'd even been married once in a shotgun wedding. That didn't work out so well. She left me when she discovered how much I was away with special forces work. Still didn't stop me believing, and that was a good thing.

Mustang snickered. "You know a lot about that cure, don't you? You have no muscles." He stepped over and pinched my bicep together. "What are they looking at?"

I swung my arm away from him as Hawk and Gunner

grinned. "I got muscles, just lined up next to you two beef-cakes makes it hard for them to be seen. I'm the lean guy, fit in tight places."

"No pun intended," Hawk said sarcastically, and the lunchroom broke out into laughter. "I'm glad I sorted that out early because you were interested in Tara. You're out here melting women's panties off. That's the word on the Guardian streets. I wouldn't have wanted to fight you."

"Man. I'm for the bro code. Plenty of beautiful women out here. We don't need to all fish in the same pond." It was true, and I planned on heading to the bar downtown with all my new spare time.

"It's pretty much the same pond here," Mustang responded with a distressed tone.

"You gotta get back on the horse, my guy. Get out there." I smacked him on the back, and he moved forward a little. He narrowed his eyes at me as he looked over at me.

"Watch it, Maverick," he growled a little, but I knew down inside that Mustang was like a bear with a sore paw sometimes.

"All right fellas, no love tapping going on over there. I wanted to get you together and let you know the latest because we haven't had any missions for so long." Hawk brought us back into line.

"Gunner, what are you going to get into?" I asked as I watched him cueing up the balls on the table.

"Sitting tight I guess until the next mission. You never know when things might turn." In saying that, I knew he was right. It made my mind flash back to an Afghan tour that I had been on for some reason. Deserted and dusty roads. Decked out in tactical gear from top to toe. Walking through a minefield of unforeseen dangers. *Literally.* Active minefields were right under our feet, that as a unit we had to navigate through in order to reach a small village. Our job was to detect the landmines present before anybody else and put a stop to people being killed.

In Afghanistan, the mines had been laid down so long ago they'd sunk deep under the layers of the earth. We were only a small team of five back then. The heat out there was a bitch, thirsty for our perspiration and making it hard for me to think straight. I kept gulping down water, but it still didn't quench my thirst. I sipped from my water flask, watching the visible heat waves float out over the dry desert, with the lack of trees making it worse.

On that day it was another scorcher, even more so since I was housed in one of those bomb suits with a mask over my face. We all were strapped with walkie talkies and were working on small sections at a time to clear. *Beep. Beep. Beep.* "I got one!" I called out to the crew, raising my arm in the air. The other members stopped as I disarmed the mine, this one designed for humans and not vehicles. Took me a good hour to tackle it. We'd marked a path in and out of the area we were working in. A tight square, and that was it for the day. The next day we would work on the next square. It was painstaking work, and you couldn't lose your patience with it, otherwise you would die. I'd learned to stay calm and was humming to myself at the time.

"Nothing new here, we're just going to disarm this puppy and everything will be swell." It's a mantra I used to tell myself when I was working on the bomb exercises in class. I repeated it as we worked on the second day.

I would never forget that day that we lost one of our soldiers and it wouldn't be the last time. I tried to blink away the image sometimes, but it stayed with me long after the event. Cliff was with me, and sweat was dripping off us from the heat with no chance of drying out. Every time I wiped it, more of it dripped. My body was relaxed in motion, but my mind was coiled like a spring, wound tight and ready for anything. Every time I worked to defuse anything, bombs or landmines, I focused with laser-like precision. One false move, and my life and the lives of my comrades would be over.

We worked diligently through the day. We only worked for four hours at a time, since after that fatigue could cause deadly errors. The conditions made it harder to concentrate on top of that. We were deployed to an abandoned village and had to sit through videos of the blasts. Children were maimed, their arms blown off. Men, women, cats, and dogs. The mines didn't discriminate; they took whatever they could. The videos we were made to watch made my stomach churn as I watched human body parts fly in the air as a child played too close to a mine. Every moment out in the field I thought about this and sticky taped it in my memory so I knew to not lose concentration at any point.

We were finishing up and walking back to shelter. The sun had dropped a little in the sky. We were about another hour away from sunset. My mind wanted to think about the ice-cold beer waiting for us. The high fives we would have when we arrived back, just to be alive another day. We all knew it was a death mission. Any day, any one of us could die. Being a bomb expert came with an intense warning label, but somebody had to do the job. Why not me?

We traced our steps, light on our feet. Testing. Moving our motion sensor equipment over the same spots, it didn't matter that we'd cleared them as we'd come out. We needed to make sure on the way back. Some landmines were secondary exploders, which meant if they didn't blow the first time they would on the second walk-over. Cliff was ahead of me, a good twenty paces out front. Nothing detected and all clear. No fast walking, just a nice easy pace. We had a few more paces to go. I watched him. I saw his swift movements. He stepped to the side. The movement was so small that I didn't register it in the first split second. In the next second I did as his heavy army boot caught the edge of the plate of a landmine. I heard it click into place, and my heart started racing. The other two men were about ten feet apart in front of him. If it set off one, it might set off the others. All of these rampant thoughts came through my brain at a rapid speed. "Shit! Help!" He stopped dead in his tracks.

"Don't move! Stay right there, Cliff. Steady," I barked as the other two men turned around.

"Holy shit, Cliff. Secondary."

"Yup. We got one. If he moves he's a dead man," Walker, one of my unit members, pointed out. Cliff was breathing heavily. I could hear it through his mask.

"*Fuck, I'm going to die.* Tell my kids that I love them. Call my wife, *please*," he asked as his voice quivered.

"Not today you're not. I got you." We'd been trained for this, and now it was time to put the training into action. It was a long shot, and we all knew it, but we had to try.

"Cliff, what I want you to do is raise your foot slowly, on your toes like we got taught." I stared into the eyes of a man who thought he was about to meet his maker. "Look at me, buddy. It's just you and me. We're just walking along down the street, it's you and me. We're going to get some of that Hershey's kiss ice cream you like." I talked to him with the melodic sing-songy voice I used when I was trying to keep shit level within myself. It worked for me, and I thought it would work in this situation.

"I can't do this. I can't. Stand back. Go back. I'm going to go. I'm going to let it go. There's too much pressure underfoot. You won't be able to fix it. I can't do it." I listened as he broke down, his body heaving with heart-wrenching sobs. His face was scrunched up and red with sunburn in places. Tears were streaming rapidly down his face.

"Don't say that. Relax every muscle. *Relax*. Up on your tiptoes. I know how these plates work. It's going to be fine. I got you, man. I'm not going to let you go out like that."

"Cliff, Maverick is one of the best. Trust him." My unit was too far away and they couldn't do anything. Everybody had to stay put. It was only me that was going to take the risk. Cliff eventually took the risk and lifted the back part of his boot off the plate. I dropped down to the loose soil on the ground and scraped off the sandy deposits on top of it. I leveled the pressure out on the plate with one of the tools we employed. It took me an hour to measure and make sure that the weight was light enough for the plate to trick it into thinking there was no need to blow.

"Okay Cliff, I want you to move that foot in front. Nice and light. One full step. Think you can do that for me?"

"Do I have a fucking choice?" he exclaimed with a terse tone.

"Ah—not so much. Let's do it. I got you," I said.

"I love my wife and kids, please let me see them again." He stepped the one foot that had been standing on the plate off it and in front with the other. I prepared myself as best I could. If it blew it was all our asses on the line because we were in such a tight grouping. Nothing happened. I fist pumped and so did the other guys, but we weren't out of the woods by a long shot. We had three more yards of mine-fields to go, but I was confident.

"Follow in our direct line. No more here. None detected at all. Stay steady, Cliff and Maverick. Easy does it. That was too close a call."

"Fuck me. Way too close of a call."

That's when it went. I got him out of one, and Cliff stepped right into the next. It happened quickly. One foot. The plate clicked. A loud popping noise. Shrapnel hitting the sky as I shielded my body in reaction. One leg severed. A finger. Right in front of me.

"Hey Maverick, you all right, bud? You look lost in space over there." Hawk brought me back to the present moment.

"I'm fine and doing mighty fine." My thin veneer of a smile wasn't cutting the mustard for Hawk.

"No you're not. What was that? You weren't even here," he pushed as his piercing eyes locked on me.

"You got me. Thinking back is all. Nothing major." Mustang and Gunner both gave me a pitiful look, knowing what I was talking about. Both of them could read it in my eyes what I was experiencing. Hawk knew as well, just probably not the extent of the memories that surfaced at the wrong time. My palms were wetter than monsoon season, and I was feeling light-headed. I needed to sit down for a minute. I plopped down on the couch, pulled out my joint, and lit her up, taking a hit. "That's better, and now the world is a better place."

"You okay?" Hawk inquired again as he gulped down water.

"I am. I had a flashback about a bomb incident. Shit tore me up for a minute, but I'm back here now," I admitted.

"Wanna talk about it?" Mustang asked.

"I should have been able to save him. I walked my guy out of one landmine and right into the next one. I still feel responsible is all," I blurted out. I didn't mean to, but that memory haunted me until this day. I wished with everything in me that Cliff was still here. I wished that I hadn't had to go to his funeral and bury him. I didn't want to see his family there crying and breaking down over his death. He had one daughter and one son. A perfect blend, and now they had no father, just a memory of a loyal man that was willing to put his life on the line for his country. My eyes glazed over for a minute as I sat there wishing to go back and change the moment.

"Hey, don't beat yourself up about it. That's rough, man. You did the best you could. There's nothing else you could do," Mustang encouraged as he munched on an apple.

"I know, just sometimes, man. I wish I could go back in time and fix the situation." The joint was starting to hit my system, and it felt good to get the situation off my chest as I sat among the guys. I watched as their eyes traveled to the door. I looked up to see Pop coming in.

"Here's our guy. What's up, Mr. President?" I asked as Pop came into the lunchroom and sat down, placing a hand on his knee. He was moving a little more gingerly these days, but still had the same sparkle in his eye as when he'd approached me.

"The sun is up. I tell you what, fellas, I wish I never let that fucking Wildcard Willy back in here. I'm hoping he will go away on his own," Pop reasoned as he rubbed his knees.

"What's the latest stunt?" Hawk enquired.

"The latest is still the same, trying to blackmail the club for money. He's saying he has some insider information, and that he'll go to the cops with it if we're not careful. He doesn't have any information as far as I'm concerned. Another mosquito that we need to squash. I'm hoping this one just flies away." Pop's gruff tone made it clear that he was pissed off about it.

"I wonder what he thinks he's got on the club?" I pondered. "He seemed like a pretty chill dude. When he gets the drink in him, he turns into something else. Like Dr. Jekyll and Hyde."

The guys sniggered. "Yeah, he's something else, that's for sure. Listen, I gotta roll. I'm taking Tara out to lunch." Hawk slapped the palms of the other guys and mine as he walked out.

"When's the wedding?" I said casually as he walked past.

"No weddings yet."

"Ooooh," Gunner chimed in, chuckling. "So there might be one. How about that? Love in the chaos of biker life. That's a beautiful thing."

# 2

## STEPHANIE

THE BAR WAS ROCKING, AND I WAS POLISHING GLASSES GETTING ready for the usual regulars to flow through the side door. It was a blink-and-you'll-miss-it door. One of the many features of the place that the good people of Edgewood loved. The place was nicknamed 'the no-name bar' and tucked down an alleyway in downtown Edgewood right behind the Plaza Loop. We had this long dark wood bar which was glazed, and I loved it. Meant I could just wipe it down and keep on moving. The stage was only small since it wasn't a big place. Most weekends gigs ran, some local musicians trying their luck. We had a slam poetry night every month and that was a real hoot and a lot of fun.

Some were pretty good, and others just plain sucked. I wasn't feeling like being at the bar, I was purely going through the motions. I'd just broken up with my boyfriend, Ralph, a few months ago, and the stabbing wound of deceit was still fresh for me. We'd made plans. Lifelong plans that I was excited about, but he'd cheated on me with a girl I used to go to school with. I not only felt sad, but humiliated and ashamed. I wanted nothing to do with any crusty man. The problem was I worked at a bar where men were all around me, *all the time,* and every other shift I was propositioned in some way.

I worked for Dustin, who had owned the bar for over a decade. He was a big, stocky guy with a handlebar moustache and a no-nonsense approach who would kick you out as soon as look at you if you were causing trouble. "Hey, Steph. How are we looking out here? We still got enough beer on tap to run for the whole night?" he yelled from the back.

"Sure do. We're good," I yelled back. A rock and roll band was warming up in the background. The Titters, that's what they were called. Weird-ass name, but they were great and a huge hit in town. I knew both the drummer and the guitarist from school. Rod and Clem. Both of them were born musicians who'd always stayed after school to practice. Some of the regulars were already huddled around the high round tables, ready to watch them perform with their hands curled around their beers. I looked down at my watch. It was 7 o'clock, and they were due on at 7:30. When they took a break, we would play the jukebox. We got all sorts in, including the notorious bikers of Edgewood. The Guardians loved it in our spot because it was discreet and it gave them a reprieve without too much trouble. The other bar they frequented was the Crookers Bar. It wasn't my favorite place, but apparently it worked for them. Can't go to the same place all the time, I guess.

Dustin kept everyone in check. He had one security guy, and it was all he ever needed. Most of the patrons that came in respected him and the space. We got the occasional rowdy drunk, but no real brawls or escalations that I'd seen in my five years working here. A few of the old ladies frequented as well to mix it up and have a good time. Bell

Marco was one of my favorites. She tipped well, and the men stayed longer so they could get a closer glimpse of her. The woman was hard to miss. Suited me just fine. She kept my bank account in the black.

On the left were pool tables—only four, nothing major, just a little break-out area for people to have a little fun on. They weren't even full-size tables, but they were popular. The bar got full pretty quickly, especially on a Friday night. In front of me at the bar were three guys and two girls. One of the guys at the end of the bar had both of those girls surrounding him, and he was lapping it up. He had floppy sandy hair, a goofy smile, and a big, dimpled grin. He seemed like a nice guy. He was kind of on the lean side, with a couple of tattoos, nothing to rival mine. I had a dragon with a heart through it on my arm and a few other special ones on the inside of both wrists. From what I could see, he was punching above his weight.

"Hey, Steph, can I get a beer?" I shifted my gaze to the customer in front of me and smiled at him.

"Hey, Dave, how are you doing tonight?" I said cheer-fully as I pulled his usual from the tap. Dave was a lonely single guy, and I suspected he came to the bar to talk to me mostly, but he wasn't my type. He stared down the length of the bar to where the guy was working his magic with the ladies. "I'm doing pretty good. Work is busy, same old, same old, you know." Sometimes Dave irritated me with his droopy attitude. If he made more of an effort, maybe he could pick up a girl.

"I do. I'm here every week, rain or shine." I poured Dave's beer and put a coaster down underneath it. He nodded his head in the direction of the guy at the end of the bar.

"Who is that guy? I've seen him in here a couple of times, but I don't know his name."

I smirked as I watched him in action. "No idea. He ordered a beer from Dustin. I haven't had a chance to talk to him."

"Oh" is all he said, but I could tell from the sunken look on his face that he was jealous. There was easy laughter and a huge amount of hair flicking going on his way, and he was on fire. Made me curious to what it was about him that was taking the women's fancy. I wanted to try his charm on for myself. Not that I was interested in anything with him, just might be fun to get in the mix and see.

"He's doing all right down there," I commented with interest.

"I mean, yeah, if that's what you're into... I guess." If his voice was any sadder, he would sound like a distressed foghorn.

"Dave, you'll find the right woman for you. She may not be in this bar is all. Don't worry so much about it."

"Easy for you to say. You're beautiful, Steph." Heat rose in my cheeks from the compliment. I knew I wasn't ugly or anything, but I wasn't a Bell Marco or one of those super-model looking women. I had my own brand of appeal, and I liked me.

"I'm sure you'll be fine," I said, ignoring the compliment he gave me.

"Maybe you're right. Just tough to find a good one in this town," he lamented, and I was thankful that a woman popped up at the bar to quench her thirst. I went straight over to her.

"What can I get you?" I put on my friendly bartender voice as I waited for her order.

"Let me get two bourbon and Cokes, both with ice."

"Coming right up," I quipped cheerfully as I reached for the bottle of bourbon. I measured out the shot and poured it into the glass then topped it up with Coke. He must have flown into my orbit when I was pouring the soda because the next thing I knew, a sandy-haired man was grinning back at me. I dropped her drinks right in front of her, and she slid her money across the bench.

"Thank you," she called out as the guy just stood there all teeth watching me.

"Hi, I've been waiting to talk to you. It's been busy here so I thought I would wait for you," he said in a charming voice. I glanced at him. Nice T-shirt, nothing fancy or ,anything just clean and neat. Golden hair that was shiny. Bright blue eyes that had a story to tell behind them. He seemed unassuming, yet the women in the bar loved him. The other two women who were getting to know him were sipping their drinks and giving me the evil eye, I could feel the heat from their salty gazes from the other end. I paid no attention to them.

"That's nice of you. What were you waiting for? A drink, sir?" I said flirtily. I was pouring on the charm like maple syrup just like him. Two could play that game.

He chuckled and nodded his head. Maybe he knew he'd met his match. "Sir?" He flicked a hand through his hair, and it flicked right back into place. "You're making me feel a little old with the sir, but I appreciate it. Can I order a drink?"

"I didn't mean to make you feel that way. I don't think those ladies down there think you're too old," I pointed out, tipping my head towards them. The band started to play as the drums kicked in, making the floor vibrate. People started to take their drinks and gravitate to the front room to listen to the band as I watched his reaction to what I said.

He didn't skip a beat. "Always good to make new friends. I'm new in town. My friends call me Maverick." He extended his arm, and I was surprised to see that he was quite muscular. His handshake was strong. I'd underestimated him a little bit. The warmth that circulated through my arm and traveled up my neck made me wonder what was under the shirt he was wearing.

"Nice to meet you, Maverick. I'm Stephanie. My friends call me Steph." We looked back and forth for a minute, taking one another in. He was easy on the eyes, and his personality seemed sweet to me.

"Nice to meet you, Steph." He raised his voice as the lead singer belted out the first song in his set and the guitar got going. He started to move a little in tune with the beat of the gritty rock music and clicked his fingers. I watched him moving his hips and couldn't help but crack a smile.

"You like them? They're not bad, right?" I added.

"They are pretty good. They have some knock-out bands in Cali, but I can groove to this." He bit his bottom lip and danced, swinging his hips at the bar as his hair swung in front of his face. The guy was actually pretty funny. I had to hand it to him. It beat drunks at the bar all night. I would much rather have his goofy dancing than sloppy men propositioning me.

"Okay, okay. You still haven't told me what you want to drink." I put my hands up, but I was laughing so hard because of his antics that I found it hard to get the request out. I was enjoying the show, and the name Maverick was just right for him.

"Oh yeah! This is great. I might just stay right here and dance for you," he offered. The two girls at the other end of the bar were giggling and whooping it up, watching him. They didn't seem to mind that he was trying to flirt with me.

I'd seen them in the bar a few times. Both of them were all over the bikers that came into the bar on a regular basis. It made me cringe for them. They were both so predictable in their moves that I wanted to puke. Obviously it worked; guys went home with them. I'd seen them a few weeks in succession go home with anyone that looked like they owned a motorcycle.

"Ah, you could, but I think my boss might come out here and wonder what the hell is wrong with you if you keep going."

"I don't want to get you fired or anything. Let me get those drinks then. I've got an order for two mojitos, and I'll take a rum and Coke."

"Okay, you're a rum guy, that's interesting." My thoughts were you could tell a lot about a man by the drinks he ordered. He seemed like he was getting pretty loose, and it might be a good night for my tip jar the way he was acting.

"Yeah, I like my drinks to be a little dark and spicy." I shook my head at his blatant flirting and moved off to mix his drinks. I came back to the bar and dropped the two mojitos in front of him.

"That's for your lady friends down there. Come back and I'll be ready with your rum and Coke." I winked at him as I served another customer. He winked right back and took the drinks down to them. I served the other guy at the bar, and Maverick swung back in front of me.

"Here you go. That's 30 bucks." I batted my eyelashes at him as his eyes hovered over my wrist tattoos.

"Those are pretty cool. I'm guessing they have a special meaning?" I held out both my arms and leaned over the bar a little. I was wearing a T-shirt, but it was open necked so you could see my line of cleavage. As I showed him the tattoos, I deliberately squeezed my breasts together. Those tips would come in handy. He ogled my chest and blinked hard once or twice, then brought his eyes back to the tattoos. Never could help themselves. A sneaky barmaid's trick.

"Mmm-hmm. This one is a fox, one of my favorite animals. The other one is a quote with a dagger through it."

"You are definitely foxy, that's for sure, and you deserve a decent tip. Here you go." He slid a $100 dollar bill split into the right money. I put the $30 in the till and slipped the rest in my bra. No other bartenders were working; it was just me and Dustin. Sometimes Melissa worked, especially on weekends when it got packed and Dustin stopped being such a scrooge about hiring, but not that night.

"Why, thank you. You have a good night with your lady friends." I winked.

"I will." His smile was infectious and made the corners of my lips turn up. I got what I wanted and he got to enjoy the flirt with me. It was a win-win the way I saw it.

"See you next time. Have a great night," he said before he walked off.

"You too." I tapped the bar as the band broke for a set break, and a swarm of customers came back over. Dustin popped up and started serving the overflow, and I was busy for the next half hour pumping out the drinks. We did well in that little rush, and Maverick came back for another round of drinks. By the time the band finished up around 10 p.m., most of the patrons were winding down on the waters or stumbling out of the door to go home. This was about the time we started swapping out drinks for water. I cut my eyes to where Maverick was sitting talking to the women. One was seated on his lap, a blonde with a big rack, nothing out of the ordinary, and the other one looked almost identical to her. I had a good idea of what was about to happen for all three of them later. These ladies were in their element when they tag-teamed.

Maverick walked up to the bar with a confident swagger a few minutes later with his hair swooped down over one eye. He was giving me playboy vibes. He puckered up his lips with a kiss as he slid a piece of paper over the bar. I wiped off the stickiness from the top of the bar with my arms, enjoying a break from the rush of patrons during the intermission. I picked up the piece of paper in a state of shock. I didn't expect for him to drop his number and I didn't expect what he did next. He walked out of the no-name bar with none of the women he had been talking to. He was riding solo, and I didn't know whether to be impressed or worried for him.

Dustin was back in from the floor and collecting drinks. "What is it? You look like you've seen the bogeyman or something."

"Close. You never know about people," I muttered, trying to come to grips with the fact that he'd left alone. I kept cleaning and resetting the bar.

"What did you say? Speak up, I can't hear you," Dustin replied.

"Don't worry about it." I didn't want Dustin giving me a hard time and hassling me about a crush at the bar.

The doors closed around 1 a.m., and Dustin walked me to my car. There were only a few others out in the parking lot.

"See you tomorrow. Get home safe." I waved as I sank into the front seat of my Nissan.

My phone pinged a couple of times, and I looked at the text. It was from my brother James.

*Hey. I need some help.*

Fuck. He was so annoying sometimes, even though we

were pretty close. Sometimes I thought we were too close. I couldn't help wondering what the hell he wanted?

I let my thumbs get to typing as a cloud of annoyance covered my face in the dark. *What?*

*Can you pick me up from the pool hall in Sedillo? My car's fucked.*

*On the way. Send addy.* James, my little punk of a brother who was in his mid-twenties, was over in an area that I don't want him having anything to do with. He was associated with the Vipers, that piece of shit motorcycle club that was killing half the town of Edgewood with their meth labs.

My hands slid over the wheel as I cranked the engine and rode over there. I knew the exact hall that he was at, and I knew who was there. It made my skin crawl driving there; the back roads to Sedillo were eerily dark and quiet. I inhaled deep breaths as I tried to release the knots taking up residence in my stomach. The streets were pitch black, and I had to flick on my high beams so I could see. Beady yellow eyes scampered right in front of the car, causing me to yelp.

"What the fuck was that?" Some creature decided to scare the living daylights out of me on my way. My super glue grip tightened on the steering wheel as the road became gravelly.

I drove down a dirt road strip, bumping along until I came to a stop outside of a small house. All the lights were lit up, and a few cars and trucks were lined up in a row. I didn't want to be close to any of them, so I parked off to the side and called my brother.

"Hey, I'm here. Come out and hurry up. I want to get home. I just finished work, and I'm tired." Two minutes later I saw a Viper with a bandana around his neck give my brother a pat on the back as he looked over to the car. I slid down a little in the seat and hid my face. I didn't want them to get a look at me at all. I wanted no part of being associated with the Vipers. I saw him staring into the inside of the car as I slouched down even farther. I heard him say something nondescript to my brother. My brother tapped him on the chest, and the Viper moved back. He opened the door and jumped in. He smelled like a brewery, and I screwed up my nose.

"What did you do, drink out of the tap?" I looked sideways at him in the moonlight. He was wearing a baseball cap and a hoodie.

"No, I had a few. You know, normal shit," he said, sniffing and wiping his nose. I took a harder look at him.

"You look toasted. Are you using?"

"No, I'm not using. I don't get high off my own supply. I smoked a little weed is all."

I sniffed the air. I could smell a whiff of it on him, that was for sure.

"You stink. I don't know why you're involved with the Vipers. They are in so much trouble with the law and all these meth labs. You need to be careful, I'm worried about you," I pressed in a concerned tone. I bit my lip as I drove away, the gravel crunching under my tires. I didn't want to get stuck out in the wilds of Sedillo. It was the last thing I wanted. I'd watched too many true crime documentaries to feel like it was a safe place, and that didn't even include all the mountain animals. The coyotes, rattlesnakes, wolves, carnivorous birds, and God know what else. James snapped me back into his hellish reality.

"Stop worrying. I'm doing what I want. You can't stop me from hanging out with them. You work at the bar with drunks and bums all the time. I don't know why you're giving me a hard time."

"There's no way in the world you're comparing my world

to yours. Mom and Dad would have a fit if they knew you were dealing. You gotta stop!" I banged my hand on the wheel.

My brother turned his head my way as the exit for Edgewood came up. His eyes were droopy from the weed as he stared hard at me and I felt the weight of his gaze like a burning sensation on my skin. "You're not going to tell them, are you?" he lashed out with force as he faced forward in the car.

"I'm not afraid of you, so you can take the tone down a notch. It's not my place to tell them, but I will if you don't get away from this. You'll wind up dead or in jail. I don't see any other outcome for you, and I don't know why you don't seem to get that."

He rocked his head from side to side. "Nuh-uh, sis. Something big is going down with the Guardians, and I'm going to be in on it. I'm telling you it's going to be huge, and it will put me on the map."

"You're not thinking straight. Sleep it off. I'll talk to you tomorrow about it." I brushed off the comment about the Guardians. From what I heard on the grapevine and at the bar, the Guardians weren't in the drug game and wanted nothing to do with it. Hawk was involved with the taskforce to close down the meth labs. I know because he told me when he came in weeks ago.

I rounded the corner to James's apartment complex and dropped him off. He was swaying a little so I waited for him to get in the place. I watched him fumble around in the darkness for his swipe card to get in the building. He belched loudly as I screwed up my nose. I wanted so much better for him, I was both disappointed and pissed off. I let go of a despondent sigh.

He waved as he got in and staggered up the stairs. I

assumed he would find a way to go pick up his car tomorrow. I wasn't his babysitter, so I couldn't help him with that.

James was never like this. He was my younger brother by three years and a pest when we were kids, but lovable. He was normal, not extraordinary, but not a class clown either. Somewhere in the middle. He did the usual annoying kid brother stuff like picking boogers and trying to wipe them on me or messing up my hair after I'd just done it. That was about all we fought over. Other than that, we got on good with siblings and spent a lot of time together; otherwise I wouldn't be the one he called in the middle of the night. As I drove the short distance to my house, my brows knitted together, trying to figure out when he went wrong.

Probably junior high, but by that time I had my own circle of friends and was doing my own thing. Like my brother, school left me bored. I was ready to go as soon as class started. I ended up skipping quite a few times, and I know my brother did too. Maybe that was it. I started working at the bar after I finished up high school and never left.

I pulled up to my house and rolled into the driveway. It was modest, nothing to write home about, but it was mine, and I loved the fact that I'd bought it. As I turned the key in the lock, Maverick popped up in my mind. I reached down into my pants pocket, panicking that maybe I'd lost the slip of paper he gave me. I didn't; it was still there. I was starting to wonder about him and what he was really about. That move of leaving the bar by himself was interesting. Didn't mean he wasn't entertaining a woman later in his home. I let out a long, tired sigh. God, I sounded so cynical. Was I really that man-hating chick now? Ugh.

I flicked on the light and rubbed my neck. It was a little stiff from raising my arms at the bar to reach the glasses. It was like an invisible weight lifted off my shoulders when I stepped inside. I kicked off my shoes and collapsed onto my couch. It was one of those cushy ones that you sank into, which I loved, except once you were in, you couldn't get out of it.

I opened up the slip of paper. Parts of the numbers were smudged from beer being sploshed on the bar, and it smelled faintly of beer. It was still readable, though, so I grabbed my cell phone and punched it in, saving Maverick's number. Then I looked at it long and hard.

*Should I text him my number back? Can't hurt.*

*Nah. Well, maybe. It's not a big deal, is it?*

I went back and forth about it and settled on no. I was fresh out of a bullshit relationship and was in the swearing off men zone. I couldn't allow myself to text him, but my itchy fingers wanted to. I put my phone down beside me, planning on resting for a minute and getting up and heading to bed. Minutes later I dozed off and was dead to the world with Maverick's goofy smile on my brain.

# 3

## MAVERICK

Tempting. The Barbie girls, but not more tempting than the sassy bartender. She was more intriguing to me. Those tattoos gave her an edge that I liked. She was mesmerizing when she made a drink, she knew how to make a cocktail, and I liked the way her lips wrapped around the straw when she conducted a taste test. The blond chicks were a little too easy, and their hands were like octopuses. I was pretty sure one of them grabbed my crotch, but I didn't protest because they'd moved their hands to another spot by then. They were like some filthy sirens from the sea. If I was being honest, they killed my vibe a little bit. If they weren't there I would have spent my time hanging out at the bar watching Stephanie make drinks and talking to her.

I sailed into the club around eight in the morning. I was working with Shadow in the auto shop fixing locks and breaking down parts since there was a hiatus between missions. I passed the main office where Dutch and Tara were talking. I tapped the glass and waved to them both. They both turned sharply and waved back.

My first instinct was to look over for Axle or Bell on the

bags, but Bell was in her mother duty bag, so no dice. You wouldn't catch me on the bags like that. I was more into land activities that were fun. I used to surf in California, but in Edgewood water was hard to get to unless you traveled a little farther and hiked to a body of water. Not quite the same as picking up your surfboard and hitting the beach. I would get back there some time, but for now I would have to be content with hiking trails and trying something different. I focused on looking for Shadow in the chop shop. The music was pumping, and I saw the back of Shadow's head as I entered.

"Hey, Shadow, what's up, my guy?" I asked in a chipper tone. My mood was up a notch after giving Stephanie my number. I wanted to know what she was going to do. If she was going to play her cards close to her chest and not text me back whether she would give me a shot. The jury was still out, and from the lack of messages on my phone she probably had written me off as another drunk dude at the bar. I was certain she got hit on all the time. She was way too cute not to.

Shadow greeted me with a quick hug. "Nothing too much, just fatherly duties with Abby and Ava." A normal statement, but his whole face lit up when he mentioned their names. Shadow was one of those men that was built to be a father. I knew that he was close to his grandfather and his father.

"The two As. How are they doing?"

"Both of them are doing good. We've got a good routine going now." He tapped my bicep lightly as he smirked. "I say that now, and it could change any minute."

I picked up one of the wrenches in the plastic container and twisted it over. "That's nice that you got yourself a family. Real nice."

"What about you, Maverick? Ever want kids?"

"Not a choice of wanting or not wanting. Hasn't been on the cards for me, but hey, who knows, seems like there's something going on in these Edgewood waters, all the old ladies are pregnant."

A grin broke out over Shadow's face. "Careful, you could be next."

"Ha! I don't know. A couple of kids running around might be nice. Speaking of nice, I met this cutie bartender last night."

Shadow stopped for a minute and looked at me. "Oh yeah? You get her number or what?"

I sucked in through my teeth. "See, I wanted to be a gentleman, I gave her my number and didn't take hers."

I grabbed a handful of tools that I needed to pull apart the upholstery from the door I was going to work on and moved with Shadow to the car hoist. "You're in the wait zone."

"The what?"

"You know that wait zone, where you're waiting to see if she's going to give you the time of day," he pointed out as his heavy frame moved with purpose.

"I guess you're right. I am in the wait zone." We were out on the floor, and Axle and Rush had their heads down both working on bikes. Rush was working with a beautiful looking sports bike with bright purple chrome. His hair was up high in a man bun, and he was bobbing his head to a rock song that was blasting on the radio. He didn't look up. Axle was working with a muffler, his eyes intense as he inspected it from top to bottom. His head was moving in time with the music as well. Both were in the moment with their work, and I had my own job to do working on a few door locks.

"It's not a funny place when you're in it. Sounds like she's playing hard to get. What are you going to do about it?" Shadow challenged.

"Ah man. I'm pretty easy going, but she got that thing, you know," I projected passionately.

"What thing is that?" Shadow enquired with a smug expression.

"That spark I like. We had this nice back and forth exchange over the bar. We were dancing with one another." I stopped and swayed from side to side showing him what I meant. "She could keep up with me."

"You have a way with words, Maverick, but those dance moves need some work. You got what you need?" Shadow cocked an eyebrow at me as we left out to hit the warehouse floor.

"Hey, you should see me when I get grooving. I'm not too bad."

"I can't even say I wanna see it," Shadow said with his quick-wittedness. Sometimes he caught me off guard.

"Yeah, I got everything right here." I slipped on my work gloves as Shadow grabbed the other end of the door and helped me move it out. He dropped it down on the ground, and we went back to grab the second one. Once we got them moved out, I sat down on the ground, so I could rip the upholstery back and tinker with the lock mechanisms.

"So what's her name? Let me know. I might know somebody who knows of her. I might save you the trouble," Shadow said in a dry tone.

"That's pessimistic, man. She's a hottie. Her name is Stephanie, and she works at the same bar that all the guys go to here," I said.

Shadow chuckled. "Ohhhh! Stephanie, okay, okay. I can't say anything bad about her. She's been at the bar awhile.

She can make a cocktail that will put you under the ground, and it won't taste like alcohol. I like her." Shadow nodded his head in approval as I got a clear look at the door lock under the fabric. I grabbed my allen key and set to work on practicing unpicking the lock.

When I looked at items, they seemed to become larger in size and I could zero in on them. I picked the lock in less than two minutes, although I was a little rusty. "You approve? What else do you know about her? Anything?"

"Listen to you! You *really* like her," he joked. "I'm not out like that so much anymore. I got my girls, so if anything I have a drink with them at home and chill out."

"Gotcha. You seem real settled. You've always seemed like a solid guy to me, but now you're like in the zone and a hell of an artist. What a combination." I admired Shadow for pursuing his passions even if they didn't match up to what was expected from a biker.

"It's been a strange ride, but I feel good about it. Me and Ava fit together. I feel complete as a man, you know. Like I have purpose. I have my little girl, and she's growing so fast. Right in front of my eyes and I want to press the stop button." He simulated the action of pressing a button on a remote.

"I bet," I said as I got ready to move onto the next lock and break down the car door.

Rush strolled over to where we were. Shadow pointed to him with his wrench. "Should ask this guy about Stephanie. He'll know what's up with her."

"Hey, Rush." I smiled as he grasped my gloved hand. I was seated on the ground, and my legs were getting a little stiff, so I stood up on my feet.

"Hey, Maverick, you working on the locks? Got new tricks?" He grinned.

"Nope. No new tricks. That man bun is a trick in itself," I teased as I got ready for the ribbing to come. He patted it and smiled good-naturedly.

"I'm catching Penn. She has hers hanging down her back now."

"Whoa. Both of you should be hair models," I laughed.

"Funny you should say that. Dara asked me to do just that for her catalog. I think I'm due there in a few weeks."

"No way! See. There you go." I ripped up the door, dislodging the fabric. I gritted my teeth as the tape clung to one spot. I eventually got it to budge and peel apart.

"I think Maverick has a few questions for you about a certain someone," he said smugly.

"Yeah? What's up?" Rush gave me a blank look as he waited for my answer.

"There's this gorgeous bartender, the bar with no name down that alleyway." I struggled to remember the spot as my thoughts went blank. "Anyway it doesn't matter, you know the one?"

"Ah. Penn knows her quite well. The old lady gang go in there on their girls' nights."

"What do you know?" I fiddled with the lock while I hummed to myself. I listened for the click of the lock mechanism to ping, giving me an odd sense of satisfaction.

"Hmm. You like her, huh, Maverick?" I fist-bumped with him, and he pulled out his phone.

"What are you doing, man?" I asked in an exasperated tone. Shadow started laughing in the background.

"I'm calling my girl. Let me get the scoop. Let's see what you're getting yourself into."

"All right, fuck it, call her and let me know." What did I have to lose except my pride? I saw the cell phone go up to his ear as he made the call.

"Hey, Penn. How's your day?" His voice dropped a little when he spoke to her. I think all men spoke to their ladies differently than how they spoke to their crew. It was a thing. "I want to ask you something... do you know Stephanie? The bartender, is she single? No, babe... what? I'm asking for a friend of mine." I laughed out loud at the tail end of the conversation. "Oooh, okay, sounds tricky. Maverick can wear her down. I'll let you know. Love you too. See you later tonight. Bye." He slid the phone back in his pocket and came back with a weird look on his face.

I put my tools down. "That face doesn't look good. What's going down, my man?" I leaned back on my hands.

"You got your work cut out for you. She just got out of a relationship. Some guy named Ralph." I stood up and bent over, stretching out my hamstrings as I flipped my hair out of my face.

"Okay, so that means I just take it slow. Get her comfortable. I can dig it. I'm not too serious about it, but I wanna hang with her," I said. "She seems like my speed. I only met her one time, so I can't know much from that."

Rush scrunched up his face. "I don't know. The guy was a biker, and apparently she might be done with guys on bikes. According to Penn she's in a man-hating stage."

"Nah, she's just hurt. I'll keep it casual, suits me fine."

"Okay. She is pretty cool from what I remember. She's a hell of a bartender and makes a wicked cocktail. I think she won some sort of competition last year," Rush said.

"Oh really? I saw her making a lot of them, but I didn't know she was that good." I got back to the lock and picked it open.

"Yup. She is." Rush walked away and got back to the bike.

Shadow was wiping his hands down, giving me a funny

look. "So what are you going to do now?" he challenged as I shot him a mischievous look.

"Nothing. I'm playing it cool. I'm going to ease her into the Maverick charm. Things will work out fine, you know. I'm not your average biker. You know that."

"That I do know for certain. I took it slow with Ava when I first met her," Shadow said in a soft tone.

"You're a real softie under there, Shadow. You had me fooled for a minute, but I see you now."

"Shh! Don't give all my secrets away. I'm trying to maintain," he said through gritted teeth.

"Ha! Secret's safe with me. Hey, have you seen Hawk? He around?" I wanted to talk to him about Tara and how that whole situation was progressing.

"He's in the lunchroom, I think," Shadow quipped. "I have to go take a run down to the construction site to grab some tools from Scout."

"Okay. See you later on." The warehouse was the same as a normal weekday. Nothing too hectic going on. Axle was focused on his car, and I admired his focus. He'd become a different man since the birth of his daughter. More well-rounded as a man. All of these babies at the Guardians were making me think of fatherhood and what I wanted. Pity no woman I'd ever met made me think I wanted to be one with them.

I rose up off the concrete floor and cruised over to the lunchroom where I found Hawk and Finn leaning over the pool table and talking. Both of them looked up with intense stares as I entered. Finn was holding a beer in his hand. He grinned when he saw me, and his hard-lined expression changed.

"Hey, Finn, long time no see. How you been?" He leaned in close for a quick hug, and I tapped him on the back. He smelled like leather, and his beard was a little longer than I remembered.

"I've been around. I've been handling a lot of business stuff at the backend, paperwork for Pop and going over the particulars with Red. That's why you haven't seen much of us around the club, but we're here," he explained. "Not to mention that I got the little one keeping his eyes open at all times of the night wanting to play. It's the best thing. You should get you one, Maverick, but it's costing me my sleep and my sanity. That's for fucking sure." I nodded my head with a wry laugh, feeling as if I'd interrupted something big.

"You gotta bring the little man in here. I want to see him," I said. "He's the future of the Guardians."

"You're right. I will, Chloe hasn't been down here for a long while. We are on the quieter side right now. Might be the perfect time to introduce Tyler to his uncles and agony aunts."

"Agony aunts? Who's one of those?" Hawk and Finn pointed straight at me.

"Are you kidding right now? I'm going to rename you as the guru of the club," Finn proclaimed.

"Me?" I pointed a finger back to myself. "That's funny. Sure, I'll help the little guy out if he needs it. No sweat...Were you guys in the middle of discussing something?" I glanced at Hawk whose face was still intense. I saw the flicker in his jaw and his eyes were guarded.

"Nah, get in here. We were talking over things. It's fine, Maverick," Finn reassured.

"No secrets here, Maverick. Just Wildcard being a royal pain in the ass. We're trying to figure him out. If we should be worried or not," Hawk added as he let a burp fly.

I raised an eyebrow and moved to the fridge to grab a beer and join them. "Why? Last time I heard he wanted big bucks. Is that right?" I flipped the tab of my beer up and sank down a few gulps.

"He did, but now he's threatening to go to the cops. He's telling us that he knows we have some dirty laundry to clean up."

"What does he think he knows? He tell you?" I asked, wracking my brain to think about it.

"Nope. I'm hoping it doesn't have to do with Clint," Hawk said slowly as he drank down more of his beer.

"Where did that come from and how does it relate to Wildcard? Isn't he on the drug trafficking train? From what I sensed he was trying to start his own up. What else does he want the money for? Got to be that." I added in my two cents worth.

Finn let out a low whistle as his arms strained against the pool table. "That's where my head is at as well. Hawk seems to think Wildcard might know something. We have a few things we dabble into, so it could be anything. What Wildcard fails to realize is that we have Edgewood police onside. Not offside. They aren't just going to believe some old prick running around town and talking gibberish." Finn opened his arm up and swung it out with his beer in hand as it splashed on the floor. Her eyes were a little glassy, and I got the idea that he'd already had a few.

"Hawk, where'd it come from?" His arms were folded over, and his eyebrows were knitted together in deep thought. "I can't shake it. Tara mentioned that she spoke to Wildcard a couple of times about having trouble with Clint. I mean it's no secret that's how she came to the club. I can't see it yet. I'm probably way off base. Don't worry about it."

"He'd left before then, Hawk. He doesn't know about that. How the fuck could he?" Finn leaned back over the pool table as I observed from the outside looking in.

"Wildcard will come good. He can't keep threatening the club. He's going to have to act. Let's run down the line." I held my fingers up. "He can go to the cops. He can get the Vipers to come for us. Pffft, not going to happen. Or he can fade into the background, like the wallflower he used to be. He popped up, and he'll wilt away again." I reached out and cupped my hands on both of the guy's shoulders.

"Let's not worry about this. He's nothing. Flow like water." Finn's shoulders started to heave as he let out a bellowing laugh, and Hawk glanced sideways at me with a *You've got to be kidding* look at me.

"You and your water," Hawk said.

"Got you guys out of your heads, though, didn't it? What did Pop say?" I asked.

"Pop he-uh got a little heated with it. Went a little too far, so we're not going to mention it too many times to him," Finn mused, and the lines around his eyes folded as he smiled.

"What did he say? C'mon. I'm dying to know," I bounced around on my feet.

"Yeah, me too. What did Pop have to say? This has gotta be good," Hawk sneered.

"He made a suggestion that we put the old man out of his misery and put him to sleep. He's not the biggest fan of Wildcard," Finn said as he slurred a little bit. Yep. He'd definitely had a few and was getting tipsy in the lunchroom. That was fine as long as he wasn't riding.

Hawk stood up and tapped the pool table with the heel of his hand. "I knew it. That's Pop all day. Take him out. He only ever wants to take people out if they cause a problem."

"A little heavy-handed from Pop, but I can see where he's coming from," I chimed in.

"You can? How? Wildcard isn't that bad," Finn stated.

"From my experience in the field, the ones you think aren't that bad are usually worse. He was a part of the Guardians, so he does have insider knowledge. I'm not saying he's going to do anything with it, but the Guardians could send a warning shot to let him know to back off."

Hawk gave me a look of confusion. "But you just said to leave it alone! Make up your mind."

"I had to think it through. I'm seeing all the angles now," I said as I made the symbol of a square.

Hawk went back to drinking his beer. "Let's just see what happens, shall we?"

"Let's," I agreed. My gut did tell me Wildcard might end up causing a bigger problem for the club in the long run. I just couldn't figure out how...

# 4

## STEPHANIE

THE BAR WAS PACKED FOR THE SECOND WEEK IN A ROW, AND I sure as hell didn't mind. Kept my mind, my heart, and my hands busy. Although I thought we could do with an extra pair of hands on deck at times. More than just the one or two times a month Dustin brought Melissa in. Would save all the agitated customers giving me dirty looks from time to time.

Another band was due on stage, and as I looked around, I could see new patrons who I'd never seen before in the bar. People were having a real good time. I was tapping my foot behind the bar and doing what I do best, mixing up a hell of a cocktail. I didn't typically get the fancy cocktail requests, I got the standard whiskey and Coke, rum and Coke, vodka and cranberry, that type of thing. I was always hyped up when I got to play a little more. Every month Dustin let me live a little with a Steph house special.

"We can't add it to the menu every week because the regulars like what they like, and they don't always come for the cocktails. We have to give the customer what they want,

Steph." We'd gotten into a huge argument over it, which is how I got the monthly slot for cocktails in the first place.

"You're not giving it a chance, that's why. We had a huge night when I came out with those fruity cocktails for ladies' night. They loved it! Give me a chance to do something here," I'd yelled.

Dustin had given me one of those *Are you kidding* looks. "We ain't one of those swanky uptown bars. Maybe you should go work up there with them. We don't have the money for extra fancy ingredients every month," he'd said as a passing comment, not thinking I would care so much.

I was fuming at the time. I'd worked so hard for Dustin and been with him for so long that I felt I deserved a little more respect than that. "Maybe I will. Give me one cocktail a month. Let's track it over the next few months, then let's see," I challenged.

He chuckled. "You're not going anywhere, Steph. I know you're not. Born and bred in Edgewood. You're a lifer here." He might have been right, but the way he said it with such certainty made me upset. The next day I came back to him for four applications. A couple of them were out of town in Santa Fe, and the other two were from uptown bars paying double in California where I spent some time before.

I'd stood there all fire and brimstone with my arms crossed. I'd always had that rebel streak, especially if I felt like something was unfair. "Uh-huh. Sure am going somewhere, if you don't give me a drink a month."

The man's face had turned as white as a ghost. "Are you really going to do this, Steph?" I actually ended up feeling pretty sorry for him. He looked like a lost puppy dog. "I can't do this without you, don't leave me, please," he pleaded.

"Then I want a pay rise and a monthly cocktail and if it works profit-wise it becomes a permanent feature every second week. I'm getting bored, and I need to improve my skills." I put my foot down. In my wildest dreams I wanted to run my own little cocktail bar, but I was nowhere near the funds I needed to make that happen, but if I got close...maybe.

"Okay, okay. Let's try it. I give in," Dustin folded and gave me a 15 percent increase in pay. So far my predictions about the monthly cocktails were working. The first two months we'd make a killing, and patrons were looking for the cocktails all the time now.

"Good. It's done. While you're at it, hire more staff. We need to expand, Dustin," I whined.

"Yeah, yeah. Let's start with this first." Now here we were with a packed bar and Dustin still holding on and acting as if he didn't need more staff. If he was any tighter, he wouldn't be able to pry his butt cheeks apart.

"I'll take a screwdriver! Can you make me one of those?"

*Sure, got you covered. Easy peasy.*

"I'll take a sex on beach. Especially if it's with you."

*I can't help you with that. Hand over your money.*

The night was moving along like clockwork. Every now and then I found myself looking at the door, wondering if I would see that Maverick guy again. He seemed like a fun, likeable guy. There was this 'thing' he had going for him, and despite my anti-man policy, he got my vote. His face kept popping up in my mind, and I kind of missed him at the bar. I had his number and it was sitting on my bedside table under my lamp, with the smudged ink and all. I didn't have the heart to call the number, though. Wasn't much point. He *was* pretty cool to talk to. The fact he didn't hook up with the Barbie twins surprised me and maybe made me more interested.

I switched my mind back from Maverick and over to the

band. They were getting the crowd really into them with their lyrics and melodic voices. The music they were playing people could bop their heads along to and dance. Some of their songs were up tempo, and I liked being close enough to the stage to enjoy them. Dustin and I meanwhile were getting slammed at the bar, and the line was three rows deep.

"We should hire another staff member, it's getting too hectic in here," I said as I did the hot shoe shuffle with him while the customers stared at us, waiting for their drinks.

He grimaced and plopped a beer in front of a customer over my shoulder. "You know I can't afford to do that right now," he said in a pained voice. I shook my head as I slammed the register closed.

"Why not? We have been running at a profit, killing it in fact for the last two months."

"Hey thanks, Hank. See you for the next round." He grinned at a customer before he turned back to me. "We already talked about this, Steph. Just because we're up now doesn't mean we're going to be up next quarter. Let's just see how it pans out for the next quarter and then, I'll hire," he confirmed as he moved to the other end of the bar. Dustin and his tight purse strings were giving me the shits.

I pressed my lips together firmly and shook my head as I wiped up the beer puddle from the last patron. We got a small break from the crowd as the band got stuck into the second set. I was in my head and wiping so furiously that I missed the man in question right in front of me.

"Hey, I think you just about rubbed a hole in the bar. You all right there?" The voice chuckled and I dropped my shoulders knowing I was being a little sulky.

"Hey, I'm just frustrated right now," I admitted, but managed to produce a smile for him.

"If you weren't working here, I would buy *you* a drink," he assured as he flipped his sandy hair out of his eyes. His strong jawline and mischievous eyes made me squirm a little, so I sliced up some more lemon so he wouldn't notice. When I looked up he was staring right at me with his arms folded over one another. He was wearing a blue collar shirt, rolled up to the elbows, and black jeans. I'd snuck a good look at him as he came toward the bar. "Looks like I came at the right time. The bar has cleared just for me." He sat down and spread his arms out wide with a cute grin. I burst out giggling; he'd broken me out of the little storm cloud moment I was having. "There we go! A laugh, just what I like to see," he cajoled. "How about a Bloody Mary to get the party started?"

I drew back and looked at him. "A Bloody Mary? I wouldn't have picked you for that type."

"Ah, I don't know about that. I like to mix it up from time to time. A Bloody Mary is on the healthy side. At least I like to tell myself that. You make a good one?" he enquired with a sparkle in his eye.

"Is that a challenge?" I scoffed. "I make a good one, but truthfully I haven't made one in a while. I'm confident I still have it in the Bloody Mary stakes." I grinned with my hands in my back pockets. Maverick's eyes zeroed in on my neckline and then back to my face, and I watched in amusement.

"Is that a line of text on your neck? Is that a tattoo?" I touched my neck and shifted my hair to one side.

"Yes, it says, *Life is a rollercoaster, enjoy the ride*. I got it when I was 18. My mother went apeshit about it."

Maverick laughed. "I bet she did. What about Dad?"

My father was a pretty laid back one and a very accepting person. He was the one I ran to if I wanted something. All I had to do was give him the goo-goo eyes and he would give it to me. He would tell me all the things I wanted to hear.

"You're my princess and you deserve to be treated like one," he would say. "If a man doesn't treat you like one then you should leave him." Obviously I didn't help myself by heading over to the dark side and dating a biker. They weren't exactly known as boyfriend material.

My mother on the other hand was another story. "I don't think you should get a nose ring right now. You're so young it will ruin your chances of getting a job."

I had to laugh at that now. I worked at a bar for a living and had two arms' worth of tatts with plans for more on my back. Most definitely if I wanted to hear the brutal unfiltered truth I went to my mother for it.

I curled my upper lip in contemplation. "Nah, my dad is pretty good. Just Mom, but I'm all grown up now, what can she say?" I held out both arms and turned them over with a smile.

"I like them. They suit you. I'm trying to figure you out, you got this edgy bartender thing going, but you seem like a real sweetie." He made a circle around my face as I batted my eyelashes in response and got to work on his drink. I opened up the bar fridge below and pulled out the tomato juice.

"Can I not be both?" I called out over the bar. The drums were kicking on a song and the singer was moving into screech mode, so I had to yell a little.

"Sure you can. Humans can be a lot of things. It's true," he reasoned with a nod. I kept making his drink and squeezed in the lemon, the shot of vodka, the Worcestershire sauce, and a dash of Tabasco, and poured it over ice. I was pretty sure I'd gotten the consistency right. I dropped a celery stick in as a garnish. A few people were looking at him with interest because some of the old-timers had never seen a drink like that before.

"Here we go, try this one on for size and let me know," I said proudly as he dropped his money on the bar.

Maverick licked his lips. "This already looks good. My God, woman." He put his lips to the glass and taste-tested, smacking his lips. "Oh yeah, this is the shit. I love it. Well done. There's a tip in there for you." He nodded to the money as he kept drinking and closed his eyes.

"You're doing too much. I know it's good, but it's not that good, is it?" I wrinkled my nose and took the money, ringing it up on the till.

"It is. You should make more cocktails." He looked around the bar and then back to me. "Maybe Edgewood isn't ready for you." He winked.

I shrugged my shoulders with my hands in my back pocket. "I mean—maybe."

"Oh, don't play coy. You *know* you're a great bartender. I'm surprised I get to talk to you like this. You're normally so busy, that's why I gave you my number. I thought you might wanna hang out sometime." He grinned. The way he got back around to that was smooth. I wiped down my station as a customer rolled up to the bar. I served her and got back to Maverick. "I was saying that I thought you might want to hang out," he repeated.

I didn't answer him, I just smiled as he smiled back with an open face looking for my response. "Maverick, what do you do to earn a crust?"

He sipped his drink a little longer and set it down. "Oh, I see. You're not going to answer me. That's all right, Steph," he said with a grin. "I can take a hint."

I shrugged again. "What? I don't really know you. I haven't seen you around. I wanna know what you do," I asked, and I really did. If he ran in biker circles there is no way I wanted anything to do with him, but he wasn't wearing a single thing to let me know he was. He seemed like he was into something corporate or something.

"If you must know I used to work in the military as special ops and now I'm retired. I do some private hire stuff. No big deal, but it keeps me out of trouble."

I was floored, and my mouth dropped open as I looked at his physique. "You? Special Ops? Are you for real? That's so awesome. I don't know... I was not expecting that," I gushed a little too much.

Maverick arched his eyebrow as one half of his mouth shot up in a cocky smile. "That'll teach you to judge a book by its cover. Yep. I sure am a military man. Anything to do with a bomb I can handle."

"This is mind blowing. I'm sorry. My bad."

"Now will you go out with me?" he laughed as two women approached him.

"I might," I sliced back.

"Welp. You got my number all right, unless you threw it in the trash."

"No, no I didn't." I looked down at the bar as the women wiggled their hips to Maverick and I rolled my eyes. Maverick had already taken them into his orbit and I was fading away. I stood firm and eyed the ladies. I didn't know either of them, but I thought them to be pretty bold as to approach when I was clearly in the middle of a conversation with Maverick. He didn't even get to reply to what I said because they were in front of me.

Both of them looked to be younger, around their mid-twenties. I wanted to see how he was going to handle the situation and if he would succumb to their tricks and go home with one of them. It was clear they were trying to get drinks out of him.

"Hi, we thought we would come over and say hello. We saw you talking to the bartender and we thought you might be lonely," one of them said as she flicked her hair around like a horse's tail. I wanted to slap her back from the bar.

*You have no right to be jealous. You don't like men, remember?*

The other girl had a short pixie cut and looked quite different. At least they were better than the Barbie twins. I coughed and held my head down to hide my smug expression. "Can I get either of you ladies a drink?" I pushed out of my mouth. The request must have come out a little stiff because one of them gave me a dirty look as in *Can't you see we're working it here?*

The one with the long hair bit her lip and twisted around a little on the spot looking at Maverick. As my eyes traveled around the bar, I saw there were plenty of eligible men in the room for the ladies to hit on. One nice-looking guy standing to the left with his friend was probably the right age for them. They were looking in the direction of Maverick and I'm guessing wondering what in the world he had that they didn't.

Further to the back of the room a group of guys—a boys' night out, it looked like, were goofing off and making eyes in the girls' direction. They would have been an option too, but no, they picked the older male sitting at the bar by his lonesome.

Maverick gave them both a pitiful look, and it made me smile. He clearly had no interest. That look made my stomach release for some reason. Why did I even care?

"Hey ladies, drinks on me. Tell the lovely bartender Steph here what you'd like," Maverick said over the music. The band had been playing for a while now, so I anticipated a rush of parched patrons trying to rush to the bar before the band's third and final set.

The one with the long hair grinned, her drink mission complete, and leaned over the bar top. "Can I get one of those Bloody Marys I saw you making earlier? I've never seen one. I want to try it one time." She sounded very young and naïve, finding her way. I relaxed a little with her and flashed her a smile.

"Sure. They do have a little bit of a kick to them, but nothing too harsh. Still want one?"

She nodded her head. "Yep!" The girl put her elbow on Maverick's shoulder as if she'd known him for years. *What is it with these women that come in here to talk to him? They seem to feel so comfortable with fawning all over him and he doesn't bat an eye.*

"And what can I get for you?" I asked the girl with the pixie haircut. She seemed a little more indecisive.

"I'm going to have a daiquiri, strawberry. Can you do that?"

I beamed. I was a little excited I got to stretch my wings with a seldom chosen drink. I was more of an experimental cocktail maker, but it was a good start regardless.

"Good choices, ladies. Be right back with your drinks," I chirped as I started to make their drinks.

"How are you ladies doing tonight? Are you enjoying the band?" I heard Maverick say as he chatted away to them. I could hear their cute laughs as he started telling jokes. As I made the drinks I saw that we were about to get hammered at the bar.

*"Oh shit!"* I muttered under my breath. "Dustin, get out here!" I yelled, and he popped right up and started to point to the swarm of people ready to trample one another to get to the bar. I got the girls their drinks, and Maverick ordered

another and tipped me really well. At that point I was back to back making drinks and in a groove. The bar rush lasted a good twenty minutes before the band saved us and everybody rushed from the bar back over to the stage.

I exhaled as I checked the kegs out the back and added more small change to the till.

"See why we need more staff?" I said sarcastically as I passed Dustin on the way back to the bar.

"You're right. I'm going to ask Melissa if she wants to come on part time. It's not fair to you," he admitted with reluctance as he watched the crowd peel away from the bar.

"What did you say?" I gasped for dramatics. "Did you just say I'm right?"

"I did. I'm a man that can admit my wrongs. I just take a while. Between you and my wife I don't know who's worse," he grumbled as I laughed at him.

"You need us to keep you on track," I offered.

"Like a hole in the head," he quipped as he restocked the vodka. I found myself seeking out Maverick. He was having a conversation with the two women, and they were laughing hard at him. One of them kissed him on the cheek, and I felt this weird pang inside my chest.

*Maybe I should text him my number after all.*

I made the decision that I would give him a chance. After all, it was just a drink, nothing serious. The band started their last set, and I did something a little bit sneaky as I kept my eye on Maverick and the girls. Under the bar I pulled out my phone and shot him a text.

*Hope you're having a good time. Anyway this is my number. Steph xxx*

I smirked and waited for him to realize. His phone was sitting on top of the bar, and he reached out for it. As he picked it up, I watched a smile lift on his face, and he looked up at me. He mouthed the words *I'll call you* to me as the two girls craned their necks to scowl at me.

I crossed my arms and gave them both a little tinkly wave. *You've got nothing on me. He's not going to go out with you.* The one with the long hair turned up her snub nose, but not before her eyes glowered at me. The other one gave me more of a perplexed look. As they kept talking, I saw that Maverick was bored as hell. I moved to the end of the bar as another customer requested a drink. When I turned back around, I saw that he'd left the bar. Maybe he would call me or maybe he wouldn't.

We made it to closing time and by the time I got home my head hit the pillow pretty quickly. As soon as I showered and washed my face actually. I was too tired to eat and smelled like a brewery.

The next morning I woke up to my phone beeping. I patted my fingers around on my bed before I saw the end of it tucked under my pillow and grabbed it. It was a text message from Maverick.

*Hey. Thanks for your digits. Let's hang and go for food. Wednesday? Mav.*

*Sounds good. I'm free then. Day off.*

*Cool. Pick you up?*

*Yes. :)*

*:) 7 ok? It's a surprise.*

*Yup fine.*

I frowned a little. I had an unofficial date. At least that's what it seemed like. I woke up slowly and got myself together. The message from Maverick put a pep in my step even though my mind was still on the cheating episode from my last partner. I didn't have to marry him. I was the resident night owl because of my job. I started late and finished early in the morning. That part came with the territory. I was watching some trash on TV when my phone rang. It was my brother.

"James, and to what do I owe the pleasure of this call?" I groaned. "Why are you calling me so early?"

"I wanted to see if you were up yet and if you could drive me to pick up my car from the mechanic's?"

I flopped my bowl down on the table. "You are a pain in the ass. Why do I have to take you? Why don't you get one of your dirty Viper friends to take you there?" For all our little bickering arguments, I was close to James, and we had a pretty unbreakable bond.

"Sister. Don't be like that. You know I love you. Come on. It's fixed now, and I need to get where I'm going," he said in a panicked tone.

I swirled the Fruit Loops I was eating around in my bowl. "And where is that exactly?"

"I'm going to see the boys. We got something cooking, and it's real good. I told you. Maybe I can even help you start that cocktail bar that you've been talking about." His voice was edgy and made me angry. I knew what he was up to. He was about to go sell drugs. If Mom and Dad knew what he was doing, it would break their hearts. I'd broken my mother's enough by becoming a bartender. It took her years to come to terms with that. If my little knuckleheaded brother kept running with the Vipers, then it would ruin them.

"Excuse the pun," I quipped sarcastically.

"What?" he replied.

"Don't worry about it, James. It went over your head."

"Oh, okay."

"I don't want anything to do with your dirty money. I don't, James. Whatever you have to do to get that money is going to cost you in the long run. *You need to stop.* I want you to stop running with the Vipers. They don't care about you at all. They're using you as a pawn, don't you understand? You're just their little dope boy," I flamed at him passionately.

"You wait and see. Just drive me to pick up my car. Come on," he begged. I looked at the phone as if he was right in front of me and shook my head. He thought I was going to pick him up so he could go drive himself to an early death.

"Nope. It's a no. Figure it out." I clicked the end call button hard. I wanted nothing to do with his bullshit. Sadness clouded my heart because I knew that it would change our relationship, but oh well, fuck it. Maybe it was that tough love that needed to be employed.

# 5

## MAVERICK

NO MORE ASSIGNMENTS WERE COMING THROUGH TO THE Guardians, so I was twiddling my thumbs at the chop shop and goofing off with the guys. It was about lunchtime, and things were moving slow.

"You want a game of pool? You don't have any cars coming in right now, come on, man," I said to Axle.

Axle wasn't a bad pool player, but he wasn't the greatest either. "You're right, I'm not up for this car right now anyway. This part is giving me the shits. It won't fit in properly, and now I'm going to have to wait another two days for it to come in if I order it and that's only if I order it today," he said with a gloomy sigh.

"Then it's the perfect time for me to kick your ass on the table," I challenged.

"You are kidding, right? You kick my ass? There's no way on this planet you will."

"Rush is the pool guy, not you."

"That may be true, but you, my friend, are no match for me. I have beaten you what? Six times already and you want to play me again? Can it be that you're a glutton for punishment?"

"All of those times, I'd had a few drinks. I want to see how I play completely sober. Those games were purely social experiments," I said in a joking tone.

We were going back and forth when I saw Pop walk in from the front of the warehouse as we entered the lunchroom. He was walking at a quick pace—for Pop anyway—and it looked as if steam was blowing off the top of his head.

"Boys, we have a serious issue that's going to need a church meeting asap." The grim look on his face gave it away.

"What's going on, Pop? We got trouble in the woods?" I asked. Anytime anybody mentioned there was a serious problem it wasn't that big a deal to me. Nothing could be bigger than watching your friends getting blown up right in front of your face. I took everything in my stride and if I couldn't take in my stride I smoked it away.

"We have trouble in the form of a Wildcard," he corrected.

Axle looked over at Pop. "Are you going to keep us in the dark or let us know now?"

Pop readjusted the hat he was wearing. "Wildcard has obtained some footage that could prove to be very damning for the club. Axle, this involves you." I watched Axle's jaw twitch as Pop handed him the phone. I couldn't see what they were looking at, but Axle's reaction let me know it wasn't good.

"*Shit!*" I could hear a sledgehammer noise from the video as Axle handed it to me. What I saw was a video taken with a night vision camera. The footage was hard to make out at first, and then it became clearer as the person holding the camera gained their footing. You could see four men carrying a body to an incinerator and tossing it in. For the first portion of the video the men all had their faces covered. That's when the problems started. I watched as Havoc pulled his balaclava off and the footage was clear as day. His beard, his facial features, the works. Axle being 6'4 along with Gunner made it even easier to pick them as Guardians. This was a shitty day. Not as bad as being blown up, but somewhere in the ballpark.

"Might have a problem if this gets in the wrong hands. If he's already sent it to you who else has he sent it to? Depending on what the cops have in the way of equipment, they might not be able to identify Havoc," I said, trying to instill hope into the dire situation.

"Maverick, you know that's a lie. This camera has the time, the date, and the vehicle plates of when our guys dumped that pig Clint off. We are in the shit. Finn will send the message. The meeting will be tonight. Wildcard just officially became more than a pest." Pop stalked out of the lunchroom as Axle and I looked at one another.

"This old dude really has it out for the Guardians. We took him in after being out in the cold for so long, and now he goes and does this. It's a real bummer. Protect thine own is the motto, but he seems to have forgotten it," I pointed out as Hawk walked in to see our faces.

"Yo, what are all the long faces about, kids?" Hawk asked cheerfully.

"Your girl," Axle added with a stony face.

Hawk's face dropped just as all of our phones beeped simultaneously. It was a message from Finn for a church meeting.

*Meeting at church 19.00hrs.*

"Tell me what that means, Axle, and don't tell Tara.

What does it mean?" He pushed as his forehead wrinkled in angst.

"Wildcard has footage of us putting Clint in the incinerator in Sedillo," he said matter-of-factly.

Hawk closed his eyes for a moment. "Shit. Tara is going to freak out. She's only just starting to feel better about the situation. Tell me this isn't happening," he moaned.

"Want some weed?" I offered meekly.

"No weed in the world is going to solve this one. Are your faces clear? Who has the video?"

"Pop has it. He's going to bring it to the meeting I presume," Axle confirmed as he shifted his weight. "Gunner had his on the whole time, so did Shaggy and Mustang.

"Who was there?" I asked.

Axle's eyes were vacant like when he went into fight mode except there was no one to fight on this one. "Mustang, Gunner, Shaggy, Havoc, and me. We set the car on fire too. You can see it in the video."

Hawk threw his head back in anguish and punched the throw cushion on the couch. "I want to kill this guy. We need to find Wildcard. That means the footage could be out already. We're already screwed." His eyes went wide as Axle pressed his hand on his shoulder.

"Calm down for me, Hawk, and breathe. We are going to fix it. We can handle this. Wildcard isn't a saint. We start digging in on him. Ain't no way I'm going to jail with Zena and neither are you or the boys. We are going to sew this up, and it's going to be another hiccup along the road," he reasoned.

Hawk sat down on the couch, and I looked up at him sideways. "When did you become so wise?" I laughed along with Axle as he cracked a grin.

"When I started changing poopy diapers for Zena," he crowed. I heard the voice of a proud father as he spoke.

"Ahh, listen to you, you big softie. Bring it in here, big guy." I reached around Axle's waist and he stood as stiff as a pole as I wrapped my arms around him.

"Maverick, if you don't get off me, I'm going to have to try out my new move on you," he hissed good-naturedly at me.

"Aww, you love me, big guy. I love you right back," I joked. He tapped my forearm.

"You're not a bad guy to have around. We'll let you stay here." He cracked a crooked smile.

"Gee thanks. I feel so privileged," I joked as I bunched up my shirt.

"If you guys are finished with your love fest already I gotta go give Tara the heads up I guess. I don't know how to break it to her. Once she hears this, it's going to send her back into a downward spiral." Hawk looked super stressed, and I felt for the guy. I wasn't one for murder, but Clint had to go.

"Let's just see how it opens up. Tara's here, right? Probably best to leave it until after the meeting and we can see how to tackle it." Hawk's eyes closed as he let out a frustrated sigh. "If she knows that I took that to the meeting without talking to her, she is going to be pissed."

"I agree with Maverick. Leave it. You want to at least give her a game plan, so she knows the situation is being handled. We should have been more careful. I had this feeling we were being watched. How the hell did he know to follow us?" Axle asked, more as a rhetorical question more than anything.

"Your guess is as good as mine," Hawk added. He was picking up the balls on the pool table and dropping them down on it in misplaced frustration. "Fuck!" Suddenly he let loose as he gripped one of the porcelain balls and let it clink another one as they rolled into the top pocket.

"Hey, hey, hey. We're going to work it out. Everybody here has Tara's back." I was trying to pacify the situation, but my guy was pretty uptight about it.

"Let's get out of here. We have to come back later anyway. The day was pretty light, and all the other boys are gone. Let's move on," Axle said.

"For sure. Let's get out of here."

As we walked to the front of the warehouse, I saw a problem. Hawk was walking in time with me. "Ah shit, we got a problem. Check out who it is," I remarked as a dark figure stood in the rolled up garage door.

"Sheriff Malone. What the hell is he doing here?" Axle and I looked at each other, putting two and two together.

"Hawk," I said slowly. "Tara just came out of the office. Stay cool, brother," I added. "Don't cause alarm, we don't know if he knows anything. Remember that Tara reported Clint, right?"

I could see the flicker in Hawk's jaw as he stalked to the front. I pulled him back. "Easy," I reminded him.

Sheriff Malone took a look at all three of us with a seemingly non-threatening smile. I knew under that smile was something else and he was sniffing around. He knew something. Shit was either going to hit the fan or be nothing.

"Hey Sheriff, howdy! You come to get your car fixed?" I chuckled with a wide grin. I was a lot more easy-going than the other guys and had a knack for being diplomatic and smoothing things over.

The sheriff chuckled as he held out his hand to me. "Maverick and Hawk, the meth boys. I'm glad we haven't had to call you in lately. That spike we experienced is calming down. We actually might be getting a handle on this thing," he added. "It's hot out here boys, ain't it?"

"Sure is. We're happy to be working on it with you, Sheriff. If we've got it under control then that's a good thing." Hawk smiled back at him, but his smile didn't reach his eyes. I caught a quick look from the sheriff as he licked his dry lips and scoped the warehouse out. Axle slipped away, sensing it would be best, I was guessing.

The sun was blazing hot, but Sheriff Malone had his hat on, and he lifted up revealing a line of perspiration underneath. He pointed as he shook both Axle's and Hawk's hands. They were wary, but the best way to counter was to be open and jovial. It was one of my tactics, and it worked like a charm. If I wasn't a bomb expert I would have been a kick-ass interrogator.

The sheriff's eyes moved past us to the office. "Would Tara happen to be around? I have an update for her," he asked.

"Yeah, I think she's right in the office. Working hard. Anything we should know about?" Hawk asked as I stood off to the side a little.

"Nope, just a conversation I was having with her in the past. Want to clear it up with her, if you don't mind," the sheriff said as he started whistling.

Hawk grimaced as he nodded. "Let me get her for you." He opened the main office door as I smiled at the sheriff.

"Thanks, Hawk. Good man."

"So, Maverick, have you been getting any private security contracts or you're taking a little break?"

"Ah, you know what? I haven't. I'm going to take it easy for a minute and see what flows to me, you know. I was doing a few before here, but since the meth lab stuff I haven't found anything as exciting for me to sink my teeth into. Once that blood gets rushing it's hard to go back to mainstream security."

The sheriff crossed his arms as if he was thinking of a solution. "You know, leave it with me. I might know someone who knows someone. I have to just see what he's up to. He used to run security at the White House and he's here now. He often gets a lot of overflow for work for capable men such as yourself. Could be good for you. It does require you to travel, though," he mentioned.

I crossed my arms to match his behavior. "Well, aren't you just a wealth of information! That's good to know, Sheriff. I'd appreciate that. Get in touch with me," I said with a bright smile. From the way he was talking I knew he had no idea about the video. Wildcard was holding that ace up his sleeve. For now.

Tara came out a little nervous, but with a brave smile. "Hi, Sheriff, how are you?" Hawk was standing guard on her right. I angled my head to him to move away from her.

"I'm good, Tara. Are you doing all right?" he asked as he studied her. She bowed her head a little and gathered her hair, sweeping it to the side.

"I am. Not bad at all. Can't complain, except about this heat," he chuckled.

"Yeah, it's pretty awful today," she agreed quietly.

"What can I do for you?" She blinked and looked back at the sheriff like a deer in headlights. I could see she was holding the edge of her sleeve in a tremor. The sheriff wiped the sweat off his brow as his face scrunched up in an ugly way from the heat.

"Sheriff, you want a glass of water?" I asked, trying to give Tara time to get herself together. Her eyes were screaming for help.

"No, this won't take but a minute," he stated. "Tara, I

promised to follow up with you. I wondered if we could go somewhere private and have a chat," he asked, looking at both Hawk and me hovering.

"I-I'm okay. You can say whatever you have to say in front of these guys. I'm just going to tell Hawk anyway." She shrugged, nibbling on her lip. The sheriff's expression was sympathetic.

"Ah, all right then," he said gruffly. "I wanted to know if you've seen Clint by any chance. It's the strangest thing. I went to see him at his address in Bluewater Complex. He's listed as living there still, but he's nowhere to be found. I asked around the neighbors, and nobody has seen or heard from the guy," he said as he pulled out a handkerchief and patted his upper lip.

"I mean, I have no idea. I don't. I don't even speak to Clint. I just, I don't-" Tara was cracking up and needed saving, but the sheriff, unassuming as he was, hit his stride with the questioning.

"Imagine my surprise when I learned that the Guardians corporation Inc. I believe it is—brought out Bluewater. That's pretty damn cool, so I guess I wondered if you'd seen him or anything because you might have patched it up with the man." He raised up his tiptoes and rocked forward. "Now, I'm not one to pry into someone's personal life for no reason, but given your experience with the man, I would have thought you wouldn't go back to him. Still I thought it wouldn't hurt to stop by and ask the question."

"Ah, I haven't seen him," she said in the smallest voice. She looked guilty as hell, and Hawk fixed his mouth to say something.

"We did buy that building and I believe Clint got a nice sum for the store downstairs. I would say he probably skipped town, Sheriff. He received a pretty penny from the

Guardians. The store was pretty run-down while he was managing it, and now we have some new renovations going on in there to revamp the place and make it great for the community again. Kind of like what the Guardians did for Martha's, you know." I patted him lightly on his flabby bicep as he assessed what he was told.

"Well then. That's a pretty good reason. I've seen the renovations with my own eyes. Looks like it's coming along real nice. I've stopped in there a couple of times. Hmm." He looked back at Tara, who looked stunned. "This true, Tara?"

She seemed to snap out of it and got her senses back as she smiled at me gratefully. "It's true. The Guardians have acquired the building, and it's coming along," she said.

"Well then, that is great. I'm glad to hear it. I wanted to do my part and make sure you were okay. You take care of yourself, but judging by the caliber of men you have around you, I'm sure you'll be just fine. You have a nice day. Maverick, I'll be in touch," he claimed as he tipped his hat and fit it snugly back on his head and walked out into the hot Edgewood sun.

We waited for him to get in his vehicle. He took another look at all three of us with the window wound down and drove off.

Hawk shook his head. "Shit. Good save, Maverick." He closed his eyes as he put his hands over his head. I could see the tears welling in Tara's eyes as she reached out to hug me.

"Thank you so much. I'm sorry I clammed up. I don't know what happened to me. I'm strong. I'm not like that normally. I don't know why I was stuttering all over the place. I almost blew it," she said in shock as she held her hands to her face. I hugged her back, and she went to stand beside Hawk.

"Hey, it's cool. Easy. You've done nothing wrong, and I

told him the truth. You would have told him too. You were just a little slower about it. Come on. It's all okay. Take a deep breath." I breathed in and stood on one leg trying to make her laugh.

She stifled her grin. "Maverick," she said in a pained voice. "Stop making me laugh." Hawk kissed the top of her head.

"Sorry, baby. I should have stepped in. I froze too. Dammit!" he said as he ran his fingers through his hair.

"Let it go. He doesn't know anything," I said to the both of them. Hawk's eyes widened as he glared at me as a warning. "It's over, Tara. He can't do anything anymore. You're good."

"Thanks, Maverick for stepping in and saving my ass. I was about to lose it."

"As per usual, we get on the straight and narrow as a club and a lurker comes. This one comes in the form of Wildcard. Now it's a little more personal on all accounts. I've called you all here because once again we're going into battle," Pop confirmed as he looked around the table.

"We all need to protect Tara. This isn't her fault. She shouldn't be haunted from the grave by this guy. She should be able to live her life and get on with it," Finn commented as he ran his hands through his thick beard.

"What's going on? What we got, Pop?" Rush asked.

"This." Pop pulled down the screen that we projected videos and movies on sometimes in the church meeting room. "Maverick, get the light." I was closest to the door, so I flicked the light off.

The room went dark as Pop pressed the remote and

revealed the footage we'd seen briefly on his phone. The screen started out blurry and shaky. It straightened up and became clear as the timer ran at the bottom of the screen. A car pulled up. Clint's car. Four men got out. Then one more. I recognized every single one of my brothers.

"Shit, is that what I think it is? Is that the tape from the Clint situation?" Rush asked. Poor guy was out of the loop completely. Mustang looked at Axle and Havoc and Shaggy. Shaggy looked as if he might piss his pants any minute.

The tension in the room was high as everybody processed what the video might mean. Pop stopped the tape and looked at me. I flipped the light switch back on. "Yes. It is. This means that Wildcard has the tape. He is using it to blackmail us, and he's feeling lucky right now. He is looking to extort us for over a million dollars." He tapped the pads of his fingers together as he looked around the room, and the chatter picked up.

"There's no way in hell we're going to pay that. We need to find him. Hit the streets and get to him before he can take it any further," Axle said in a defiant tone.

"Trouble is how far has he gotten already?" Finn jumped in.

Havoc slammed his fist down on the table in frustration. "I shouldn't have taken my mask off. I mean, how can the police identify us anyway? That's in the dark, how are they going to pull evidence in on that?"

"They can. They have all kinds of technology to be able to do it. At the very least it will give them just cause to start sniffing around here." Pop set the record straight, and I felt compelled to update the room of the afternoon's visit.

"That part is already happening. The sheriff came nosing around because Clint is missing. Tara put in that restraining order so he was following up," I threw out. Shaggy started to rub his temple.

"This is shit. I can't believe it," he said.

"It's not. Sit tight. We have good dealings with Edgewood. We can clear this up. This is not a guy that anybody wants on the planet. It's going to be a problem when the parents start digging or not being able to get a hold of Clint. I suspect they will file a missing persons report at some stage," Mustang put in. He seemed unconcerned, and given all we'd been through military-wise, this was child's play to us. Personally I was worried about my guy Hawk and how it would affect him and Tara.

Pop swung back in his seat. "Axle. I want you to find him. I suspect he is trying to set something up somewhere. If I know anything about Wildcard, he's cooking up something. Excuse the pun. From what Hawk and the boys have told me it has something to do with those meth labs. Edgewood has them under control, but my guess is he wants the money for it."

"I'm on it. He won't get far," Axle declared as he cracked his knuckles.

"Last we knew he was at Bluewater..." Red chimed in.

"We know he's moved on. If he was talking to the Viper boys, then we know he's probably over in Sedillo country with the other scumbags," Hawk added. "He was asking me for the breakdown of the meth operations, so I know that's what he's planning."

"I want everybody in this room to hit the ground on this. Report back. Edgewood isn't that big that somebody won't know where he's hiding out," Finn directed.

"What about the cops?" Shaggy asked. He looked as if he was going to lose it.

"What about them?" Pop raised a bushy eyebrow. "Wildcard isn't going to them yet. He's trying to get his money. We play him at his own game. Regardless of the video footage where is the evidence? Where is the body? There is none. It's gone." Pop darted his eyes up to the ceiling and blew out a breath as if blowing into a sandbag. "Poof!" The whole table broke out guffawing and laughing at Pop's antidote. "Meeting over. Resume when we have more information."

Chairs scraped along the ground as the boys got up out of their seats and moved toward the stairs. The only person in the room that wasn't laughing was Hawk. He had a storm cloud over his head as he stormed out of the meeting room and down the stairs. I wanted to talk to him, but I thought it was best to leave it.

Don't know why I was nervous, but I was. I looked around the door frame of Steph's house. Nice enough place in the suburbs. I knocked on the door two times.

"Hey!" She bounced to open the door a little out of breath.

"Well, hi. Don't you look great."

"Thank you." Her cheeks flushed crimson as she ushered me in the door. "Come on in."

"Okay, thanks." I came in and looked around. She had a small walk-through section with pictures on the walls of her loved ones. On the right was a small open plan kitchen. Faintly in the background I could hear Metallica playing.

"You like Metallica? Are you into rock?" I asked her. "I'm more into Indie rock myself," I established, trying to find common ground with her.

She scoffed. "No, that's what's playing right now on Spotify. I am into alternative music though." Stephanie was wearing a long form-fitting dress with boots, and she had this real quirky vibe to her that intrigued me. Her hair was in the two long dark braids, and she smelled like coconut.

"Where are we headed?"

"Ah, you know the place. It's not far from here," I smiled without giving anything away. When she moved to the outside, she would see that I rode a motorcycle, so I thought it might get a little hairy. I was willing to take the risk and to let her know that not all bikers were dirtbags.

"You're not telling me anything. Something is going on." Her little nose scrunched up, making me want to touch it.

"You'll see. It will work out." I walked ahead of her in the hallway to the evening light of Edgewood. As her eyes adjusted to the light, she saw what I was talking about.

"Ah you're a goddamn biker. I should have known." She expelled a heavy sigh.

"I am, but I'm not a bad guy. Come on, give me a chance. Let's go out this one time," I coaxed.

She closed the door behind her. "You're here, and I'm letting you take me out, so I guess let's just see," she said with hesitation.

"I don't bite, I promise." I saw the shadows of doubt cross her face and knew I had my work cut out for me as I handed her my spare helmet. "All right, let's do this."

She slipped it on as the night sky got darker. "You look really cute in a helmet. I want to give you a few instructions first. I want you to put your hands right here." I tapped my waist area. I knew not to wear my cut; I didn't want to scare her off. In my mind it was *If we get past the first date then I'll show you who I really am*.

"It's okay. I've been on the back of one plenty of times. Lean this way, lean that way." She rocked from side to side.

"Pretty much how it goes. Come on then, let's go." I

mounted my bike and felt the weight of the bike shift as she got on the back. Her arms around my waist felt good, and we were about to cross the first hurdle. I started the engine, letting the bike rumble under us. I sped off into the night, a hot girl on the back of my bike and the power of the beast under me. Best feeling ever.

We made it to Martha's within ten minutes, and I killed the engine. She pulled off her helmet.

"Ahhh, Martha's. This is a great place. I haven't been over here since the fire." She smoothed down her braids and the smell of coconut wafted off her in waves. It must have been in her shampoo or something.

"I'm glad. The whole place has changed. New décor, everything. The front and the back have been extended. My buddy Shadow is an artist, and he's got his paintings here with his girl, Ava."

She swung her head back to me. "You know Shadow? He's from the Guardians. He used to come into the bar a lot. I remembered him mentioning that he was an artist. That's pretty cool that you know him." So she wasn't completely against bikers.

"Yep. That's him. Great guy." I hoped that she would think the same about me in time. The place with its warm family glow was lit up inside, and people were sitting in the diner style booths closest to us. Most of the booths were packed, but I was smart and had made a reservation. Fairy lights were twinkling along the edge of the timber steps, and the cicadas were buzzing from the woods across the street. From the back deck I could hear people laughing and the low hum of chatter.

I opened the front door for her. "Ladies first." Her eyes were fixated on absorbing the new additions of Martha's.

"Thank you," she mumbled as she craned her neck to

look behind the back of the restaurant. In doing so, her foot slipped off the step, and I grabbed her around the waist. Holding her close to me made me want to stay there. Her waist was slim, and her body radiated heat. Her hands latched on to mine as she gasped.

"Shit—sorry. Clumsy. I was trying to look at too many places at once."

"It's okay. I'm glad I could catch you," I murmured softly as our eyes connected. I could still see the pain in them, not knowing whether she should respond.

"Thanks." They shifted back to the front door as we walked through. The grill was flaming, the mouth-watering smell of burgers cooking, and that fried onion smell I adored was in the air. At Martha's there wasn't always a host at the door. Even though they'd expanded, they kept the same traditions. Something I really admired about the place, that and their bacon and egg sandwiches were pretty damn good.

We went straight to the front, and the waitress gave us a seat out back. "Wow. I can't believe how much this place has changed. This used to be some run-down diner that served sloppy joes and great coffee. I hate to say it, but the fire looks to have been a good thing for them."

"You might be right about that," I replied. "How are things for you? Are you feeling good about being at the bar?"

She rubbed the bridge of her nose as she picked up the menu. "Yes and no. I want Dustin to hire more staff. It could really be something, you know? He could expand out back with a bigger stage for the performers. More cocktails. Different promotions. I'm frustrated if I'm honest."

"Do you like working there?" I asked as my eyes settled on what I wanted to eat. She looked at me for a moment.

"I want to run my own bar someday. I'm not holding out for it, though. I'm just saving money now." A woman with dreams. I respected that. A wisp of her hair was blowing around in the breeze as it drifted over her face. I pulled it back behind her ear. Really I wanted an excuse to touch her skin.

"Thanks."

I smiled. "That's huge. You should go for it, you got the smarts for it. I liked that Bloody Mary you made, sure got the party started for me." The waitress came and we placed our orders and went back to talking.

"How come you're here in Edgewood if you used to work in the military? This seems like the last place you would be."

"Ah, I'm a throw caution to the wind type of guy. I like to take chances and Edgewood, well I thought why not." A tiny flicker of guilt flickered over me. I was omitting the fact that Doc had called me here. I would have been pretty sweet staying in Cali where I was.

She narrowed her eyes at me as our drinks came out. "Really?"

"Really." I sipped on my beer, taking my time with her. "Tell me why you don't like bikers?"

Instantly her back went up and I watched her stiffen in her seat and her hand grip her glass as she wanted to crush it. "I went through a breakup recently and the guy happened to be a dick who rode a bike. One of those bad boy types."

"Ahhh. I get it." I sighed. "Not to sound cliché, but I'm not like those guys. I wouldn't ever treat you like they did." That part was true, we were still getting to know one another, but this little Maverick intuition of mine knew she was different from the rest. She blinked into her drink as the cicadas helped fill the gap in our silence.

"I'm not trying to get into a relationship or anything. I

just thought you seemed like a decent guy and I wanted to find out more about you," she admitted, which I appreciated. Always good to know where you stood.

"Sounds fair, and likewise. We can take it slow, we're just getting to know one another here. Everything and anything is possible," I reassured her with a smile. I would win her over eventually. The fading look of skepticism on her face made me think I might have a shot.

"So do you have family here, Maverick?" Tricky question. Technically I regarded the Guardians as family. I shifted my beer back and forth on the table as I tussled with telling her the truth.

"Ah, I have friends that I regard like brothers here, so in answer to your question, yes." Not a bad save, but I couldn't keep on lying to her.

# 6

## STEPHANIE

THE PRETEND DATE WAS PRETTY GOOD. I THOUGHT I wouldn't end up liking him, but I did. He seemed like a pretty decent human being. I learned a little bit more about him, but my gut told me there was more to him than he was giving away. There was no goodnight kiss at the door—I didn't want him getting any ideas so I wanted to keep it light and gave him a kiss on the cheek.

"I'd like to see you again, I really would," he'd said with his cute way when we got to my door. I could see his hopeful pupils shining through the dark. My past was still clouding my future, and I wanted to say *no chance*. My heart was still red raw from the last man that had mishandled and trampled it.

"Uh, I mean sure. I had a nice time, and it can't hurt, can it?" I justified to myself more so than to him.

"Okey dokey. I will give you a call. Take care." He did lean in, but it was for a kiss on the cheek. I hated that I tensed up my whole body as he did. I caught the whiff of his cologne as he pulled back.

"You too, see you soon." The crunch of his biker boots

faded away, and I watched him mount his motorcycle and take off into the inky night littered with stars.

"What am I doing?" I muttered under my breath as I untied my braids and stepped inside. I headed for the bathroom and wiped off my makeup, taking myself off to bed. The next morning was a little rough. I was used to sleeping in until noon and getting ready for work in the afternoon and working into the dead of the night. Waking up at 9 a.m. was unusual for me.

My phone beeped next to my bed, and I uttered a low groan of disapproval at being woken up so early. The text message was from my brother. The words on the screen automatically ignited a flight or fright response in me as my heart started to palpitate.

*Lunch? Don't worry not in trouble :)*

I texted him back. *Good. Okay.*

I plopped my head back on the pillow. At least there wasn't any trouble for now. I willed myself out of bed at what I deemed to be an ungodly hour and shuffled to the kitchen. My stomach started to rumble, which made me detour to the kitchen for breakfast. I ran through my daily routine in a fog and sat idly on the couch. Mid-morning rocked around soon enough, and I was barely awake when a knock came at the door. Irritation flashed over my face.

"What now? Who is this?" I pressed my hands into the couch and stomped to the front door, barely able to grasp the door handle because I was so mad. "What th-" As I flung the door open, I was greeted with a sight that made me want to hurl.

A Viper. Not just any Viper, the same one that had been staring at me when I went to pick my brother up in Sedillo. His whole aura bled violence. From head to toe he was dressed in black with dark stones for eyes. He was of

Hispanic descent and a purple bandana was wrapped around the bottom of his neck. "Surprise," he said as he held his arms out. I gulped down my fear and moved my feet behind the door. I saw him look past me into the hall-way, and I closed the gap.

"What can I do for you?" I asked in an ice-cold tone.

He zoomed in on me, undressing me from top to bottom. "You can't do nothing. I was looking for your little bro. Is he around?" He talked as if he had some authority and we were old friends. My heartbeat was pounding in my chest, boom, boom, boom, and the blood rushed around my ears.

"Excuse me? I don't even know you. My brother doesn't live here. He has his own place. Why are you here and how did you get my freakin' address, you creep?"

"Your brother told me you live around here, and I know your car from our little meeting last week," he said matter-of-factly with an ugly sneer.

"Back to my question... Why are you here? If you're trying to threaten me, I'm going to call the cops," I replied. I wasn't afraid of him. I was taken aback and upset that he'd found me.

He ran his tongue around the rim of his lips as I strug-gled to contain my shiver. "Okay, Ms. Bartender. He said he was coming here, and I have to deliver some important information to him. I won't bother you again." His tone was menacing as his dark eyes glanced down to my bare feet and back up again as he chuckled. I slammed the door shut and watched him walk to his bike.

I stalked to the kitchen and picked up my phone to call my brother. My teeth were grinding together from his stupidity, and now he was dragging me into his bullshit.

"Hey sister, sister. I'm going to be coming on over real soon," he answered.

"I want you to get over here now. I just had a visit from one of your stupid Viper friends looking for you. I don't want them coming to my house ever!" I screamed, letting out all of my pent-up feelings.

"Shit, he came there?"

"Yes! Do you even know who you're fucking with? These are dangerous people, James. Seriously dangerous people. I told him the next time he decides to make himself known at my house I was calling the cops," I said.

"No, no. no. You told him that? Shit. Maybe you shouldn't have done that." The warning bell came, and the pang in my gut came back.

"Get over here now." I patted my hair, knowing it resembled a bird's nest because I could feel the tangles and knots that I would have to straighten out before I went to work.

"Okay. I'm there." That thin line of what is right and wrong is the one I was dancing on. The tightrope was a difficult one. I wanted to tell Mom and Dad, but I knew if I did that it would cause a huge rift between my brother and me. He was all I had in the way of siblings, and I wanted him on my side. My cereal was getting soggy, and due to the privacy invasion, I'd lost my appetite.

The throttle of a motorcycle is the next thing I heard, and this time before I opened the door I checked out the side of the window. It was James, and his expression looked horrified.

I opened the door, fuming at his antics. His fist was balled up, ready to knock on the door. "I beat you to it." I kicked him in the shin with my toe, which hurt him more than me.

"What was that for?" he whined as he ducked under my arm and into the living room.

"That's for bringing that slimy guy to my house. How did

he get my address, fool?" Spit flew from my mouth, and my brother dodged it. Even with my yelling, his face stayed blank.

"That part I'm unsure of. I didn't tell him about where you live, I swear," he said as he grabbed both my shoulders.

"That's even worse. Give me one reason why I shouldn't call the cops on him. Tell me right fucking now." I directed my finger to the ground as a thunderous cloud of rage enveloped my body. I wanted zero things to do with any bikers. If it wasn't work, it was my brother or the stupid drug fucked bikers infesting Edgewood. My life was a complete mess.

"Relax. I was supposed to have been at a meeting yesterday, but I missed it. Slept in, so he was probably coming to check if I was good for the next one. What did he say?" he asked earnestly without any regard for the fact the guy could have killed me.

My brother's eyebrows shot up as I contemplated slapping him senseless. "He said he had some important information for you. Why did you miss the meeting with them? Not that I want you to be involved, but if missing a meeting means they come hunting you at your sister's house then you better work on your time management," I fired at him as I went back to the couch.

"You're right. That's my bad. I'll tell them to stay away from here. Sorry. I really am." I slanted my head forward and massaged my forehead extensively. "Hear me out. This is going to put us on the map."

I held up my hand. "We? I want nothing to do with your maps. Forget it," I declared.

"You will when I start raking in the millions." My brother's eyes went wide as if he was flying off to another planet.

"Wildcard has a plan for us all, and it's going to make us a whole lot of money, baby."

I groaned loudly. "James. This is bullshit. Get a job like a normal person."

"Nope. This is my ticket out of this hellhole called Edgewood," he gloated. "Twenty meth labs coming up. We got the product to move." His mouth was salivating with the thought of the money.

I grabbed his wrist and sat him down on the couch. "You can't do that. You're going to get caught, and you're going to go to jail. If you get busted you will get shot. You can't live this life, James." I lowered my voice, thinking that might be a better way to reach him. It didn't work, his eyes were glassy with the taste of living a rich, fast drug-fueled life.

"I don't care. Let it ride. I can help you with the cocktail bar, don't you see?" he begged.

"No. I don't." I shook my head vigorously. "No, I don't see," I croaked as tiredness seeped in. I wanted no part of it. "I don't want a cocktail bar if it's coming through you. I don't. Leave me all the way out of it. You're becoming delusional."

"Am not," he quipped childishly.

"Are too. I would rather have a brother who is alive and well than one who's dead."

James paced my living room floor like a caged lion and poured himself a drink. I wasn't going to let up on him. At least he wasn't using the stuff. If that started, it would be a dark and dirty downward spiral for him.

"How about this... I do it for a little bit. Like say until I get the money I need?" He sipped his water as he stood in my kitchen.

"You're trying to negotiate being a drug runner with me? Oh, James, you are out of this world, brother. No. No. No.

Not going to be a thing between us. If you are dealing with the cartel across the border, which I assume you are, they don't negotiate like that. Sorry. Get out now."

"Pfft. Forget it. You'll see. Wildcard has something on the Guardians. They are going to get what they deserve. This has been brewing since that shootout a few years back." He put the glass down on the counter and kissed my cheek as I stood there not able to speak with the news he just relayed. "I'm out. I'll make sure you don't get any more visits. Stay chilled, sis."

I sat glumly on the couch and watched him walk out of the door and into an unknown world that was going to cause him a lot of pain in the long run.

*Another date with Maverick, a few days later...*

"We're here again. You and me. Did you think it would happen?" Maverick's goofy expression made me grin.

"Yeah. I did. I think you're a nice guy." We were sitting downtown in Edgewood facing the street with coffees in our hands watching the cars pass by. The coffee shop was pretty dead, but a few people were roaming around doing what they needed to do. Edgewood wasn't the busiest shopping precinct. It was more of a drive-through town. You didn't actually stay here if you could help it. We were having a quick coffee before I went in for my shift. I assumed I would see him there later at work, since he invariably showed up for a drink.

"A nice guy," he repeated unblinking as he took a sip of his coffee.

"Yes. What's wrong with that?"

"You might not think I'm such a nice guy when I tell you

what I have to tell you next," he confessed. The light was shining on his sandy-colored hair, making it appear extra yellow. I pulled my sunglasses out of my bag and slid them on my face.

"What do you have to tell me?" My brain had nowhere to go on this one. It could be anything.

"Promise not to flip out. It's not as bad as you think it is." He was trying to ease me into something, and I wanted to be told the truth whatever it was.

"I'm a Guardian." There. Right in my face. I closed my eyes and put my palm over my forehead.

"You're a Guardian? Is that what you just said to me?" I squeaked as I swiveled my chair and stared into his eyes. I started to laugh hysterically and covered my mouth. Maverick kept his gaze looking ahead, calm and still like he normally was, but he reached to the side and pulled out a jacket. I touched it, feeling the leather as I took note of the skull crossed over with guns on the back of his jacket.

"Still don't believe me?" he asked as he put the jacket on the seat next to him. I processed what he'd just shown me and that same feeling I had when the Viper showed up to the door came rushing back. Was this a set-up? A sick game. Why was I in the middle of two motorcycle gangs having to deal with this?

"Why would you not tell me this? Why would you keep it from me in the first place?" I questioned him.

"I shouldn't have, you're right. I wanted you to know because I like you. You seemed like you were hating on motorcycle gangs, so I didn't wanna push it with you, but hopefully you see that I'm a decent guy," he said, but I was already upset that he lied to me.

"I knew it. I knew you weren't telling me something. So

when you were explaining about the private contracts, that was a lie too?"

"Nope." He shook his head. "That's all true. I do privately contract, and that includes for the Guardians," he explained as he searched my eyes to see if I was about to run. I wasn't. I wanted to find out exactly what he did. My fingers unfurled from my cup as I turned back around to the front.

"I don't exactly forgive you for leaving this information out, but tell me what you do."

"We are a team of four, and we work with the Narcotics Unit to shut down the meth labs. Things have gotten so bad around here that they had to call in the big guns, aka your guy Maverick."

Shitballs. "You umm—shut down meth labs?" This had to be a horror movie gone wrong. If I told him what I knew it might put my brother in jeopardy. If I didn't tell him, my brother might go to jail.

"Yep. So we are the good guys. We only go after bad people, not pretty bartenders." He grinned as he drank the rest of his coffee.

"Ha. What else? If you have no missions then what do you do?" I asked. I steadied my nerves and allowed my breathing to come back under control. This was the good guy, and James was the bad guy. I was in a world of confusion right now.

"That's where the private contracts come in. That's what I was doing out in Cali before I arrived here." The pounding in my chest was subsiding to a dull drilling as I listened to him. The more I did, the more he seemed legit.

"What do you think about the meth labs here now? You think it's over with?" I wanted an overview, and being in contact with Maverick might be a way to keep my brother safe and give him a heads up.

"Hmmm. Hard to say, but at least for now it seems like it's under control. It got so bad. The kids when we were pulling them out. Twenty to thirty people living and working in these houses, barely any food, pipes everywhere, unsanitary. It's been sad to see how many people have been hooked on it in this town. I'm glad I've been a part of it. I don't want there to be any more missions." The sadness in his eyes when he described the kids made me feel guilt-ridden.

"I think we've all known an addict in our time. Thank you for telling me. Don't lie to me next time. I'm a big girl, I can take it," I told him.

Our eyes met, and Maverick picked up my hand and kissed it. His warmth seeped into my hand and made me feel a little more alive. His goofy nature didn't overshadow his sex appeal. His two-day beard growth was appealing to me, and that strong jawline made me want to stroke it. "Yes, you can. I'm sorry. Didn't want to scare you off," he admitted.

"Takes a little more to scare me off," I shot back and changed the subject. I wanted to keep him talking. My feelings were unresolved, and I wasn't sure what to do with them at this point. "So what did you do before you started with the Guardians? Like in the military?" A few more people streamed in and out of the café as we kept on talking. I was conscious of the time I had to get to work shortly.

"I was the bomb guy. Still am. Not so much danger as back then, but a little bit." He pinched his fingers together, and that adorable smile made me grin. "I'm a man that likes to go to the edge of the cliff and look down." He pretended to look down a cliff face.

I giggled "And what do you do when you look down?"

He wrinkled up his nose. "I say nah, I'm good. We can go back now." He was so easygoing that it was hard for me to believe that he was a bomb guy. "What is it? Have I got something on my face?"

"No, you? A bomb expert? You're so calm, so—I don't know, just yourself," I admitted.

"Who else should I be? The calmer you are, the better. If you're jittery and scattered when you're dealing with a life-threatening bomb then that's not helpful. Those suits don't help either. You sweat heavily inside of them. It's crazy."

"Wow. You're not what I expected!" This guy was a whole world of something else, and I was trying to figure out what that something else was.

"Is that a bad thing or a good thing?" he asked as his mouth twitched.

"No, it's a good thing," I cleared up quickly. I slicked my hair back as I looked at the time. "Maverick, I have to get to work. It's going to get crazy tonight; we have a happy hour going on."

"Cool. Let me pay, and we can go." As I watched him go, my eyes bugged out, and I slapped my knees. A biker. A bomb guy. Enemy to my brother and hot. I could not tell him about my brother. I just couldn't.

He paid and came back to where I was already standing and ready to go. "Are you ready, my lady?" he joked.

"Yes I am. I don't know about my lady. I'm a a little too rogue to be a my lady," I said truthfully.

"That works for me. You are perfect the way you are." He naturally took my hand as we walked out to his bike.

"Ready to ride?" he asked as he handed me the extra helmet he'd brought.

"Sure am," I said in a somber tone. I wanted to keep

seeing Maverick, but in light of what I knew I needed to keep my distance. The problem was the little butterflies that were fluttering around in my stomach every time I saw him. If they weren't there it would be easy to ignore him and move on. I was shocked I had any feelings left. I thought my ex had annihilated them completely. I wrapped my hands around Maverick's waist and held on as the wind whipped my hair. He was lean, and I got to touch his chest and feel that he had a rather nice six pack. I loved the feeling of being on the back of the bike, and I loved the freedom it represented. I was toying with getting one for Christmas. A little present to get myself as a treat. I'd learned to ride from my brother. He had a Harley, and I presumed that's how he got talking to the Vipers in the first place—through bikes.

I got to work right on time and dismounted. Huge, dense dark clouds were holding what looked to be like buckets of rain, and I wanted to get inside as quick as possible.

"Shitty weather incoming. Looks like a storm, that wind is picking up," Maverick remarked as he lifted his leg over the bike. He took his helmet off and I eased mine off and handed it to him. He tucked it under his arm and held the other one in his hand.

He stood with his nose wrinkled up as the first droplets of rain presented themselves. One dropped right onto the middle of Maverick's nose. I giggled and wiped it off with my finger.

"Ugh. Here it comes. So before the downpour comes let me get out of here. But first..." He came closer to me watching my every reaction as he moved. He closed the gap and kissed me on the lips. He didn't use his tongue, just placed a nice tender kiss on my lips. He didn't try too hard; it was just a nice simple kiss, and that's all I wanted. A rumble sounded off in the sky as large plops of rain came between us, and the pitter patter sound of rain filled my ears. The once dry ground started to soak in the raindrops falling from the sky, and I knew if I stayed any longer I would end up a drowned rat.

I tapped Maverick's chest. "I gotta go! I'm getting wet." Maverick's sandy hand was plastered to his head, and he was blinking away the water. That's just the way I left him. What he didn't know is in my mind that would be our first and only kiss. Being involved with him would put me in danger, my brother in danger, and Maverick. Best that I keep away from all of them for the time being...

# 7

## MAVERICK

She was sweet and a little sassy, and she had this rebellious streak that appealed to a man like me. Coming from a background of blowing up bombs and working for the Guardians, I needed a little spice in my life. I wanted to keep spending time with her. It had been a few days since I'd last seen her. We'd been texting back and forth, but we weren't able to link up for some reason. Our schedules just kept on clashing. I ended up smoking a little weed on the couch, but that was becoming too much of a habit. I needed to get some private gigs. Not for money—that I had enough of—but to keep my mind and my body productive. I was itching to call the sheriff and ask for that favor he'd promised. The more I thought about it, it seemed a little weird given that he was probably looking into Tara's case. I was about to shoot off another text to Stephanie when Hawk called.

"Hey, Maverick. Ready to be busy for a little bit?"

"Hell yeah, what we got going on?"

"We got a meth lab outside Sedillo, home based. The job is this afternoon."

"Yup, I'm ready. I'm on my bike right now to come over there. What's the story with it?"

"Nothing out of the ordinary. A start up, the neighbors in the area called it in. A lot of men and bikes coming and going at all times of night is what was reported."

"Ahh, everybody in? Gunner and Mustang?" I enquired. I assumed they were, but we hadn't been on a mission in a while, so it was possibile they had private contract work going on.

"Yep. They're in. If you can get in here in the next hour, that would put us in good time to run through a brief. You cool with that?" Hawk asked.

"No problem. I'm on my way over right now. Don't worry about the one hour," I said. I was ready to move and get some action going. I wondered if that was a bad thing to constantly crave the adrenaline rush. The high was something I craved from my days in the military. Some days it cost me my sanity, but other days I lived to have that feeling back.

"See you when I'm looking at you."

"Okay, my guy. Let's do this." I pulled myself up and off the couch launching into action. I bounced off to my room where I had all my equipment stored in one spot. I pulled out the special drawer with my Smith and Wesson, my parabellum bullets, bullet proof vest, my leather gloves, my bomb kit, and my face mask. I was meth lab ready. I was like a dolphin seeing water for the first time. Now my purpose was re-ignited. I was back in the saddle, baby. I mounted my bike and let her rev for a minute, then spun my tires as I headed out of my street to the warehouse.

I tapped on the office window as I strolled in. The first thing I noticed is that Tara wasn't there. I moved through to the lunchroom where I knew we were meeting with my bulletproof vest in my hand. The music was cranking, and Axle fist-bumped me on the way through.

"Hey man. How you hanging?" I said cheerfully.

"A little to the left. All good here. Got some news for you," he said with his eyes glaring at me in intensity. Some part of that stone cold killer was still inside Axle even though he'd fathered a baby girl from his loins.

"What is it, big guy?" I asked. The deep expression on his face led me to believe it was huge news. I could see Hawk, Gunner, and Mustang peeping at me through the glass.

"Keep on the lookout in these meth labs. I think Wildcard has something to do with them. I heard word from a dealer downtown at the bar that he was scouting out places." He patted me on the shoulder as I nodded my head.

"You went out? Let's talk about that! Bell let you up for air?" Axle shrugged his boulder-like shoulders.

"What can I say? I had a job to do, right? I have to get the word on the street. What can she say about that? It used to be her job too," he pointed out.

"Thanks. We'll report back if we see or hear anything. Good looking out. That part about Bell. You make it sound as if she has retired. Has she?"

Axle rolled his eyes. "Bell Marco retired? *Noooo.* There's no way. She is just enjoying the time out. She's going to be back, badder than ever."

"I was going to say. That doesn't sound like Bell at all." Even though Bell was fast in motion for mother of the year with Zena, all I could see was her ready to start teaching her to kick box the next man into oblivion. I missed hearing the heavy pad being beaten up every morning. If that heavy bag was a person, it would have died a thousand deaths.

"Never say never. She has talked about branching out

and getting into fitness videos," Axle said. I heard a whistle call me from the lunchroom, and I knew it was Hawk waiting for me.

"All right, bud. I gotta go. Report back."

"Cool. Let me know if you need anything. Safe mission."

"Always." I winked at him and jogged into the lunchroom.

"I'm here. I'm here. Just getting the lowdown from the big guy what to look out for on the next mission. Hawk glanced up from his map coordinates with his knuckles on the table.

"He didn't tell me anything. I must have missed it," Hawk mentioned as I fist-bumped Gunner and Mustang. Gunner's stoic face was on and Mustang was sliding on his vest.

"He said that apparently Wildcard might be involved with this one. I don't know. He said he heard a street whisper about it when he went to the bar. I'm just the messenger passing it on."

Hawk nodded. "Okay good. Let's see what goes down when we get there. Everybody feeling all right? We haven't been out in a while," Hawk asked.

Gunner cricked his neck and bent his hands back. "I've been waiting for this. I'm good to go."

Mustang was stretching out his hamstrings on the floor. He glanced up and put his hand up with the OK symbol.

I clapped my hands. "We are ready, Hawk. Details, baby!" I shouted, and all the crew looked at me as if they were ready to send me into the looney house.

"You've been bored, haven't you?" Hawk raised his thick eyebrows at me.

I shrugged and danced around the comment. "Leave me alone. I've been hanging with Stephanie a little bit, so I'm not all the way bored. She won't return my calls right now. She might be busy or something."

Mustang guffawed as he stood up and stretched out his hamstrings. "You blew it already? Pun intended," he added with a sly grin.

"Have some sympathy for your fellow man, my guy. I'm trying here."

Hawk and Gunner were staring at me with pity eyes that I didn't want or need. "I've got it under control. We are taking it one step at a time," I said.

"Okay. Let's get on track here. This is the location we are headed to." Hawk pointed to a section of the backcountry of Sedillo on the map. "I've spoken to you individually about it, this is a residential meth house, and it's been called in by the local community. I don't know who, or what. Apparently this one is a little more disorganized. It may or may not have security involved. According to the locals there are all kinds of goings on night and day throughout the house." Hawk paused for a minute and looked around. "This seems to be a nice easy one, but let's take it seriously like we always do and get ready for anything and everything. Note that we are heading into Viper territory."

"Vipers. Those stupid snakes wouldn't exist if it wasn't for the Devils. Those guys have become non-existent right now. Most of them are locked up, in jail or dead from the shootout, right?" Mustang asked for clarity.

"Yes. That's right, but don't count them out. There are a few members left, and who knows what form they will take on? That shootout was to put the feud to rest once and for all, but you never know," Hawk said as he folded up his map.

"Time for us to go and kick some meth-cooking ass," I

said in a cheery voice. Mustang, who was closest to me, squeezed my shoulder.

"Let's do this, Maverick." We slapped hands and moved out to the van. The back door slid open, and we jumped in one by one. The van engine turned over, and we backed out. We were traveling to the meth house in broad daylight to catch them unawares. I could feel the blood rushing through my ears and the adrenaline pumping through my veins. It let me know that all of my senses were alert and ready to execute whatever task was required.

I had a question for Hawk, so I shouted from the back at him. "Hey, Hawk. What's going on with Tara? Everything okay?"

I saw his eyes in the mirror go dark. Something was up. "It's not so great. She took a few days off. The sheriff hasn't been in contact, but it made her a little upset. Wildcard hasn't come back with anything yet, but I'm sure he will and now we're in limbo. He was last seen out here in Sedillo. Keep your eyes and ears open. If we happen to run up on a Viper let's see what we can find out."

"Okay." I tapped the seat in front. Half of the road to the meth lab was sealed, and the other half was dusty and full of pebbly rocks. We were on the latter part as we bumped along into the suburb.

The van pulled up a few blocks down from the large weatherboard house that was conveniently at the end of the street and next to a wide-open field. I guessed that would make it easier for them if they had to escape. All of these meth labs had a similar setup. Every now and then we got an anomaly. Hawk pulled out his binoculars as I heard the click of Gunner preparing his sniper gun. "You're not going to pull that in a residential area, are you?" I yelled at him.

"Relax, Maverick. You're supposed to be the easygoing

one. I'm prepping. I'm a sharpshooter, why are you doubting my skills? Shut up," he snapped. My senses were tingling and telling me that Gunner was in one of his moods as I looked at his tight biceps and the straight grim line on his mouth. No smile. Mustang mouthed the word *no* to me, and I left it. I didn't want to get him riled up. I directed my energy back to Hawk.

"Whatcha see, Hawk?"

"Ahh, we got activity. Three men just came out. They are moving in and out of a vehicle and putting stuff in it. I can see one guy sitting on the front porch. There is no security from the outside. I can't quite see around the back from this angle. I think we can play this one straight." He clicked his finger to Mustang. "Mustang, I'm going to need you close by." He flipped his gaze to Gunner. "What can you do from here?"

"Ah, not much. I can close out a person or two at a pinch, but it would be risky business." He squinted as he looked through the viewfinder.

"Okay, do we need to bring the van closer to the house?" Hawk asked as I put my mask on.

"No. I can get out and do what I need to do. I don't just have the sniper gun. I've got another gun here," Gunner said as he patted the Glock in front of him on the van floor.

"Okay." Hawk gave him a thumbs-up. His fierce gaze turned back to us. "Mustang, you lead, and I will drop in behind you. Maverick, you back up from behind. Are we good with that?"

"Yes," all of us replied in unison. The street itself was quiet. I spotted a few people out on their porches sitting and enjoying the sounds of nature, but that was about all.

We moved in quickly, and those people quickly stood up and made themselves more apparent. Mustang for a big man was incredibly nimble and supremely confident. His gun wasn't cocked at all; it was still in his shoulder holster. I stayed steady behind the other two, knowing we were backed up by Gunner from afar.

Five paces. Four paces. Three paces. Two paces. One. We were at the house. The music was blaring, and the door was wide open. I could hear words being spoken in Spanish.. My mind instantly thought of the cartel and their connection. A younger man was standing inside the doorway of the house with a cocked rifle. His face went pale white as he spotted Mustang coming into charge.

*"Holy shit!"* the guy screamed. He couldn't have been older than 25. I looked past him. It was the typical scene. Chocolate paper wrappers were strewn everywhere, and tattered clothes and rags were all over the floor. Glass paraphernalia as well. The place smelled like a whole plethora of toxic chemicals. On the left was a series of trestle tables lined up in arrangement. One person was cooking up ingredients in preparation on the stovetop, stirring with a ladle. Thick, acrid smoke was rising in the air. The other was a woman who was arranging plastic packets along the tables ready to be bagged. A teenage boy was in the line-up moving the factory line production along. He was helping bag the contents as well. Another younger man was next to him and shuffling the drugs into the bags with record speed. He had a gun, and when he heard our footsteps, he turned with the gun and raised it. Mustang disarmed this kid with an elbow. He dropped the gun, and it slipped from his fingers to the ground. He looked petrified; terror was painted all over his face. "Hey, what are you doing? Where did you guys come from?" he asked with a screechy voice.

"We came from the dead. Come outside now. Who are

you working for?" Mustang grabbed him by the front of his shirt. He had a fistful in his hand, and he was snarling.

"I can't come out the front if I can't move," he said, licking his cracked lips. I smirked and covered my mouth. The kid had a point. I kept moving to the left with soft foot-steps as I listened to Mustang.

He sang like a canary. "The Vipers! The Vipers. Man, you're fucking up the plan. You are."

"Good, I like to mess up plans, I'm like the Grinch of fucking up plans," he said in the only voice that Mustang could speak in. He was on a roll, and I wanted him to stop, otherwise I would drop my gun myself. The kid—well, I called him a kid but he really wasn't—looked familiar.

Mustang shook his head. "Wise guy, huh?" Mustang had the kid lifted up off the ground almost. Hawk was scanning the rest of the building. I heard the back door open. He was checking the perimeters. The others swiftly turned around to face us. I pulled my gun and shoved it in a skinny woman's back and shook my head. She was the one cooking.

"Don't think about it. Turn the stove off now. Let's go," I directed her calmly. She put her shaky hands up to the ceil-ing, and I whirled her toward the front door.

"Please, please. I'm just trying to provide for my family. Don't shoot me. *Please*." She was crying. I sighed hard and put my gun back in my holster. She wasn't a threat.

"All right, relax. How long have you been here?"

"We've been here about two weeks cooking," she said with a tremble in her voice. She was pasty, with a few sores on her neck. It made my stomach turn. She was caught up in the cycle, and now she was cooking as well. I squinted in the heat of the sun. I needed some water. I had one small bottle tucked in my cargo pocket. I hesitated and pulled it out. I had more water in the van.

"Would you like a drink?" I asked her. Her eyes went as wide as saucers.

"Yes. I'm so thirsty," she said. I was cautious she might run, but I liked my chances if she fled.

"Let's take a seat on the step here. Talk to me about what's going on here. Who called you to work here?" Her brown eyes darted back and forth as she brought the water to her crusty lips.

"A guy named Wild—" She tapped her forehead. "*Shit!* I can't remember. I don't know. I think there's some other part of his name that I'm missing." Her words came out like a hurricane. I tracked her movements, and she wasn't going anywhere. She was sitting on the step. It almost seemed as if she was grateful she'd gotten caught. Hawk walked the others out the front. All of the people that were inside their homes were peeping through their curtains. The once quiet street was now alive with concerned and nosy citizens. What she told me confirmed my suspicions.

"That's okay. I know the guy you're talking about. What did he offer you?" I asked.

She looked at me with her matted hair, trying to bring moisture to her cracked and what looked to be sore lips. "He said he would ease me in and if I was loyal, like stayed with it, he would give me a pay raise," she said, her voice breaking.

Hawk beckoned with his fingers that we take it to the van. I tapped her shoulder. "Come on, let's go. We can get you some help."

"Thanks," she said as she hung her head in despair. She walked with a limp as we entered, and Gunner was already packed down. He must have seen us coming.

"What's your name?"

"Susie. My friends call me Suz, though. I'm sorry, man,

we weren't trying to hurt anybody. We were just trying to make a little extra cash, you know?" Her eyelids were heavy, and the kid who was acting as the pretend security guard said something.

"Shut up, Susie! They don't care about you. Shut up about it," he hissed.

Gunner shouted at him, "Hey! Shut up. You're in enough trouble as it is." The kid shook his head but sank back in his seat.

I stared back at the hollow faces in the van. The kid was staring back at me from across the van with bitterness in his eyes. His nose and his eyes seemed familiar to me. I couldn't place where I'd seen his features, but I knew I had. It was bugging me, and I didn't know why I couldn't figure it out.

We drove the short distance back to Edgewood as Hawk called in the pick-up to the narcotics division. Another successful meth lab take-down. This one seemed easy enough and that tidbit of information from Susie would help us in the long run.

My phone started to vibrate, and I pulled it out. Axle. Last week we had no activity and now all of a sudden, everything was popping off. I answered.

"Yo. Talk. We're in the van," I said as I pulled into the Edgewood Police Station.

"Someone is trying to get rid of Pop. I was with him. Another drive-by," he stated.

"And?" I asked. Gunner was giving me a curious look. He knew something was up.

"Clipped them, but they drove away, someone out there has a shoulder wound. If you see or hear, let me know. Church meeting no doubt. They didn't expect it. I stepped in front and fired."

Strangely, I wasn't worried. It was all part of the business to me; it was what I loved. If there was warfare, I was equipped for it.

"We got ourselves a party then. I have to go, but I'll tell the crew about the situation. Take care, big guy."

"You too. How many? All good?" he questioned.

"Eight total."

"Okay. See you later on at the meeting."

"Done."

As I hung up the phone, Hawk parked, killing the engine. Gunner was closest to the back of the van door and slid it open as I got out next, and he directed the culprits out. "Come on. Let's go," he commanded as he walked them into the station. Hawk was heading up the front of the line.

All in a day's work. Once we processed the paperwork and dropped off the meth labbers, I grabbed water from the back of the van. I checked my phone, hoping there was a message back from Stephanie. There was nothing. Maybe I got it wrong and shouldn't have told her I was a Guardian. We rode back to the warehouse, and I sat up front with Hawk. I wanted to be the one to tell him first.

"You know, Axle just called me," I said as I let the water soak my throat.

"He did? What did he say?"

"He said he just saved Pop's ass. Another hit has been put out on him." The guys heard from the back.

"What?" Hawk's hands got a little shaky as I relayed the news to him.

"Whoa. Keep your hands on that wheel, dude." I placed my hands on the hot dashboard as he swung the van back into alignment. I pulled them back, not having realized how hot it was. I rubbed the pads of my fingers as Hawk glimpsed at me.

"Sorry, I was thrown for a moment. Keep talking."

"Yeah, he stepped in front and clipped the guy. I got this feeling, man. I think Wildcard has something to do with it. He doesn't like Pop at all, and he can't get what he wants. He's trying to nail these screws into us. Susie, that cook, told me that a guy called Wild put her up to the meth lab. We both know who that is, don't we?"

"Sure do." He glowered.

"Wildcard Willy," we both said at the same time. "Man. Shit's about to get rough. Tara went back into the office today, and the sheriff paid her a visit. I didn't tell you earlier."

"What? Why? What's his deal?"

"He's asking more questions. He asked Tara flat-out if she knew anything about Clint's disappearance. The parents are involved now. They know that Clint's gone."

"We gotta get to Wildcard. I should have asked that lady how she got in touch with him. Shit! That's my bad."

"Don't worry about it. The crew is on it too. Axle is going to hunt him down, don't worry about that. We all need to be on high alert." Hawk swerved the van into the warehouse parking lot. He was in a hurry, that was clear. I guessed he wanted to see Tara and make sure she was okay. I heard objects sliding around in the back of the van as he abruptly stopped.

He yanked the keys from the ignition. "I gotta go check on Tara," he panted as he leapt out. He really loved that woman; it was clear to see. Mustang and Gunner stepped out of the van, both of them stretching.

"You hear what I said?" I asked them quietly. Among ourselves, we had this other code of ethics. We were about to show the Guardians why they needed us in the first place.

"I was listening, I heard it," Gunner said.

"Me too." Mustang was cracking his fingers and pulling them out.

"You know we gotta find Wildcard, right? We gotta clear this up right now."

"Agreed. I'll be at the bar tomorrow, and I can find out more there. I'll put money up. Let's see how that goes."

"I have some contacts. I will talk to them. See what's going on," Gunner said as his jaw twitched.

"I'll do my part too. I'm going to ask Stephanie what she knows." Gave me an excuse to go see her at the bar to check in. I would give it one last shot and cut my losses if I came up empty. A silent agreement between three men. We all walked into the warehouse ready for the debrief with Hawk. I saw Tara in the office with Hawk hugging her. She was crying into his shoulder. I figured that meant the questioning hadn't gone so well. My happy-go-lucky was fading. I needed a hit of weed to get back to center. I sped up my walk to the lunchroom, where the big guy Axle was hunched over the fridge with a beer in his hand. He looked up as he saw me in the door.

"Want one?"

"Yup. Load me up," I said.

"Here." He handed me the ice-cold brew. It was soothing my fingers from the hot dashboard I'd put them on earlier. He tilted his head to Mustang and Gunner, who followed closely behind me, and handed them beers as well.

"You heard, fellas?" Axle asked as both of them nodded their heads. All of our phones beeped together. I looked down at mine and saw the same message they saw from Finn.

*Church meeting. 1700hrs.*

"That's in another half hour. He means business," I said out loud as I broke into my beer and sipped. I put it down on the counter as I reached into my pocket to bring a joint out of my cargo pants, sparking it up. As I took in the first draw, I felt the ease drop into my body. The guys were used to me sparking up in the lunchroom so much that no one even flinched.

"He does. Pop's safe now. Red's with him. We are going to be round the clock with him until we get to Wildcard," he stated.

"How are you doing with that? Being away from Zena?" I asked as I blew my smoke up.

Axle's big, broad chest heaved in and out. "Not great, but I'm the Guardians' enforcer and Bell understands. She knows it's part of the job. I don't want to leave her at all. This is what I've been afraid of. That I would be taken away from Zena and not able to spend time with her." I could see Axle visibly grinding his teeth together at the situation.

"That's a tough situation, and I don't envy you."

"It just means I have to crack heads quicker so I can get back to my little girl."

"I guess we'll find out what's in store in half an hour," Gunner said.

"Damn straight," Axle said. "Gotta be Wildcard."

"You too? That's what we all think," I agreed.

"I definitely think it's that bastard. He has a lot to answer for."

We were back in church except this wasn't a place to redeem your sins. It was a place where sins were cast out and a place where other people's sins were judged and weighed accordingly.

Pop was wearing his beret and smoking his cigar as if he

hadn't been shot at. His throaty laugh carried across the table as the fellas streamed in. I was mellowed out and relaxed, but I worried about Tara and Hawk. Hawk didn't come in for debrief, but he was at the meeting. I flashed him a smile and saw his eyes were dead inside. I would have to speak to him after the meeting.

Pop cleared his throat. "We've been quiet for a while now, and we've enjoyed it. We've rebuilt stronger than ever with new additions. Mustang, Gunner, Maverick, Scout and Dutch. A fine crew. We've linked in with law enforcement and have had a good reputation with them up until now. We are now under attack by an insider. One of us." Pop looked around the table at all of us for a long moment and held all our gazes one by one. The man could be intimidating when he needed to be to get his point across. "A traitor who has no boundaries. That one is Wildcard Willy, if you didn't know. Today, I believe from reliable sources that he tried to put a hit out on me. God was smiling on me once again. Axle was with me at the time and saved the day. Now the hitter has a severe shoulder wound for his trouble." Pop released a dry chuckle while shaking his head.

Shaggy looked over at Pop. "You going into hiding, Pop? Maybe you should lay low and take it easy for a while. Wildcard is really gunning for the club."

Pop's eyes turned into blazing furnaces as he looked at Shaggy. "No!" His voice was booming, and it made Shaggy jump in his seat. "We didn't back down during the shootout, and we aren't backing down now. Let's draw him out." He gestured with his fingers. "He's going to mess up, and when he does, I want to be right there. Bulldog never should have let him into the club in the first place. When he helped Finn's father it was only so he could get into the club. I want

Wildcard dead. If he's gunning for me, I'm gunning for him. Any reports?"

Hawk nodded his head at me. "We were out today and on a mission with this residential lab. Nothing heavy. Pretty standard, but the cook said that she was hired by a guy named Wild. I assume that's Wildcard. So he's trying to get his drug operation started. Might be a guess as to why he's trying to extort," I said.

Pop picked up his whiskey and sipped. "Hmm. I believe it to be true."

Axle spoke up. "I'm going to be guarding Pop around the clock until we sort this Wildcard situation out. Red is going to be there too. I need everybody to ask around. Put down money if you need to. We have to get to him." Axle didn't usually talk so much in meetings, so for him to speak let us know that things were hot.

"Hawk? News on the Clint case?"

Hawk looked down at his drink and swirled it. "The sheriff asked Tara if she killed Clint outright. He was pretty brazen about it, but she said no. Technically it's true. I did. I'm the one that shot the gun. If I have to turn myself in I will. It was self-defense, and I have more of a chance than anything of getting off. I don't know, I think it's the best thing to do. Beat Wildcard to the punch."

"*Like hell you will!* You did act in self-defense, but you know as well as I do the sheriff is not that reasonable. He will be looking for a lockup, and the parents are involved now. We are going to get rid of Wildcard before he can make any more demands. So far no word from him, but I suspect he has something up his sleeve that he's waiting to release," Pop advised.

"We ain't letting you turn yourself in," I said. "Don't fold, Hawk. You held your old lady down, and that's what you're supposed to do. Nope. We are not going to let you fall like that. Protect thine own is the motto and we stick to that right fellas?"

"Yes." Those who had glasses raised them in the air. I could tell by the light that had gone out of Hawk's eyes that he was tormented with the decision. He was wanting to turn himself in. Dealing with Tara's insecurities and fears from the past trauma would have been weighing on him heavily as well. I felt for the guy.

We were about to have a war of a different kind. One I'd never experienced, but I'd come to know the Guardians as family, and I was ready to fight as one for them just as I fought for my country.

# 8

## STEPHANIE

I saw the text messages, but I refused to answer them. I knew I wouldn't get away with that. I had this feeling that Maverick would come see me at the bar. I was ignoring him, half of me was doing that because of the threat with my brother and the rival gang, and the other half was preserving my heart. Problem was the butterflies in the bottom of my stomach were still there and making me question myself.

Edgewood was in fine form as her morning light shone through my bedroom window way too early, causing me to grumble and remove myself from the sheet unceremoniously. I padded to the kitchen with my dark hair hanging in my face. I hadn't heard from my brother in a few days and that was normal most of the time, but the way we left things the last time I saw him was terrible. I had to release him from my life for the time being. Too much drama. I couldn't be seeing a Guardian while my brother was affiliated with their rivals, the Vipers. That would be a murder in waiting. I was surprised at my cavalier attitude considering a Viper had come straight to my door. I should have been scared, but I wasn't. I was angry and annoyed that James' choices were reflecting on me as a family member.

My phone was ringing, and I was all the way in the kitchen. "Grrr!" I said in frustration as I bunched my fists up at my sides. "The fuck do people want this early in the morning, seriously?"

I snatched it up from my nightstand. James. I had half a mind not to answer it. I picked it up anyway.

"Brother."

"Sister."

"What do you want, James? Are you in trouble again?" I said sleepily.

"Yeah, kind of," he answered sheepishly.

I woke up then. "What?" I shoved my hair back behind my ears as the water boiled on the stove.

"I got picked up by the cops. Or some cop-looking guys. They were Guardians. I think they're working with the cops or something."

"Who were they? Do you know?"

"I don't know who they were, but there was a guy who was asking a lot of questions. Some Maverick guy. Real pain in the ass." I stopped him there.

"What did you say? Who?" I asked. I was pretty damn sure he said Maverick.

"This Maverick guy. Some other guy named Mustang was there too. He tried to take me out, and he put me in a sleeper hold. Shit got nuts." My whole body was lit up with anger. Maverick was involved. This was the biker drama I wanted no part of, and now this news confirmed it.

"How are you talking about this like it's nothing? They could have shot you. You could be dead," I shrieked into the phone as my fingers started to tremble. I moved over to the stove and turned it off.

"Hold on. Calm down about it. Everything will be just fine. It was a really small lab, and it was like a test run. Wildcard knew they would probably come for that one. He was setting up shop with another one. We got 20 people in that house getting all the ingredients ready. All I have to do is keep guard," he said proudly.

"Listen to how stupid you sound. Keep guard? You couldn't even do that. You got caught. I can't listen anymore."

"I'm home. I'm chillin'. Stop worrying about all this shit. Doesn't matter anyway because the Guardians are about to be in a whole world of hurt. Wildcard is putting down an ultimatum that will land them all in jail if he pulls it off. They shut down one, but they can't shut down 20 all at once."

"Maverick was there? How do you know his name? I never told you about him," I said in confusion.

"What are you talking about? I never said you knew him. I know him because he's part of the Guardians crew. I have to make it my business to know. Do you know the guy? Why are you asking?" he accused.

Silence. I put my big fat mouth into it. If he knew that I'd gone out with Maverick, shit would hit the fan.

"No. Seen him in the bar." No lie told there. It was the truth.

"Anyway. I'm okay if you wanted to know, but I do have to go to court. Fucking sucks, but the money I'm about to make is going to fix that right up." I was sitting on the phone having a surreal conversation and realizing that my brother had no regard for his life.

"I would sound like a broken record if I kept going. You're going to do what you're going to do. I'm not helping you anymore. If Mom and Dad call me and ask, I'm telling them. Too bad, so sad."

"Wha-" He tried to speak, but I pressed the end call button too fast. I wanted nothing to do with it. I knew it wouldn't be that simple. If my brother fucked up with the Vipers, they would target his family next. That would be me. They already had my address. Felt like a good time to go register for a firearm for self protection. I scribbled a note to myself on the kitchen counter for it.

I picked up my phone again as I saw the caller ID for my brother. He was trying to call back, but I wasn't having it. I pressed the hang up button with force. I wanted to clear my head and make some decisions about the situation.

I stared at the clock. It was 12 p.m. I'd slept in, and nobody had been calling me early. I felt like I was starting to lose it as I tapped my knuckles on the counter. I closed the kitchen blind because the sun was beating on my neck through the glass. I could see my neighbor mowing his lawn. He waved, and I waved back at him. Stan was a little too nosy for my liking, but we got along well enough as neighbors. I'd stopped waving and knew he was probably on the other side still looking and hoping I reopened the blind.

If James went to court, Mom and Dad would find out, it was an inevitable course of events. I hadn't spoken to them in a little while, so I dialed Mom's number.

"Hello! Steph. How's my favorite daughter?" she said in her usual upbeat tone. My mother was the classic mother figure and always the bedrock of the family. She tucked me in at night, she sang me lullabies, she picked me up when I cried, and she cried when I left the nest.

"Hi, Mom. I'm your only daughter," I reminded her, feeling better for hearing her voice.

"Yes, well, you are still my favorite. Are you getting ready for work at the bar?" she asked.

"Yeah, I'm close to it. I wanted to know if you've heard from James yet," I asked, trying to keep my voice from sounding as if I was up to something, but I wanted to teach him a lesson. If Mom was after him, it would scare him. Not in the sense that she was a tyrant, but more so she would be disappointed, and the hot serving of guilt that our mother could slide on was enough to make anybody beg for her forgiveness.

"So there's something going on with him? Are you going to be the one to tell me, or should I give him a call?"

"I'm not the right person to tell you what's going on, but he should call you about it." I gulped down the lump in my throat. I should have thought through the call before I made it. I was about to put my brother knee deep in the mud, but it might be the thing to save him. My belly tightened up as I listened to the calm breathing on the other end of the line.

"You should at least give me a clue... has he knocked somebody up?"

"No, Mom, he hasn't done that. It's a little worse than that." The more I kept talking, the more I was digging the shovel deeper into the ground for James.

"Hmm. This does sound serious, and you won't tell me. That's the rude part," she added indignantly.

I let out a frustrated sigh. "Ask me something else about my life rather than his."

"Okay, any potential suitors for you?" she asked in a charming voice.

"Nope. No suitors." White lie. Maverick might have been one had I given him half a chance. I didn't tell my mother that, otherwise she would want his full credentials, and it would be a long-ass conversation of grilling and require-ments to see if he was 'marriage material.'

"That's a shame. Maybe I should get into the matchmaking business. Surely there's someone for you," she fussed.

"Mom. Stop it. I don't need your help with finding anyone. I'm not looking for anyone right now," I said in an agitated voice.

"No need to raise your voice. I'm only looking out for you. I just want to see you happy and settled," she said.

"I am. Just our versions of happy and settled are way different." She paused, and I took solace that she might be listening to me.

"That's true. I will let your father know you called. You can catch him on his cell," she said.

"I'll give him a call. Give him a big kiss from me," I said.

"I will. I'm going to call James right now and find out why you're being so evasive," she snipped. I wasn't the one in trouble; it was him.

"You'll find out, and you will be as shocked as I was, I'm sure."

"That's it, you're making it sound worse and worse the more you talk. I've got to go. Talk to you soon and don't be a stranger, Stephanie. I love you."

"Love you too, Mom."

I shook my head with the madness that was happening in my life and headed for the shower. I let the warm water clear my muddy mind and prepare me for the night ahead at the bar.

It was my official night with the Stephanie's specials, and a lot of women were in the bar, which meant there were a lot of men in the bar too. I was testing out this new fruit tingle drink that I thought the women would love. The colors in the glass looked amazing as well.

"These drinks are going down well. This was a good idea to make this a permanent fixture. I'm proud of you," Dustin claimed as he stood beside me at the bar. There wasn't a band, just me, my drink specials, and the DJ.

"I told you it would work. I do have ideas that work sometimes."

"You do. Are you still looking at those bars in California? Or are you happy here?" Dustin asked with a wobble in his voice as he chewed a fingernail.

I scoffed as I wiped off the remnants of alcohol from the last drink I'd made. "Dustin, I did that because you weren't listening to me. I do have to tell you, I'm not going to work in the bar forever. I am going to move on. I have to do something more with my life. I do like drinks, but I feel I need to step up somehow."

I'd dropped a bombshell that I didn't even know I was going to drop. The words just came out of my mouth. "I fully understand that and listen, I know." He was making circles in his hand which was a little nervous habit he had. I knew he wasn't happy about what I said. "Whatcha thinking about doing?" He was fishing around, but I wanted to keep some cards to myself for now. I wasn't sure about the cocktail bar dream, and I didn't want to hurt Dustin's feelings, so I played dumb.

"Nothing fully formed yet, and I would let you know for sure. I would give you plenty of notice," I reassured him.

"A lot of notice. Like a year's worth. That's how long it would take to even get anyone close to your standard," he said dramatically.

"You never know. There could be a budding bartender

out there that you just have to discover for No Name and you just haven't discovered them yet."

"You are not funny."

"I wasn't trying to be." I did think there was a possibility. On that annoying note, he pivoted and moved over to the stage to check on things. I served another two young women at the bar and Maverick strolled in to sit on the barstool. Smack bang in the middle of the bar. Normally, he would sit either end of the bar, but not this night. Right where I could see him and I wouldn't be able to ignore him. My heart rate sped up rapidly. He was wearing his patches proud and true, and the jacket suited him. He had a black T-shirt on underneath and blue jeans from what I could see. His smoky eyes were zeroed on me as if I was his next target. I hadn't seen the man go out with any women from the bar since he started talking to me, so I bit the bullet and went over to him.

"Hey, Maverick, nice to see you again. What can I get for you?" My head was speaking before my heart. When I said it, the words came out frostier than I wanted them to. I stared at him, noticing that even his nose was in perfect proportion.

"Have we not met before? You're giving me the cold shoulder now and you're acting as if you don't know me. Did something change?" Maverick asked with a pensive look. "I sent you a bunch of messages. I guess I just wanted to hear it from you first that you weren't interested." He seemed calm as always, and it was throwing me off.

I pressed my lips together. They were coated with deep purple lipstick, going for a gothic feel, and I thought I might keep the look. I felt so bad, but I couldn't let my heart get in the way of the decision. I *wanted* to be with him. To at least go out with him a few more times, but I would be putting his life in danger and my own. I put my hands on my hips. The bar was clear momentarily, and I wished it was busier so I didn't have to face him.

"I'm just coming out of a breakup. You know that. I think that—I don't know... the whole biker thing. Anyway, can I get you a drink to start with?" His facial expression showed disbelief and confusion as he took his wallet out of his pocket.

"Ah—okay. To me it hasn't been anything heavy going on between us, Steph. We shared a kiss, and I get that you're scared. I get it, but to shut me out completely?" He made a funny trumpet sound with his lips as he pushed his hand through that sandy blond hair I loved. "I don't know, Steph. Sounds fishy to me. If you don't have any interest, we can be friends and call it a day. I'm a reasonable guy. Just let me know something," he added logically, but there was sadness in his voice. I didn't want to be responsible for that and to dick him around, but I couldn't see how we could get things worked out between us easily. If I did go out with him I feared guns and warfare would be involved.

*If only it were that simple, Maverick.*

"We just went out on a mission to close a meth lab down. I'm not a bad guy biker. I'm not like your ex." He stared right at me as if he was looking through me. "Granted I do blow stuff up, but I'm still no threat to you. I don't know why you can't see that. What am I missing?" Hairs stood up on the back of my neck as I fiddled around with the tap in front of me.

*So it was true what my brother said. I have to warn him. I have to say something.*

"You aren't missing anything." I leaned over a little at the counter, giving him the courtesy of looking him back in his stormy eyes. "Let me get you a drink. On the house." I was feeling bad, so I wanted to give him a little consolation. Not that he would need it with the way some girls were ogling him from the dance floor.

"All right. I'm going for the plain old regular today. I'll take whatever beer you got in that tap right there," he added in a flat tone as he pointed to the middle one, which was an ale.

"Okay." I pulled the beer. "Was this your first mission in a while?" I wanted to find out a little more before I dropped any more hints. "Tell me about it." It would be hard to drop right into the friend zone, but I was going to give it a go.

I put a coaster on the bar and slid his drink over to him. "Yeah, it was." He tapped the side of his glass as if he had more to say. "We picked up a few people, a few kids, which was sad. We got this guy named Wildcard that's after the club. Do you know anything about him? Has anyone been talking?" Maverick asked as he sipped his beer. A line of creamy froth sat at the top of his upper lip. I giggled a little, which broke the ice between us.

"What is it? Now you're laughing at me?" He rotated his right palm up to the sky.

"You have a beer moustache, and it's cute," I told him as an involuntary smile lifted on the corners of my lips.

"Ahhhhh. See, you are trouble, Stephanie. Trying to have me look bad at the bar. I see your tricks now." He swiped the froth away with a tissue. I served a lady at the end of the bar, a young woman with blond hair who had her eyes set on Maverick.

"I will have a beer, whatever that guy's having," she said in a flirty tone. I tried to hide my eye roll as my lips clamped together.

"Sure. Be right back." The beer tap was in the middle and closer to Maverick. I could talk to him in front of it.

"To answer your questions, I have heard that new meth labs are popping up. That there is some sort of operation going on," I told him in a casual way. I pulled the beer and stepped down to the young blonde. Now she was joined by a girlfriend with mouse brown hair. Safe enough for me to tell him that I thought.

"There you go. Same as the older gentleman at the other end of the bar." My tone was super sarcastic, and I knew she felt it. Both of them gave me the stink eye.

"No need to be so rude, but thanks. He doesn't look that old," she cut back at me. I lifted my eyebrows and put my hands on my hips. Unfortunately, Dustin was behind me before I could tell her that the guy was double her age and that she needed to go find some college boy to slip under.

"Be nice to the customers, please. We want them to come back," Dustin said as he narrowed his eyes to slits, daring me to say something to him. "We started off busy, and now it's dying off. I don't know sometimes with this place. "Maybe I need to change the music. You think?" He scrunched up his nose, wanting guidance from me, but I was in no place to give it.

"Try it. Can't hurt, can it?" I ducked in front of him and moved back down the bar to Maverick.

"How do you know about the meth labs? Who is the source that told you?" he asked in a low voice.

"Well, everyone knows about them. It's been all over town. You would have to be living under a rock not to know we have a drug crisis going on." I tried to cover my tracks as quickly as possible. "Besides, I can't tell you that. Bartenders' code. I do know that the source is highly accurate. I'm confident you will have more missions to go on. I do think you should be careful," I added quickly as Maverick stroked his chin and checked me out. He was close to finishing his beer, and I prompted him, "Another one?"

"Yeah, I will have another one," he said blankly. "You are being evasive. I think you know more than what you're telling me, Stephanie. It's weird that you're backing up from the connection we had going. Is it because you know there's more meth labs popping up? Is that it?" The man was persistent I would give him that, but I was digging my stubborn heels in. That naughty sparkle in his eye was so appealing to me. His humor, his laidback California vibe was so different from anything I'd known. You didn't get guys like him in Edgewood. I wanted to take it further, but I would have to leave it. It was just too dangerous.

"Don't read into it too much. People talk to me, you know. Locals, out-of-towners, it's no big deal. I do know that the meth labs aren't finished, and it would just be good if the Guardians kept an eye out. I don't think for a second you don't already know that," I bluffed. I didn't want Dustin thinking I wasn't busy doing stuff, so I moved a little further down the bar past Maverick and started cleaning up the shot glasses.

"I don't get it. I really don't, but I guess there's nothing to get huh?" He swallowed down a decent gulp of beer as one older woman approached him, a brunette with long legs and a mojito in hand.

"Hi, handsome, you all on your lonesome? That can't be right." She cut her eyes back at me. What was with all these women giving me evil looks all the time? "You can't talk to the bartender all night long." She stroked his forearm with two fingers, and Maverick regarded her with amusement. That's the look that was best described on his face. "I'm here to keep you company." I gave Maverick one last glance. I knew this was the turning point, and I had to let him go.

That's all I heard of the conversation, and that's all I wanted to hear. I was single, he was single. I had no right to be mad at him for anything at all. His smoky eyes did seek mine out and lingered. I pulled my eyes away from him and got to cleaning down the bar. From the way he was engaging her in conversation and his face lighting up, it appeared like I'd blown it big time.

## 9

## MAVERICK

"You are so handsome and cute. So what's your name, sugar?" A lady in her late forties was hitting on me. Why did I get the extreme ends of the spectrum? Never the in-between. They were either too young or too old in this bar, and it was the oddest thing to me. I wanted Stephanie, not this lady, but we were talking, and I'm a polite guy so I threw her a sympathy bone.

"I appreciate all the compliments. You look nice and your hair is pretty." I threw her back a few compliments as well, keeping it as nice as I could. She was good looking enough, with brunette hair hanging down past her shoulders, heavy eye makeup, and botoxed lips that were a little over the top. Fish lips is what I called those girls back in Cali, but some guys were into that. It wasn't my place to judge what people preferred on their faces. She was wearing a halter neck top and she had the girls out on display. They were a decent size and not over the top, but I knew the way she flaunted them she'd had a boob job done. Her slender legs were in blue jeans, and she definitely rated herself highly. I kept sucking down my beer, my mind in two places at once. I was trying to work out where I went wrong with Stephanie. From what she told me about her source, it was the only logical explanation as to why she wouldn't want to see me anymore. My attention was drawn back to the overzealous woman in front of me. She jutted out her chest and flipped her dark hair back over her shoulder.

"Thank you for the hair compliment, helps you have a good conditioner and to get rid of split ends." In my mind I was thinking; *What the hell is she on?* It must be good, and can I have some? My face read a little differently externally, but I decided I would go with the flow of it.

"Oh yeah? I like that Pantene stuff. I throw a little gel in it at the end of the day and keep on moving right along," I said, laughing with her. She moved in a little closer and tried to wedge her slender leg in between my thighs. I closed the gap real quick as she licked her lips. I didn't want her getting in that close. I didn't know what she would do. She might bite my face. From the way she was swaying, it seemed like she'd had a few.

It's not like I hadn't met women from all over the globe or that I was averse to female attention. Back in my heyday when I was really getting down, I used to have one in every city I got stationed in. Some long-term, some short-term, but there was always one. I let dating take its course mostly, and I cruised. I was lucky in the department of getting women, but not necessarily keeping them. I promised myself I would let Stephanie go and this would be my last attempt, so that's what it was going to be. I returned back to the woman in front of me.

"My name is Sally. I see you got your patches on. You be a biker boy. Which one are you with, the Guardians or the Devils? I know a few of the Devils."

I lifted an eyebrow as I gently pushed her back a little bit. "You do? The Devils or do you mean the Vipers?"

Her eyes were glassy as she looked at me. "Vipers, Devils all the same right?" She ran her fingers over the leather of my jacket and sniffed it. "Mmm. I like the smell of leather. I have a leather crop if you want to try it out on me, later. What do you think? You bikers are into that kinky shit, right?" She got close to my ear, and I jerked away.

"Not all of us are, yeah, but maybe some are. If you think I'm taking you home for the night, I'm not, okay? You want water or something?" I cleared it up as quickly and as frankly as possible with her.

"Why not? Could be fun. Nobody has to know. My friends are getting ready to leave. I wanted to see what you were getting into tonight." I looked past her to see these friends she was talking about. I couldn't see anybody at all. To me she looked to be on her lonesome.

"I can't see any of your friends. How many people were you with? That's pretty shitty that they just left you here like this." She stroked the side of my face, and I drew back.

"Oh come on, give me some sugar." She puckered up her lips, and I turned my head to the side. Now she was just being plain desperate. She was definitely about to topple over, and I needed to call her a cab. I scanned the bar again. There were a few leery men in the corners lurking, and I wanted to make sure she got home safe.

"No, not tonight. How about I call you a cab? Come on, let's go, I'm about to leave anyway. That's the best thing we should do here." She was starting to get on my nerves, and from the way she was moving around her knees looked like they would buckle under her any minute. I rose up off the bar stool, shoved my keys and wallet in my back pocket, and grabbed her lightly by the elbow. I knew Stephanie was thinking I was leaving with this woman. That might have been a good thing.

"A cab? Are we going to your place? That would be good if you called one," she slurred her words.

*Let her think what she wants to think. Women. I'm lost on what to do about them.*

Sally's arms were like octopus hands all over me, and she was giving me the special beer googly eyes. I held my face back from her, but she was so quick and awkward with her movements that she managed to land a kiss on the corner of my mouth. Her saliva was on my skin, and I didn't like it one bit. With one arm I straightened her up, and with the other I wiped it off.

"Back off, Sally," I warned gruffly.

She smiled and gave me puppy dog eyes that were not attractive. "I got you. I got you!" She waggled her chipped red polished nail at me. "Ha! Ha. I got you good. You got nice lips. You would like mine. I had them done by Dr. Salvos. He's the best. So good," she said, sluggishly making fish lips movements. A smirk found its way to my face. I had to laugh because only I ended up in these types of situations with women. She was busy making duck faces at me when one of the leering men who was dressed as if he was going on a hunting expedition spoke. His fingers were wrapped around a beer, and he was sneering at me walking her to the door.

"That's a nice piece you got there. I'd be happy to take her off your hands for the night," he said darkly.

"That's what I'm afraid of. You drink your beer and shut up," I said in a rough tone to the douchebag.

The man looked taken aback by my comments and went back to drinking his beer. "I was trying to help you out there, man." I glared hard at him.

"You tell 'em, baby. Thanks for looking out for me," she

cooed as she attempted to stand up just like a baby deer would when it had just been born, all legs and arms. I dug my fingers a little firmer into her bicep to keep her away from my face.

"Oh no. I have enough kisses from you. I cherish the last one you gave me," I said sarcastically. We walked out to face the bite of the midnight Edgewood air, and my arm hairs became covered in goosebumps from the chill. I pulled out my phone from my left pocket and made the taxi call.

"You cold?" She didn't seem to be or maybe she wasn't feeling it because she was warmed up with copious amounts of alcohol in her bloodstream. She started to spin around, with her hair flying out around her and yelling out loud.

"Whooo! Whoo! I'm spinning." Yep. She was drunk as a skunk. I shook my head at her antics. At least she was having fun. I wondered how many of Steph's specials she'd drunk. I knew she was going to have a sore head tomorrow, and if she kept on spinning she would be liable to throw up. I wanted that to be in the back of the cab and not when I was around.

Nobody was in the parking lot, just me and her, so nobody could hear her yelling out to the moon like a wounded coyote.

She did stop spinning and held her head for a minute. I kept my distance, predicting there was about to be an emptying of contents from her stomach, but it didn't come. She giggled and held her head with both hands. "Are you having fun over there?" I called out.

"Not as much fun as I would if I came to your house," she pushed.

"Nope, look, your cab is here and that's where you need to go. Tell me your address, do you know it?"

"Yeah, I know it. I live right over on Church St. right near

Denny's." Her eyes lit up as if she'd just discovered the world's greatest invention. "We should go to Denny's and eat! Let's do that," she said excitedly. The crunch of asphalt from tires moving made my gaze look out into the night and over to the taxi approaching us. I let out a sigh of relief. I was about to put her in the cab and get her out of my hair. I was happy that the driver was a woman as well. I didn't know if I would feel entirely comfortable if it was a man driving her home. Not a common sight at this time at night in Edgewood. Not a common sight in the first place for a woman to be driving, but at this moment I was happy about it. She had a grill to separate her from her customers and a bobble head figurine on her dash. I opened the cab door and gave the driver some money. More than enough to get Sally where she needed to be.

"Can you take this young lady home?" I asked, leaning inside the window to the cab driver.

"Yessir I can." The lady driver smiled with an understanding that she had a very drunk patron on her hands. I helped Sally get inside the cab.

"There you go, watch your head now. Get home safe and sleep it off." I tapped the window of the taxi as they drove off. I walked over to my bike and mounted it. An interesting outcome, but one that I could live with. Maybe she would come around down the line, but by then I probably would've moved on.

The beers prepared me for a heavy sleep. When my head hit the pillow I was out like a light. When the morning light hit, I got up early like I did on most mornings. That trait I'd picked up from my special forces training and I didn't want to give it up. I was a lot fitter back then, but all that hard-ass training, running through wind, hail, sleet, and snow was something I'd left behind. I let myself be normal for a while, but I was still in pretty decent shape by civilian standards. The sun was high in the Edgewood sky, and I was ready to see what the good word was at the warehouse. The Guardians had a lot going on.

I loved the smell of the air in Edgewood, New Mexico. My house was close to the bottom of the mountains, and it reminded me of Big Sur in California, where I would hike when I came back to the States from overseas. My life had been a colorful one, to put it lightly, with every touch of the rainbow in it.

I'd been all over the Middle East saving men, women and children in villages from explosive bomb sites. I'd seen the whole world. *Almost.* Some parts I still wanted to see, and I'd fought alongside valiant men who were still in service and hadn't seen their families for more than six weeks at a time. I'd gotten out while I could. I saw that it wasn't leading me in the right direction and that I would have been caught up in the military lifestyle for the rest of my life. The next step would have been to step behind the scenes at a desk, but I wasn't that guy. If Pop hadn't called me up when he did, I would have been floating around the Cali area sitting at the beach and cruising. I would have taken more private contracts and maybe worked at teaching people how to defuse bombs. This was better. I got to be a part of something that wasn't as high pressure as the special forces but was still fulfilling enough for me to feel good.

My bike added to my natural sense of freedom. She was clean as a whistle, and I loved my Harley. She was in mint condition all the time. I kept her this way, and she served me well. I let my ears enjoy the rumble of the engine under me. I rode into the warehouse with a lot on my mind, I was thinking of Tara, of Stephanie and Pop. No messages came from Finn, so I assumed no news was good news.

I dismounted, and Pop was there at the front with his hands in his pockets. "Maverick."

"Hey, Pop. You good?" I asked as I shook out my hair.

"I'm doing better than ever. We have received news on an address for Wildcard. Mustang has the details. He is hiding out right in Sedillo as expected where he has cover from his cowardly minions. I may need you to run a mission of your own, except the crew would be different. It would consist of you, Axle, Mustang, and Gunner. I believe you boys would be the right ones for the job. Would you be up for that?" Pop's bushy eyebrows lifted as I processed what he was asking.

"I don't see why not. It's going to need a stakeout. We can't rush in there. There's a cartel involved, that's what Hawk told me. We have to tread lightly, Pop. This is what he wants. He's trying to derail you. We can't charge in, it would be a death mission," I said patiently. I knew from other circumstances that Pop on occasion was one-sided in his thinking and wanted to charge at anything and anyone who threatened the club.

His forehead creased like old leather as his eyes came to the recognition I wanted him to understand. "Second attempt on my life, Maverick." He was visibly shaking. "I have a granddaughter I want to be around for. I can't let this man of all fucking people ruin the Guardians. Bulldog would be turning over in his grave if he could see what's going on. God rest his soul." He shook his fist as a vein popped up on his forehead.

"He won't, we have a strong unit here," I reminded him. A roaring blast of more than one bike flooded my eardrums as I watched Shadow, Shaggy, and Rush ride forward and park. I was grinning ear to ear. It was good to see the boys. A wood-grained Jeep followed the boys in and made me sit up, alert. I peered at it to take a closer look. I was having a hard time making out the face of the person as I squinted. The Jeep parked, and I put my hands on my forehead when the facial recognition set in.

"Shit. What the hell is she doing here?" I yelled.

Shadow grinned. "Women stalkers, Maverick? You really got it going on in Edgewood. You putting voodoo on these women or something?"

"No, I'm not. I just put her in a cab hours ago. I don't even know how she's driving. She was smashed."

The guys started laughing at me as I walked over to the Jeep. The last thing I wanted was a woman stalker.

"Sally? What the hell are you doing here and how did you find out where I was?"

Her face was withdrawn a little, but she looked a damn sight better than last night. "I came to warn you all. I made a mistake last night with you." She looked forward and not at me, and I assumed she was embarrassed. "I didn't think you would be a nice guy, but you are. You're real decent. You didn't have to put me in that cab last night. Not too many men would do that." I noticed the fine lines around her eyes. They didn't make her look unattractive; if anything, they added to her appeal. Her words were sharp and fast. She was sitting in her car with her hands firmly attached to the steering wheel as if it would fly off at any moment.

"Wildcard sent me to you, and he paid me some money to do it. I thought why not?" She shrugged her slight shoulders. "He knew your weakness was women." She blinked her big eyes at me rapidly while I stood and listened to her in mild shock. "I'm sorry about last night. I made a fool of myself, but I got paid a decent amount of money." I shook my head, not in surprise but at the fact that we were underestimating Wildcard. He had a good handle on reading people, and he knew what to do to get under their skin. Sally looked at the guys as she parted her wavy hair. She seemed a little jumpy, but that was understandable given the details she was unveiling.

"Interesting" is all I said.

In the light I saw she had these big bright beautiful blue eyes, and she wasn't so annoying in the morning. "I have to get this out. I messed up, and I'm sorry."

"Why? What's he got you doing now?" I grilled her. I didn't respond to her apology. She didn't owe me one really. I did what I would do any other night of the week. I wasn't in the business of taking advantage of drunk women.

"Nothing, but you need to know that the Devils are still out there, and they got their eye on the Guardians. Don't think it's over. That shootout has increased their rage for you all. I should know; I dated a Devil." She dropped the bombshell, and boy was it a good one.

"Why did you stop?" I questioned, keen to soak up every bit of information I could.

"He was abusive. If I can help y'all I will. I really will, just be careful."

"Are you okay? Are you away from that now or you need cover?"

"No, I'm good. You ain't gotta worry about me," she said as her slender leg shook inside the vehicle.

The guys all had their eyes on me, and I knew they thought it was some heart to heart, but it couldn't be further from the truth. "Do you know what Wildcard's got planned? Where he lives?" I raised my arm on the top of the driver's side window casually as the answers flowed from her lips.

She crouched her head forward as if someone was standing on her neck. "He was in Sedillo, but he's on the move. He keeps jumping every week or so. He knows you're after him.

He's got some meth labs that are up for grabs near Bluewater. He's been working on them a while, and he's got the cartel as backup. That's what he told me. I'm telling you 'cos I want the Guardians to win. I'm outta here now and getting on a plane. I have to get out of here and fast, but I wanted to come here and let you know." She nibbled on her bottom lip as tears pooled in her eyes. So Wildcard sent an insider. He'd done a good job. I had to hand it to him, he was living up to his name. He had us all hoodwinked, but I knew being on the run like that would wear an old man down. He couldn't run forever. Mustang and Gunner's speciality was hunting and ambush, and this would be a real treat for them. Sally kept talking, and this time I was all ears. "Thanks for everything and being the first man to treat a lady how she should be treated." She grabbed my hand, and this time I didn't pull back from her. I hugged her.

"Take care. Be safe and hurry up. Go! We got it."

"Okay. Okay. Bye and nice meeting you. It truly was and I hope I find a good man like you where I'm going." She blew me a kiss as I let all the information sink in.

"You will. Bye, Sally, and thanks. You've done good." I waved as she screeched off.

Shadow was clapping and so was Shaggy. I waved my hand at them to calm down. Pop knew what I knew. I could see the look in his eyes. "What she tell you?"

"You know?" I confirmed with him in a low voice, parting my hair with my hands.

"Any woman coming at you like a bull at a gate has a message. She's not trying to get a date. I could tell by the way she was driving." Shadow's and Shaggy's facial expressions changed from laughter to shock after Pop spoke.

"Oh wise one," I joked. "Wildcard sent her to seduce me and get information. He's on the move. Bluewater is up next.

The meth labs will heat up around there. Not smart since it's so close to us. She said he's got cartel backup and that the Devils are still after us, but they're laying low for now." I ran through the dot points just like I would if I was in the service.

"Fuck! The cartel? We are not strong enough to take them on," Shadow flew back with. "They will ruin us, but it doesn't make sense that they're here. They have to get over the border first, and unless Pop smuggled them in, then I don't get it."

"No. They won't come here. They'll stay over the border, it's too risky for them as well. They may have support from the distribution points I presume she meant. Looks like another church meeting needs to happen so everyone is on alert," Pop confirmed.

"Aren't you glad you held it together and didn't take her home? He got the weakness wrong this time," Pop concluded with a wry grin.

"She's not my type." I cleared it up quickly. Shadow and Shaggy walked in with me as I looked in on Tara and Dutch. I tapped on the window and waved. Tara waved back, and she looked better. Stronger. I opened the office door and peeked my head in.

"Hey, Tara, Dutch, I wanted to check in on ya. How are you this morning?" I wanted to keep it light; I knew she would be freaked out already. She rubbed her knees and gave me a weak smile. Dutch looked calm and studious. His eyes were glued to the computer and gave me a flippant wave. She got up and pointed to the door to step outside. "Hey, what's going on?" I whispered.

"Did you know the sheriff came by again?" she said nervously as she bit her lip.

"Yeah, I heard. Is he opening up an investigation? Why did he automatically accuse you?" I said in a low voice.

"I don't know, Maverick. I'm worried for Hawk -the guys." Her hair was long and dark, and by all accounts she looked like a little mini version of Bell. Made it weird sometimes and had me wanting to call her that by name. It wasn't until you got closer and saw her unique features that you knew it wasn't her. "He must have some extra information to just outright accuse me like that."

I put my hand on her bicep. "Don't stress out about anything yet. There is no evidence other than what Wildcard has, and we are tracking him. He can't run forever. No leaks of the video have come out from other sources so we can sit tight for right now. Probably best that we have the Guardian legal team prepare though," I said objectively. She looked down at her hands in her lap for a minute and then back up at me. "Remember at the end of the day, it was self-defense." I was doing my best to reassure her without being too whimsical about things. She crossed her arms and kept nibbling at her lip in thought.

"You're right. Thanks, Maverick. What did that woman want?" she asked.

"Oh, that's a whole other story, and I don't have the time to tell it."

"Okay. I'm going back in, got a lot of paperwork today," she said hesitantly.

"Sure. See you later on," I said and moved through to the chop shop. Axle, Havoc, and Shaggy were huddled together talking.

"Hey crew. Shaggy, you telling them about outside?" I asked.

"Yup I sure am telling them about it. That was crazy he sent that lady to you. We gotta get rid of Wildcard. You think Mustang and Gunner got some skills to sniff him out?"

I nodded my head. "Yeah, I do. They are on it. They'll get to him and they're the best at what they do," I clarified.

"Why are you so calm about this, Maverick? You know something we don't?" Havoc inquired as he looked me up and down. I'd spent less time with Havoc, but when we did speak we got along real well.

"Yep. I know who we are. I know I'm special forces and so are Mustang and Gunner. I know the Guardians were in a shootout and survived. This is nothing. It's going to be poetic justice in the end. Stop worrying about it. Now, I'm going to get something to eat at Martha's. Does anybody want a breakfast sandwich?" I rubbed my hands together.

The boys looked at one another, shellshocked by my admission.

"When you put it that way, what do we have to worry about?" Shaggy grinned. "Can you get me one of those?"

"Done."

Havoc was still assessing what I was saying. "I see your point. You're right." He tapped me on the shoulder as he stepped away and back to the bike he was working on.

"You don't want anything?" I called after him.

"Nah, I already ate. I'm good."

"All right, I'll be back soon," I called out and walked out of the warehouse with steady resolve. What they didn't know was this was what Gunner, Mustang, and I lived for. We were right back in the field, and that could activate something good or something very bad. I wasn't sure which, especially with Gunner. He had a loose cannon element to him that would need to be kept in check. For me it was good; for Mustang I would have to see. He seemed the most disciplined out of all of us. That didn't mean he had no triggers, I'm sure he did. I thought about it as I rode over to Martha's. Hawk had become like us in style. We'd trained him that way, and he'd worked beside us for so long it was inevitable that our training and tactics wouldn't rub off on him. I parked my bike in the packed parking lot and sat for a minute enjoying the fresh air. Martha's was close to the woods, so it felt a little different than eating downtown. You could really breathe and enjoy the low hum of cicadas.

Martha's gave me such a good feeling every time I walked in. New paintings and photographs were on the wall, making me smile. Shadow and Ava, what a place they'd built for the community of Edgewood. The whole of the front section of the diner was packed with the locals, and the door was swinging open, back and forth as the morning breakfast traffic flowed in and out.

Dark hair tied up high in a ponytail is what I saw. A guy with his back turned to me in the diner booth. I moved a little closer in the door as I heard that tinkle of laughter that I knew so well. The tattoos on the arm which was lit up by the light shining through the window. It was Stephanie sitting with another man. My stomach dropped. She was single, after all, or maybe I was reading too much into it. My gut told me to go over and confront her, to at least say hello and let her know there were no hard feelings. She could do what she wanted to do. I walked over to her and my blood pressure rose through the roof when I saw who she was sitting with. The young punk kid from the meth lab. All I saw was blackened rage as Stephanie's eyes went wide as she spotted me. She put her hand over her mouth in shock.

"Maverick-" she said in a shaky voice as I shook my head in disbelief and anger. I looked right into the face of the kid who was smirking at me.

"You little bitch!" I snatched him up around his shirt as

onlookers gasped in horror. "What are you doing here?" I hissed. He slapped my hands away. I lost it completely. I wanted to fuck him up. I tried to reattach my fingers to his shirt again, and he slapped my hand down again.

"Calm down. Calm down," the kid said in a weird voice. "Get the hell off me. You've done enough already."

I held him in position as Stephanie tugged at my cargo pants. "Maverick, stop! It's my brother. Please. Stop," she pleaded. All the eyes of the diner were on us, and my heartrate was spiralling out of control as I managed to snatch up his shirtfront again. I dropped him like a hot potato at her confession.

"Your brother, Stephanie? Why wouldn't you tell me? What are you into? You with the Vipers now? Huh?" She was opening her mouth, but no words were coming out. I was panting a little, and my eyes were glowering with the rage of betrayal. "Answer me!"

Tears welled in her eyes. "Maverick. I'm sorry, look... I was trying to protect him. It's my brother, what do you want me to do?" Her fingers were wrapped around my wrist, and she was crying. I'd lost my shit, which I never do. I smoothed my hand over my hair as my jaw muscles jumped. "I don't have anything to do with them. I don't. I want him to stop running with them." Her voice was petrified, and I wanted to reason with her, but I was already in another zone, and it would take a lot for me to calm down.

I stared down her brother as I balled up my fists. "You need to be real careful about what you're doing and who you're running with because it's either going to end in death or misery for you. Tell your buddy Wildcard we are coming for him. We got some special forces action for him. How about that?" I spat out as I glared at Stephanie, who was holding her head in her hands. The whole diner had stopped in motion, and you could hear every little nuance of sound. It was as if we were in a time warp, and I didn't care one little bit.

"At least I know why you didn't want to date." Her eyes were begging me to stop and to leave the table. I could tell. She swiped away a tear, but it wouldn't do any good for me. Anger was coursing through my veins and making my heart hammer. "Good luck with your life, Stephanie," I said bitterly.

"Maverick, don't talk to me like that, listen to me. I wanted to—" she begged. Too late I was already on my way out.

I stalked out of the diner and slammed the door behind me without the breakfast sandwiches I'd been craving.

# 10

## STEPHANIE

"Don't worry about it, sister. You'll find another guy. He's not worth it anyway," James said dismissively as the whole of the diner gawked at me. I wanted to close down and never open again. I wanted to crawl into the deepest, darkest hole and never come out of it.

"Shut up, James! You're the reason I'm in this mess," I hissed as I brushed away the tears.

"Why didn't you do something when he tried to snatch me up like that? Why didn't you defend me?" he snarled as he threw up a hand. As I looked at his darkened eyes and listened to his hard-nosed approach, I realized he wasn't the brother I used to know. He was some alien replacement for mine. I was sitting opposite him with tears streaming down my cheeks, and he was talking to me like I was the scum of the earth. He wasn't taking any accountability for anything he'd done.

Considering I was the eldest, it was time for me to take a stand. I was about to blast him when the chef from the back came over and started walking toward our booth. I gasped because he never came out from the back. He had a long white handlebar moustache, and he looked livid. He placed his knuckles down on the table and leaned over it.

"Do we have a problem at this table?" His voice was deep and booming. My brother looked up at him and so did I.

"No, I'm sorry about that. A little tension between men. It won't happen again." I tried to put out the slow burning fire that was about to turn into a full-blown flame if I didn't douse it with water.

"Looked like more than that to me," he observed correctly. He turned to face James and wiped his hands on the striped tea towel hanging out of his pocket. "That man that just came in here is a good friend of mine. A Guardian. From my little hairy ears perking up did I hear that you run with the Vipers? Would I be right?"

"None of your business if I was running with them," James said in a prickly voice. The chef was clearly angry. His face was turning red and my stomach was rolling itself into knots as I knitted my fingers together under the table.

He slammed his thick, veiny hand down on the table as his eyes popped out his head. "Enough! You will not come into my diner with all of our patrons as a Viper. You're not welcome here. You have time to turn it around. You're just a kid." His voice simmered down a little as he considered a more measured approach. I could tell James was listening. "This is a community diner. The Guardians helped build this place, and you won't bring it down with your type of bandits coming in here," he said loudly.

"Bandits?" James tucked his shoulders in, scoffing and rolling in the booth with laughter. He sat back up. I pinched my fingers together at the temple; there was about to be a showdown. The chef clipped him around the back of the head with a heavy hand, and he fell back over in the booth from the blow. His face held the shock that he'd just been hit by the chef. I didn't jump in. This time I thought it was the right action and it was probably something my father would do when he found out that James had a court date for drug distribution. If I'd had enough strength and thick hands like the chef did, I would have done it myself.

"Get out now!" He looked at me next. "No Vipers allowed. I like you, and I know your family, but your brother can't come in here anymore. Shadow and Ava are like blood to me and so is her mother. We don't do rival gangs in our diner." His cold words were final. I sat silent, nodding my head. I'd picked my side, by sitting silently and not saying anything. James looked at me with the eyes of a wounded tiger.

"You're on this guy's side? I'm your brother!" he shouted. It was good we were farther away from the door than the others. I was hoping the wind carried our voices away so they couldn't be heard, but the slap was heard by the booth behind us, and they clambered up out of their seats to crane their nosy necks and take a look. I wished they would just sit back down in their seats and mind their own business. The chef understood the fragility of the situation and flipped his palm downward to them.

"I'm on the right side of the law, James. You are either going to jail or going to end up dead. I can't support you in it," I said in a grave voice. The large chef had his hands on his hips and nodded with a *hmph* sound.

"You heard what your sister said. Pick the right path, my friend. If you pick the wrong one, it could have devastating consequences." His eye squinted at my brother for emphasis.

"Fine. I'm fucking leaving. All of you can stay here and rot in this deadbeat town." He pushed past the chef as he slid out of the booth and rocketed through the front door. Mostly people had gone back to eating, and I was left alone in the booth crying and patting my eyes with the dinner napkin. Not the greatest look to go into the bar with puffy eyes and a sourpuss disposition. The chef, who could barely fit the wide girth of his stomach in the booth, sat down in replacement where James was. He put his large hands over mine.

"Always tricky when it's family. I'm sorry, dear. I *did* have to do that. We can't have him in here. I hope you can sort it out with Maverick there. Seems like a nice man. Would be better than that other biker guy you were dating." He winked as my mouth hung agape.

*Does everyone in this town know my business?*

"Yeah, he's a lot better. I don't know, I think I blew it."

The chef smiled, and his moustache lifted with it. "You haven't. Trust me. Maverick is a very cool, calm and collected guy. Comes in here every week and gets his break-fast sandwich, and he's cheery and talking to all people. For him to get so riled up over this at your table is man-speak for he really likes you. He'll come around, give it time." I frowned as he provided the clarity I needed.

"Thank you for what you did. I appreciate that. I've been trying to get through to him. I don't know that it did anything, but at least he heard it from two different males," I reasoned as I slouched back in my seat.

"Trust me, he heard it. It's up to him now. Be safe and stay well. Your breakfast is on the house. I think you've gone through enough this morning," he said with a smile.

"Thanks, but you don't have to. I'll pay," I assured him.

"No you won't. I know you like your coffee to go, so you can pay for that and that will be it." He gave me a stern look as I got up from the booth with a few eyes ogling me and waited near the counter. Safe to say I wouldn't be coming back to the diner for a little while. I would take a few days' breather and then return. Maybe they would forget until the next scene arose. Martha's was becoming famous for biker scenes. The last one was when Brody hid the little black book of that killer cop in the women's bathroom. The diner had been through a lot with bikers.

A few people were lined up, so I waited on the side. Five minutes later, my hot coffee was placed on the bench. "Here you go. That's four dollars, Steph," the waitress said giving me a smile.

"Thank you. See you next time."

"Yup. See you next time."

What a fucking morning. One I would rather forget. I never thought Maverick liked me that much. I'd never seen him explode like that. It was kind of hot in a way, but I didn't know if I should be happy about the way he was yelling. I thought about it a little more as I drove home to get ready for work. Highly doubtful I would see him again, though. That was the problem. I got to work in the afternoon, and I was grateful because I knew it was going to be busy. It was a Thursday night and that was band night. A band called The Jezebel Cutouts were playing. Another strange band name, but it fit because the members were good-looking millennial boys from Edgewood.

We drew in a younger crowd every time they played. That movement of the younger women coming to the bar drew out the older men as well. That was the icky part. I made it my duty as a female bartender to watch out for any predatory behavior from the men. I would bring glasses of water to the girls for every drink they ordered. They were busy bouncing around with their mini dresses and their long hair. Sometimes as they bounced around, their breasts were half hanging out, and they didn't know that the local men in their fifties were standing around the bar stools salivating and hoping the young ones would have their beer goggles on and pick one of them.

Technically there would be nothing wrong with that because everybody was of age in the bar—from what I knew. I could only do so much as one person, but Dustin did extensive ID checks at the entry point and at the bar while I ran the drinks. The last time they played was over a month ago, and we got perpetually slammed for the night. That's why when I strolled in I was happy to see Melissa with her smiling face behind the bar.

"You're here! How are you? I'm so happy you're working," I shouted so loud that Dustin raced out to the front to see what was going on. I was mid hug with Melissa and we were bouncing around. He frowned when he saw there wasn't a fight.

"All the noise, Steph. What are you on?" he said like a big grumpy bear.

I narrowed my eyes at Dustin. "Same as you. I see that Melissa is here. I'm excited okay? You're becoming this brand-new person. Hiring staff, expanding, letting Steph's drink night still run. I'm proud of you, boss," I said sassily.

"Hardy har. I'm not the boss. I just run the place and pay the bills it seems like," he sighed in an Eeyore tone of voice as he stroked his handlebar moustache. "Fair deal, I suppose. As you suggested, Stephanie, I hired the lovely Melissa part-time, and she is willing to come on board and accommodate us with the request. If you can please train her and show her everything you know. I'm going to leave her in your capable hands. I will be back here slaving away and finding more money for us to expand with. I may have something exciting for you, Steph, but I can't confirm it just yet."

The day was a mixed bag, and all I could do was let go and surrender to it. Anything was going. Shit. "Stick a fork in me, I'm done. This day has been a doozy of a day, and I haven't even started work." A groaning sigh left my lips as Dustin took what I said the wrong way.

"I thought that announcement would add some joy to your day. Why the pouty face?"

I hugged Dustin around the waist. Hard to get my hands around, but I managed as Melissa pulled a face and laughed at me. "No. I'm sorry. It's not you, it's me. A guy and a little tiff I had this morning between him and my brother. I'm just bummed about it is all," I added.

Dustin peeled my arms off him. "Hands off. You know I detest touching." I frowned at him. I didn't know how he had a wife and two kids then. He couldn't have hated touching too much. "It's not that blond-haired dude that makes bedroom eyes at you at the bar, is it? Apparently that guy is a badass and can fuck you up," Dustin speculated as he leaned on his back foot and imitated a ninja move with his hands. Melissa was busy in the corner of the bar doubled over in extreme fits of laughter and tears streaming down her pretty face. *I got it.* The whole exchange from the outside looking in would have been hilarious. My head started shaking, and I had to crack a smile as well.

"Dustin, where did you get that from? Who told you that?" I smirked at him.

"A few people told me that. Come on now. I'm in the know." He pointed to himself and started grinning. "You're not the only one that talks to the customers. I do own the place. Sheesh," he replied dramatically.

"He is the one I'm bummed over. Don't give me a hard time over it, and no I don't want to talk about it," I jumped on, squashing the dissection of my love life right away because I knew both of them would be more than happy to do it. Both of them were in relationships and took that to mean I should be in one with their top-notch advice.

"I'm trying to help you here. I tried to save you from that reckless biker you last went out with. How come you can't see that?" he nagged, cupping his fingers together.

"Not today, Dustin. I can't deal with it. Go back there and do your paperwork." I cleared him away from me and started talking to Melissa about the new drinks at the bar. "Hey, so we should test run a few drinks, what do you think? Maybe a taste test," I said with a glint in my eye. Personally I wanted to be the one getting hammered, not serving drinks to people who wanted to themselves. The more I tried to stay out of the way of trouble, the more it found me.

I set up the drinks station with orange, pineapple juice, Bacardi rum, and ice. "Okay it's going to get busy up in here later tonight. I know it. If you want to run this side of the bar for the night I would be grateful." I was talking about the stage side. Between the sets, the groupies and hot sweaty young girls would come to that end of the bar—not that they wouldn't seep over the sides to the other end because they would, but I wanted Melissa to get the full experience. She would learn quicker that way. That would allow me to watch her and provide training on how to keep the pace during busy periods.

"Your girl is ready! I've been here when a few big bands have come through, but Dustin has put me on during the quieter periods lately," she commented.

"I noticed. I don't know why on earth he did that? Worst thing ever for him to do. Why not put you on the roster when we need you? Speaking of that, what days has he got you working?" I asked.

"Mmm, he has me working on Thursday, Friday and Sunday."

"Not bad. Me and Dustin can handle Saturday." I exhaled. "Sorry I sound so whiny. I'm going through it right now, and things are getting on top of me," I confessed. Melissa and I had been working side by side for a number of years, and I knew her well. She was an excellent bartender, and customers loved her. Helped that she was super cute too. She was a couple years younger than me and at college, which was why she worked at the bar in the first place.

"Don't be silly. I'm here now to help out. Should relieve some of the stress for you. I'm glad to be here tonight. I wanna hear about this band. People have been saying good things about them. You like them?" she asked as her tawny eyes twinkled.

"If the customers like them I do. Some of their songs are okay. Not my style of music, but I appreciate them for it anyway." I brushed some loose strands of hair from my face as I washed my hands and got ready for the cocktail lesson. Melissa followed and rinsed her hands off as well. I grabbed the silver canister, poured equal parts pineapple and orange juice in and two shots of Bacardi rum, and poured the spicy orange rum cocktail over the ice. I demonstrated and then she repeated the steps. The drink was not hard to make, but women seemed to love it.

"Easy, right?" I asked.

"Yep. Easy. I can do it. Is this going to be the game winner tonight?" She grinned as she swung around.

"Yes it is. That rum gets things flowing. Sometimes I add

a little twist in it for kicks, but that's it. The next one is slightly trickier," I warned as I narrowed my eyes at her and she giggled.

"You're scaring me now. We can't just let these drinks sit here, we gotta drink 'em right?" I looked at her as if we were about to steal something and nodded as I bit my lip.

"Yup. We gotta do it, right?" I wrinkled up my nose and took a big easy gulp of the fruity spicy rum sensation we just made and felt the fire of the alcohol rouse me to life.

"That is damn good if I do say so myself. Shit hot drink! I wouldn't think to put the rum with it. What's the twist part?" she asked as she took another sip, closing her eyes.

I grinned, poking my tongue out between my teeth. "A lime squeeze. One fist squeeze of it."

"Ohhh shit, yeah! That would add a tang and it goes well with the rum. Me likey." She high-fived me, and I felt the disappointment of the day fading away a little bit. We got the place set up as much as we could, and the band members came in early to prepare with a soundcheck for their stage show. We fed them all free drinks which was part of the deal with some hot snacks.

The sound of the drums and bass kicking in with the groan of the electric guitar made for a good start to their rehearsal. "They sound good already. I'm excited!" Melissa started bouncing around on her toes, and I started to pretend to headbang. We were having fun already and goofing off behind the bar.

"Melissa, has it been a while since you've been let out? Is that the problem?" I teased her.

"Yep. Can you tell?" She whimpered.

"A teensy bit. Ha! I'm glad you're here. You're lifting my spirits already. How's school going?"

"It's going. I have one more year to go and then I will

graduate. I can't wait to finish and then I can get a real job." She rolled her eyes and clapped her hand over her mouth. "Sorry, I didn't mean to offend you. You're the manager so it's okay."

I smirked. "No offence taken, and you're absolutely right about getting a real job part. Someday I will own that cocktail bar I want," I said wistfully. I heard Dustin's footsteps coming out from the back as he dropped in beside me with the floats for the till. I looked up from polishing the glasses with a smile.

"Good to go?" I questioned.

"Yep. Good to go," he said quietly as he slipped out back again.

"Hmm, don't know what's up with him, but ah well." I shrugged. Just another man that I couldn't figure out.

"That cocktail bar comment if I was to take a guess, and maybe the getting a real job part. Just as a small hint." Melissa raised her eyebrows as she checked the tap beer and cleaned down the grate.

"Too bad. I never said when. Probably won't ever happen. Really? You think it was that?" The singer's voice kicked in with his catchy melodic tone, and I bopped my head to it. He didn't sound half bad. Maybe I would look them up a little later to see if they sounded good on an album.

Melissa and I waited for the customers to come on through the doors at five. The customers came in drips at first. One person. Two people. A group. A few excitable young women ready for what the night would bring. A bunch of young guys. Oh yeah it was going to be a busy night for us. I remembered the day when I could party like them and ruin my perfectly good liver. Now I was slaving away at the bar to serve them. It made me think of Maverick. I liked it when he was sitting in front of me. He was a good conversationalist, and I loved hearing about all his travels and his exciting life, which took me away from my little sheltered existence in Edgewood. In a way, I was living vicariously through him. I sulked for a moment because I felt like I blew it. The whole breakfast scene had been my fault. The only part I didn't like was him yelling at me like that. I wondered if he had a serious temper problem.

I should have told him. He probably would have been okay about it or at least I could have given him the option. With his childlike demeanor and sense of fun I knew he would be easily snapped up by the next woman.

*Three days later...*

Sunday night and Melissa and I were back at the bar again. Thursday night was a huge success, and the bar was packed at intermission. I loved every minute of it. I even tried out a new drink for a customer. I loved the pace when all eyes were on us for the fuel. It gave me a weird sense of empowerment. Melissa didn't skip a beat and managed the crowd like a pro. We didn't have to send anyone home, and we made a pact that when we saw any young women looking worse for wear, we would give them water and send them away.

"Last night was way tamer than I thought it would be. I thought I was going to be a nightmare. Those young ones were a little too well behaved. This is Edgewood! I don't get it," Melissa noted.

"I know. Might be because of the police crackdown since all the meth labs have been in town. Who knows, but I agree they were tamer."

It was about 7 p.m. and the night was slower than normal for a Sunday. We didn't have such a big band playing, but we had a local group that the regulars enjoyed sure enough.

I finished serving one of the Sunday regulars when the man I'd been hoping to see walked into the bar. Maverick was all smiles, back to his cheery self with his Guardians jacket on, blue jeans and white T-shirt. His eyes didn't waver when he saw mine. He smiled warmly, and it gave me reassurance that he was no longer angry at me.

He pulled his hand out of his pocket with a small wave. "Hi."

"Hey, Maverick. Nice to see you. Glad I didn't scare you away from the bar," I said wryly. I felt the breeze of Melissa walking behind me onto the floor to collect the glasses.

"You didn't scare me off, but you did shock me. I didn't mean to rough your brother up or lose my cool at Martha's, but it was pretty shitty what you did." His forehead was creased with worry as he straddled the stool and sat front and center of the bar.

"I know what I did was wrong, but you have to understand... me and my brother are close. He's all I got. I gotta look out for him. I have to make sure he's okay. I hope you can understand."

"I don't know. It was sneaky, and if you're lying about that, what else are you lying about?"

"I'm not a sneaky person. Told you I was protecting my brother," I reinforced as Maverick narrowed those sexy smoky eyes at me.

"I heard you the first time. I'm not deaf. Can you give me a beer?" He was still mad; the little snappy jaws of his were biting me, and I could feel his anger simmering under the surface.

"Sure. I can tell you're still mad. I'm really sorry. I fucked up. I know that I did, but you need to calm down and stop talking to me like that. I don't appreciate it," I snapped back at him.

"I was so scared. I have to tell you something. I have to tell you what's going on." I moved towards the beer tap and poured him a beer, placing it down in front of him.

His sullen attitude changed as soon as I said that. His hands gripped the beer as a few strands of his hair fell forward. His head jolted up to look me in the eye. "What is it?" he asked firmly.

"James told me a few things about what's going to happen with the Guardians. I want to pass on the message."

"We probably already know, but go ahead with it," Maverick said. I paused for a minute as I looked away.

"Are you going to keep up with the steam coming my way or can we really talk? I'm sorry, Maverick. How much more do you want me to grovel?" I asked as I threw the towel down on top of the bar.

"I don't know. A little bit more. Just a little bit. Your brother sucks right now, and he should know whatever he is involved with with Wildcard won't last long." Maverick's eyes were full of fire, but his voice was calm and peaceful. How did he do that? Maybe it was part of his training. I know if I was mad you would be able to see it. Everybody would know about it.

"More groveling is not going to happen. Can get you another beer later on though. I can promise you that." I laughed and I saw a smile crack at the side of Maverick's lips and it let me know we were at least on speaking terms. "My bro is in the pits right now. It's hard to know what to do. Mom and Dad don't know either." I paused for a minute and looked at his face. He was listening to what I had to say at least.

"Both of them are going to go nuts. He has a court date

pending as well." I put both hands on my forehead and pressed. I was stressed to the max about it.

"Hey. I *was* mad. I'm lukewarm now. Gotta let a guy thaw out for a while after news like that. Tell me what you know, Steph."

I pretended to clean. I didn't want Dustin to have an excuse to make a passing comment, even though I wouldn't listen anyway. "James told me that Wildcard had some grand master plan and it involved millions of dollars. He also told me that there are going to be 20 new meth labs cropping up."

Maverick absorbed the information for a moment as he took another sip of his beer. "About right. We have news of where the next meth labs are going to be."

"Okay, you're too calm about this. You must know something else too."

"No I don't. I'm ex special forces. This is not a big deal for me, and I know you don't want to hear that, but it's not. The Guardians are a strong unit. We just have to find Wildcard. If you hear anyone speak about him, let me know. When you talk in millions, those were his words? Is that millions in street product, or your brother was told he's going to make millions?" Maverick raised an eyebrow and glanced over the bar at me.

"That's a good point. I don't know which, but I know he wants money, and that's all he's thinking about. Hang on, I have to serve a customer." Past Maverick on the right I served one of the regulars, and they wanted to chat at length.

"Hey, Marsha, I haven't seen you in here for a while. You been all right?" I asked. I poured her a white wine, which was what she liked to drink. She was a retired taxi driver and came in from time to time on a Sunday night by herself.

I think she came in for the conversation and to talk about her week. She was in her late fifties, I would say with a few lines around the mouth and eyes, but for the most part she looked pretty good for her age.

"I've been good. Did a little gardening, but all I can get to grow is the cactus," she said sadly.

"Ah, rain will hit soon. It always does here. Might not last long, but it will be here. I have a few cacti and they're doing pretty well," I replied. If you couldn't grow cactus in the desert, then I didn't know what you could grow.

"I agree. Listen, I have to get back down the bar, enjoy your wine. The band will be on soon." I let go of her quickly. I saw the flash of rejection in her eyes that I was leaving our chat, but I was already walking away as I started talking. I cut back in front of Maverick as I put the money in the till.

"Can I ask you a question, Maverick?"

"Sure. Hit me."

"Why were you so mad when you left with that blond lady?"

Maverick's eyes crinkled at the corners as he finished the rest of his beer. "Steph, if you hadn't noticed. I'm into you, and I'm sorry for yelling at you the way I did. I don't do that normally. I didn't go home with her at all. She was super drunk. I put the lady in a cab and sent her home." He became animated in his speech and sat up.

I nodded my head at him and searched out his eyes for any sign of deceit, but I couldn't find any there in his smoky eyes. "I believe you. Okay."

"Thanks, I'm glad you do." He smiled and kept talking. "Get this, my gentlemanly ways paid off because she was sent by Wildcard to seduce information out of me."

"What the fuck? Why would he do that?" I asked. This whole Wildcard thing was getting more and more twisted.

"He is trying to find out information and blackmail the club. He's willing to go to extreme lengths to do it, or that's what it feels like right now," he said. Maverick's beer was finished and now we were just talking. I felt like we were back on solid ground and over the hump. A warm glow ran through me when he told me he liked me.

## 11

---

## MAVERICK

I wanted to hear more from her own lips. To hear her side of the story. I'd lost it at Martha's and I knew it was because I had feelings for her. I hadn't even had sex with her yet. This was the strongest set of feelings I'd had in a long time for a lady. Stephanie made me think of my future, and to try and work out the jigsaw puzzle of my life after the military. I'd been floating like a lost ship not knowing what I wanted to do with myself. Coming together with the Guardians gave me the feeling I was to stay with them. I'd been inducted in and taken a solemn oath.

When I saw her at the bar I was sure. When she said sorry I wanted to just tell her *Hey it's all good*, but my Maverick pride got in the way. She could have gotten her brother killed. If she'd told me earlier I could have prevented him being roughed up and warned him some-how. She kept it from me, and that made things ten times harder. I did respect her for it, though. It let me know she was into her family, and that mattered.

I was on my way up the stairs to the church room where we were having an emergency meeting. Chairs were scraping along the floor, Axle was standing up and gave me a quick pound. Hawk saw me and did the same. I hugged Shaggy and Havoc, and a female face made me light up.

"Bell Marco! Retired asskicker, come over here and give me a hug." She rolled her eyes at me but came towards me and hugged me tight. I pulled back to get a look at her. She was glowing, a little softer and her hair a little longer.

"Hey, Maverick. Looking good. Nice to see you."

"You too. You look radiant. Motherhood looks good on you."

"Ugh. The little rugrat is keeping us both up at night, so I'm not sure how good I look or feel but I'm managing," she said warmly.

"You're doing a great job, I bet. What are you doing here? You felt like you needed to come?" I whispered as Pop with his short legs came up the stairs.

"Yes, I do. Axle is not at home, and I need to know what is going on firsthand in case I need to take any precautions around the house with Zena. I want to know the latest."

"I get it. I'm glad you're in here."

She saluted. "I'm not retired, though. Let's get that straightened out."

"Oh, word on the grapevine is-" I joked, and she pinched my shoulder hard, leaving it throbbing.

"Ow. Shit. If your ninja kicks don't work that pinch can be added. That's lethal."

Bell smirked. "Serves you right for trying to put me in the washed-up pile. I'm onto you, Maverick." She waggled her finger at me, but it was all in good fun. Bell and I had a great relationship, and I regarded her highly. If not more so than the guys.

Red, who I barely saw, spoke. "We are back in here again. For the second time in the last couple of weeks, which brings me no joy. Wildcard has to go. Axle." Red gave him a telepathic message almost. Axle nodded as soon as their eyes met. "You know what to do. This means I'm going to be on guard with Pop along with Gunner. Hawk, if you need Gunner back for the missions let me know and can make arrangements."

Mustang stood up. "With all due respect, Axle has a family. Let me hunt down Wildcard. He won't expect it. I can find him quicker than you know, and I'm adept at tracking." Red nodded his head as the others sat in silence around the room.

"Appreciate it, Mustang, but Axle is our enforcer, and that's what he's trained to do for us. We need you for missions. However, if you find out any information during your missions and you can act on it... I give you the green light to hunt him down." Red was a serious guy most of the time, a little harder to read and well spoken. He was more on the quiet side and seemed to be enjoying his family time with Brody and their baby.

"Okay. No problem." Mustang folded back in the shadows to sit on his stool. Privately I thought Mustang's idea was the best option and if left to him he would find Wildcard in a matter of days and put the old man out of his misery.

Red pointed a finger at me. "How about you tell the rest of the story, Maverick, and what happened with the mystery lady from the bar."

"For sure. Wildcard sent a woman to seduce me." My whole team of brothers started laughing at me, and I threw my hands up in mock disgust.

"You? She picked you? Maverick, you lady killer!" Dutch chimed in as I held my hand up in exasperation. The whole room that was supposed to be serious were cracking up at my expense.

"Why does everyone find this so hard to believe? I'm a nice guy, fellas. Women like me. Let me get this out. Come on."

"Hurry up, Maverick," Hawk cajoled with a grin on his face. Bell was snickering behind her balled-up fist.

I pointed to her. "Bell, don't you laugh." I sighed. "Like I said... Wildcard sent a woman to seduce me. I didn't go for it. I put her in a cab, and she came to see me here. She told me that Wildcard is hitting up Bluewater Complex next to start meth labs. She also told me that Wildcard is moving around and is no longer in Sedillo. I got some extra information from the bartender, Stephanie. James, the kid we picked up on the mission, remember guys?" I glanced in Hawk's general direction and then Mustang and Gunner.

"Yep. I remember that kid. He was trying to stop that meth cook from talking to you."

I pointed quickly at Hawk. "Yep, that one. That kid is her brother, and he is working with the Vipers. Apparently there are millions of dollars up for grabs." I read the room.

"Millions. Hmm." Finn tapped on the table. "Smells like Wildcard is playing with fire. He's talking to the cartel. Do you think, Pop?"

"He does have history with them. I wouldn't put it past him. He's probably doing the same thing he did to me." He sounded deeply regretful that he'd let Wildcard back into the club.

"What's that, Pop?" I asked.

"The sweet talking and bringing up the past connections and memories. He'll do a few favors here and there and make it look good. He's forming his alliances, that's exactly what the old badger is doing. Axle, take him out! I want that tape. Extort it out of him," Pop's eyes were glowering with anger as he balled up his fists. From my time at the Guardians I'd only seen Pop angry a few times, and this was one of them. If someone was trying to take me out, I guessed I would be angry too.

"Done, I'll take him out," Axle said without hesitation.

"Then it's settled. We are now officially on a Wildcard hunt..." Red confirmed.

*"Protect thine own!"* everyone called out in unison. Safe to say Wildcard was a dead man.

Shadow, Axle, and I were at the bottom of the stairs, and Shadow looked as if he had something to say.

"What is it?" I asked. "You got that look in your eye."

"Are you dating Stephanie?" Shadow inquired.

I scoffed as we walked out into the depth of the violet night. "I was trying to. I saw her and her brother in the booth at your place—Martha's. Shit made me wild, Shadow."

"You shouldn't trust her if her brother is hooked in with the Vipers. You know she lied to you once, she would do it again. Family ties are huge. From what I know she's pretty close to him. How do you know she's not doing the same thing to you that Sally was contracted to do?"

I sighed. "No, this is different. She's not with her bro on this. I can feel it in my bones. We're connected somehow. Hard to explain it."

I could just make out Shadow's face in the dark. The whites of his eyes were gleaming. "Maybe so. I don't have to tell you to be careful. I know you got it covered. Good luck. See you tomorrow." Shadow walked off to his bike, leaving me there standing with my own thoughts and loud doubts about Stephanie.

Stephanie wouldn't leave my mind. She was circling in there like a hamster on a wheel, and I wanted it to stop. I wasn't one of these obsessive types of men, but right there at the back she sat there. I didn't want to ignore it since it was there.

The next day I dropped my pride and called her. I knew she would have gotten home late from her shift, so I called her around midday. I was sitting on my back deck watching the birds fly over my house.

"Hi, Steph."

"Maverick? Hey. Nice to hear from you." She seemed hesitant, and I didn't want the conversation to be stilted, so I kept talking.

"I wanted to know if you want to hang out sometime. I was thinking about mini golf. Feel like a game?" Nice and slow is how I wanted to take it. I wanted to ease back into things with her. We got off to a bumpy start, and I wanted to smooth things out.

"I'd like that, Maverick, and I'm glad you called me. I didn't think you would after...you know, everything with my brother. I messed things up."

"Trust me, I still have some feelings about it, but I'm not a man to hold grudges. If we didn't have that obstacle in the way, then maybe we would stand a chance," I ventured and hoped she wouldn't leave me hanging out on a limb.

"Maybe we would. We can only see, right? Let's go play mini golf. I haven't been in so many years, I think it would be a lotta fun. I have a day off today, which is rare. You must know something," she joked.

"*Maybe*! You didn't answer me at the bar when I told you that you were the only one I was interested in. What do you think about that?" There I was feeling around trying to get a sense of what Stephanie wanted.

"I think that... I'm into you too, Maverick, otherwise I wouldn't go out with you. What time are you coming to pick me up?" she asked.

I pumped my fist behind the phone. A small step in the right direction. Steph and I getting together at this point had been like pulling teeth. "How does one sound? I can pick you up."

"I'm in. Do I need to wear a golfing outfit?" she joked, letting me know we were back on track.

"That question could go so many ways you have no idea," I said to her. My mind started to drift to golfing outfits I could put her in. One of them involved a miniskirt. I let the bubble dissolve and came back from the fantasy land I was in.

"I'm sure it could. I walked right into that one willingly," she said with that sassy tone I knew her for.

"What can I say to that? You did, and I'm not mad. I'll see you at one, Steph. Get ready to get your butt whipped!"

"We'll see. I'm a little rusty, but I should be able to at least keep up," she countered. "Bye, Maverick."

"See you soon, Steph." I got off the phone with a huge grin on my face. The conversation made me motivated enough to go clean up my bike, so I headed out back and started to polish her up. I made the chrome and the silver on her gleam. I could see myself in the reflection of the bike.

"Now she's ready to ride," I praised myself out loud. I got cleaned up and pulled the bike out into the Edgewood sun. Yeah. It wasn't such a bad place. It was as good a place as any to settle down and have a family. Time to throw in the towel on being casual with Stephanie. I wanted something with her. I rode over to her house and knocked on the door. She opened it, and as soon as I saw her I knew what to do. I pulled her into my arms and held her face with my hand. I crushed my lips against hers. She didn't resist; she wrapped her arms around my waist and the kiss changed. She opened her lips slightly, and I slid the tip of my tongue in as the kiss deepened. She drew back slowly. "That's a greeting and a half," she said breathlessly as her blue eyes twinkled.

"I like to make a good first impression," I answered in a husky voice.

She raised her eyebrows and put her hand on my chest as I held her waist. "That you did. Are you ready to go?" She looked up at me through her lowered lashes.

"Yep, ready when you are, my rock queen," I said.

"Rock queen?" she questioned with one eyebrow up.

"Yep, you look like one today with your lipstick and your leather pants. Very cool." She was incredibly beautiful to me with her long dark hair and her dark plum lips. She was wearing minimal makeup and leather pants with a cute T-shirt. I took her hand as I led her to the bike.

"Thank you. I like to switch up sometimes," she said.

"Nothing wrong with the switch up. You got it," I praised. I admired her shape as she slid her helmet on. She definitely looked like the classic biker chick with her badass tattoos, the dark hair, the lipstick, and the leather pants. She even had the leather boots to match.

We rode out to this little mini golf place I'd found when I first moved to Edgewood. I'd played there a couple of times with Hawk and beat him viciously. If Steph wasn't any good I planned to go easy on her. The place was nondescript and out in the middle of the desert—or at least it felt like it. The front path had a cactus garden on either side of it, it was quite unique. Bees were buzzing from the flowers around them. Some small shrubs were scattered around the cacti as well. Daves's Mini Golf is what it was called, and it was perched on the outskirts of town. Attached to it was a café and a golf center. I led her through a small gate and as we entered inside.

"Welcome to Dave's Golf. Are we playing today?" a large boisterous man behind the counter asked.

"Yes, we are. Two people." I held up two fingers.

He rang the tickets up as I exchanged money with him, and Steph squealed, making me smile. I liked making her happy, and I wanted to make her mine, but I didn't know how to bridge the gap to the next step with her. I guessed I would find a way over the course of the day.

We picked up our golf clubs and headed out to the little mini golf world. The first putt was a hole in the middle of a castle. "This is pretty fun, I'm happy you brought me here. First hole. Prepare to be beaten," she said cockily.

"I don't know. This hole is deceiving, it's a little tricky to get past, but I want to see it. Let's go."

I watched as Stephanie planted her feet and gave a little butt wiggle which I liked and lined up the putt, knocking the ball toward the hole. It ended up just off to the side and missed by a few inches. She stomped her foot.

"Shit. I was aiming for a hole in one." She clicked her fingers in frustration.

"Patience, patience." I was calm and steady as I lined up my putt and pulled back my golf club and followed through to the hole. The ball clinked around in the hole, and I looked back over my shoulder at Steph, who was standing there mortified.

"You rigged this, didn't you? You set this up, you've been practicing," she accused.

"No practice. I just think of the hole as a landmine that I

have to clear. Focus, trajectory, and aim. Want me to help you?"

She snubbed her nose at me. "Maybe on the next hole. This one is close to the hole. I can get it in." She proved herself right and knocked the ball straight into the hole.

"Good job. Let's move to the next one." The heat was starting to kick in, and I didn't know how long we would last out in the sun.

"Do you want a drink? It's getting pretty hot here. They have slushies inside. I can grab us both one," I enquired as the sun shone on the top of Steph's head.

"No, let's do the next hole and then we can do a drink break." The next one was an alligator in a swamp, and the hole was inside its mouth. It had to curve over a mini hill and roll down into the mouth.

"Okay, you ready for me to help you on this one?" An opportunity to get a little closer to her is what I was working toward, and now was the chance.

"Sure, you can help me," she said. I stood behind her and sank down into my knees. "Bend your knees, baby. You gotta get down low with it. You wanna tap the ball lightly but give it enough so it gets over that hump," I whispered into her ear and nipped it with my teeth. She jumped and hit me on the thigh.

"Get off me, you're trying to sabotage my shot," she replied playfully.

"Me?" I pointed to myself. "I would never do that. Come on, not my style." I beamed as she took her shot, and the ball hung in the balance, deciding whether it wanted to go back or forth over the hump or not. It moved forward and slid down the hump and right into the hole. Stephanie raised her arms in the air and butt-wiggled again.

"Yes! I did it." she cried out as new people entered the green and waved at her. She waved back. I laughed.

"See what the help of a good trainer can do?" I added. She side-eyed me.

"Yeah, right," she responded with those gorgeous eyes of hers twinkling. I ran inside and got us those slushies to cool us both down.

"Here you go, one slushie for you and one for me." I handed her the raspberry cola one she'd asked for.

"Thank you." She took it and sipped hard through the straw and closed her eyes, then her expression changed, and I realized what happened as she started to hold her head.

"Brain freeze?"

"Yes, that'll teach me for being greedy," she chuckled as she touched my shoulder.

"I used to do that on purpose when I was a kid," I grinned.

"Do what?" she questioned. She was still trying to shake off the freeze.

"Brain freezes."

She smirked. "That sounds like something little boys do. I used to play with mud pies and throw them at my brother, so I can't say I'm much better."

"Mud pies! My favorite. Bake them in the sun and let them dry. No problem at all."

"Pity my mud pies don't turn as well as my real pies," she added.

"Me neither. Thank God for the bakery," I said. This was good. We were having a nice light conversation, and everything was right back where we needed to be. We kept playing, and we were neck and neck until the 12th hole. This hole was the toughest one, and it meant the ball had to flick upward to a treehouse. I don't know anyone that I'd played with that got the hole in one.

She didn't do too badly, and neither did I. I flicked the ball up to the treehouse, and it landed close to the door. Once I climbed up to the flat part, I was able to make it in two shots. If Stephanie made it, we would tie. Her ball was a little farther away inside the door of the treehouse. I waited and made funny sounds in the back to put her off. I'd always been a big kid, and that's what people loved about me.

"Stop it! I'm trying to putt," she moaned with a frown.

"That's why I'm doing it." She ignored me and did well to focus on the shot. The ball went in, and she raised her arms again.

"There we go. I think we have ourselves a tie, Maverick." She was proud of that fact as well.

"Looks like we do. I think that deserves a winner's kiss."

"It might." She leaned in, and I kissed her on the lips lightly. She took her thumb and wiped her lipstick off me. Didn't bother me one bit; in fact, I'm pretty sure my face had a goofy look on it all the way back to dropping off our golf clubs.

We walked hand in hand back to the bike, and I took the risk. "Steph, you wanna come and hang out with me at my place? Stay for dinner? I'm having a great time, and I don't know about you, but I want to keep it going." I was facing her, and we were in front of my bike. She dropped her eyes to the leather upholstery and skimmed her fingers over the seat.

"Yeah, I would." She squinted up at me with one eye. "I'm having a fun time too."

"All right then, let's go." I handed her helmet to her, and she swung her leg over and wrapped her arms around me. I ran my fingers over hers and interlocked mine with them. I turned my bike engine over and hit the road. The golf place was about a 15-minute ride away from my house so we got to get out on the open road together and enjoy it. I pointed out a few landmarks on the way, and she gave me the thumbs-up. Made me think she would be perfect to take on a longer road trip.

We approached my house, and I was feeling good. I walked her to the door as she came inside and placed the helmet on the kitchen bench. I'd left the back porch door open.

"Shit!" I exclaimed. Edgewood's break and enter rate was high. Thank god I was in a decent neighborhood, but it was still a mistake to leave it open.

"What?" Steph asked as she twirled her hair around her finger.

"Ahh, I left the back porch door open. Not a good idea."

"Oh. This is a good area, I think you're safe. This place is niiiice. You've done well, Maverick, and you're clean. Wow."

"Right now I am. You caught me on a good day." I smirked. She looked around the place some and looked in the fridge to see if there was anything I had to offer her to eat.

"Are you hungry, Steph?"

"I am a little. All that beating you at golf has worn a hole in my stomach," she teased as she came back out with her hands in her back pockets.

"You are something else, but you're too cute, so I won't say anything."

"Good choice. What do you have?"

"Hmm, nothing. How about we order takeout? It's close to late afternoon, that's practically dinner." She smiled as she stopped near the counter and tugged at the edge of my shirt. A stream of fire ran through me as I stared into her eyes.

"Chinese is my pick. Pick a bunch of menu items I don't care. I like it all," she added nonchalantly. I grabbed her fingers and ran mine over them, kissing her hand.

"Easily done." I placed the order, and we waited for our food. I sat down on the couch and patted the couch cushion. She slotted in easily next to me.

"Are we Netflixing and chilling? Is that what we're doing here?" she asked as she ran her hand over my thigh, and I felt an ache run through my cock. She was trying to seduce me before the food arrived.

"Maybe, maybe not," I said, and Stephanie hitched her legs up and in toward her and faced me.

"What do you want, Maverick? You have women hanging off you all the time and you don't seem like the type of guy who wants a relationship. I'm not getting back into any situations where I'm getting cheated on again." She lowered her eyes as she revealed her cards and put them on the table.

"I'm not that guy. I swear I didn't go home with that woman, you know that. Yes, women do come up to me, but I don't want them. In my past I was a little wild, a little free, whatever. I'm not that anymore, and it's not what I want." I grabbed her hand and rubbed it reassuringly. "You've put some kind of spell on me. Must be in the drinks you poured. I don't know what you did." I paused and took the time to really look at her.

"Me put a spell on you? Might be the other way around. You've been unexpected." Her eyes were so tranquil. I would have no problem gazing into them for a long length of time.

"Is that a good thing?" I was looking for any light at the end of the tunnel she would give me. Even if she could just keep going with me the way we were it was better than nothing to me.

"I didn't want to rush you. You're coming out of heart-break. We have a lot going on around us, and I can see how this is the worst idea on the planet." I raked my hand through my hair in irritation. "But to me it still feels hella right. Can we try it? I won't let you down. Give me a shot, Steph." She looked down and started circling her hand on my thigh. "We don't have to move like the speed of light. We can take this thing slow." I tossed it up and out there for the universe to decide.

"We have great chemistry together, and I'm always happier when I'm with you, so I don't know, might be the way to go," she said as she nibbled on her bottom lip. She stopped circling my thigh and stared at me.

"No pressure, but know that I want you. I'm not cruising around town with any other Edgewood chickie babes." I laughed to break the tension.

She started laughing hard, and I pulled her over to my lap. She arched her back, and her hair covered us in a bubble. We were entwined together, and the body heat between us was like a furnace of hidden desires coming to the surface.

I cupped her face in the middle of it and kissed her. My hands slid down from her face to cup her ass in the tight leather pants she was wearing. I sat her right across the bridge of my upper thighs so she knew what I had waiting for her. Her mouth opened a little as I smiled and concen-trated on breaking her lips apart with my tongue. She was lightly panting as our hands started exploring and dancing over one another's flesh. We were starting to get hot and heavy, but the death of our desire came when the doorbell rang. Steph lifted her leg to the side and groaned at the interruption.

"I guess the food is here," she muttered as she flipped her hair to one side.

"Hold that thought and that position," I said as I jogged to the door half-mast, and she giggled. I mouthed *no* and pointed to her to let her know it was her fault. The guy at the door was a young male, and I was standing behind the door frame trying to will my cock to go down.

"Hi, delivery order, Chinese corn soup, sweet and sour, beef and black bean, and plain steamed rice with six spring rolls."

"How much?"

"25 dollar special today. Thanks, sir." The delivery guy was starting to give me a weird look as he heard Steph laughing in the background. I jogged over to the kitchen counter and ran back with the money.

"Here you go. Keep the tip," I said quietly. I took the plastic bags, and thankfully the guy didn't look down past my waist; he kept his eyes up top. I was still half-mast, and desire was flooding my system. Steph and I hitting the sheets had been a long time coming in my mind. It was a fantasy, though, and I didn't want her to think it was the only thing I was after, but she was a knockout and it would be a lie to say I didn't want her.

"Thanks. Have a nice evening." I closed the door quick.

"Timely." I put all of the bags on the counter, and she jumped on me before I could put the last bag down.

"You said hold that thought. How about I hold that…" She reached forward and rubbed my cock through my cargo pants, and I groaned as I moved her back over to the couch. She was a feisty one, and I liked it. The ache was increasing, and a fire of red-hot adrenaline coursed through my veins.

Steph lifted her T-shirt over her head and dropped it to the floor. I could hear the raspiness of her want in her breath. I wrenched my shirt over my head and balled it up next to me on the ground. She grazed my chest with her fingers, touching the small tuft of hair I had on my chest. Her fingers on my skin were electrifying. I unzipped my jeans, keeping my eyes on hers. I wanted her to see. To know. My cock was now full and ready for her. She moved her hands up to touch the flesh on my chest again as I spun her around and sat back on the couch and let her take the lead.

She wriggled out of her leather pants, and due to the heat they took a moment to get off. "Oops. Not so sexy," she said as we finally got them free.

"Plenty sexy to me," I said in a low voice. Sex didn't have to be linear to me; anything could happen along the way. All the mishaps made it fun to talk about the next day. I skimmed my hands over her thighs, which were shapely. She straddled her slender legs over the top of me again. I unhooked her bra and discarded it to the side. Her round breasts were revealed. So perfect and supple. Her nipples were raised, and I ran my fingers over them first and listened to Steph sigh. She was enjoying herself, and that was a good thing. I cupped one of the perfect beauties and put it into my mouth. I heard a little moan, and knew I was on the right track.

We were already a little sweaty from the Edgewood heat, and it only added to the spice of the moment. I cupped her other neglected breast, running my hungry tongue around its edges and back to her swollen areola. She ran her hands softly through my hair as I continued my exploration. I smiled at her because I knew what I was about to do. She frowned for a moment as she opened her eyes, wondering why I stopped. I bent her backwards with a steady hand on her carved abdominals, and she leaned back over my legs as I supported her back. I pulled her plain blue bikini briefs down and slid a finger to her dripping center. She groaned a little as my fingers stroked, finessed, and made her moan a little more.

I lowered her gently to the ground and slid her forward to the carpet, crawling to her center. I bent my head and licked the inside of her thigh. She slowly responded, opening her slender legs as I ran my palm over her pubic bone and stroked. I found what I was looking for and nibbled, tasted and caressed her with my mouth. I plundered my tongue there until she cried out, and her body shattered to pieces in bliss. I wiped part of the sweat off her and rose to my knees as she lay panting. I jogged quickly to the bedroom to find my condoms. I opened my bedroom drawer and cursed. I didn't want to lose the fire of the moment, and I was about to if I couldn't find them quick enough. I found one in my jacket pocket and raced back to her.

"Sorry," I replied as I ripped the packet open. She didn't answer; she was too wrapped up in the moment. She looked so glorious lying there with her legs spread and a hand on her beating heart. I rolled the condom on and dropped down to her. She stayed still, licking her gorgeous lips. I felt as fierce as I had the day that I'd walked into Martha's and seen her and her little brother James together. I teased the tip of my penis at her entrance as her eyes closed. She was ready. Panting and needy. I slowly dived in as I held her hips. I thrust forward as she wrapped her legs to grip me. I grunted with exertion as my body felt as if it might explode inside her. Her body was pliant with mine, and we rolled in time together. The ticking bomb of internal explosion flooded through my cock, and I exploded and fell into a heap onto the carpet next to her in a long sigh of pleasure. I put my hand on my chest as I felt the sweat dripping down my body.

"I think we earned our Chinese food now, what do you think?"

We both laughed, and I rolled over and kissed her breast.

"I think we did too," she said, glowing next to me. We lay there cooling off and staring at the ceiling.

"I never gave you an answer about us. A real one. Now that I know you have the goods -just kidding." I grinned. She shot me a pained look. "Sorry cheesy, bad joke... No, seriously I want to be with you. Let's try and we can take it as it comes."

"I can do that." I searched her face for any uncertainty. There was none, just smoldering beauty and dark hair covering my carpet. I circled one of the tattoos on her inner arm.

"Good. I'll take care of this." I put my hand on her heart and kept it there for a minute. It was beating loud, but steady and true. I'd never been this serious about a woman ever. It was a new adventure for me, and this time I was staying put in Edgewood so I could be more committed.

Gloomy and wet was the forecast with a touch of thunder for Edgewood. I rode slower as I knew the roads would be slicker, but riding in the rain was feeling real good. Steph and I stayed up late keeping one another company and talking about the beauty and the struggles of our childhood. We ate on my floor in my living room; it was so intimate, so perfect for us both. Hawk sent an early bird message that another mission was on. We all knew it was coming. It was playing out just as we'd said. The next one was at the Bluewater Complex of apartments where Wildcard used to live. I strolled into the warehouse and tapped on the office window like I always did, and Tara and Dutch waved. I whistled and strolled along. I was a man redeemed. I thought about how just a few sweet hours ago I'd kissed Steph goodbye and taken her back home.

Hawk caught me halfway through the warehouse with his maps in his hands. I looked down at them.

"What we got?" I said.

"We got an old lady who was given a lot of money to cook. The police aren't getting out of bed for that one, so they sent us." Hawk rolled his eyes.

My cheeks filled up as I burst out laughing. "I haven't seen that trick pulled since I was in Serbia. One of the older women in the village had a son she was hiding who was in her basement building bombs to blow everyone up. Is she alone cooking? Why were we called to it? Why didn't the sheriff just bring her in?"

"She's not alone. That's the part I don't know about. We are about to find out. The second one is in the same complex, different floor level this time. More meth cooks." Hawk sighed as we entered the lunchroom.

Mustang was sitting on the floor and stretching out. Gunner was counting his bullets and placing them meticulously into a small cardboard box. Both of them looked up as Hawk and I entered.

"Fellas, we got an interesting assignment. Now we all know it's coming. We are headed to the Bluewater Complex." Hawk bent his fingers back and opened up the maps he had.

Mustang groaned. "It's going to be a tight squeeze and a

lot of civilians. It's going to be hard to contain anything. We will have to be real careful. Minimal force and only apply it if necessary." Mustang's jaw was tight, but he looked to be in good spirits.

"Correct. No force unless we need to. We want zero homicides today. That's our aim. We want to be able to walk these people straight out of the building. They are likely to be harmless, when I tell you the age groups and the demographics you might be shocked," Hawk tossed out.

"Doubt it. I just about seen it all," Mustang claimed with a dry tone. "Try me, though."

"We have Grandma in apartment 10C. I don't know who else is working with her on it. She is apparently a cook. This is inside whispers, and the narcs division has sent us in to check if it's true. Apartment 5D—there's hardly anybody on this floor. Maybe only five tenants, apparently there is a group of teenagers running drugs through the complex. Apartment 15A. A lady early thirties, cooking with weird smells coming from the apartment. Vipers have been seen here dipping in and out of the apartment complex at varying times of day and night. Footage has been provided. We don't have time to look at it, but I can guarantee that Wildcard is on with this." Hawk grimaced as he looked up at the others.

Gunner polished the last piece of his hardware and zipped up his sniper rifle bag. "Won't be needing this, I don't think. We hit the lowest point first and work our way up. If the upper apartments become aware of what's going on, they have to come down and out of the building somehow. They got the stairwell that runs around the back, the elevators and the shop they can run through." Gunner's eyes were steely and dark. He was ready for some action.

I slapped him on the back. "Gunner is readddddyyy,

baby." Hawk grinned as he rolled up the maps and shook his head.

"The nitty gritty part of what Gunner has pointed out is at either end of each floor is an elevator if you want to know the layout. There is only one stairwell and the shop has a back entrance to the first floor. Gunner, you wanna lead on this one?" Gunner's silent reply was an outstretched palm. Hawk slapped it.

"Sure. This will be fun." Gunner typically didn't smile. There was a reason for that, and I guessed it was because his smile was an awkward, creepy one. He tried, though, so I had to give the man credit.

We rode out in the van in silence and with no tension. For all of us this was an easy mission and one we would accomplish easily. We arrived at Bluewater in under three minutes. It was so close to the warehouse that we didn't have far to go. The crew practically lived there at times. Especially now that we owned it as a club. The whole vibe of the place had changed since the departure of Clint. New staff were placed in the convenience store, and they were much nicer. Tara was involved with the new extension of the store, and it was great. It had now turned into a coffee spot. A lot of the residents sat downstairs and met up. It fostered a real sense of community among them all, and it was a shame that Wildcard was trying to dismantle it.

Sheets of rain were coating the streets and making it hard to see clearly, but we would make do. None of us had qualms with wild weather. We'd seen it all in our time. Gunner started the mission off by wrenching open the door to the van and hopping out. I looked up at the complex, nothing too flashy. The convenience store underneath now outshone the dingy complex because of its shiny new renovation. Gunner bypassed the store as we punched in the code to the apartment complex.

He pulled his gun and cocked it low. Hawk went next, Mustang third, and me last. There were no weak links in the foursome. We'd all learned to play to one another's strengths. We moved steadily to the elevator and got off at Level 5. Out of all the levels we had to visit, this was likely to be the most volatile from the information given to us. The hallway carpet was a dirty brown color when it should have been gray from the looks of it, and it smelled like rank piss. The apartments were set up like hotel rooms, and as we got closer to the door of the apartment, I could smell the stench of harsh chemicals. It wasn't hard to identify the apartment that we needed to bust into.

Gunner did the polite thing and knocked. A teenager shouted out from behind the door. "Who the hell is it? We're not ready yet. Come back tomorrow."

Gunner smirked and looked at all of us. "He said come back tomorrow? You hear that?" All of us smirked back.

"Ask them how many are in there," Hawk whispered.

"How many guys? When can I get a cut?" Gunner yelled out.

"Excuse me?" Gunner had his hand over the peephole so he couldn't see our faces. The kid swung the door open, and Gunner pointed the gun in his face.

"Whoa. Okay, okay. We're just a couple of kids. Don't shoot. Do you want some supply? We have a little bit cooked up. We're working on it right now." The boy, whose words were racing off his tongue, looked no older than 16. His hands shot straight up as we entered and started to look around. A little less paraphernalia. They at least had decent mattresses and bed frames. The place was half decent in that it didn't have clothes and pipes all over. They were purely cooking.

"I won't shoot if you go turn that stove off now." The young boy with blond hair turned it off, and we all sat down at the dining room table on the right hand side. What a sight to see with four burly looking guys pulling up in your apartment. It wasn't a group of teenagers; it was two young kids. How wildly wrong they'd gotten that. The adrenaline spike in my system simmered down, and I stopped reaching for my gun.

"Who put you up to this, and how did you get this apartment?" Gunner asked in a stern voice.

The young kid looked as if he'd seen a ghost. He shielded himself by crossing his arms. "A guy named Wildcard. He gave us some money and food and paid for the apartment. We are cooking for him. He gives us the ingredients and stuff." The scared kid handed a sheet to Gunner, and on the blotched paper was a list of ingredients with a recipe scrawled in pen. A recipe for meth preparation along with diagrams.

"Look at that," I said as I snatched it from the kid. "You don't want to do this anymore. Trust me. This right here is a recipe for disaster. You will die if you keep messing around with these chemicals." Both of them clapped their hands over their mouths.

"We didn't know. He fed us, gave us some clothes. We won't have a place to live. Are you bad guys or good guys?" he asked, squinting at us.

The smaller blond kid with the big blue eyes and an even bigger megawatt smile—had to be no more than six— climbed on Mustang's lap and sat there. Mustang looked at the kid as if he was bananas. Mustang had a serious kid allergy. The tension we all felt running into the apartment dissipated. These were glorified street kids who'd been taken advantage of, and it made my heart drop.

"Do you know where the guy is?" Mustang asked the kid as he tried not to touch him. Hawk was covering his mouth, trying not to laugh, and I smiled at the kid and gave his little hand a high five.

"I think you're the good guys! That's what I think. I'm six, and my name is Michael. They call me Big Mike. I don't like this stuff. It smells, and it makes me cough," he said. As soon as he said it made him cough, I felt anger flowing. I wanted them out of the apartment and pronto.

I looked at the guys. "Wait. I have the number of the guy who we talk to."

Hawk took the phone from him. "This is a different phone from the one he contacts Pop on. We can draw him out with the number. Thanks, kids. Let's get you out of here, and I promise you will have a place to stay." The problem with what Hawk said is he couldn't guarantee that. If they got caught up in the system, they might end up in a monster's hands. Damned if you do, or damned if you don't was what I thought.

"Okay," the little one on Mustang's lap said. He turned to hug Mustang, who had no idea what to do. He reluctantly patted the little boy's back, and I instantly loved Big Mike. This big open-hearted kid that didn't know the evils of the world.

"Can we risk Mustang staying here? I think he has it covered. We can deal with the others. It will be fine," I said. If I had my way I would stay with the kids myself and make sure they were okay.

"We can do that," Hawk agreed as Gunner stood stoically in the corner.

"Hang five. Let me get some masks for these guys." It

stank badly even though the curtain was blowing in the breeze behind them. I refocused on them both as the older one stood by Mustang's shoulder and the younger one was comfortably leaning back on Mustang's chest. He didn't look as twisted up about it as before, but he was still a little weird-looking with all the attention. I smirked as I bent down to their level and lifted my plastic face cover to talk to them. "What's your name? I know that's Big Mike, but who are you?" I put my hand lightly on his shoulder.

"My name is Justin," the older one replied.

"Good job looking after your brother, Justin," I said as Hawk and Gunner stood, but nodded in quiet agreement that they would wait for me to come back with masks. I ran out, took the elevator, jogged back to the van, and returned without mishap with two masks. I showed them how to put them on, and Mustang opened up every outlet of air in the apartment that he could. That included the front door.

"Fellas, let's go. We got the next to go, 10C—the grandma. Don't be fooled she might be an angry one," Gunner remarked. I laughed. This was the most interesting meth lab takedown yet. We took the elevator and stepped out in the quiet hall and knocked on the door. Gunner first. He was leading the charge today.

"Hello, ma'am, we have a delivery for you," Gunner lied.

"I didn't ask for a delivery. Is that you, Wildcard? You got my money?" Gunner had his hand over the peephole again as Hawk and I looked at one another with raised eyebrows. This was the right apartment.

"No, it's not, but it's somebody that knows him." We heard a shuffling sound behind the door and wondered what she was doing. Gunner signaled to both Hawk and me to get ready. Gunner did a two-step to the right and stood away from the door. We followed suit. I heard the click of a gun on the other side of the door. Grandma was armed. I shut my eyes.

"You gotta be kidding me. Grandma's packing heat? Fuck is going on here?" I hissed to Hawk.

He was neck and neck with me. "You got me stumped. This is fucked up."

"Put the gun down. Otherwise I will have to kick the door in. Put it down."

"You get out of here now. I don't know you." Her voice trembled.

"You got 20 seconds to get away from the door. I'll give you some time. Ready for the countdown?" Gunner was trying to be respectful due to her age. This mission was getting funnier by the minute.

"Oh, shut up. I'm putting the doggone gun down." The clasp to the door unlocked, and she let us in her apartment. It smelled like mothballs and roses. There were no meth lab cooking utensils. No mess. Just an old lady apartment with doilies on the table and knitted throws on old worn leather couches. In the middle of her coffee table, she had a teapot. Next to the teapot was what was unusual. A bag of pills.

"What are these?" Hawk asked as the old lady with her glasses put her hands on her hips.

"They are some things I'm selling. It's doing better than Avon, I tell you. I've sold out." Her old, watery eyes were lighting up. She was old, but she had a pep in her step and pure white hair that made me want to put glasses on.

Hawk and I shook our heads as Hawk took the bag. "We are working on behalf of Edgewood police, and we need you to come down to the station with us. Who gave you these pills?"

"Wildcard. He's a good guy, my age. That's why I trust

him. He told me I would be able to make a little side change," she said.

I lost it at that point with laughter. Hawk tapped me on the chest, but he was trying to hold in his laughter as well.

I would have to add this to my storybook of experiences. I would call it the Meth Lab Diaries. Stephanie would get a real kick out of this when I told her.

## 12

# STEPHANIE

MAVERICK. MAVERICK. MAVERICK. HMM. HE *WAS* WHAT I wanted. Powerful. Magnetic. Charismatic. Funny. Had me in fits of laughter after sex and before. One man with all the qualities I'd ever think of having in a man. He chased away my sadness. Ex who? What? No longer in my stratosphere. Be gone.

A few days later, I was still thinking about him and me on his couch. He was a cuddler too, which I loved. He told me he was a good guy, and so far he was showing me that's exactly what he was. He was busy on missions, so I hadn't seen him, but I'd talked to him on the phone a little bit. It had been longer since I'd spoken to my brother. I wanted to make sure he wasn't in any danger, but I didn't know how I wanted to reach out to him. I knew he was harboring resentment toward me at the showdown from Martha's. I sent a text instead before I left for work.

*Hey little bro. Miss you. Come meet me at the bar for a drink. Love you.*

I waited for a bit. No answer. I was disappointed about it, but I was powerless to do anything. If he was going to run with crims, then it was the end of the line. I got ready for work and headed down to the bar. When I got in, I couldn't see Dustin. I figured he might have been out back and getting stock ready. I sighed, ready for another day at the office. I dropped my bag off and tucked it behind the bar. When I stood up, Dustin was standing there with a sad face.

"You want to run your own cocktail bar?" At first I was confused and running the sentence through my mind. I let the wheels turn, and it clicked.

"Were you eavesdropping on my convo with Melissa by any chance? If you were, I said I *wish* that would happen for me. It's more of a pipe dream to be honest." I looked at his expression and saw that he'd taken me rather seriously.

"I want to help you with that. When you leave. Seriously, Steph. You deserve it. You just have to train someone up to be as good as you before you go," he said grimly.

I was so startled by what he was saying that I had to stand back and think about the gravity of what he'd just said.

"You would?"

"Yes. I'll help you. I'll give you the start-up money. I've seen your eyes light up when you get to make your own drinks. You love it, and you seem so much happier. I want you to go on and be your best self," he said in a sulky tone. I spontaneously threw my arms around Dustin and stood like a ramrod.

"Ugh, Steph, what did I tell you about my hug policy? I don't want your cooties."

"Oh yes you do. I know you do." I squeezed him tight, and he patted the side of my hand.

"Okay, get back to work or something," he mumbled but with a smile.

I did just that and started to prepare the bar. We still had half an hour before the club opened.

It was a quiet night, and I knew I would be able to cruise this one in. I heard my phone beep in my bag. I pulled it out and looked at it. A text from Maverick. I slid the text open.

*Wait till I tell you about the latest. See you tomorrow night.*

I smiled. His message added an extra boost to my day. I liked hearing from him. Once I got all the stations set up, I opened the club doors. The first people to come through were my tried and true locals. Some of them were so local they could stumble home for the night.

One of them was Luke. "Stephanie. Here's my favorite lady. Boy, have I been looking forward to seeing you all week," he said wearily as he put his beanie on the bar.

"Oh yeah? You can tell me about it over a whiskey." I smiled warmly at him.

"Nothing out of the ordinary. I'm just feeling sorry for myself, but I have heard a few interesting things around town. Tickled me." I poured the amber liquid in a tumbler with a few cubes of ice and put it down in front of him.

"What's the word on the street?" I grinned. Luke was amusing to me and half of what he said was fabricated, but it was fun to listen to when I was in the mood.

"Word is that the Bluewater Complex got raided the other day by a bunch of vigilantes. My people saw it. Apparently there were some drug operations going on. About four men decked out like the S.W.A.T. team or something." Luke's eyes grew wide as he moved his hands around in a circular motion.

A truth from his mouth. His sources were good this time. At least it sounded true. Maybe that's what Maverick had to tell me. I figured I would get the lowdown tomorrow.

"Really? That sounds interesting."

Luke drank a sip of his alcohol and chuckled to himself. "Doesn't it? I would have loved to have been there. There must be some bad guys over there. I never go over there meself. I have all I need at the corner store up the street."

"I know."

I screwed the whiskey bottle top back on and placed it back on the shelf, and when I came back to the bar, my brother was there.

"James, you came through," I said softly. He was all in a huff with his hands shoved in his pockets and his hoodie over his head. He yanked it back, and I saw the darkness developing in his eyes. It was as if he was changing and not for the better right in front of me.

"You texted me, so I'm here now," he forced out with an attitude.

"Are you okay?"

"Yeah, I'm fine. Give me a drink." He tilted his head up and signaled to the bar with a cocky sneer.

"Back up a minute. First, I'm still your older sister and I will kick your ass. Second, you will buy a drink like everybody else here, it's not open bar. Third, don't talk to me like that."

He sighed. "You are such a pain. Fine. I want a bourbon and Coke. Here's your money." He pulled a crumpled note out of his pocket and put it on the bar. I slid it off the bar and placed it on the till making his drink while I watched him sit on the stool.

"How's the big fancy druglord plans? Still working out for you?" I mocked in a passive aggressive tone.

"Great. Be quiet about it." His eyes were shifty as he looked at Luke, who appeared to be oblivious to the conversation, but I knew his ears were perked up ready to soak up any gossip that he could take back to the streets. In a way I wanted him to hear so he could pass it on. In other ways I knew the Edgewood wire was like a bunch of Chinese whispers that sometimes were believed and other times they were dismissed and thrown out with the trash until the next town rumor came along.

"Please, James. If you didn't want to be known, then you picked the wrong profession."

"That's true enough. Were you seeing that Maverick guy? Is he your friend or something?"

I smiled when I heard his name. "Seeing. Meaning current."

Anger flashed in James' eyes. "I want you to stop seeing him," he commanded as Luke snuck little glances here and there at him. James was quick enough to catch him looking and glared back. He made a motion of lunging at him, and Luke scrambled off his seat and to another section of the bar. I pressed my lips together.

"Did you have to do that?"

"Yeah, I did. Old man was listening to our conversation. He should mind his own business," he snarled.

I stared hard at my brother. He looked unkempt, with facial hair sprouting from his chin here and there. He hadn't been shaving properly. His eyes looked a little wild, and his usual cool personality was gone.

"When's your court date?" I hammered out.

"Next month. It will be fine. I have enough money for a lawyer," he said.

"You do? Do you have enough money for bail? Do you have enough money for when you get convicted and Mom and Dad look at you like the biggest failure in life? All the therapy you're going to need after you come out of jail?" I grilled him.

"You're being dramatic," he said quietly. I was getting

more and more frustrated by the minute with him, and the hope of reconciliation was slipping away fast.

"Stop seeing Maverick." He pointed to his bourbon for a refill.

I poured him another one and topped it up with Coke. He slammed another crumpled note on the bar, but this time he smoothed the paper out. A small gesture, but it didn't go unnoticed.

"Why?" I strained.

"He's going to make a last run at the Guardians, and it could get ugly. I don't want you to get hurt. Wildcard has the cartel on his side, so even if the Guardians have full firepower, they will lose the fight. It's going to be huge, and I want you to get out now." James rocked his tumbler back and forth over the coaster as I watched with my eyes glazed over for a moment. I couldn't believe what I was hearing.

"You are involved with what cartel? Who? A particular gang?"

"I don't know the name of them. We've met them a couple of times."

"You're kidding. You don't even know who you were talking to? That's a stupid move. How do you even know they were cartel members? Wildcard could be feeding you a bunch of bullshit. Which is what this sounds like. Was Wildcard there to bail you out when you got picked up by Maverick?" I was shouting now. There weren't many people in the bar, so my voice carried. Dustin came out front to see where all the noise was coming from.

He saw James and grinned. "James! How you doing, buddy? I came out here wondering whose head I had to crunch and it's you. What you been up to?"

I folded my arms across my chest at that question as

James continued to look down into his drink. "I've been busy and setting up a few things," he replied timidly.

"Good to hear. You must be aggravating your sister if she started getting stuck into you so early in the night," he sneered. "Don't worry. It's a wrath I've had to encounter in the past."

"Thanks, man. We're good, just a friendly conversation about a few family matters."

"I will leave you to it, then." Dustin scanned the floor and moved past the bar to talk to a few of the patrons.

"Wildcard came to see me after your boyfriend's arrest. Or whatever you call that. Does he think he's G.I. Joe or something?" Blood was rushing to my cheeks, and in my mind, I saw myself flying over the bar and slapping the shit out of James.

"I think that we're done with the conversation. Thanks for the heads up. You take care out there." I polished one spot of the bar with my cloth for about 30 seconds, and I knew I looked like a maniac.

"That's it?" he asked. I'd put my sword down and I wasn't picking it up again. Come what may to him.

"That's it, little bro. I wish you good luck out there and all the best, okay?" Detachment was the key now and I was backing right off the pedal. I trusted Maverick and the Guardians to be able to handle whatever Wildcard was about to throw at them. They were a hallmark of this town and weren't going anywhere as far as I was concerned. My brother's eyes were lasered in on me as I loaded up the tumblers through the glass wash.

He cocked his head back and downed the contents of the first bourbon and now was on to the second one I'd made for him. "You should ask your boyfriend about the murder. Ask him about that. Wildcard is going to expose the

Guardians. Maybe your sweet Maverick isn't as clean as you think." James tilted his bourbon to his face and drank half of it.

My gut felt like it had taken a few punches as I turned around to him. "What murder?"

James flashed me a smug smile. "You're going to have to ask your boyfriend about that," he said in a mocking tone.

"No. You tell me, James. What the fuck?" A drop of my spit flew out of my mouth and I wiped it off the bar.

"That's another one we got on them. So we are going to hit them from all sides. It's kinda fun. See you, sis." James looked over his shoulder, quickly sunk the last half of his bourbon down, and walked out, leaving me floored.

Murder? Huh?

## 13

---

## MAVERICK

THE LADY ON THE TOP FLOOR OF THE BLUEWATER COMPLEX wasn't there, and we weren't doing a re-run. It was her lucky day. We took the kids down to the Edgewood police station, along with Grandma. One of the funniest sights you ever did see. All of them wrapped up in Wildcard's hare-brained scheme to sabotage the Guardians and to ravage the town of Edgewood with drugs. When we walked in with our unusual suspects, Chloe, Finn's wife, looked at us with puzzlement in her eyes.

"Hey guys, what is going on?" she said slowly. Mustang saluted her, Hawk shook his head, and I just shrugged my shoulders.

"You never know who or what, Chloe," Hawk said to her.

"You got that right, why am I not surprised?" Chloe replied. She rolled her eyes but gave Grandma a winning smile. I saw the same heartbreak that crossed my face when she looked at the kids. Both of them waved at her, their eyes innocent. She waved back, especially when she looked down at Big Mike. This kid didn't realize anything bad was going on. He was excited about coming to the police station and wriggling around with his brother holding his hand. His brother knew, though, and I saw the sad look on his face. The grandma had taken a liking to them.

"When we get out of here, you can both come to my house for milk and cookies," she said. "I have some nice oatmeal ones that I whipped up. They are yummy."

"Really, cookies? I love cookies. Yay! Justin, can we go for milk and cookies? I want them. *Pleasseeee!*"

"No. We can't. She's in trouble like us. No." Justin's face was full of hurt. I didn't abandon either one of them, but it had caused a world of hurt for them both.

I spoke at length to the sheriff that wherever he put them I wanted to go together and that I wanted to know where so I could go check on them.

"I'm going to make sure the boys are good. Thanks for looking out for them and good job to all you boys. You're doing great work out there," Sheriff Malone commended us. We left out the part where we knew who was in charge of the latest spate. If we revealed our hand, then it would possibly lead to Clint's murder tape being released. We as Guardians would have to take care of Wildcard ourselves.

"How is young Tara? Last time I spoke to her she seemed rather distressed," Sheriff Malone pulled me to the side and asked. I knew he was looking for me to take some kind of bait, but there was no way in hell I was about to do that.

"She went through a lot with Clint. You know that. Domestic violence is not an easy thing to recover from." I was on Tara's side and wasn't about to let anything slip from my lips that might incriminate her. The sheriff regarded me slowly as he rubbed the stubble on his chin. "Sheriff, you coming around to accuse her of murder probably heightened the distress for her, don't you think?"

He considered what he was about to say next. "We'll see

how everything plays out, Maverick. Thanks again for your diligence and your service to the crackdown on drugs in Edgewood." A contrived speech, but there was a hidden code between us that I knew he understood. *You don't mess with us and we won't mess with you* was the undercurrent.

"Can you do me a solid, Sheriff?" I whispered to him.

"What's that, Maverick?" His ears were perked up in curiosity.

"Can you make sure the boys get some cookies? A small thing, I know, but can we get them for 'em?"

Sheriff shook my hand. "We can do that. That's one solid I can guarantee." I shook his hand back. I trusted him to do the right thing by the boys.

In the chop shop, Havoc and Axle were standing side by side and sharing moves. Axle had been away for the last few days defending Pop, so to see him meant Pop was with him.

"Hey, big guy. You're in." He hugged me, or as much of a hug as you're going to get from Axle with his rock-like chest. Every inch of him was machine-like.

"I am. Short and sweet. Pop is talking to Dutch about a couple of things, and then we gotta go."

I scanned him. He was wearing a bulletproof vest. He had a gun in his hip holster and the top of something silver around his ankle. "That bad?"

"That bad," he replied stonily. The Axle that I knew at the start was back. That cold-blooded killer had been re-ignited in the defense of Pop, and he was ready to pounce at any moment. I knew this look. Same one that Mustang and Gunner possessed when they went into a bigger mission. Axle's eyes spelled destruction. "Another hit was taken on

Pop. He had a meeting yesterday—late afternoon for a new construction site. Shots were fired. He wasn't hit, but I have to put a new side door panel on Pop's car."

"Must be running close. He's trying to distract you. He knows you're the club's enforcer and that you're after him."

"True," Havoc said as he nodded at me.

"You make a lot of sense, Maverick. I found out he's hiding near that wildlife park. I got a tip-off. I'm going out there today. Wish me luck." He grinned.

"What's Pop doing?"

"He's staying here until I come back. He's safe here. Wildcard doesn't have that much of a death wish. All of us are armed in here, including Tara. High alert."

"Smart. All right, big guy. You going alone?" I asked.

"No." He pointed to the lunchroom and beckoned Mustang out. They could have been twins. I shook my head at them. They were like two Hulks together.

"Ah-hah. Even better. Have fun." Mustang was munching on a sandwich and tearing it to shreds as he walked over to the group.

"What's all the chit chat?" I waved my finger like a magic wand at his mouth where mayonnaise was dripping down his prickly chin.

He mopped it up in a manly fashion as he grinned at me. "My bad."

"You going out to mix it up?" I tapped Mustang on his chest.

"Sure am. Living for the dream. Time for this Wildcard guy to take a hike. We know he's near Wildlife West Nature Park. Sounds about right. I hope a hog gets him. Hawk gave us a few maps to take with us. If we can get this cleaned up today it will be good. If not, I'm confident we will get the job done in the next five to ten days." Mustang's expression was full of confidence, and I backed him on it as well. He was the man. I smiled and crossed my arms.

"You live for this, don't cha?"

A humongous grin swam on his face, casting a dark glow over Mustang. "You know it."

We slapped hands. "Go well, brothers. See you both when you get back."

Havoc and I looked on as they fist bumped one another and moved to the front of the warehouse. "Think they'll find him?" Havoc's face spelled skepticism.

"If they don't, they will have some clues to get to him for sure. I know Mustang, and once he has his mind set on getting something or someone he will get it, trust me."

"Same with Axle. Let's go check on Pop. I'm worried about him a little bit. This is the second hit on his life. The last time they almost got him."

"I hear ya. I wasn't here for it, and neither were Mustang and Gunner. You got extra protection now. It's a different story."

"You're right about that."

We moved into the lunchroom, and Pop was tapping his foot and watching TV. He didn't look like a man whose life was under serious threat. He and Gunner were laughing about something. Bell was on the stool with little Zena on her lap. She was dressed in white and pink with a huge giggly smile on her face. Bell's leg was bobbing up and down, and Zena was flapping her chubby little arms around. I could tell she was loving it.

"You guys are cozy in here, Pop, nice to see you," I said as I moved to the fridge.

"Going to take a lot more than a few stray bullets to take me down, Maverick. I am well and truly here as to be expected. Wildcard is now my personal pet project. I'm hoping Axle and Mustang come back with his scalp today," he answered in a disgruntled tone.

I grabbed a water from the fridge and gravitated to Bell and kissed her on the cheek.

"Pop. You are just a little bit on the crazy side. You know that. You would have done well in special forces," I noted.

Pop chortled as he folded his hands over his stomach. "Ha! Don't I know it. It's served me well up until this point." My attention moved to the little one that had everyone captivated.

"You brought Zena in here. She's growing so quick. Is she walking yet?" I asked as I grabbed onto her little fingers and danced next to her. Waves of black hair were forming on her head. She was so vibrant and full of life and energy.

"Yep. I wanted her to visit her godfather. Where is Hawk?" She looked around the warehouse.

"He's probably in the front office canoodling with Tara. Those two are going to get married soon. I can feel it in my bones," I joked.

Bell snorted in laughter. "I don't see that coming so quick. They need to get rid of a few things before they can get to that. Ya know what I mean." She kissed the top of Zena's head and squeezed her tight. "If I didn't have this love bug I would be out there kicking Wildcard's ass as well."

"I know you would, Bell, but you have more important things to take care of. Doesn't she, Zena?" I bent down to face level with Zena and let her grip my face. I kissed her cheek, and she giggled and bubbles of spit formed in her lips. "You are so cute," I cooed. I didn't realize how enthralled I was with the kid that I when I stood back up, Pop, Havoc, and Bell were staring at me.

"If I didn't know any better, I would say someone is getting a little baby fever..." Bell smirked as she held Zena out to me to hold. Zena agreed and held her little chubby arms toward me.

I pulled her to me, and she tucked right into the crook of my arm and I rocked her in my arms. Everybody's eyes were on me in amazement. "I'm good with kids. I looked after a few when I was in Afghanistan. Look at this little butterball. She is the cutest thing." As I walked with her she fell asleep on my chest.

Bell gasped. "I've been trying to get her to sleep for so long. How did you do that?" she said in absolute shock.

"Kids, they just want you to pay attention to them."

"The kid is on my boob half the day. Yeesh. You're killing it. Love you." Bell blew kisses at me.

"No problem," I said. "The problem is going to be when I give her back to you." I carefully guided Zena back into her mother's arms, and one of her little blue eyes opened and looked at me. I mouthed ssshhh to her and she did. She remained quiet and stayed asleep as Bell took her.

Pop smiled. "You won't be long away."

I grinned, but it got me to wondering if Stephanie wanted kids. She would be a good mother. The way she cared about her brother and how she was willing to go to bat for him. She would defend her family. I was going by the bar later, and my heart was jumping. I hadn't been enthused about a woman in such a long time, at least not for the long haul. I'd numbed my heart for such a long time, and a lot of it had to do with my job. Never being able to stay. Never being able to lay down roots and really love. Every time the going got good with a female I was uprooted to another assignment across the globe.

Time was ticking for me, though, and I wanted to stay in one place, and now I'd found my brothers and the brand of excitement that kept me in one place I knew I could sustain a relationship.

My mind drifted back to the lunchroom, and I sat down next to Pop as Havoc perused the channels with the remote. "Do you know who the hitter was?"

Pop elevated his eyebrow. "Gang members are involved. Wildcard's old contacts, I suspect, or it could be the Vipers. I haven't pinpointed the exact men, but I'm close. Death threats to myself and Red. Notes dropped off at the mailbox. I'm not moving an inch. I'm going about my business, and they won't stop that." I nodded in response.

Dutch was muttering to himself as he stumbled into the lunchroom. "The sheriff is here. He's asked Tara to come down to the station," he said, his nose twitching.

"Hawk there?"

"Yes. He's there."

"Then she'll be fine. He can't take her to the station without evidence. She would have to go voluntarily."

Dutch scratched his head and considered what I said. "I guess. Okay."

Pop tapped his leg, and Havoc seemed nonplussed about the unfortunate news that Dutch blew in the door with. Zena started to stir and grumble a little, making Bell walk out of the lunchroom bouncing with her in her arms. I assumed she was going to walk up and see Hawk in her travels.

The Guardians were under some heat. Wildcard was up to something bigger, and Bluewater Complex was too close for comfort, it seemed like too much of a weird move from him, so to me it was coming across like a cover-up. We were in a race against time and all connected to the Guardian's past.

It's true how the past can catch up with you if you leave loose strands hanging.

It was time to go and see my lady at the bar, but before I did I took inventory. I looked at myself in the mirror. Not bad for 40. I hadn't been working out, but the residual muscles from the missions and the countless hours of military training were still intact. I dabbed a little gel on my fingers and teased it through my sandy blond hair. I'd been that lucky guy that everyone hated. My hair color hadn't changed, and I had no grays in sight. Yeah, I was that lucky bastard.

I splashed some cologne on either side of my neck and poked at my stubble. Steph told me she liked it, so it would stay. I choose the collar shirt and my blue jeans. Feeling good, I strode to the living room and shrugged into my jacket. Smack bang in the middle of the jacket was my patch, the skull and rifles, which was the code the Guardians stood for. I picked up my keys and shoved them into my jacket pocket along with my black biker helmet, locked the door, and headed to the bar downtown.

The sound of cicadas and the distant sound of coyotes filled the fresh night air. The mountain trails were notorious for coyotes; I'd encountered a few of them on my rides out of town to the back country of Sedillo. The sound comforted me and made me feel right at home. There was something so sacred about Edgewood. It was this gritty-sidebar of noth-ingness, but deep in the underbelly of its streets was danger, deception, warfare, brotherhood, and most of all, love. Just right for a man like me. A little bit of everything. As I pulled up, I noticed a few bikes were in the parking lot in a row. None of them I knew, but I wanted to know who they belonged to. Harleys. Not the Guardians. I knew those bikes by heart.

I pulled open the door to the bar and strolled in a little after eight. Classic rock was playing in the background, and the place smelled like whiskey. In the back I saw a couple of bikers and it made me strain my eyes to get a closer look, but I couldn't see properly. Steph was serving a customer and giving them her usual charm. The same charm that won me over. Her hair was up in two cute space buns that she liked to style with from time to time. She was wearing crimson lipstick, and her tatts were on full display. Her slender frame was covered with a ribbed white tee and black jeans. It was as if we had mental telepathy between us as her head lifted as soon as she finished serving the customer that was in front of her.

She grinned at me, and I grinned back, we were in this bubble of just me and her together whenever she came into sight. I sat up at the bar and drummed my hands on the wooden counter.

"Hey, you," she said.

"Hey. How are you?" I scanned her and I took it she was pretty good with that big smile of hers gracing her face.

"I'm doing good, and my night just got even better now that you're here. Whatcha drinking?"

"A cup of you would be good," I flirted.

"Shucks, you must say that to all the girls." She fluttered her lashes at me. We both laughed at my smutty joke. Wasn't my best work, but I liked to see her smile, so it did the job I intended it to do.

"I'll take a whiskey and Coke."

She slanted her eyes at me. "You look good. Did you go out on any more missions?"

"Thanks. Nope. Not today, but we are under a lot of heat though."

A disturbed look covered Steph's face. "I have to tell you some things, Maverick." She sounded serious as she put my drink down in front of me.

"That look on your face isn't a good one. What did you find out?"

She grimaced as her pretty crimson lips twisted. "James came in last night." She put her hand to one of her buns and twiddled with it.

"Ah. James. What's he doing now?" I asked. Her brother was vexing me to the max. He wasn't about to win this war and he thought he could. I knew for a fact that Axle and Mustang were out hunting Wildcard, and his house of cards was about to come tumbling down. Cartel or not.

"Warning me off a relationship with you. He told me that the cartel was involved and that I might get hurt in the process if I was with you." She dropped the bombshell, and I threw back my drink. I beckoned with my fingers for another one. This shit was depressing. How could I protect Steph? The only way would be to have her with me. I looked away for a moment to the bikers in the back.

"Who are those guys? Where are they from?" I questioned hotly.

"They're nothing, Maverick. They're old timers. They come in when the wind blows, and they've been coming here for the last five years. Ever since I started here. Did you hear what I said?" she inquired with a look of aggravation.

"I did. How did we go from having a nice cheerful start to this?" I sat up straighter.

"I don't know, but you still haven't answered my question." Her eyebrows were raised, and I had no escape. She wasn't going to let it go.

"You're right. I want to say your brother is wrong, but if he is planning something and he's warning you then there's a little bit of truth in what he says. I don't want to stop seeing you. This just means that I have to keep you safe. Now you have no choice but to come home with me tonight."

"I'm not opposed to that. I have to tell you something else. Don't get mad. This was before we got together."

"What? Out with it." I braced myself for the worst of it.

"A Viper came to my door looking for James."

I shook my head at her, not surprised. "You gotta shake him loose for a minute, Steph. We are after Wildcard. Once we get to him, the whole operation will fall. The Vipers won't hold it up. They need partners. The Devils. Now Wildcard. They don't hold much weight. Wildcard is the instigator." I was feeling a little loose myself with the whiskey starting to infiltrate my veins. It allowed the words to flow a lot better.

"I trust you, Maverick. I'm with you. I can't help him anymore. I missed him and it was the last chance for me to connect with him. I know it's over and he has to bump his head. I just hope he doesn't bump it too hard." Steph looked worried, but that family loyalty might be the thing to get her killed.

"That was almost poetic, Steph. What time do you knock off?"

"Hmm, depends on what's going down here. Maybe around 2 a.m. or something? That's after I clean up and pack down. You know."

"Okay. I'll be waiting. You just give me a call when you finish up. You can come to my place."

"Okay, Maverick. I'm down." That smile would melt any man's heart. She put her hand out on the bar, and I put mine on top of hers. I could feel the heat running through it and straight to me.

"I had something funny to tell you about the last missions that I finished up, doesn't seem so important anymore."

"No, please tell me. I want to hear something funny," she pleaded with her vibrant eyes.

"Okay. Part of it is funny and the other part not so funny. You be the judge. *We picked up this grandma...*"

## 14

---

# STEPHANIE

SHEETS WERE RUFFLED, PART OF THEM CURLED AROUND OUR bodies as we made love after the bar. All time was lost, and it was just us. I brushed the pads of my fingertips over the outline of Maverick's square jaw as he moved inside me. Our lips finding one another in the darkness, we found hope in one another. Lost in one another with soft moans of ecstasy as our tempos matched. I cried out as he took me to the promised land with my heart skipping a beat. We lay in the dimness for a while, assessing what we were going to do. One of those make or break moments of well-that's-the-last-time and-I'll-see-you-around type of dating experiences. *Not for me.* I was invested, and I'd made my decision to keep seeing Maverick even with our backs against the wall. So far it was just talk from my brother. Nothing bad had happened to either one of us.

I sat up and so did he. "I can't hear you talking, but I know that mind of yours is ticking away. Let it out. What's in there?"

I stared at his deep eyes in the dusky light. "Fears. What

if one of the Guardians kills my brother when you go out on the next mission?"

"I know who he is, and we are on missions together as a team and I can identify him quickly. Not saying it couldn't happen, because it could. Absolutely," I wanted to put the truth out to her plain as day so she could decide. "Or none of that could happen and Wildcard Willy will get taken out." I put both my hands out as if I was juggling the options.

"Fuck it. Let's ride it out. I'm here now and I'm happy with you," I asserted as I ran a finger down the middle of Maverick's chest. He didn't work out much, he was on the lanky side, but he had a six-pack and his arms were veiny and sinewy as if he did. I didn't get it, but I wasn't complaining.

"I've been in from the day I saw you at the bar. Took me a little while, but that's not a bad thing for either of us. I see a future with you, Steph." His words were tender and genuine. They caught me off guard. I didn't expect that depth of feeling from him.

"I see one too. Hard to deal with us when our deaths are being plotted," I pointed out, but I did see something down the line with him; I was just unsure.

"No, don't say that. They're not being plotted. I do want you to learn to shoot a gun. Do you want me to take you to the gun range? I think you should learn being here in Edge-wood anyway."

"I think... that's a good idea. I was thinking I should buy one and have it handy."

"I'll organize for you to go with the best in the business. Gunner. He is a qualified sharpshooter and the sniper of all snipers. He's the one to teach you," I said proudly. I nodded and snuggled into Maverick's shoulder. He kissed my head, and we fell asleep in one another's arms.

I woke up to the sound of Maverick's phone beeping. I wiped the drool from the side of my mouth and looked over to Maverick, hoping he didn't see. He was still fast asleep. I tiptoed out to the bathroom and washed my face.

I sighed as I went to the front door and stepped out onto the porch. Morning dew was on the ground and I knew that I was up way earlier than I normally was. The pavement out front was cold, but I still walked to the mailbox, enjoying the still quiet of the early morning. So this is what the morning looked like. I must have only slept for four or five hours because it felt like I'd only just left the bar. I sat out on the front step of Maverick's house and listened to the birds chirping. So peaceful and calm, unlike my life currently. I didn't want to think of my brother anymore, so I let my mind drift to better times when we were kids.

*"You can do it. If I can ride my bike, you can too."* I'd been encouraging him to take the training wheels off his bike when he was younger. We were riding down the middle of the street in our neighborhood.

*"I can't. I'm scared, Steph. What do I do?"* He had the cutest face back then, vulnerable and innocent. Now he was a complete villain who I didn't care to know. I wanted my sweet innocent pain-in-the-ass brother back.

"You just stay steady in the middle and pedal with your feet." James was always a little slower to get things. What might have taken me one or two times to get would take him three or four times to figure out. Not a big deal, but now I wondered if that trait was going to lead him to deep waters that he wouldn't be able to swim in.

I sat for another 15 mins. Thinking. Hands massaging my shoulders drew me out of thinking mode as I flipped my hands up to touch his fingertips. He was massaging the knots out of my tight shoulders with such strong fingers that I melted, and my mind went to mush.

"Good morning. You are up mighty early, night owl. This is a first for you if I've ever seen it."

"Yes it is. Kind of cool to see how the other half lives in the light of day. You have nice things. This morning dew business is cute." I pointed to the blades of grass with little droplets of water on them.

"Yeah, we got the good stuff in the morning. Like coffee. Want me to make you one?" He offered.

I leaned back against his legs. "I would love one. Thank you."

"Coming right up." Maverick moved away from my legs, but the heat of his hands was still on my shoulders. I got up from the spot, following him in.

"I can't stay long, but you're welcome to stay the night again." He slid a key off the chain and put it on the table. "Here you go." The key. A symbol of commitment. A huge move. Combining one another's spaces.

"You're giving me a key?" I squeaked.

"Yes. I am. Does it bother you? I thought you might feel more comfortable here. The alternative is me sleeping on your couch or in your bed at your house. I'm not leaving you with what's going on now." His dimpled smile made me melt even if he was trying to coerce me.

"My own personal bodyguard. I'm fine with it. I just didn't think you would want to give me this." I toyed with the key in my hand as I let the insecurity I had lodged in my throat come out. "If we weren't in this circumstance, would you still give me the key?"

"Hell yeah, if you asked me for it." His smoky eyes assessed me as I stood off to the side of the kitchen bench.

A slow smile drifted to my lips. "That's good to know. Where you gotta go?"

"Mission." He shook his head as I enjoyed his physique from the back. "These locations are off. The next one is a store downtown. I feel like we're on some wild goose chase with Wildcard."

"What store is it?"

"China Chef Takeout. Where we order from. He's playing games. Apparently at the back of the restaurant, a meth lab has popped up."

"This whole thing gets crazier by the minute." An exhausted sigh left my lips as I sat down at the kitchen table.

Maverick came over to kiss me deeply before he made coffee for us both. He placed the hot steaming cup in front of me, and I blew on it and took a sip.

"Give it another week, and the whole thing will be over. Mustang and Axle together are a powerful force," he reasoned. A girl could get used to this type of treatment. I could barely be bothered to make my own coffee so it was nice to have someone to make it for me. He didn't do a bad job of it either.

"This coffee is actually good. You're a man of many talents," I mused.

"Wait till I make waffles for you. You won't recover. Drowning in maple syrup and goodness. The secret is in the special flour I have. I learned to make them on base. So good." He touched his fingers to his lips.

"What else don't I know about you? There seems like a bottomless pit of things to learn." I sipped some more.

"I would say that makes two of us." Maverick fast-tracked his coffee and packed all of his things up. I watched in fascination as he laid out his wardrobe in military precision. Masks, his vest, his gun, his cartridges. He was a fun guy, but he had this other serious-minded side that was emerging. I liked both of the sides.

He kissed me lightly on the lips and left me alone in his apartment, which was surreal. I drank my coffee and made the conscious decision that I'd seen enough of this morning time business and I would head back to sleep for a little while.

I was the quintessential night owl.

Melissa was out near the stage of the bar ready for another night of mayhem. Tonight was band night. A Thursday night. Dustin was in high spirits, Melissa was doing great and adding her great energy to the space. The band was fine-tuning on stage and were prepped and ready to go. I was feeling excited and nervous about me and Maverick. The only question mark was my brother. That cloud was big enough to be permanently stuck at the back of my mind.

We had about five minutes until opening, and it was about to be on for the night. The routine didn't change. A drop. Then a trickle. Then a bigger group of people. More trickles until before we knew it the No Name bar was full of people drinking, dancing, laughing way too loud, and sharing gossip from the Edgewood grapevine. I was laughing at a joke that Melissa had made when Dustin thumped me on the arm.

"Dustin! That hurt. What are you doing?" I held his arm for a minute.

"We got company. Isn't that you know who?" he said through gritted teeth. I looked forward and standing in front of me was an older man with white hair and a long scraggly beard. As the man approached the bar, I saw that he had a limp. You could hear a pin drop. It was as if the world stopped. I pinched Dustin on the upper thigh.

"Oww," he said loudly as the whites of my eyes became more prominent.

I narrowed my eyes, trying to look scary. I don't think I pulled it off. His eyes were as dark as lumps of coal, and his aura was pitch black. He was wearing a long trench coat that looked like it needed a wash. I was happy to put it in the trash for him. He seemed worse for wear by his appearance, and his food-stained white wifebeater was a real turn-off, but when I looked into his eyes all I saw was cloaked determination and brute courage. I folded my arms over my chest in defiance.

Dustin stood in front of me, and Wildcard bared his teeth. "Stand down. I didn't come here for a fight. I came here for a chat and a whiskey neat on the rocks. Top shelf. Let's go." He waved his hand at me to put me to work. He flattened his palm on the counter. I watched him for a moment and slowly people in the bar went back to their drinks, conversations and whatever else they were doing. I thought about it logically. Wouldn't be smart for him to off me in the bar.

I fixed his whiskey neat on the rocks and slid it over to him. His eyes were keen, and he opened his gnarled fingers and captured the glass, lifting it to his lips and sipping. "Ahh, not bad." He shook his head. "Seems like you've been looking for me. Now here I am."

"It's not me that's been looking for you. I want nothing to do with you, and I want you to stay away from my little brother. You're an old man, don't you have something better to do with your time?"

"I would say you're looking for me, you're with the enemy, Maverick. I would advise you to move on from him," he said with a menacing stare. I was trading shots with the devil himself, and I wasn't about to stop now.

Dustin was standing guard, but he was giving enough space for us to have a conversation. He stepped forward and placed his weight over the top of the bar. "Any Guardian that comes in here is a friend of ours. Can't say the same for the likes of you."

"Your breath is kicking. Now stand back. I'm having a conversation with the little lady right here and not you," he bit back gruffly. Dustin frowned, stepped back, cupped his hand in front of his mouth and blew into it to check.

"My breath is not bad. It seems like peppermint. I don't know what you're talking about," he grumbled.

Wildcard started to break out into crackly laughter. "Gets people every time. You fell for it. Stupid." He downed the whiskey and held his crooked fingers up for another. "This time put a twist of lime in it. I want a taste of extra zip."

Melissa seemed awestruck. The man did have power, that was a surety. The whole bar had stopped for him when he came in. I moved past her and tapped her on the thigh as well. Everyone flipping out over this man was starting to grate on my last nerve. I wanted them to stand up to him like me. "Uhh-sorry. He's just so—something... fascinating about him. He's like a wizard or something. Don't you think?" she whispered and gushed with her fingernail in her mouth. I pulled her hand down.

"Please. He's an old extortionist. Stop it."

"All right. I like him in a way," she said wistfully. I think she was thinking of him as her grandfather, but he was far from the Father Christmas type, regardless of the beard.

"Ugh, Melissa. Get away from me right now." I squeezed the twist of lime, adding an extra twist of resentment for good measure. I slid the glass down to him just like I had the last one, and he dropped his dollar bills on the bartop counter. I smirked in satisfaction as some of the drink splashed out of the glass and onto his hand.

*Lick that off, old man.*

"Take this money."

"Gladly." I took his money and rang it up in the till. "I hate you. You have my brother wrapped up in your evil drug-fueled world. You know you're being hunted as we speak. You'll be lucky if you make it through the night. Once the Guardians find out you've been here, they are going to hunt you down like a dog," I snarled as I flipped my hair behind my ears.

"You think I'm stupid? I have security surrounding this place. I wouldn't want your little bar to get shot up or anything," he chuckled. "Don't ruffle your feathers too much. What we got planned for the Guardians will keep them well out of my way for some time to come. I came here as a warning to you, sweet girl. Stay outta my way and break up with Maverick before you get hurt." The old man stood up then and slammed the rest of the whiskey down his throat.

"That's some damn good whiskey. You have yourself a great night. Rest well, Stephanie." The almost threat rolled off his tongue, and I looked after him with hate in my heart. One man had caused all these problems in the town.

As soon as he left, patrons pushed one another and rushed to the bar to talk to me.

"You should call the police."

"You should call Axle now."

"You should leave now. I heard that he has a samurai sword in his bedroom."

"You should take a leave of absence, but never come back."

All the white noise was doing my head in and making me want to explode. "Everybody shut up! Just shut up!" Silence. Back to the pin dropping.

"Somebody's a grumpy pants. Don't worry about us, we're trying to save your life over here," one of the patrons said. The bar got back to normal after another 20 minutes. Melissa saw my distress and made me a drink.

"Here, drink this shot. Clear your head a little bit. Sorry I got carried away a little. I hope you're okay."

"I'm fine. I'm just tired of it all. I'm going to text Maverick. I'm sure Wildcard is long gone." I fished around in my pocketbook and found my phone. I shot off a message to him.

*Wildcard was just here.*

*I'm on the way with the gang. Are you safe?*

*Perfectly fine.*

Maverick was on the way. I wish that I had acted quicker and snatched up my phone, but if I did that in front of him there was no telling what he would have done. Dustin broke me out of my thoughts.

"Do we need to call the cops? Or is this a motorcycle gang thing?" Dustin was smart and knew the code of bikers in Edgewood. Some things didn't require police involvement.

"No police. The crew are coming down here. I know he's gone," I said to him. He nodded.

"Now I have to get extra heavies at the door. We can't have him coming in here again, scaring our patrons."

I rolled my eyes. "You think they were scared? I think they were loving the entertainment."

"There was that too. That pinch hurt, by the way. I'm

going to have a bruise there tomorrow. How do I explain to my wife that I got beat up by my bartender?"

"Very easily. I got beat up by a bartender!" The tension behind the bar lifted, and I got back into a normal rhythm of serving customers. That normalcy was probably because I knew the Guardians were coming to save the day.

The thundering sound of motorcycle engines filled the bar and could be heard even over the top of the music playing in the background. I smiled, and the tension I didn't realize I was holding in my belly eased. Hawk first, Maverick second, Mustang third, and Gunner last. More gasps around the bar. I wanted them all to stop. The band was still playing, not perturbed by the unannounced entrance. After all, the show must go on.

Maverick didn't bat an eye when he saw me. He straddled the bar stool as the others spread out, and Melissa grinned. I could tell she was intrigued by all of them being in the bar at the same time. I would be too. All of them were in great shape and pretty impressive with their rugged biker ways.

"Got away too quick?" he asked. I nodded in response.

"Yep. He told me to stay away from you. Same thing that my brother said. He said he had something on the Guardians that would bring them down. Can I get you all some drinks?"

Maverick circled. "Make it easy, four beers." I smiled at him.

"Thanks for coming here." I poured the beers, and out of the corner of my eye I saw Melissa talking to Mustang and striking up a conversation. He seemed to be enjoying it, and his eyes were on her the whole time. Melissa was attractive, so I could see why.

"In a heartbeat." His eyes met mine as he touched my

hand over the bar. "Mustang and Axle know where's stay-ing." He wiggled his eyebrows as I handed over his beer and distributed the others to the crew. I put the one that was for Mustang in front of Melissa so she could give it to him. We gave each other a secret smile, and she slid the beer to Mustang and their hands touched.

Dustin was standing with his hands on his hips, grin-ning from ear to ear. "*On the house!* The beers are on the house. Glad you guys are here. I haven't had a chance to meet some of you. Maverick I know. Gunner, right?" He pointed to Gunner, who looked stunned. He didn't know of Dustin, but Dustin knew him.

"That's me."

Dustin put his fist out, and Gunner bumped it with his reluctantly.

"I have heard so much about you. You're the sniper guy, huh? Man. Thank you for your service to this country. I salute you."

"Fan club over here," I said out of the side of my mouth.

"Ha! He's great. I have a lot of time for Dustin. Were you scared?" Maverick asked with concern.

"No, but I was angry. This stupid old man corrupting a whole town."

"That he is, but he's got some moves. I gotta give it to him. He's not doing too bad for a man on the run. We can't go get him just yet. He's been hidden, and there are cartel members involved. Might get a little tricky. We have to play the waiting game a little bit." Maverick was relaxed, and this made me relaxed. I sniffed his shirt and caught the faint whiff of weed.

"Are you smoking?"

"Not as much as I used to. I don't smoke that much. Only now and then."

"Okay. We can talk about it another time." Hawk was close by, so I didn't want things to get too personal over the bar.

"Sure." As the band were playing their last set, we got one last rush to the bar, and I ended up being busy for the rest of the night. Maverick stayed for another half an hour hoping for a break in the crowd, but it didn't work out. He waved goodbye and made a phone signal with his hand to his ear as he and the boys headed out. I waved goodbye as they left. I didn't know how I felt inside about it all; I was torn in a lot of ways. I wanted to have my brother *and* my new boyfriend. In normal life, this wouldn't be a problem, but in our relationship it was a sticking point.

I didn't want to wish death on anyone, but I was starting to wish that Wildcard got sick or hurt really soon, then my new life could start without all these hiccups.

## 15

## MAVERICK

"Can you get to him during the day? Or do you have to wait until night? Can we get Gunner to pick him off? Let's get this old battle axe out of the way. Can't be that hard." Some of the Guardians crew were hanging around in the lunchroom the next day. The chop shop was dead, and in a way winding down due to all the real estate properties the club was investing in.

Some jobs were slowly being reallocated. Rush loved working on his custom bikes and had a specific set of skills so he was always in the warehouse working on a bike. Axle loved his classic cars and restorations so he was a permanent fixture in the warehouse. Havoc could float, I don't think he cared for the cars as much as Rush, Shaggy and Axle did. Shadow could float and do whatever. Quicks was a floater, but I hadn't seen or heard from him so much. He was never around the club so much anymore. I was starting to think he didn't exist.

"Six Mexican cartel members. Two guarding the place at the front. Two inside, I saw them come out. Two out back I saw them through the binoculars. I can take them out. I have to find the right spot. We sat there for half the day, didn't we, Axle?"

"We did. He doesn't come out that often. Mainly he comes out back to talk to the guards for a minute and then goes back inside. I can't see inside so it's going to be too hard to peg him from inside."

"Only six? You can do that with your eyes closed, Gunner."

"The tape," Hawk chimed in.

"I say you risk it with the tape. Fuck it," I said casually.

"Worth it to think about it. We're not sitting there negotiating with him. He's told Pop that we need to drop cash off in bundles in three days. We all know Pop is not going for that."

"Sure the hell not. Get Gunner involved. Not like Mustang can crush him. The cartel will spray him. We gotta find out who these guys are. Mustang and Axle, get a look at their signs or symbols. Check their bodies for tattoos. Has to be a clue and then bring it back. I can decipher."

"All right. Next step. We're about to go out right now as long as there's no missions," Mustang looked to Hawk.

"Nope. None. We do have a small one, but nothing major."

"Okay, Axle, let's go." Both of them lifted themselves up from the couch in the lunchroom and moved through to the front of the warehouse. It was me, Hawk, Rush and Red.

"Red, I haven't seen you around the club so much. All okay with you?" I asked.

"Fine. I've been working a lot on the books with Dutch and Scout on new ventures for the club to get involved with that's why. I'm also working with Pop to look at expanding the club. We have the financial means now, and I think before the Vipers get any more stranglehold on Sedillo we should look at branching out."

"Ahhh, you're the brains behind the operation. Do you think the chop shop is going to stay?"

"It will stay for now, but I can see that the club will evolve. Brody is in charge of the chop shop crew mostly. They are doing pretty well, moving the cars in and out without much trouble."

"All on track then except for this little hiccup we got with an old family member." I grinned as I spread my arms out on the back of the couch.

"Well, sometimes families fight. I know you got it under control. Pop is still getting those death threats."

"You know which cartel members are involved?" I asked Red.

"No, they aren't signing off on anything. I'm starting to wonder if it's a big circus and that Wildcard doesn't have any cartel members on board at all."

Hawk shook his head. "Axle and Mustang saw them on the stakeout. They are hunting him right now as we speak."

Red's lips were locked in a grim line. "That means nothing. From the way Pop spoke about Wildcard, that's how he confuses people. He uses smoke and mirrors to get people thrown off. This might be the same thing."

"I have other problems to worry about. The sheriff has called Tara in for questioning," Hawk said.

"Use the club's legal counsel," Red jumped in with a solution.

"I am. She has a meeting with them in a couple of days," he replied.

"Good. I know she will be fine. This thing is dragging, and I'm sick of Wildcard. He's having way too much of an effect on the club." Red moved up and off the couch.

"He really is wild. Whoever named him got it right," I observed.

Red looked at me. "The irony of that is that Bulldog named him that and now that same Wildcard that he brought into the club has proven to be a thorn in our side."

"Would you look at that?" Hawk frowned as a call came through. He moved to the outside of the lunchroom, leaving me sitting inside. That gave me time to check in on Stephanie.

"Hiiii. Wake up, sleepyhead, it's after lunch," I teased. She was at my house which made me feel better. If she was at hers I would have been worried all day. A Viper had paid her a visit last time, so there would be no reason for them not to visit her again, and if he did I would be the one hunting.

"I know, but Dustin gave me the day off. He and Melissa are going to work at the bar tonight."

"Wow! He let you off on a Friday? The happy hour night? *I'm* happy about that." She didn't want to let it show; no, she was too strong for that. I knew that she missed her brother and thought she'd lost him for good. To me she hadn't, it would just take a little more time to pull him back from the dark side.

"Me too, my feet are sore. I want to sleep for a week. I think I need to," she groaned.

I spoke with a deep voice into the phone. "I plan to rub your feet when I get home."

"You will? That would be nice." Her voice lifted from its dullness momentarily. "Even better if you find that Wildcard loser and get rid of him."

"Axle and Mustang are out right now, going to work on that very thing. What are you going to do with all your free time?"

"I'm going to sleep and relax and watch your TV. Lots of movies back to back is my aim and not move from the couch once."

"Ha! I thought so. I-" My mouth was about to slip and say something that I wanted to confess to her but was struggling to do. Hawk interrupted me, his face white.

"Hey, Steph, I gotta call you back, all right?"

"Don't worry, see you later tonight," she replied cheerfully. I clicked off without even saying goodbye properly. The color drain from Hawk's face was one I'd never seen before. I stood up.

"That meth lab tomorrow. The Narcotics Division called me about it. It might be small, but it's mighty. Mexican cartel members are running it. They gave me the rundown of their convictions, and the list is long. It includes a high murder rate. All of them are straight killers and all of them are armed."

"So the narc's division planned on sending us into a death mission? What kind of shit is that?"

"No. I don't think they did. As soon as they get the information we get it too," Hawk explained as his brows knitted together.

"We need the full crew on deck. There goes the manhunt for Wildcard. Damn. He's not bad, is he?"

"He sure isn't. I wish Pop never let the bastard in here. I got my nephew trying to come down here and work on cars, and I don't want him hearing about all this crap. He's doing so good."

"Your nephew, he's a good kid. I like him. He hasn't been around as much, has he? Or maybe I missed him."

"No, you didn't. He's had school and other stuff. He's killing it right now. If you met him today you would never have known that he was ever on drugs."

"Speaking of kids... I wanna find out what happened to Michael and Justin. I want them to go to a good home. A stable one. Hawk... I've seen kids having their limbs blown off. I hate when shit happens to kids. They haven't even had a chance to live this life. You know what I mean?"

"I know. I think I would probably feel like Axle did at the start about having a child of my own and being involved as a Guardian." I reached down in my pocket. This was a time that called for a little more relaxation. Bringing up the kid that I'd seen being blown up made me feel nauseous and clammy. The memory was so vivid that I wanted to throw up. When the bomb went off in the small Afghan village, I couldn't save him.

The bombs don't care about the person, they care about blowing up their target. His arm came clean off as he stepped on the land mine. His little brown face was etched in horror and anguish. The screams would ring in my head if I didn't stop them. I closed my eyes for a minute, giving the hard moment time to pass through my brain, and laid my head back on the couch. The joint was already rolled and hanging loosely in my hand.

"Flashback, Maverick?" Hawk guessed.

"Yeah, how did you know?"

"I've been around you long enough to see and know what's going on with you. I know you don't want anyone to know that. I see you helping out the other guys, but what about you? There's a reason you know all the stuff about PTSD." Hawk peering into me was unnerving, but he lived up his name too.

I shrugged as I lit up my weed. "A mild tranquilizer. I suffer sometimes too. No shame in my game, but I smoke less now I'm with Steph. She has a grounding quality to her that I can't explain." I winced as I thought about her sweet face. "I can't use her like a crutch though. It's something I have to work through, Hawk. The memories sometimes are so clear it's as if they're replaying right in front of my face. Mustang is the most stable out of all of us. That guy has a mind like a steel trap or something."

"Steph is a cool chick, and I think you're not giving yourself enough credit. You're pretty level-headed too. I would come to you for advice and not Mustang. Hell. I do! Smoke your weed. No harm."

I chuckled. "I don't mean to be soppy, but you're a good guy. A real good one." I sparked up my weed and sucked in for a long hit. I blew out the smoke and let the plant take its course through my veins.

"You've always been soppy, Maverick. This ain't new. What do they say? You're in touch with your feminine side? Something like that. For what it's worth, I think you and Steph make a great couple. I haven't heard a bad word around Edgewood about her," Hawk mentioned as he sank into the couch. "She knows about your little weed habit?"

"I think I'm a pretty sensitive new-age guy, until I'm in combat, then it's a different story. I turn into a machine." I paused for a minute. It's good to have some contrast as a person in life. I felt like I was a pretty well-rounded guy. "She knows, you guys know. I'm open. I don't have a problem speaking to her about it, but we got bigger fish to fry than me smoking a little weed." The way I figured it, I was doing everybody a favor by smoking and keeping people calm.

"Sure do."

"I was about to tell Steph I love her before you said something to me. You saved me."

"You're not safe. She's living with you. It's going to come out, and she's going to know how you really feel. Head over heels is what you are. I'm only telling you because I tried to hold it in too. Women have this special power that's unseen, you know." Hawk burst my bubble. He was coming through with a lot of wisdom lately. Seemed to me he was becoming more mature.

I turned my head to look at Hawk with a smile. "You know me a little too well. I'm not sure about that. Let's talk about you for a minute..." I changed the subject. It was my turn to grill him.

"You and Tara, if all the roads were clear would you be having babies now? Would you be married?"

Hawk didn't say a word, but I knew he was thinking it through. Out of all the guys in the group I would say that Hawk was my best friend. The one who I could have these life conversations with. Mustang and Shadow too, but Hawk and I had a different type of bond as brothers. Since I didn't have a real-life brother he was as close to one as I would ever have.

"My answer is boring. I don't know. I don't. I know I want them in the future. Especially since I have Zena in my life now. She means the world to me. I know how I feel about her, so I can only imagine what I will feel when I have my own child."

"That's a good answer. You'll work it all out when the timing is right. I want kids. I think I want them with Steph, but I don't want to scare her with that conversation. She's the one, Hawk. She's it for me," I said with conviction.

Hawk lifted his head off the couch in surprise. "Yeah? Wow. That's huge."

"It is. I just have to ride it out with her and take it slow. What's Gunner say? I always hit my target?"

"Gunner... ahhh, not quite the same." We broke out into

,laughter and I finished smoking my joint. I was back to level and the zen calm that I was known for returned.

"Tomorrow we find out about this mission, what is the Narcotics Division doing to assist?"

"They're coming back to me by tonight and then we can decide how to play it. My question is how did they get over the border? If the cartel is involved, they can't stay here. Let's see what's in store."

"Okay."

"Gunner, I want you to send a warning shot in. Fire one close, and let's check their reaction from there." Through my binoculars I could see five men, one with a rifle hitched over his shoulder pacing around out front. I moved my line of sight to the back of the meth house, where another one with a rifle paced around a courtyard area at the back. The house looked to have a side entrance, and another man was guarding this. He didn't look to be armed. It didn't mean he didn't have a weapon tucked somewhere. Another one of the men would peek his head out from time to time on the other side of the house.

The dawn of first light was shining over the top of the hill. We were at what we all deemed to be a more dangerous location for a meth lab takedown. The Mexican cartel was involved. Once we knocked them off, we couldn't just run in there. Every worker inside would be armed—that's where the task force made the call they would take it from there. All we had to do was the initial heavy lifting. All four of us were in camouflage gear and laying low in golden grass on a hilltop. The meth house was on the outskirts of Edgewood, right near Juan Tomas Canyon. Gunner's sniper setup was ready and in position. There was a spot in the hilltop that would lead us to the bottom of the hill, and we could run in from the back.

"Gunner, can you take out the guy in the back without being seen? Can you pick him off?" Hawk asked in a low whisper.

"I can, but it's going to get trickier once you guys come in and with the taskforce. I have to be able to identify you pretty quickly and you have to do your jobs on the ground."

"Good point. Hawk, how much involvement do we have with this mission? Seems like they don't need us," I asked.

"They haven't given me many details, but that's what the radio is for. It's one of those play it by ear situations. If they are getting picked off and can't handle what's going on inside, they may need our help." Hawk paused, and I knew what he was about to say. "This doesn't feel like much in the way of missions, but this one is dangerous and could involve the loss of lives. I'm not entirely prepared for this one, and I know that sounds stupid since we could die at any one of these."

"You're so dramatic, Hawk. This is nothing. Not a single hair is going to be out of place. We will be sipping beers in the lunchroom before 3, watch. They won't call us. I got a feeling they will be able to handle them. I'm looking into room one inside, and they may not be armed. Those curtains make it hard to see in there." Mustang was straining to see through the translucent curtains. I could make out shadows, but that was about it.

Hawk's radio communication came through. I saw him press the receive button. "We're in position, locked on target one at the back. One rifle. Ready to go on your command."

"Proceed. We have them surrounded. Make your way to the bottom of the hill and wait for my next command."

"Over and out," Hawk replied. "Gunner, do what you do."

Gunner was bent on one knee squinting through the viewfinder. His chest was rising and falling, his whole body poised with every muscle in preparation for the important first shot.

"There we go. Stay still. That's it. You don't move a muscle, you big oaf," he said in a quiet voice. Hawk was on his feet and crouched low in the grass. We also had to be aware of another enemy: whatever snakes and other creepy crawlies were inside the grass. Mustang was behind Hawk, and I brought up the rear. We maneuvered over the sharp rocks as Hawk glanced over his shoulder every now and then to check. Gunner pulled the trigger. The gun had a silencer on it, so when it reached its target not a soul would hear it. Hawk immediately raised his binoculars to the post at the back of the house.

The man dropped to the ground. *Bingo*. Target one. This would be nothing for Gunner. He would see this as a day at the range. That could either be taken as a good thing or a bad thing. In this case, it was a good thing. Hawk pressed the button on his radio.

"Hawk, we got the back covered. Stay put at the bottom of the hill with your team." My heart started to race, adrenaline coursing through my body. The next moves would be crucial. We saw the shadows of the task force approach the house. So far nobody had seen the dead body at the back. It was business as usual.

"Got it." That's when the figures emerged from the shadows, all dressed in black with the task force logo on the back. I knew Gunner was aiming the front once he knew they were entering from the back.

Hawk warned him on the radio. "Gunner. Pick off the

front now!" We were in limbo; due to the slope we were on at near the bottom of the hill we couldn't see the front of the house now.

The taskforce was quiet, no big announcements, they just snuck in the back door of the brick house. That's when the yelling came from security out front. As the hits came, I heard them speaking in Spanish. They had no idea where the shots were coming from. I watched as they looked upward toward us, but we weren't in the line of sight. We were tucked too far in to be seen. They turned in circles with their hands up, cursing at one another. They were too busy in-fighting to stay focused. All three of them left their posts. A bad move by all of them. I watched as the security on the side of the house moved to the front. I saw his huge bulk slump to the ground. Gunner had done his job and put a clip in him.

My body wanted to get up and pounce. It was so hard not to run down the hill and be a part of the action, but we had to wait for the call. None came.

Gunner hit the radio. "Got 'em. Two targets down. Task-force are entering the front. I think we're good." We had a seperate channel on the radio just for the crew. I hit the button on my radio.

"Good job, Gunner. Nice shooting, baby."

"Still got it," he replied. A voice came through Hawk's radio.

"We got it from here. Twelve inside unarmed. All threats have been disarmed. Good work, team." That adrenaline spike descended, and all three of us loosened up. We didn't take any chances, however, and crouched low back to the post where Gunner was. He was still in position.

"Well, that was an anti-climax."

"I don't know. I'm good with the anti-climax. I feel like

living these days," Hawk sighed.

Mustang stood up straight. "We get paid, so it's all good by me. I can get my gym session in later today and rest my tired muscles," he snorted.

Hawk grinned and patted him on the back. "I think we should all do breakfast at Martha's. This is a good time to do it."

"Great idea. I can redeem myself. The last time I was in there, I might have caused a little bit of a scene." I grinned as we climbed down the hill.

Mustang frowned. He had no idea about my antics. "What you do?"

"I got into it with that kid we picked up from the meth lab, that's when I found out he was the brother of my lady."

"You're kidding. This I want to hear! You've been holding out on me, Maverick. You official with that bartender? I thought you were getting close with her. I saw something you did with your hands over the bar." His thick eyebrows lifted up and down. I grinned as I watched Gunner pack down. He zipped up his prized sniper rifle and looked at us for the next move.

"I'm ready for Martha's. Those fluffy eggs they make are calling me," he groaned as he rubbed his belly.

"Yeah, I forgot about those. Let's go eat. This drug business is hungry work," Mustang rubbed his six-pack, and among all three of us it was all smiles.

We scrambled down the hill and caught a closer look at Gunner's handiwork. Hawk almost fell on his ass as one of the loose rocks rolled out under his foot. I yanked him up by his bicep. "Whoa. I gotcha. Watch your footing."

"Pebbles," he grumbled as we trudged down the rest of the dusty hill. Women and men were being ushered out and into black vans. By the time we got to the entrance of the meth house I counted ten being taken out. All of us had sunglasses on, and it was a smart move so none of the people apprehended could look us in the eye. Once they were all safely in the vehicle, the sheriff approached with a stern face.

"Thanks for your help. I know it didn't seem like too much today, but we couldn't have done it without you. Gunner, you are a hell of a shooter, buddy. We could use you on the team. If you ever want back in, let us know. I'm sure we could find a spot for you," he coaxed.

Gunner flashed him one of his stiff smiles. "No. I'm good. I'm happy with the missions, but if your team needs some training, I'm happy to come in and do that."

The sheriff nodded. "That's probably a good idea. I'm sure there's a lot we can learn. I'll hold you to that." He pointed to the house as other deputies walked into the house with their gloves and masks on. I saw the bodies of the man that Gunner shot being wheeled out on gurneys. "This operation is a little more sophisticated than normal, but nothing we haven't seen before. When we identify the bodies we'll be able to tell you if they are cartel members or not. It's doubtful. I know you were concerned, but they may just be gang members from the local area. I will give you a call a little later today once we've found out. Thanks again, team."

"No problem," Hawk replied, looking on with a puzzled look on his face. "This is what Red was talking about. He said that Wildcard was most likely bluffing about the cartel. Where did that rumor start anyway?"

"Mmm. Given his antics, it sounds about right that he would do something like that."

We made our way to the van after a light morning for the Guardians.

# 16

## STEPHANIE

AN ADJUSTMENT WAS BEING MADE IN LIVING WITH MAVERICK, and now some of my stuff was stored in his place. I had exactly three different outfits with me and was staring at my overnight bag thinking I might need more. Maverick was out on a morning mission, and I was contemplating going to my house to pick up what I needed.

I was thinking twice and second-guessing myself because of that untimely visit from a Viper. I plonked down on the bed and threw myself back on it, and my head bounced.

"That was dramatic. I'm glad you had a soft landing." I shrieked and jumped out of my skin. I turned around to see Maverick standing there with a coffee tray and a brown paper bag.

"Oh my God, you scared the crap out of me! Where did you come from? I thought you were out on a mission."

He sighed as he dropped the coffee down on the bedside table along with the contents of the paper bag. From the smell wafting to my nose, I took it to be a bacon and egg sandwich of some kind. I was hungry and was dreading making something to eat. I wasn't much of a cook, so the smell was making my mouth water and my stomach rumble. My stomach agreed with my head and let out a growling sound that shocked even me.

I giggled and patted my stomach. "I think I'm ready for some food."

"Then I got back right on time. Here you go. It's bacon and egg, and I got you a coffee." He leaned in for a kiss on the mouth, and I lingered waiting for a longer one, but he pulled back with a light laugh.

"You are incredible, but... why are you back so soon?" I was happy to see him, and he looked sexy in his mission gear.

"The anticlimax of missions. We went to the location and really the only person they needed there was Gunner. He picked off the shooters – sorry, I know you don't want to hear the details. The main thing I want to tell you is the cartel members might not even be cartel members like we first thought. They might be gang members from the local area. The cops are getting back to us later today on it."

"Wow!" I took the coffee from the tray and sipped. "So good," I crowed. "So good."

Maverick sat down on the bed and wrapped his warm hands around my body, kissing my shoulder. "I'm happy you're safe." I reached back and cupped his face.

"Even with all my shit everywhere? I've pretty much taken over your room." His smoky eyes were melting me. He really was cute.

"Even with your shit everywhere. You haven't been back to your place so much... how do you feel about that?" I reached over and tore open the brown paper bag and opened it to a juicy egg and bacon sandwich just like I thought. I licked my lips and picked it up as some of the juices flowed out. I took a bite and chewed, groaning while Maverick sat there smirking at me. I chewed a few bites and washed it down with coffee.

"You saw me plopping down on the bed because I need to go home, Maverick. I have to check my mail. I have to water my plants, which are probably all dead, and my house will probably have cobwebs all over it. I do have to get back there."

"I got it. It's been great having you stay here, but this was only a temporary situation because of Wildcard. I do like it, though. I won't lie. I want you to be safe first. Can you go and come back? Get what you need and then bring more back for the time being?"

"How long is the time being?" I narrowed my eyes at him as I wiped the crumbs off. I wanted to go home and get some things, and I wanted time. Time to figure out if this train that Maverick and I were on was too fast.

"Ah, give it a day or so. Let me find out about whether these cartel members are fake or real," he said as he lay back on the bed. His arms were behind his head, and he seemed relaxed about things.

"And if they *are* real?"

"Then you stay. No questions. Life or death, Steph. Which would you prefer?" His face was solemn, and his smile was gone.

I nodded my head in agreement. "Life. I choose life." I stroked one of his fingers with mine, realizing I was falling harder than I thought for Maverick, and that scared the shit out of me.

Was I even ready for a full-blown relationship? Or was

this thing just forced on us by the circumstances we were in? I kept nibbling away at my egg and bacon sandwich until it was almost finished as I let my mind drift over things.

"Good choice. I can run you back over to the house and I'll be right out front in the living room. I won't bother you one little bit. I promise. Scout's honor?" He closed his eyes and tried to look as noble as possible as he put his hand up.

"You don't give me boy scout vibes. Please, but yes you can drive me back to my place so I can have some clean clothes to wear and not look like some bum when I go into work tonight," I sighed. My belly was full, and now the morning grumpiness had worn off.

"With that cute a face you could never be a bum. I'm ready when you are. I got up early for nothing."

"Not for nothing, that's for sure. You shut down another meth lab. I don't think you understand what an impact you're having on the town. It's huge what you're doing." I kissed him full on the lips and marveled at the green flecks hidden in his eyes.

"Thank you. Who knew you were so sweet? We have to get to Wildcard. That slippery guy keeps ducking our punches, and I want Axle and Mustang to get rid of him."

"Why can't you go get him?"

"When we find out about this meth lab later tonight then it's all systems go, don't worry about that." Maverick inched his way to the edge of the bed as raindrops started to fall outside his window. I got up and pulled the curtain back.

"It's raining again. It's been this miserable ick weather for the last few days. I want it to be sunny," I pouted as I closed the curtains back.

"No you don't. When it's hot and your armpits are trickling sweat you'll be asking for a little rain shower. I like this. I get to snuggle up with my girl. Feels good to me."

"Am I your girl, Maverick?" We were facing one another, and he was playing around with my fingers.

"To me you are. Am I your guy?" He chuckled. "I feel like we're back in high school with those tick boxes asking if you would go out with me. Do you remember them?"

I laughed out loud and covered my mouth. "Yes, they were so cool. Back to simpler times. I filled one of those out!" Maverick and I laughed easily together as he gathered my hands together in the middle of us and kissed them. He looked up at me under his long lashes.

"And what did you say?"

"I said no. He was a nasty little boy that picked his boogers. So no," I said gently. "But if it's you asking me, and I had to tick a box... I would say yes."

"Ha! Good answer." Maverick's mouth closed over mine as he held on to my waist. We stood there lost in a time warp with the rain providing her bountiful supply for Edgewood. As our lips merged and I inhaled the essence of Maverick, my heart was telling me that he was the right one. There was comfort and reassurance and a whole lot of laughs. We emerged from our embrace, and I grabbed my overnight bag.

"I have to take this bad boy and refill it. Let's go now. I have to be at the bar a little earlier. Dustin wants to discuss some paperwork with me. I don't know what he's up to, but I will find out soon, I'm sure."

"He's a cool guy. I like him."

"He can be. Depends." We left Maverick's house and went to mine. I opened my mailbox to three envelopes, and I had no doubts that they were bills that I needed to pay. I sifted through them and wanted to throw them in the trash. It was as I suspected.

"Bills, bills, and more bills."

"Can you pay them, Steph?" he asked with a tinge of concern as I stepped to my door and opened it to the stale air of my little place.

"Yep. I can. Just don't like seeing them. Wow. It smells a little stale in here. Let me open the windows." Maverick and I opened all the windows around the house to let it air out.

"It doesn't smell that bad. It's just you haven't been here for a few days," Maverick commented. I moved through to my bedroom and rifled through my clothes drawer and picked out some outfits. I sniffed them to see if they were okay.

"Yup, that's clean and that can go in there," I was speaking out loud to myself as I packed up some reasonably decent looking outfits and shoved the articles of clothing into my bag. I made the next trip to my bathroom and picked up some things from my cabinet. I didn't need any more shoes. I had two pairs at Maverick's. I stopped for a minute. I wanted the whirl-wind to end, to see what Maverick and I really had in real life, not this souped-up battle zone kind of intensity that we were being initiated into. An hour later and I was done. I'd gathered up what I needed for another three days and after that I wanted to come back to my home. I didn't see the reasoning for us living together yet. I wanted to slow us down a little. I was going against my heart, but I wanted to be sure this time.

I did one last thing that was on my mind, and that was to message my brother. I found my phone and sent a text.

*Hey. I hope you're okay. Give me a call. I miss you.* Normally I would get an immediate reply from that type of message. He would call or send back that he wanted to do lunch. That burning sensation in my heart kept cropping up when I thought about him. I'd gone through the full spectrum of emotions worrying about him, and now he was willing to turn his back on me so quickly, just for some money that he would blow anyway. He was 25 and still blowing his money on video games. I didn't want the doom and gloom of my thoughts to cloud the rest of my day, so I called out to Maverick.

"Maveriiickkk! I'm ready. Can you believe it?" I joked as I grinned at him. I'd taken a shower and he'd done what he said he would and stayed put on the couch watching TV. He was eating a bag of my potato chips, and I dipped my hand in the bag to grab one.

"You ready? Then we can move on out. For now. For now. Don't get all riled up."

"I never said that I wouldn't want to live with you. I just think we're under pressure, and I want us not to be."

"I see your point. You're scared, that's all it really is. You'll see." Maverick winked at me as if he knew something I didn't.

Dustin greeted me at the door when I walked into work and all the lights were on. "She arrives." He ushered me inside, and I frowned at him. He seemed to be acting weird.

"I do. What is so urgent that you brought me down here so early?"

"If you look on that table right over there you'll see." I rolled my shoulders back and dropped my purse over the back of the bar like normal. On the table was a thick bunch of documents with a bulldog clip on them.

I picked up the papers without sitting down. The front

page was titled 'Cocktail lounge bar proposal.' I saw what I was looking at and the penny didn't quite drop. *No. Shut up.* The location was listed on the document. An old cocktail bar that had closed down in the middle of town. The site price. The approval. A deposit to be paid. "Whattt is this Dustin?" I asked in a high-pitched tone with my hands shaking. I pulled them together to hold them still.

"It's an offer to you," he said slowly. "I want to make you a bar owner and a business partner with me. I've seen you, Steph. You can do better than you're doing. You are better. I want you to step up and train people and leave. I want you to run this bar and get it going. You can manage it and run it how you want." I went to complete shock as I stared unblinking at the paperwork in front of me. This was huge.

"Dustin, you would do this? What would you want out of this? This isn't for free, I assume," I narrowed my eyes as my suspicious side kicked in.

"I would take a percentage cut, like an investor. It's all in here. Take as long as you want to look over it. I think you'll find that the offer is really generous. I believe in you that much, and I know you can do it. I know you want this. I saw you with that far-off look in your eye when you talked about running your own cocktail bar," Dustin said, trapping me with my own words. He was right. I wanted the bar. To me it was one of those things you say like when people ask you who you want to be when you grow up. It was like that.

"I don't know what to say. This is so crazy. Let me look over all the documents. I don't know what to say. I don't -"

"You don't have to say anything yet. Just tell me that you'll think about it," he replied as he beamed.

"I will. I will. Dustin, are you sure?" He pulled his large frame up from the table.

"It's not me that needs to be sure. It's you. Take your

time," he reiterated as I got up with him and looked around the bar and thought about how I would want mine to look and feel like.

"Done. Wow. Crazy. I have so many questions, but I'm going to take this home and look over it. How long have you been planning this?"

"Hmmm, pretty much since you threatened to leave here and go take a job in another state. That does things to a man. I couldn't let you leave like that," he said with a mock sad face.

"I only said that, Dustin, because you were being a stubborn mule," I reminded him as I rounded the bar, locating the stock sheet in preparation for a stock count for the night and to check on the kegs.

"I hear you, but the knife has still been buried deep in my chest ever since," he cried out as he put his hand on his forehead.

"Stoppp it." I pulled out my stock sheet and got to work on supplies. "Just out of curiousity, if I did take your offer, when would you want me to start training staff?" I asked with my clipboard in hand.

"Yesterday. And I'm going to need two of you. Okay?"

I smirked. "You're not wrong there. It will take two of me to get the job done. We will, though. Say no more. This does sound like the most amazing thing in life. I'm having a hard time accepting that you offered it to me in the first place."

"Believe it. It's Saturday night, and I brought Melissa in, so you got your tag team buddy ready to go with you."

"She sure is. She would be the first team member I would train. She can easily run this bar. I've seen her under pressure, and she's steady. She's friendly, and she's pretty. The regulars know her, and I consider her a friend. I trust her to run a bar."

"Tell her all that yourself, boss. She's right behind you." Dustin was behind the door to the back room, and only his fingers were visible now as he attempted to sneak away. Me, on the other hand, wanted to talk to Dustin about all the different types of drinks to make and what trends I was seeing with the customers and countless other things.

"Hi, Melissa! You're here."

She smiled at me. She looked really good. Her hair was up high in a ponytail with two diamante clips, and she was wearing a red halter neck top with blue jeans and boots.

"You're in good spirits. Something or someone must be putting you in a good mood," she teased, looking for me to say more.

"You could say I have two men putting me in a good mood, how about that?" Her blue eyes lit up as she giggled and dropped her bag behind the bar.

"Oh my! Tell me. I want to know all the gossip. Spill all of that tea over here." She clapped her hands together. "This is the most exciting thing. It has to be better than my study nights. I'm exhausted most of the time, and I don't know half of what's going on in class." Her shoulders slumped with defeat as she talked about her studies.

"Do you like what you're doing? Or are you doing it because you think that's what you have to do?"

She saw the stock sheet and what I was up to. She stopped to look at me. "Yes. I do want to do it. I just get bummed out with all the bookwork. It will be better next year when I can do real work. Do you need help with this stock sheet here?"

"Yes, can you count the rest of the items for me while I put the floats together for the two tills?"

"I can do that, but when I finish counting I want to hear about these two men keeping you happy."

"It's not what you think, and one of them involves you possibly."

Melissa twirled around to look at me. "Say what now?"

"Stock count first, then the gossip, and I'll show you how to make a new cocktail drink tonight. I have this new drink I want to test out." Now more than ever I was determined to perfect my drinks. I had an incentive to come up with something great.

I'd gotten used to the routines of the bar. I knew what drinks were a favorite with my patrons, and I knew when to rotate stock. I knew what wines of red and white to stock and which ones were in season. I had a knack for ordering just the right amount of alcohol. I counted out the change into the registers as Melissa tallied up the rest of the stock sheet and handed it to me.

"Thanks. Maverick is one of the men, but it's kinda messy. This whole Wildcard bullshit and my brother has thrown things off course. I'm living with him and it's been good, but I don't know if I should move back to my place. It feels like it's too soon." I was rushing my speech, and my stomach was tied up in knots.

Melissa grabbed my wrist. "Sheesh! Slow down, woman. There's nothing wrong with you and Maverick, you're just scared. You can take it slow, but if it's feeling right, don't question it. Let it go. See where the river flows is what my mama used to say."

"Sage advice from her. My mother would tell me to take all my piercings out and to stop dying my hair." We both giggled at that. "You are so right. I felt like I've lost a limb, my brother..." Tears were pooling in my eyes and I refused to cry over someone who thought it better to take dirty money than to stick with their own sister and possibly put her life in danger.

"Are you okay? You shouldn't be crying over a relationship this early, that comes after the first fight."

I swiped the tears from my eyes. "No, the tears aren't for Maverick. They're for my brother. I've lost him, Melissa. I don't know why he would do what he's doing."

"You haven't lost him. He's still your brother. A little misguided, but he's there. He'll come around. You have to leave him to fight his own battles, and he might have to learn by taking a fall."

"That's what I'm afraid of. His moments of shittiness, though, could end in death." I grabbed a tissue and wiped away the rest of the tears. "Let's talk about happier shit!"

"Yes, and let's make drinks that people can drown their sorrows in."

"Sorrow-making drinks I like that. That other guy making me happy for once and not grumpy is Dustin. I can't say too much, but I wanted to know something from you," I said. I was about to ask her a question, but she cut it off.

"No, you can't do that. You can't say Dustin is making me happy and then take it back with I can't tell you now. What is it?" I opened the glass washing machine and pulled out a rack of clean wine and beer glasses. I grabbed my polishing cloth and Melissa did the same. Both of us automatically started polishing the glasses together as we chatted.

"Well, that cocktail bar comment went a little further."

Melissa gasped. "*Nooo*. Tell me something good." Her fingers started to work the glass she was polishing a lot more.

"I haven't even gotten it out yet! Wait for it," I told her.

"Okay, but you're taking so long to tell me I could have had my car detailed by now," she pouted.

"Dustin offered me my own cocktail bar." I pressed my

lips together as I put the polished wine glass up on the wine rack holder. She gasped loudly as her mouth opened.

"Wow! How—I don't have any words."

I nodded my head triumphantly. "That was my reaction. I haven't taken it yet, don't tell anyone. I have to look over the contracts first and make sure I'm happy with it. I need someone to look over the paperwork. The reason is... it involves you—if you want to join me, that is. You can either come work with me in the cocktail bar or I can train you to manage this place. It does mean working full time, and I know your studies are important to you." I let a moment go by in order for her to absorb the news I was telling her.

"Wow. So huge. I have to think about it too. This is big and it's not what I expected when I came into No Name today!" She bounced around on her feet, and that infectious energy of hers reminded me why she was great to be around. She was rubbing off on me.

"Me neither. This is the last thing I was thinking of. I said *one day*. I guess Dustin made the decision that one day is here!"

"Sure is. We need a drink. Let's try out your new recipes for your new bar."

"I don't even have the bar yet. I don't want to count my chickens before they hatch," I told her cautiously. I nibbled the inside of my lip with my teeth as I thought about it.

"Count 'em! I say. Count them suckers. I want to come and work at the cocktail bar with you. I wanna know what drinks you're going to whip up. I know you have some fancier drinks in the bag that you haven't taught me. I can feel it. You're just not bringing them out, are you?" she questioned as I set up the glasses in a row.

"I will in time. I don't think everyone who comes here is ready for my brand of drinks. I hope to introduce the chocolate dream that I learned how to make with a few twists of my own. Now *this* drink is out of this world and will blow your mind. I love it, and it goes down so smoothly you don't think you're drinking. Some of the ingredients are chocolate flakes, coconut cream, Baileys, cinnamon, and a little chili spice." I licked my lips. "Scrumptious!"

"That sounds like a dangerous drink, and I want one immediately. I want two or three. I think," Melissa added. "What are you calling it?"

I shrugged casually. "I don't know. I have to brainstorm and come up with some ideas. Chocolate Dream, Chocolate Casualty, Chocoholic, Chocolate Drop. I gotta play around. I've been at Maverick's house, so I haven't been able to get in my kitchen and whip up drinks and practice."

Melissa wasn't listening to the last part; she was stuck on the naming of the drinks. "Hmmm. I like Chocolate Casualty. That has a sophisticated air to it. It feels fancy."

"That's the problem. I wonder if I'm doomed. Maybe a cocktail bar is too much for Edgewood, and I should think about something else. Is it too much?" I'd polished the same glass for the last few minutes, and Melissa was staring at my hands.

"You might want to move on to the next glass, you've worn that one out," she observed as I looked down and placed the glass into its slot in the wine rack. "No. You're overthinking it. It's not too much. Think about other things. Women like cocktails; they love them. Gives them a lush feeling when they go to the bar. We want to feel like we're queens even though we live in dreary Edgewood. I think it will be a hit. Think about your drink nights here. They win the people over every time. You have to restock all the ingredients, and you're shocked every single time it happens, but you're *that* good." Melissa made a convincing argument which I had to stop and consider for a minute.

"Way to pump up my ego, thanks."

"Not what I was trying to do, but you could use a little ego boost right about now. How long we got before opening?"

"We've got 20 minutes. I put a special cocktail on the list tonight called The Slider."

"Is that the one you showed me last week? If it is, I already know how to make it. The one with the Kahlua, whiskey, and milk?"

"That's the one. Except the type of whiskey is important. We're using Makers Mark every time. If you use another whiskey, it throws off the composition of the drink."

"Well then, Makers Mark it is. It's a fine drop."

"Yes, it is. Okay, we're close. Let me set this music in motion. Earl was complaining last week that we didn't play enough rock. He said we were playing too much 'young people's music.'" I made air quotes as I said it and reached to turn on the speakers.

"Earl schmerl. He always has something to say to that guy. He's a gossip. Last week he was telling people that the cartel was coming in here with militant soldiers to take over Edgewood. The guy is completely off his rocker. I wouldn't listen to a word he has to say. I tell you what, though, if you want to listen to an entertaining story then he's the one to talk to."

"Nope, he's not. You'll find out a bunch of he said she said type stuff. You ask him the same thing the next time you see him, and he'll have another story for you about someone else."

"Hmm. A couple of times he's been right about a few

things." I rounded back behind the bar and shook out my shoulders.

"I'm sure the rumor mill is on overdrive with all that's been going on here."

"Edgewood, New Mexico, the place to be." I gave her a wry smile as Dustin came to the front to open the doors.

"Ladies, are we ready to do business? I do believe it's time to open these doors on up."

"Yes, let the hooligans join us in the bar for good times and merriment," I joked.

"Here they come." Dustin opened the doors, and six customers were already waiting at the door, all of them women. As I tried to take them in as they came to the bar, I saw that three of them were the old ladies from the Guardians. One with short blond hair that looked like a rock chick, another one looked like the girl next door, and the third had an interesting Bohemian look.

The other three women were in a separate group and a little older. There was excited chatter among all of them, and I was happy they were here so early. It would make the time pass much faster. "Hi, ladies. Nice to see you in here again. Girls' night out?" I inquired.

"Yep, Steph, it is. We keep hearing about these great cocktails that you make, and I came especially to drink one. I'm Dara, by the way if you forgot." She held out her hand to me. She had a real sparkle to her, a light that made her stand out.

"I remember, you have that hairdressing salon downtown."

"Yes, that's me! You should come in sometime. I would love to do your hair. It's so lush and long. That color you have is to die for as well." She scrunched her fingers at my head. "I would love to get my hands on it." I laughed as the gypsy-looking woman pointed at her friend.

"Don't scare her, Dara. You want her to come to your salon, after all."

"Sorry, I get carried away sometimes. I just see a head of hair I like, and I want to play," she said in this deep, husky voice.

"I could use a trim, that's for sure. Do you want to try the slider I have on the menu to get warmed up?" I handed over three menus to all of them to look at.

"I don't need to look, I'll try it," Dara said.

"I'm going to have your Tropical Paradise drink. It's been raining here, and if a drink can make me feel as if I'm in the tropics then I'm all for it," the bohemian one said.

I felt bad that I didn't know her name, so I asked. "Are you one of the Guardian old ladies? I see you've got your jacket on."

"Yep. Red's partner. I'm Brody, it's nice to meet you in person by the way." She held out her delicate hand, and I shook it. They were piano playing fingers. "We've heard a lot about you. You're well-known at the club." I figured that was because the Guardians came to the bar over the years, and I'd gotten to know them. Maybe they were speaking about the bar and where to get drinks from.

"Makes sense. The guys are in here a lot."

"No, that's not why. Maverick. He talks about you all the time. Since he first started coming here, he's been talking to the guys about you. Then they tell us. They're pillow talkers. All of it's good talk." She smiled. My body flushed with warmth, and my cheeks were becoming hot.

"That's so sweet. He's a great guy. We have a lot of fun together."

"He is. Very generous, kind-hearted, and pretty good

with bombs. A winning combination. I'm Rosemary, I'm married to Havoc."

"Ahh! You're the mayor's daughter. I've seen Havoc in here a few times."

"Yep, he comes in here on his boys' nights. I'm going to take the slider as well."

"Right, coming right up, ladies." I pulled out three martini glasses and prepped my ingredients. Maverick was talking about me. Made me feel stupid to be worried about living with him. He was the first guy to treat me with respect and to care about me, and he made me feel alive. The little butterflies were coming back into my stomach, which made all the other bad stuff going on fade away.

I finished the three drinks and made sure to add the little garnishes. Those extra touches were what made people come back for my cocktails. "Here we go, ladies. I hope you enjoy them." I put my hands in my back pockets as I watched their faces.

"Yummy. I can't wait." Dara sipped her drink first and closed her eyes. "Oh my God. This is fantastic. I cannot wait. Let me go in again." She stopped and drank a little more. "The tang in that, the flavor is so good." When Dara smiled, her whole face changed. "Do you do private events? I'm trying to shake some things up at my salon, and I would love it if we could do a cocktail hour. Like a V.I.P. experience. Would that be something you're inter-ested in?"

"Yes, please. I would love that. Do you have a business card?"

"Here we go." She flicked a card over to me between two fingers. I took it from her and slid it into my purse under the bar.

"Thank you so much." Their encouragement was the

boost I needed to get me thinking positively about the cocktail bar. I could do it. I could run it.

"I wholeheartedly agree with Dara. Your drinks are fantastic," Brody announced.

"Endorsed!" Rosemary called out. All three held up their drinks and clinked their glasses together. As the night wore on, it kept getting better and better.

## 17

---

## MAVERICK

I was dead to the world when Stephanie got in from the bar, but as soon as I felt the weight shift I woke up and put my arms around her. Her flesh was cool to touch, coming in from the outside. It had been raining on and off all day. I slid one of my hands up and cupped her breast, spooning in with her.

"How was work?" I kissed her shoulder.

"It was good. Dustin offered me a cocktail bar." She said it in such an off-handed way it made me double take and look at the back of her head.

"Huh?" I opened one eye and shifted my leg through the middle of hers so we were wrapped together. She snuggled into me, and I knew we wouldn't need the covers because it would be too hot with our body heat combined.

"Yeah, I didn't mean to wake you. I wanted to tell you. I wanted to call you as soon as I heard, but I thought you might be out on a mission."

I kissed her shoulder lightly again, and the contrast of cold to warm was nice to me. "You should have called me. That's amazing. I know how great your cocktails are."

"Thanks. Anything interesting happen while I was away?"

"No, and let's stay on this for a minute. We have to celebrate." News from out of the blue but it was nice news. I was glad to hear it.

"Not yet. I have to look over the contract first and find a lawyer to help me read it and make sure it's what I want. Dustin is going to invest in the bar for 25 percent of profits basically. I don't know the first thing about this type of stuff," she said nervously.

"Easy. The Guardians have a contract lawyer. A few of them, with all the real estate purchases. I'll ask Dutch tomorrow if you can get his number. Remind me in the morning."

"Wow. Okay. One step. Thank you! I'm nervous and happy at the same time. So much to think about I'm overwhelmed." I loosened my grip on her a little to give her some breathing room. She grabbed my arm and brought it back across me. "No. I was good there, put it back," she asked in a soft command.

I smirked. "I'm the blanket, am I?" I grinned into her shoulder, enjoying the quiet beauty of her in the darkness.

"Yes. It's cold outside," she remarked softly. There was silence for a minute. Just us breathing. No problems from the outside world. "A few of the old ladies came in today. I got to meet Brody and Rosemary. They seem very nice."

"They are. Real sweethearts. I don't see them much anymore. They used to be at the club all the time. Quicks I don't see either." He was quiet as a mouse at meetings, but he spoke to Shaggy a lot. They seemed to be pretty good friends. I would have to start talking to him more, get to know him.

I saw her playing with her fingers in the shadows. She

wasn't sleepy, I could tell. Neither was I now that she was here with me. "They said some things about you." I could almost see her smile, even though her back was facing me.

I retracted my foot from between her legs and sloped my body up, propping myself up by the elbow. "What did they say about me? Turn and face me so I can see you when you're talking. I wanna hear this."

Her lucid eyes were clear in the night as her dark hair snaked around her and she leaned on her elbow with a sweet smile. Her hair hung in front of her breasts, and she looked like a goddess that deserved to be painted.

"They said you were talking about me since the first time you came into the bar. Is that true?" she asked as she narrowed one eye at me.

"You're putting me in the hot seat. Okay. I'll take that heat. I did. Something intrigued me about you, and I still haven't put my finger on it, only to say that it's what I like." I touched her hair and ran my fingers through it, admiring her beautiful curves. I stroked the curve of her hip as she lay sideways.

"I'm wired from my shift. You were sleeping peacefully, until I woke you up." She lay on her back and crossed her leg over at the ankle.

"It's a good type of wake up. I have something to tell you, and you don't have to say it back or anything. I just want to tell you because I can feel it in my heart, and if I don't tell you now, then it's going to be a problem for me."

"Phew, that was a mouthful. What do you have to tell me, Maverick?"

"That I'm in love with you." Felt good to get the monkey off my back. She said nothing for a long time. I guessed she wasn't ready to say it yet. I wouldn't feel any differently toward her if she didn't say it back. I'd wanted to tell her either way. I smirked as I thought back to the conversation I'd had with Hawk in the lunchroom.

"I'm getting there. Thank you. I might be a little slower out of the gate to say it to you, but when I do it will be for real," she said, kissing my lips.

"It's okay. I can feel it from you. I know you do and when you're ready. I don't want you to feel forced to say it to me. That's fake. I want it to be real between us."

"What we have is real. I can tell you that for sure."

"Then that's all we need right now. You and me and real-ness." I twisted a little of her hair in the dark and dropped it.

"Thanks for understanding. I care so much about you." She was giving me an apology in a way because she wasn't ready to say those three little words. I didn't want sympathy. I was okay to wait for the real thing.

She changed the subject, and I could see the underlying discomfort there. "I messaged my brother, and he didn't answer, so I guess this is it between us. It's over." She was really cut up over her brother, and admittedly I didn't understand the close bond. He seemed like a real shithead to me.

"It's not over. He's just not in his right mind, and he's working for someone who isn't either." I tried to remind her. Wildcard was running a Wild Wild West production out here, and it was starting to annoy me now. He was taking away my zen state, and when I got to that point things changed within me. I redirected my energy back to my girl. "Are you ready to go to sleep or are you getting up?"

"I might get up for a while. Too much going on in my head."

"Okay. See you when you come back." A little distant, but I knew I would win her over. Step by step and building the bridges between us. There wasn't a need for me to force anything. Things were starting to heat back up at the Guardians, so it would give us time to get to know one another more. At least we were taking a chance. I drifted back off to sleep, and when I woke up in the morning Steph was right where I wanted her to be. In my arms.

I was up early, and Steph was still sleeping. Hawk sent through a text message with a new mission. *Mission 9am at the clubhouse.* Business was increasing, and it was time for me to go kick some ass. I laid out all my gear. I had my levers that I made. These levers were multi-functional and were good for getting in and out of things.

My studio wasn't getting much of a workout because of the quick adjustment I had to make with Stephanie living with me. Not that I minded so much. She was the night owl, and I was the early bird. In front of me was everything required for the mission. In the next couple of weeks, I would have to top up on supplies, and I would need more masks for sure.

I was up and out into the fresh crispiness of the Edgewood air by 7 a.m. I was built for this, and this is how the special forces carved me out to be the man I was today. My helmet was in one hand, my bag in the other. I strode to my bike and mounted her, slid on my helmet, and took the ride to join my brothers.

Hawk's bike. Axle's bike. Mustang's and Gunner's. The gang was ready. I saw Rush's bike as well. I breezed on in and tapped the office window, giving my good accounting folks a wave. Straight to the lunchroom where Hawk, Axle, Mustang, and Gunner were already here. I frowned.

"Man, I thought I was early, but you're here already. Did you have a secret meeting before I got here or something? Fuck! It's 7 a.m."

"I live here now. Didn't you know that?" Axle grinned,

but the smile was hollow, and so were the grooves under his eyes.

"Axle, what's going on, big guy? You look like you've gone twelve rounds with Tyson."

"I have. The national park where Wildcard is posted up at is swarming with snakes, the Viper variety. We staked the place out, and I saw Wildcard in clear sight. I took a shot at him, but he and his heavies knew how to shoot. They retaliated and slipped out of my sight too quickly. That guy that tried to clip Pop had his arm wrapped up, and now we know he is a Viper team member." Axle paced around the pool table, knocking balls in, and then came over to me.

"Axle, you went rogue? Why not take one of us with you?" I questioned. "The man is old, why can't you catch him? Shoot the bastard and let's move on with our lives." My voice was elevated, and Axle feigned shock until his eyes locked in with mine.

"That's how you feel, huh?" His bottom lip bent out, and he bobbed his head at me. He pointed to Mustang. "This guy was with me. Happy now?" he said icily.

"All right. Out of line. He's fucking up everybody." I was on a rampage, and the military fire was resurfacing.

Axle's black obsidian eyes were boring into me. "Never question me again. If you think you can catch him, then you go out and do it, Maverick." Not one part of me was scared of Axle, even with the imminent threat of getting my head knocked off.

"Big guy. I will. What's his address? Let me go take a run at him. Can't hurt."

Mustang let out a low whistle. "Not that easy, Maverick. I know what you're thinking, but he's crafty. We circled back to the spot and tried to hit it again, and the whole crew had left. The place was deserted. So I assume he has a new hiding spot. We're trying a new tactic. I paid a dealer to get information, and we'll see what comes up."

"Okay. My bad, Axle." I held my fist out for the bump. He looked at it and I thought for a minute he was going to grab my hand and crush it, but he fist-bumped lightly, letting me know there were no hard feelings.

"I was up with the baby too, so I'm not a happy man," he said grumpily.

"Fair enough. I can't argue with you there. If I can help out let me know." I changed my tune. I was too amped up and ready to fight.

"That's what Wildcard wants, everybody out searching for him instead of staying focused. He specializes in chaos, which none of us are used to. Don't fall into the trap, Maverick."

I sat down on the stool, defeated. "I feel like we are spinning our wheels. We think we got him. Then we don't. We think we got him and then he slips right out of our hands."

"It's only a matter of time. Guy's going down. If he catches the end of my sniper rifle, it's going to be an execution style shot." Gunner made the gun symbol with his fingers and squinted. "Pow, pow. You're dead, Wildcard." Mustang's expression made me laugh as he made a funny face behind Gunner's back.

"He was bluffing. Those weren't cartel members. I found out from the police last night. I wanted to tell you all first thing. Let's get that out of the way. Second thing is Finn is calling a church meeting, and you should get a text message soon. We're meeting as Pop has a plan for the Wildcard issue. Third, Maverick, this mission involves these gang members, and one thing they don't understand is bombs. We want to scare them. Can you make one? Nothing serious. A couple of car bombs. So we are going to start hitting these meth labs indirectly. Sneak in, sneak out and make them voluntarily leave and run them into the task force's hands. These missions are going to be a little easier, but more tactical and strategic."

I rubbed my hands together. My body was buzzing with excitement that I was about to get back in the swing of my old profession. A beep came through on all of our phones.

Church meeting. Another one. Now. I slid the phone back in my cargo pants pocket. "Where we headed today?"

"Behind a church called Mountain Haven. Apparently they are running a meth lab out of the back of there." Mustang made the symbol of the cross.

"They're tainting holy ground or are church members in on it?"

"No idea, but it's another weird-ass location," Hawk frowned. "Let's get this church meeting over with and then we can head there. From what's been passed on to me is that there are 15 known people involved. Obviously on this one, we're going to run it like normal. On the next mission, Maverick, you can lead with the bomb as a diversion."

"Okay."

Quicks, Dutch, Scout, Shaggy, Rush, and all of us intersected and came together as Finn entered from the back door and punched in the code to lead upstairs. One by one we climbed and settled into our spots. It was too early in the morning for alcohol, but a few of the guys had takeout coffee in their hands.

Chatter lit up the dark room while we waited for Pop to enter. He was a little late coming in approximately ten minutes later. He looked fit and healthy. His small eyes bright, he seemed to come to life whenever there was battle. Much like myself—maybe that's why I admired him. He had on his beret that he liked to wear. "Gentlemen. We find ourselves back here once again. I have to say it's been a long time coming for us to get in the ring again and fight. Wildcard is asking for money, we all know that. He wants a drop. We can employ the same tactics we employed for the shootout. Dutch, wanna fill them in on what we have planned?"

"We are searching for some fake money options. Wildcard asked for money, and he can have it. The money just won't be able to be used by him. We can drop it off at the location of his choice and wash our hands of it."

"Pop, this sounds like the Devils shootout. We don't want more bloodshed. It's taken us over two and half years to rebuild. Our boys died." Shaggy spoke up with passion. He was one that kept to himself as well unless it was a conversation about motocross.

"Shaggy, did we win? Did we make it through? You did a great job back then, and you were a hero, so what are you worried about?" Pop asked in a callous tone.

"I don't want to lose anyone else either, and as the road captain I say we go with Dutch's option. Give him the fake money and let it go." Hawk's jaw was twitching. I knew he was close to the old treasurer, and it haunted him. We'd had a few in-depth conversations about it.

"And what do you think is going to happen when Wildcard finds out we've given him fake money? He's coming at us with retaliation in the form of the tape. I've watched that footage a hundred times, and yes, a couple of you pulled off your masks. The clarity of the shots are so-so in my opinion. Let it go to the cops. He wants money and he wants revenge, and that's what this is really about. Let the games begin. I want everyone available on the drop night in two days. Wildcard is sending the location, time and date, so presumably we have two days. If you see Wildcard, you shoot him.

Pull that trigger and think nothing of it. Then we move on with our lives."

"You're making it sound simple, Pop. It won't be. We are in the same loop as we were in the shootout."

"Shaggy, why is it you that has something to say whenever it's time to step forward and fight for the club? You must remember you are a prospect for the club. You're not far away from your patch. Careful." Pop shot him a glare that would make any man rethink what they had to say. This was the first meeting I'd seen where my brothers were experiencing a little tension between themselves. Mustang, Gunner, and I were observing everything and staying quiet.

"Pop, he's not the only one. I agree. We can do this differently. Bloodshed and carnage is not the answer all the time," Hawk backed up Shaggy.

"Thanks, Hawk." He tipped his baseball cap that he was wearing, and the noise started. The muttering. Finn's brow was creased together in worry, and it looked like he had something important to say as well.

"Pop. I don't think it's a good idea either. We cannot lose any more men. You had a hit out on you already. You were shot at. This reeks of history repeating itself."

Dutch pushed his glasses up on his round face. "Some of the money will be provided. Not much. A maximum of $1,000 and those dollars will float on top of the bundles so it seems legitimate at first glance. If anyone has any other viable options, please present them."

"We kill him. Simple. Kill him," Axle stated.

"Agree with Axle. Kill him and be done," Mustang's deep voice boomed.

"Sure, but you boys have had some time to do that, and he's outfoxed you all every time. You have two days to find him, otherwise we go with my method. That's final." Pop stood up on his final note and made his way for the stairs, not letting anyone get a word in. Finn and Red were still sitting at the table, and the noise of the men talking was getting louder.

Red banged the palm of his hand down. "Shut up! I can't hear all of you at once. Let's go with the kill Wildcard option. The sooner we can work on that, the better. Axle, go. *Now.* Mustang, when you finish your mission join him. Gunner, make yourself available. Clear? We can't fall apart like we did at the shootout. I'm on your side, I don't want the drop either, so Axle, I need you to hunt this guy down and make it very uncomfortable for him. Make it so unbearable that he has to come out in the open." Red's eyes were blazing, and he was ready to rumble. This was my first time seeing the Guardians in a fight for their territory in the truest sense. For me it was more frustration building inside than anything else.

Those involved nodded yes, and we all split and made our way out of the building. Hawk, Mustang, and Gunner were all congregating at the front near our mission van, as I affectionately liked to call her. "Let's roll out."

We rode in silence to the location and parked in front of an old red brick chapel. "I can't see shit going on here. This must be a hoax," Mustang said. He was looking out as we made our approach.

"Wait for it. Let's give it 20; we're getting paid for it anyway." Hawk was parked on the opposite side of the street, and we were all looking directly at the church. The main door was open. Not all the way, just halfway. Five minutes passed, nothing. Eight minutes passed. Nothing. Fifteen minutes. Nothing. Then I spotted a movement from the back of the church, a figure. Then another. There was something going on. Whether it was criminal or not was another story.

"Hawk, I think we got the wrong angle on this thing. Ride around the block. Can you get to the next street over or do a U turn up further and turn so we can see from behind?"

"Good plan. You see something?"

"Yep. I did, a few people in single file coming out from the back of the church. That doesn't mean there's any criminal activity going on, but we can take a closer look." The van started to roll as Hawk took the U-turn option and headed up the suburban street farther and turned around, parking on the same side as the chapel so we were facing it.

"Ah, I see them know. That's a casket coming out of the church."

"What?" Mustang, whose hooded eyes were closing in extreme boredom, sprung to life. "What's in the casket? Is it a funeral?" I turned the knob on my binoculars for the zoom function and noticed the men carrying the casket were bulky and they weren't carrying one casket. They were carrying three out.

"That's funny. I don't see anybody else around them, and we got ten men carrying a casket between them. Me thinks there's something special inside. What you think, fellas?"

Gunner sneered and tapped Mustang on the shoulder. "I think so too. Look where they're taking them. To a large van. This is interesting. We need to follow that van when it leaves, Hawk."

"Why not? I don't have anything to do today. Let's see where they're going."

We all watched through the microscopic lens waiting for the burly men to close the van doors and drive off. They stacked the three caskets on top of one another. Another oddity occurred. When I turned my focus back to the church, three ladies were standing there with masks on their faces and what looked to be a pastor.

"You see that?" I was talking about the man and the three women standing at the back of the church double doors.

"Yep, I sure do. I would say there's a little something going on in Mountain Haven church," Mustang agreed.

"We following the van?" Hawk was looking for confirmation from us.

"Yep. Follow that van, Hawk." He started the engine and established a good distance from the van. I wanted to know where they were going. I wanted to know if they would possibly lead us to Wildcard. The van made a turn onto Route 66, heading toward Sedillo, and a funny feeling in my gut told me they were going to lead us to something. What it would be was another story. The van got up to speed, and Hawk let some cars fall in the gap between so we didn't look as if we were tailing them. We kept them in sight, and Hawk called it into the narcotics team via Bluetooth. When we went out on missions, they waited in the wings with their team in case backup was required.

"We have a lead on the church, three caskets with ten men. We are now on our way to Sedillo. We suspect they weren't funeral caskets. Backup required. Route 66."

"Hey team. Okay, we're in the vicinity. Whereabouts on Route 66?

"East Mountain Food Pantry. We are heading in that direction."

"Great, we'll head them off at the fire department and stop them for a search. Thanks, crew, we got it from here."

"Okay. We can leave it with you? Do you need the plate?"

"Nope we know what the van looks like. We can see you. Thanks, Hawk, we'll be in touch."

Hawk hung up from the call but kept driving; the next turnoff wasn't until the fire department. He was stunned, I could tell. "They aren't letting us play anymore. They call us in to help and then once we give them what they need we're discarded. They don't need us. Why call us in then?"

"I'm wondering if this has anything to do with Clint's death," Hawk speculated as he turned the van around and we headed back to the warehouse.

"No. If it did, they wouldn't let us on any missions at all, would they?" I tossed back to him.

"Who knows? Sheriff Malone called Tara in for questioning. She's prepped with the lawyer, and she's going to be in there with him this afternoon."

"You didn't tell me that. I don't know why I thought it was a while away."

"It is what it is. She's ready. She'll be okay. If anything, I feel guilty."

Hawk didn't have to finish the rest of the sentence, but his guilty conscience was coming from the fact he'd killed Clint. The Guardians had just helped clean up the dirty work.

Gunner was on his phone, I presumed trying to locate Axle. "We're done. I'm heading back to the warehouse. Where are you?" He nodded as Axle gave him the directions and hung up the phone.

"He hasn't got any leads. He's retracing his footsteps around the same areas that Wildcard has been known to be. Questioning people," Gunner said.

"He's not going to catch him that way. The best and most likely way that Wildcard will be caught is when we do the drop. The Guardians are going to have to do it." To me it was clear as day. Hawk looked up at me in the mirror and nodded.

"Last time was horrific. To do what we did as a club then would be crazy."

"Back then, you didn't have special forces watching your back. It's not the same. We know he doesn't have a cartel backup. He's going to come with a bunch of gangsters who essentially have no power. We are going to outsmart, outwit, and outmaneuver every single one of them. The more I think about it, the more I believe the chase should be called off and we wait for the drop and ambush them from there."

"Maverick. You're pretty smart sometimes," Mustang noted. "I like that thinking."

## 18

---

## STEPHANIE

I WAS ADAPTING TO THE CHANGE AND FEELING GOOD. JUST AS I got used to the idea that I might have to stay and live at Maverick's house for a little while, he told me that I would probably be okay to go home and the decision would be mine. Edgewood had finished crying its tears from the sky and now the sun was shining again and wearing her happy pants. I took Maverick up on his recommendation to see the club lawyer and was meeting with him at Martha's in the next hour.

"Are you ready with all your questions and paperwork?"

"I've got it all. I don't know about all the questions. I don't know what I don't know. I can't wait, I know that Dustin wouldn't do anything to fuck up my life so I can't imagine that he has put anything in the contract that's not above board," I reasoned as I pinned my hair up.

"You look great, very polished and professional, but you don't have to interview for the lawyer. He's just going to look over your contracts." Maverick made the jibe, and I opened my eyes wide at him.

"Maverick! Are you jealous? Is that a jealous streak that you've got?" I said.

"Nope, not one in my body. I promise." His devilish grin led me to think otherwise. I bent over the seat and kissed him on the lips.

"The way you said it makes me think you are!" I challenged as I bent forward in my seat and kissed his lips and he dragged me down to sit on his lap. I slid my arms around his neck and ran my hands through his sandy blond locks. I pulled them back and kissed his forehead and dragged them back down again.

"How long before you have to be at this meeting?" he asked in a low voice.

I touched his chest and put my hand over his heartbeat. "We already went two rounds last night," I whispered in his ear.

"I know, but you're irresistible. What am I supposed to do? I have to make sure you know before you leave to go home," he growled sexily as I ran my finger over the top of his lip.

"I'm not going anywhere. I'm only going back to my house which you're only going to be at half the time anyway. It's been fun living with you, and I appreciate you letting me stay here, but I have to try and go back home and get a few things back on track at my house."

Maverick's square jaw was twitching, and I ran my finger over it. "I knew the day was coming, I didn't want it to come so soon is all. I wanted to spend more time with you. I feel like we've gotten to know one another better by living together. I think it's made us stronger now. I know your little habits. The inner workings of Steph," he said in a heartfelt voice that made me want to stay.

"You left the soppy speech until I was about to leave so

I'll stay? That is a nasty trick, Maverick." He cast his eyes down as he linked his fingers through mine.

"No trick. Just the truth. I had so much taken from me and seen so much, so I know that things happen in life, and I don't want you to not know how I feel."

"I've learned about you as well. I know you're an early bird. You squeeze too much toothpaste out of the tube and don't close the top. You like a hot breakfast in the morning no matter what. You're incredibly disciplined with your routines. You sing to yourself in your sleep sometimes. You hog all the covers, and I can never get them back." Maverick's eyes narrowed.

"That last one. That's you that cocoons yourself in the blanket. I can barely stay warm. It's a joke." He pretended to be mad.

I laughed with him. "No, I swear it's you. It has to be because I would never tangle myself up like that in blankets. Never." I grinned, and Maverick squeezed his hands around my waist.

"You are trouble and I like it," he said playfully as he started trying to tickle me.

"Nope! I have a meeting and that involves no tickling before it starts. I have to get ready to go," I said.

"Okay, I'll let up. Promise," he said, smirking, and I knew he had another trick up his sleeve. He didn't try anything else, but I was already laughing and in a playful mood, so it didn't matter. Maverick brought that childlike nature in me out, and that was a good thing. I got up and kissed him goodbye.

"I'll call you later and let you know how it goes, okay?" I said as I kissed him one last time.

"Awesome. I think we might have another mission, but I can't be sure. Speak to you later on and you can tell me when the celebration party is being held. I'm happy for you, Steph. It sounds like an amazing opportunity," Maverick said sincerely.

"Thank you." I couldn't wipe the smile off my face, and my tummy was full of butterflies of the good variety. I gathered up all my paperwork and all my things that I'd left at Maverick's place and shuffled myself out of the door. I looked back with a flustered face as I was trying not to be late and Maverick pushed me out of the door.

"If you left anything. I'll courier it to you," he called out.

"What?" I squinted, looking at him not knowing what he meant as I walked down his driveway.

"I'm joking. If you've left anything, it can stay here for the next time you come."

"Oh, I get it. Bye, Maverick," I said, shaking my head at the unruly man with the big grin.

"Bye, you gorgeous thang. See you later on, and good luck with your meeting."

I waved and got in the car feeling better about life. The rest of the chaos going on around me I could do nothing about. I drove straight to Martha's to meet with the lawyer. Once the meeting was finished I planned to go dump my stuff at my house and spend some time reacquainting myself with my own house. By the time I got to Martha's it was quiet. It was brunch hour. Normally, the door would be opening in and out with people rushing in and out, but today the crowd was minimal. Once inside the doors I thought I was looking for someone corporate in a suit, but a wave from the far right corner showed me an older man in shorts and T-shirt with flip-flops. I raised my eyebrows as I walked over to the booth.

"Hi. Richard?" I asked.

"Yes. That's me, and you must be Stephanie." Relieved

that I'd found the right person, I held out my hand to shake. His grip was firm but not too tight. He had a mixture of salt and pepper hair, and his face was open and friendly.

"Yup, that's me." Richard raised his hand and asked the waitress to come over.

"Order what you like, and we can eat, drink, and talk over your contract. I find it's always easier to work on a contract over a meal. That's just my motto. I'm not a board-room kind of guy," he said.

"I'm happy with that. I guess I was looking for a suit and tie guy, but I see you're not."

"No, no. Not unless I need to."

The waitress was in front of me and waiting for my order. "I'll have a coffee with cream. Thank you."

"Coming right up."

I diverted my attention back to Richard, who was drinking his coffee. I dropped my bag down off my shoulder and pulled out the thick ream of documents for him to look over. I handed them to him. He took them and immediately started scanning. Richard made a few sounds, mmms and ahhs as each of his fingers moved through the pages.

"This is a pretty good contract overall. I'm going to need to take it away and study it and come back with any changes or discrepancies I see, but from first glance this looks like a pretty good deal."

"I thought it would be, but I wanted someone to look over it. Can you tell me what it means in plain speak?" I asked.

"In plain speak it means that Dustin is offering you start-up capital for the bar and funding for 25 percent of the profits every month. Now initially that is good for you, but if the bar does become a hit then that's a quarter of your profits going out the window. The flip side of the coin is you don't have to deal with putting up your own money."

"Can we build in an escape clause? i.e. if it's sinking and I can't make enough per quarter that a lower percentage can be taken?"

Richard looked at me and bobbed his head. "I don't see why not. That's a smart idea."

We spoke for the next hour, talking over the possible avenues I could take with the contract and what I needed to consider. I wanted to go and see the site with my own two eyes as well. I wanted to see if the building needed any changes made to it internally, and I wanted a walk-through. This was just the first step of my new venture, but it was a powerful one.

I left Martha's feeling great about the next chapter of my life. I practically skipped to my car. The sun was shining and so was my heart. I headed home and stepped back into my house. It felt odd at first when I walked through the doors. I was used to being at Maverick's place, and it was like I had a new home. I dumped my bags in my bedroom and opened all the windows up. I peeked my head in all of them to see if anything had changed. Nothing had. I came back to the couch and sat down. My shift was starting in another four hours so I thought with all the activity I would get a nap.

My phone had other ideas, but I was stuck on the couch and couldn't get up. I stayed put, flicking on the TV. There was nothing on but the midday soaps, so I dragged the cushion behind me down and started to close my eyes. The phone rang again and wouldn't stop. This was the second time. My stomach started to swirl a little as I started to worry. I got up and moved through to my bedroom and found my phone on the bed. The call was coming from James.

Panic was rising, and my lip quivered when I answered. "Hi, James. What are you doing?"

"I could ask you the same thing," he said in his doom-ridden voice.

"Why are you talking like that?" I questioned. He was speaking to me as if I was a stranger and I didn't know him.

"Talking like what?" he snapped.

"You're speaking to me as if you don't know who I am and with this stupid deep voice thing you got going on. I'm your sister, and I know you better than anyone."

"Fine. I was trying to scare you," he said in an exhausted tone.

"Thought so. I'm already scared and not because of your voice. Where are you?"

"Some shit place. I wanna go home, but we have a couple of days to go before we can finish up. The place has rats, and it's dirty here. It won't be long and it will be all over, and I will be a rich man. I might even give you a cut." His arrogant tone pierced through the phone as I heard birds in the background. I was doing my best to listen hard to see if I could pick up his location.

"I told you once before I want nothing to do with your dirty money. *Nothing.* I bet you haven't received one dime at all, have you?"

"I've gotten an advance. I've seen some money." He was too hesitant when he said it, so I didn't believe him.

"Yeah, right. I'm not on the phone to argue. Why are you calling?"

"I didn't call you to argue either. I called to warn you. Guardians are delivering money to us in two days. You have to stop seeing Maverick."

"Pfft. You tried that one before, remember? Your boss even paid me a visit, so that won't work anymore."

"It's not a game. Stop seeing him. If you don't, I can't guarantee your safety. You're dating a Guardian and your brother works for the Vipers and a former Guardian. Think about it. It's not a good idea. You're going to be kidnapped if you don't. The cartel is involved now and wants to use you as a pawn. Now will you listen to me?" he asked with urgency in his tone. A crackling noise was coming through the phone, and my head was rushing with blood. I felt like I was going to be sick. My own brother. My own flesh and blood doing this to me.

"You. Pig. Stay the fuck away from me. You are not my brother. I disown you, and I'm calling Mom and Dad. Wildcard isn't your family. He doesn't care about you. The cartel doesn't care about you. None of them do. I used to until you just told me you're trying to have me kidnapped." I could barely catch my breath, and my voice was cracking.

"Please just listen. Two more days," his voice peaked with desperation. "You think I want my sister harmed? No! I don't. Listen, break up with Maverick now. Sever your links with the Guardians. You have to. There are street spies everywhere, and they've seen you. Do it now," James barked through the phone.

"James, you are being ludicrous." I didn't get any further into the conversation. I heard scuffling in the background. How did this get so out of control? It went from James doing a few little deals to me covering for him to me being involved and potentially kidnapped. My head was spinning around, and I didn't know how to stop it. The pounding didn't help. I wish he'd never called me. Sometimes it's better not to know things if it's bad shit. I held my head in the hope that the jackhammer feeling would subside. It didn't do anything.

"Shit. I gotta go! Do what I said, otherwise you will die."

The signal dropped as I dropped the phone from my hands. Day one back at my house, and I wanted to run back to Maverick. The loud knocking from my heart in my chest was making me feel pressure there. I tried to open my lungs up and breathe deeply, but all that came out was shallow, raspy breaths.

*Break up with Maverick. Break up with him. It's more trouble than it's worth. Break up with him.*

I was up on my feet with my phone in my hand when another call came through. Blinded by tears, I looked at it. Private number.

*No. Don't answer it.* I hung it up.

The phone rang again. *Have courage. Answer it so you can find out once and for all. Find out. Answer the call.* A voice was egging me on, and I was busy trying to ignore it.

I answered the call. "Stephanie." A man with a slight Hispanic accent spat out my name.

"What do you want?"

"I wanted to call and let you know what your brother told you is true. You break up with this guy now. If he suspects it's to do with us, you're dead meat, and so is your little brother. We've met already. You know me. I came to your house, remember? We had a nice first meeting, and you sure were looking sexy." I put my hand on my hot forehead, and I felt like I was running a temperature. The Viper that came to my door. I didn't even know the guy's name. I was so casual about the encounter that I didn't even ask my brother who he was. Now I wished I could snatch that moment back.

"Keep your hands off him! You don't know me."

"You have no idea who you're fucking with. You do what we tell you. Otherwise I will send you a nice little video of your brother. This is from Wildcard's crew. Do it. It's not too much to ask if you want to save your life." Confusion reigned in the moment as the caller hung up the phone. I fought through the tears to figure out what to do.

I called Maverick on the phone. "Hey baby. You miss me already? Come on back over and drop your stuff off," he joked.

"Hi, Maverick." I sniffled into my arm as I silently wiped away the tears. "I can't see you anymore. I have to end it here. I can't see you." My words were all over the place as I thought about what the Viper said. I'd been complacent. I didn't take it further when I should have, and now I was filled with regret over my actions.

"Steph. Who called you? I'm coming over there." I was weeping and trying to hold it together long enough to convince him nothing was going on, but he already knew it wasn't true. He guessed it, and I wasn't the best at bluffing. That's why I didn't do well with poker when I used to play with James. My face always gave me away.

"Nobody, it's a decision I made on my own. I'm back in contact with James, and there's some things we need to work on as a family."

"So does that mean he's not part of the Viper crew and running with them anymore?" he asked calmly. It was hard to fool Maverick. I knew when I told him he wouldn't believe it was over, but it was. I was too young to die, and I wanted to keep everyone safe. This was the best option. I'd made up my mind. I was thinking the best place to be would be my parents' house.

"I guess so." I wanted to keep my answers short. If he got a sniff of anything wrong, Maverick would figure it out.

"You guess so or you know so?" His voice was smooth and even. The normal steady waters that Maverick was known for being.

"I know so."

"I don't believe you at all. I don't."

"Please, Maverick, don't make this harder than it needs to be. I want to be friends, and I will see you at the bar."

"No, you'll see me before that. This isn't you. I know it's not. You tell whoever has a hold on you that I'm coming for you, and they won't be able to stop me. Is anybody with you? Talk to me, Steph." Now the inflection of the voice changed. He'd gone up into a higher octave. Now the force of fire was behind his words.

"I have to go. Don't call me anymore." Finality is what I attempted to deliver to him. I hung up before he could keep grilling me, and my lies unfolded to reveal the truth.

I made the next hard call to my parents. My mother answered. She wasn't the voice that I exactly wanted to hear. It was more my father that I wanted to speak to.

"Hi Stephanie. I haven't heard from you in awhile." Her tone held a serve of contemptuousness, making me feel smaller than I should have. This is one of the reasons I never called her. "I thought I might have to file a missing persons report. How are you, sweetie?" My mother and her subtle ways of poking at me. I don't know why she couldn't be honest.

"I'm not too bad, Mom. I might be the owner of a new bar soon. I wanted to come and see you guys."

My mother squealed on the other end of the line. "Oh, goodie! You're going to own something. That's exciting, Stephanie. I'm proud of you. I would love to catch up with you, but we can't this weekend. We are going on a little sexy weekend retreat, just me and him. We haven't been away in so long."

Shit. I wouldn't be able to stay there, and I had to work. There wasn't anywhere for me to run. I had to ride this thing out and stay put. If Wildcard and the Vipers were coming to get me then that's what would happen. This wasn't a cop matter either. It would expose James if I went to them, and as much as I hated him right now, that's not what I wanted to do.

"Sounds great, Mom. I hope you have fun. Are you going far?" I asked just to keep the small talk going. That's about as far as we got these days. Not that we couldn't get further, but it would be me who would have to make the effort.

"Far enough. We decided to go to Santa Barbara. We will be gone for three blissful nights and four days. Can't wait. You know your father, though, he's a workaholic even if he tells me he's not."

"That's Dad for you. Okay well, I'll check in with you when you get back." I was disengaged from the conversation and so was she. I knew my mother loved me, but at times the wires were crossed in a million different directions.

"Okay, sweetheart. Good to hear your voice and take care. I hope you've heard from James more than I have."

I stopped myself from pressing the end call button. "You haven't heard from James?"

"No, but I assume you have since you two are so close," she said.

"Not as much anymore, but he's okay if you wanted to know," I said smoothly, and even though I wanted to throw in some sass, I left it. Wasn't the right time for it considering my brother was the reason I was under threat in the first place.

"Oh, I wouldn't worry about it. Siblings might fall out every now and then, but you two have always been close even when you were little. I don't see that changing anytime soon," she said with a hint of nostalgia in her voice. So she did care a little bit. "I do have to go, I have an appointment to go to, then I have to come home and pack. Your father has no idea about packing."

"Okay, Mom. I will see you later. I love you."

"I love you too. You sound strange. Is everything okay with you, Stephanie?"

"I'm okay, thanks. See you later, Mom." I quickly got off the phone before the tears came.

"Bye, Stephanie. Talk to you when we get back and you can tell me all about the bar."

"Bye." I clicked off the phone and put my head in my hands. It felt like I was losing my family. One by one. If my parents were going away, the Vipers and the cartel couldn't target either of them.

I lay back on my bed and wept. This was the worst feeling in the world, and I wanted to rewind back to the start of the mess. I wanted to go back to the first moment when James told me of the gang involvement. I would have nipped it in the bud then. I would have gone to Mom and Dad and not just threatened to tell them. I would have gone to the cops on him and taken the tough love approach. I knew it wasn't my fault, but it felt like it.

I decided to take my chances and head into work. I got up and walked around the house and closed up all the windows and checked the locks of every single door. I showered and made a single braid with my dark hair. I put on a light layer of makeup and fuschia lipstick. I even put on some smoky eye color. I was putting on my battle armor before I went to work. Now the news of getting a new bar downtown had been tainted with the news of a rival motorcycle gang wanting to kidnap me.

I made it to work unscathed but not without me checking my mirror numerous times for anyone who I thought might be following me. As soon as I got in, I headed to the back office where Dustin was fumbling around in a gray metal filing cabinet.

"Shit. You've dressed up for the bar tonight. Looking good Steph," he remarked good-naturedly.

"Thanks. I need your help, Dustin." I sat down in the chair in front of him, and he left the filing cabinet open and looked at me.

"Shoot."

"Let me start from the top." I was huffing and puffing a little bit, but that was okay; I had to get it out. If I could get the bar and the people to rally around me, I knew they would protect me. I had a game plan of my own.

"I started dating Maverick, he's a patch at the Guardians," I said.

"Yeah, I know. Good match for you. Seems like a good guy," Dustin observed.

"He is. The problem is my little brother is on the side of the Vipers with the meth labs and this guy called Wildcard. He's trying to run the Guardians out and cause all types of havoc. James and I have fallen out over it," I pressed on. "This Wildcard guy is apparently involved now with a Mexican cartel, and they are focused on me now. My brother called me today to tell me to stop seeing Maverick and that I would be kidnapped if I didn't. This Wildcard guy is going to extort money from the Guardians."

Dustin leaned back in his seat, making his stomach stick out as his facial expressions shifted during the retelling. "That was a whole jumbled-up mess of words you just told me. What I gathered from it is you need some protection. Where's Maverick? He can sort this out. I hope you didn't stop seeing him because of this threat. If anything you need to go to the Guardians. They can cover you." Dustin put his two cents on the table and every word he uttered made more sense than what I had come up with.

"I did, Dustin, I broke up with him. I was so frantic, I didn't know what to do," I told him in a pained voice.

"You think Maverick is going to get shaken over a little kidnapping threat? This man is special forces trained. He has seen things you would never believe. Don't be fooled by Maverick's demeanor; he's not to be fucked with. I've heard a few stories—and speaking of stories, you've confirmed a few of the rumors that have been floating about James around here. I was hoping it wasn't true, but from the sounds of it... it is."

"Shit. What do I do?" I asked Dustin.

"We got you covered at the club. Nobody is going to do shit to you under my roof. I'm going to make it known to a few others. Everyone in this town will cover you, Steph. You're less alone than you think. Haven't you got the number of one of the old ladies now from the Guardians?"

"Yes. I do. Okay. Okay." I felt the knots shifting inside my stomach. I'd made another mistake in rejecting Maverick. Maybe he would want to forget about us. I kept messing up my own happiness. A tear started to run from my face, and I wiped it off before it could ruin my makeup, and Dustin saw.

"Call Maverick, he will sort this right out. He will," Dustin confirmed as he scooted back in his chair and got up. He forgot the steel filing cabinet door was open and banged his shin against it.

"Moses, Mary and Joseph. My leg." He was trying not to use expletives, but I definitely would have used a whole bunch in his case.

"Oooh. Is it bleeding? I'm sorry, that's my fault." I winced as I peeked down at his leg. There was a small trickle of blood coming from where the pointy tip of the desk had pierced through skin.

Dustin was busy attempting to regain feeling back in his shin and rubbing it. He dipped a tissue he had in water on his desk and put it on his lower leg. "See the pain I go through for you? See what I do?" He grimaced, but a tepid smile lifted the edges of his mouth.

"Sorry. I'm messing it all up today."

"No, you haven't. Trust me. What's the bet Maverick comes in here tonight?"

"None. He won't. I made it clear," I replied dimly.

"He will. That's not a man that gives up easy. I can see that when I look into his eyes. He's in love with you if you didn't know." Dustin presented a smug smile as if he'd discovered a new invention.

"He's said the three little words to me."

"Then don't you know that a man who loves their woman will go to the ends of the earth for her? Trust me, he will end Wildcard for good, and you'll be the motivation." Dustin winked. "Now let's go out here and serve these drinks. I have my rifle out back, and it will be loaded. If I hear of anybody trying anything then it's on. You're covered here. I'll follow you home if need be."

"Thanks, Dustin."

After work, Dustin walked me to my car. The night sky was littered with stars, so perfect and true. Not a single soul that I didn't recognize was out in the parking lot. Patrons walked out with me to make sure I remained safe. Just like Dustin had said, the whole of the Edgewood community was behind me. As I drove home, I saw a flash of light. One headlight. One bike. I dug my hands into the wheel. When I looked at the rider, I knew it was Maverick. I could feel his energy, the rider's legs. Toned, and tight just like my man's. Black jeans. I straightened up the mirror. Yep, it was him. He was watching out for me. Once I got into my street, the mystery rider idled at the end of it. I pulled into my drive-way, and the rider pulled off his helmet. That rider was my love. Maverick. As soon as I got excited about the possibility, Maverick slid his helmet back on his head and rode off with a gray plume of smoke behind him.

# 19

## MAVERICK

As soon as the words left her lips, I knew they were bold-faced lies. She was under threat, but I let her play it out. She didn't trust me enough yet to know that I had her back no matter what. There was a panicky tone in her voice, and I strained to hear if there was anyone in the background. She sounded muffled on the call. All I knew is that calm still water that most people could swim in with me was gone. The water had turned stormy and dark, and I was ready to drag somebody under especially with Stephanie. She was being pushed to break up with me, that part I could feel in my soul. I wasn't so cocky to think I was the best guy on the planet, but the strong and what I deemed to be impenetrable bond that Stephanie and I forged had been built over several months. The intensity of the outside influences hadn't helped us move forward any and here they were again trying to destroy the castle we were building.

I was halfway out the door when she called mid-morning. We had another mission to face, and I was implementing a small bomb. I'd been working on it all night, testing the components and soldering the circuit boards necessary to make it work. It was a diversion tactic to use for the meth lab missions, and this was to be the first mission I would use it for. This was the last mission before the ambush, and I was curious to see how the Guardians were going to handle it.

I wasn't accepting her breakup. If she wanted to break up with me for real, she would need to do it in person. The threat had something to do with her brother. Down the line when Steph and I got married we would have a lot to clear up because all I wanted to do was fuck him up.

I shook off the phone call and got myself together. My agitation levels were through the roof, and I was sick and tired of hearing the words 'Wildcard' and 'Viper.' I didn't want to hear either of them ever again. I let myself calm down by doing some deep breathing that I'd learned in an ashram in India. I'd gone there after the bombing of my friend. The memories were so strong that my body started to shut down. I had been depressed for months and months when it was suggested to me that I go to India by another soldier in special forces who'd used their techniques and seemed so calm in and after every battle.

"I know a place. A guru that can assist you. He'll help you clear the memories. This meditation stuff works. It's the training of the mind. It's not easy work, but it's work that will help you process some of that hurt in your heart. Try it. This is the place." He handed me a white business card with a number on it.

"Thanks, man. I don't think it will work, but thanks for trying." But when I sat in the dark and the nightmares and sweats came, I knew I had to do something to shift the pain away from my heart. I called the number and spoke to a man with a heavy Indian accent.

"Maverick. Ah, I've been waiting for your call. You come to India. You stay with me. We eat, we talk. We share."

"How did you know it was me?" I thought at that point the guy was psychic, and I was convinced I had to go see him. I didn't need to speak to him anymore.

"Ah, your soldier friend told me you might call." Both of us laughed after that. His name was Dhakaan. He let me know about himself and his enlightenment and his practice. He told me about the hundreds of students that were sent to him. "Now it's your turn, Maverick. You come to India. I teach you how to stay fluid and calm in your missions and battles in life. To keep level in all your dealings."

"That would be nice. I feel like I'm losing it, Dhakaan."

"Sometimes you have to lose it in order to find it, dear man." We exchanged details, and I went to see him. One of the most enlightening and game-changing experiences of my life. I tapped in to the knowledge that Dhakaan taught me and sat down on the floor in a cross-legged position and meditated until my heartrate got under control. Once I tapped in and settled down, I rolled up the last of my weed and rode on out to the clubhouse. It was in full swing. I heard the thumping of a bag and was shocked to see Bell back on it ploughing a hole through the bag. There was a crib set up behind her where Zena was standing and giggling, watching her mother.

"Bell Marco! Back in full effect." She was in warrior mode, I could tell, and the expression on her face spelled death for her opponent. She glanced over momentarily, and when she saw it was me she stopped, leaned in, and kissed my cheek.

"I'm here. Have to get back into it before I lose all my hard work," she puffed as I wiped the excess sweat off my cheek. "Sorry about that, consider yourself christened."

"I've been christened, how about that Zena? Your Uncle Maverick has been christened by one of the baddest women ever." Zena had no idea what I was saying. She was just having fun and jumping up and down in her playpen. I went over to her and kissed her rosy cheek. Her chubby fingers went to my mouth, and I kissed her little fingers.

"How are you holding up, Maverick? I heard you've been sent out on these crazy missions," Bell asked.

"Yep, not crazy by my standards but dumb. We had one the other week with caskets of product being moved out from behind a church. The cops took over that one. Turns out inside was millions of dollars' worth of crystal meth. Wildcard is behind it, and he's trying any and everything. The guy is relentless."

"Tomorrow will sew it up. Once the ambush goes down it will sort it out. Wildcard will get got," Bell said with clarity.

"You seem sure about it. Are you in?"

"Wouldn't miss it. I led the boys out last time. Zena is going to stay with Brody for the night."

"Wow. You're in on this?" I quizzed. Bell put her hands on her well-toned hips.

"Yes. This is when I come out to play." Bell flattened out her fingers which were protected by boxing wraps and started to unravel them.

"Don't stop. I wanted to say hi is all."

"It's fine. That was the cool down. I'm finishing up now. I have to get this one to the nurse for her check-ups. She's growing so fast." Bell swooped in and patted her daughter's nose with one finger.

"Both of you look great. I got another little problem with the woman I've been seeing—her brother is connected with the Vipers and Wildcard and told her that the Vipers would kidnap her if she kept seeing me. Unfortunately, she took the bait." Bell started laughing, and I could see all her teeth.

"That's funny?" I asked as Dutch came out of the office to see where the noise was coming from.

"Yes! You're not going to let that fly, are you? The Vipers are so stupid, that's the thing. They don't have the ability to not botch anything up. They do it every time. I don't believe the threat. Steph from the bar, right?"

"Yep, guys tell you?"

"Yup, that's how the Guardians grapevine works. She's awesome. She's protected already Dustin won't let anything happen to her, you won't, and neither will we. Tomorrow this thing will end." Bell flexed her fingers and pulled her leg up into a quadricep stretch as she put her hand on my shoulder for balance.

"I hate that somebody is coming after her."

"It's rough, but it's the game of the motorcycle world."

"Pretty much. I want to check in with Tara and see how the questioning went. See you at the brief later tonight."

"You will." Bell kept stretching. "She did good, but the sheriff shook her up real hard. She'll be all right; she's a tough cookie, my twin." Tara was a mini version of Bell to most of us, so we ended up calling them twins. If you knew them both, you knew they were like night and day.

I looked over to the office window and I could see that Tara was stacking something. "See you tomorrow, Bell. Glad you're going to come and kick some ass with us."

"Me too. It will be the most action I've had in months." I smirked and walked over to the office.

"Hey Tara, Dutch, Scout, what's going on?" Dutch was helping count money with Tara, and they were stacking bundles of cash into a bag from the safe. Dutch shut the door behind me.

"Come all the way in, Maverick." He gestured with his hand. "We are setting up the cash for the drop tomorrow night. We are mixing in the actual notes with the pretend ones."

"This is how it's getting done. Nice job, Dutch."

Dutch handed me a twenty dollar bill. "Can you tell the difference?" He handed me what looked to be a fake bill. I yanked the paper from both sides, and it didn't come apart. It looked like the real deal and it felt like the real deal. It was tough to see the difference. I held it up to the light. Nothing.

Dutch scrunched up his nose to hold his glasses in place. "Pretty good for a counterfeit bill right?"

"Yeah, what's the catch? How do you know?"

Dutch pointed to the missing space where the eagle was supposed to be. "You see no eagle, not real money. It doesn't have the surname Jackson at the bottom either. A couple of small intricacies that will throw a wrench in the works for Wildcard."

Scout grinned. "Yeah, baby. I got the good stuff. These might come in handy. We have to make sure that we don't mix them up with the real money."

"That would be a trip. Give the 20 dollar bills to the enemy and then we end up using it." I made light of the fact and Dutch scowled at me.

"Don't start putting that out, we would look like fools." He was a very conservative guy, and it made me curious as to why he would be working for a motorcycle club in the first place.

I cupped Dutch's shoulder. "It's all right, Dutch. The counterfeit secret is safe with me." I cut between Dutch and Scout over to Tara.

"Hey, I wanted to come and see how you are doing. How did it go with the lawyer?"

Using her nylon gloves, Tara tucked her long dark hair behind one ear. "It went well. I answered all the questions, and my lawyer was there. He did grill me, but he was respectful. I like Sherriff Malone. I think he's doing his job. I was scared at first, Maverick, but I trust all of you. I know you won't let anything happen to me."

"Good."

A little twinkle shone in her eyes, and she was holding back a smile. "A little birdy told me you were in love," she poked.

"I am. I can admit that. Steph is wonderful. She doesn't believe in me enough, though. We're not together, her choice. We broke up a couple of days ago."

Tara frowned hard as Dutch and Scout loaded more money into the cheap duffel bag. "You were going so well. What happened?"

"The Vipers and her brother warned her off me, that's the crux of it. A little more complicated, but that's a pretty accurate depiction."

"No. So it has nothing to do with you and her?" she asked with a touch of investigation to her questioning.

"It does. She should trust me, anyway. I don't want to get into it. You got work to do here. I'll see you all at the debrief tonight." I gulped down my own reservations I was having, like why the hell Stephanie didn't trust me. I wanted her to, otherwise we just weren't going to work. I knew that in time Stephanie and I would sort things out, but we had to wade through the muddy waters just like I had to in Vietnam to get there. Not World War Two, just Vietnam to disassemble a number of heinous bombs on behalf of the United States of America.

"See you later, Maverick," Tara called out as her quick nimble fingers sifted through the dollar bills. Dutch's face was marred with a frown as he ran his finger down the computer screen. He was muttering to himself as he counted. I didn't want to break his focus, so I said nothing to him. I put up one finger in a goodbye gesture to Scout, and he mirrored it back.

"See you tonight, Maverick. Go get your girl back." He winked as I shut the door behind me and walked through to the chop shop.

Shaggy, Havoc, Rush, and Quicks were all in the shop, and each one of them was working on a vehicle of some kind. Shaggy was working on a car that resembled a rust bucket, Havoc was working on a bike, and Shaggy was working on his all-time favorite—a dirt bike.

Rush was working on a custom bike and screwing on the fender for it. He was closest to my eyeline, so he was the first person I spoke to.

"Hey, Rush." The radio was up loud and playing rock music. His tongue was licked out in concentration, and he was in the zone with the music. He looked up and stopped when he saw me. He gave me a low five when I stuck my hand out.

"Mav! How are you? Are you ready for this ambush thing tomorrow night? I'm freaking out, man." He shook the wrench he had in his hand and darted his eyes around as if the guys would think less of him if they knew what he'd said.

"Why? You've been in worse," I said bluntly. I didn't want to seem like I wasn't compassionate, because I was. From my perspective it was just another mission, and I knew for sure that Gunner and Mustang would be thinking like I did.

"That's probably why. We're starting to think about how it turned out. Ever had one of your brothers die, Maverick? Do you know what that feels like?" Rush's face was scarred by anguish, and I could relate a little too much.

"Yes, I know that pain. I've lost my unit members, I've seen children killed, so I know how you feel," I shared and watched the expression on his face morph to one of shock.

"You have, man? This is too much for me. I want everyone to live. I don't want to go to the ambush at fucking all," Rush admitted in full disclosure.

"I don't want to either, but this will draw Wildcard out into the open and give us the best chance to get at him," I explained.

He flicked his finger at the bottom of the fender of the bike he was working on. "I know we gotta do it. I'm just going back in time and remembering how crazy it was here. Shit was rough back then. We were all fighting and not getting along. I can't take it if it's that again."

I looked him in the eye. "It won't be. Trust the process. I gotta find Hawk, but I'll see you tonight for the debrief."

"See you then, Mav." Rush resumed working on his custom bike, and I changed track and went to the lunchroom. The others were hard at it so I would see them later.

Walking into the lunchroom with Red, Hawk, Mustang, and Gunner I knew this was where the nitty gritty of the ambush operation was happening. Hawk wouldn't be able to help himself, and neither would Mustang. Both of them could discuss tactics all day.

We all got greetings out of the way. Hawk had a large map rolled out with the pool balls holding the corners down. He had a number of large red circles in certain areas of the map and other areas were marked in different colors. All of the guys were either standing or sitting on a stool around him as he spoke. Hawk meant business and was a road captain and a half. If you would ever want someone leading you on the road, then he would be the guy. He was knee deep in conversation with Red and looked up halfway with a grin. "Hey, Maverick. I'm showing the crew the areas that we need to be aware of for the ambush tomorrow night."

"What are we up against?" I asked in general to the group.

"Gang members from an unidentified group. Not a cartel, so we don't have to worry about that type of backlash. Wildcard and any contacts he may have. The place is an old warehouse not far from the shootout. I don't know if he did that to make it emotionally scarring for the Guardians because it was already a killing floor or what," Mustang revealed as he cracked his knuckles.

"My guess is he did that on purpose. He wants the Guardians to be scared and anxious. He is playing with us all. It seems obvious to me. Gunner, he knows about you. He's going to have the perimeter surrounded. He is going to try and use his front line to cover himself. I know his type. He's not concerned for his team. He only cares about Wildcard." I drew upon all my knowledge from the military and put myself in the shoes of Wildcard, who was after money, retribution, and fighting for his pride. Pop had turned him away, so naturally he wanted to hit him where it hurt him the most. His fellow riders and crew.

Gunner was eating a peach, slicing it with a hunting knife and dropping the fruit into his mouth. "I'm going to pick them off one by one. If he lines the perimeter, then I line it as well and get rid of his sharpshooters. Simple. Pop. Pop. Pop goes the weasel." He sliced another part of the peach and chewed on the fruit, laughing to himself as the guys stared at him in stunned silence. He was still having a laughter party to himself and slicing his peach. When he saw that all the fellas thought he was crazy, he stopped.

"What? That's what I'm going to do. You all know that. I just know it's funny. Pop goes the weasel—the guy is a weasel. I'm telling you the truth."

A humorless smirk came from Mustang. "Gunner, there must be some happy juice in that peach. Give me some."

"Here, you want a slice?" He held out a slice of the peach to Mustang, who reached for it. "I'm not serious. You keep your peaches over there thank you very much." Mustang's eyebrows drew together and now the humor came as I chuckled.

"He's right. That is what he's gonna do. Where's the lie?" I questioned as I hunched up my shoulders and got closer to the map. The guys nodded but didn't say anything. They were stuck on Gunner's chilling delivery.

"Hawk, I have a little bomb that I've been working on. I heard that you used a similar tactic?"

Hawk grimaced because he knew that I was talking about the shootout. I saw his face change and a flicker of pain dance in his eyes. "We dropped a smoke bomb so it would give us time to get in position."

"Got it. Slightly different. This is specifically designed to be a car bomb. I've made two so far. Both of them I already had. I've been adjusting them and now I think they're ready."

"You think they're ready?" Mustang parroted.

"Correction. I know they're ready," I countered.

"I guess we have to wait for the meeting now."

"I guess so."

Church meeting number I-don't-know-what. All of the crew was seated around the table, and the room smelled of leather, cigars, and alcohol. Most in the room had a drink of some sort in their hand. Dutch came upstairs with the suitcase. I guessed he was going to show us the counterfeit money and reassure the team about what was to come next. Red was at the head of the table, and Pop was beside him. Red was whispering something into his ear, and Pop was raising his eyebrows from time to time as he spoke. The meeting was due to start at 11 p.m., and I had a feeling it would be right on closing time for Steph, so I planned to ride over and make sure she got home all right. I knew if she was at work she was safe. Dustin and the townspeople loved Stephanie, besides I thought that Wildcard was bluffing about the kidnapping.

Pop cleared his throat as Hawk pinned the large map up on the back of the church meeting room for everyone to see. "Everybody is here. All members are accounted for. Welcome, gentleman and honoraries." He was speaking about Bell and Tara being in the room. Tara was looking around and I guessed this was her first time at a church meeting.

"This is a debrief meeting. We have now graduated to the stage of the ambush, and we need to prepare accordingly. Red is going to run you through the plan overall, and Hawk will let you know how that will translate to the road. We will tease out any open gaps in the plan here tonight." Pop paused and left space for others to jump in. Nobody did. "We don't leave here until the plan is established, and everyone is clear on their roles." Pop glared at everyone around the room. "Are we good with it?"

Men raised their glasses as the answer. "Yes," I replied. I chose to forgo the drink. I wanted to keep clear sighted, and when I did my drive by on Stephanie I wanted to be alert and make sure she got home safe. The quicker the meeting finished, the better to me. Axle had a drink in his hand, Mustang too, and Red was drinking a beer. Shaggy and Quicks were on the water like me. Bell had a beer in her hand and was sitting next to Axle. Her focus was on the map, and I saw the fight in her eyes. The Guardian crew was unstoppable in my books. I felt confident that we would overcome this mission and win like we did all the others.

"Okay then, let's start. You're up, Red." Red was next in line on the Guardians throne, you could say. He could take that throne now if he wanted to. Pop was a little more hard-nosed than Red and wouldn't listen to reason. Red would and had this ability to bring all the skills of everyone in the club together. He was wearing his jacket, and his long hair was touching his shoulders. He stood up with his drink in hand.

"The details go like this. We have a location drop off. Route 66 Saddle Spur Road at a large warehouse. I've studied it and ridden past it on the bike. There's nobody staying or living around the premises that I could see. It's just a drop location. This site might be triggering for some of us. This is incredibly close to where we had the shootout three years ago. Wildcard would know that. Stay steady and lean on one another. Back each other up. We went on a run to the gun warehouse and what you can see from there is on the back table here. Collect your weapons. All guns are registered and above board. If you have your own weapons that you want to bring, by all means bring them. We don't know what we're walking into, so pick wisely. Any questions so far?" Red scanned the faces of the room, and nobody said anything, so he carried on. "Hawk is going to lead us out as always. What we know is that these aren't Mexican cartel members, these are gang members from Cedar Crest and Sedillo. They are young, most of them, and inexperienced. They are drug traffickers and known to run girls from over the border. What they lack in experience they make up for in ruthlessness. Three of them have been involved in multiple stabbings and shootings. We are looking at a crew of over 18 in size, and they've got numbers on their side. Wildcard thinks he's won this because we're going to the drop. Let's prove him wrong."

Hawk tapped the wall. "If we all want to take a look at the map, I can tell you how we're going to run. I'm going to lead out. Bell will ride behind me, then Axle, Havoc, Shadow, Shaggy, and Rush. Quicks, I want you in the middle of the pack. Mustang, Maverick, and Gunner, I want you at the back of the pack as the lookouts. I don't care which order. Finn and Red, I want you to take a back door route and come in another way. I will point that out on the map. Pop, Dutch, and Scout will be in a separate car. They won't come in to join unless absolutely necessary. Maverick, tell us about your car bomb idea and can we pull it off."

"I think we leave it. I can bring it with me, but I would need a distraction on site so I have enough time to rig and attach it to the underside of their vehicle or bike. If I can I will."

Hawk nodded. "Okay, that's the rollout from me. Pretty simple, but hard at the same time. We are flying blind and have no idea what Wildcard is going to pull out of the bag."

Gunner put his hand up. "Go, Gunner, don't worry about a hand. We're not in school." Axle sneered.

"I would say I need to fall back and relook at studying that map. I'm going to work the perimeter and keep you safe so you can roll in on command," Gunner clarified.

"Absolutely. Thanks, Gunner," Red said. "Radios are on

deck charging. We need to be here at 5 p.m. tomorrow. The drop is scheduled for 7 p.m. Everyone got their bulletproof vests? If not, we have spares," Red yelled out. "Dutch, take us through the drop and the money."

Dutch had a few beads of sweat on his upper lip, and he was visibly nervous. "Ah—we, ah, have acquired excellent counterfeit notes, and these notes are hidden under the real money we are going to distribute to Wildcard. All up there is $1500 dollars available to him. Pass this around and take a look and see if you can spot the difference. It's really quite remarkable." Dutch passed around two 20 dollar bills, and the crew examined them closely. I saw Bell and Axle pore over them and not pick up the missing symbols.

"I can't tell, but I have baby brain, so that's my excuse," she exempted herself.

"You can't say that anymore. Zena is one," Axle pointed out.

"Yes I can. You try broken sleep and hard boobs all day and come back to me." She backhanded Axle, and he grinned and raised his eyebrows, mouthing *I love it* to us. Bell and Axle's love tiff broke the tension in the room as the guys laughed. He caught Bell's fingers so she couldn't slap him and kissed them. The mad look on Bell's face quickly faded to a sweet smile, and they were lovebirds again. I found myself yearning for Stephanie in the middle of the meeting. I wanted her to meet the crew and come to the clubhouse and rock with the old ladies. I know she knew them from the bar, but I wanted her to know them personally. I missed her. A lot.

The notes kept floating around, and Dutch and Scout looked very happy that nobody had been able to figure it out. Scout looked less impressed, and as if he wanted to go and had things to do. When the notes got to Finn, he held it up and then put it down again. "Mmm. The symbol. The eagle is gone and the name. That's what it is."

"Yes! Yes. Finn, that's it. That's exactly right. The symbols are gone."

Finn's smug smile made Shaggy tap him. "If I got the chance to play the guessing game I would have gotten it too."

"I'm sure you would have, Shaggy. Wildcard is gonna be pissed when he finds out. He is going to lose his shit. Can this money be traced back to the Guardians in any way?" Finn enquired, and it was a good question.

"No, it's all covered. The originator of the counterfeit has never been caught either. It may be something we can utilize in the future should we find ourselves in this position again," Dutch added in a hasty tone. Tara wasn't talking—verbally anyway. She was making eyes at Hawk, and he was making them right back at her. I knew what they were going home to do. Made me feel a little jealous that I wasn't together with Stephanie, but I knew that soon enough we would be.

"We won't be in this position again because Wildcard will be dead. I don't have to tell you twice that if you sniff that dog turd out I want you to shoot and kill him. No hesitation, no feeling sorry for him because he was a former Guardian. Kill him." Pop's menacing stare penetrated every single one of us at the table.

"I will gladly get rid of him for you," Axle confirmed.

"Me too. Pop. Pop," Gunner said as he made the sound with his lips. I smirked. Gunner had this off beat slightly serial killer type of humor that you only got used to if you knew him. He was really a good guy.

Dutch cleared his throat. "Once the drop is made, we will step back. It should be simple. The plans for attack are only if they attack. Wildcard doesn't seem to be too bright, so I don't think he'll pick up the counterfeit money, but if he does we might need to prepare."

"So this might be easy and we don't need to worry *or* it might turn into a shitfight is what Dutch is trying to say," Finn got the raw roots of what Dutch wanted to portray.

Pop rose from his seat with his glass in his hand. "The motto, let's not forget it." He thrust his arm higher as all of the men raised their bottles and glasses.

*"Protect thine own! Protect thine own! Protect thine own!"*

The meeting finished up after that, and the fellas moved in their separate directions. I waved goodbye knowing this would be my first time going into battle with my fellow bikers. I was pumped about it and feeling as if we'd already won. I knew we would end it for good.

I had one more thing to do, and that was check on Stephanie. I rode into the cool of the night, letting the wind hit my face. Felt damn good. I slowed down as I parked in the lot and waited. I was in the back corner watching patrons come out. It was 1:30 a.m. The bar closed at 2. I just needed to see her walk out to her car, and then I would follow her home. I was amused by the stragglers as they staggered out. Some others were upright and walking straight with no problem at all. It was 2:05 a.m. when she came out to her car and Dustin was with her. He looked around the parking lot and there was nobody there. Everyone had snuck off into the night, and it was just Dustin's car and hers. She looked so beautiful in the moon-light, with the soft curve of her jaw and the smile she gave Dustin. I missed that. Her hair swayed behind her as she got into her vehicle, cranked the engine, and I followed her home. I kept my distance, not wanting to freak her out by making her think I was one of the Vipers. She knew my bike and she knew me. I wanted her to have the space to think about being together, but if I was being honest with myself if we hadn't had that church meeting, I would have been front and center at the bar.

I sat at the end of the street, knowing that she would notice me. I took my helmet off for a minute and rearranged the strands of my hair. I saw her look in my general direction, but before she had time to think about seeing me at the end of the drive, I was gone.

The next night, the sky was in that in-between stage where it hadn't made its mind up about the sun going down and calling it a night. At 6 p.m., the whole Guardians crew unified, ready for battle. High levels of adrenaline were racing through my system. Hawk was there with his black bandana wrapped low around his neck, leather gloves, a gun on his hip and one in his shoulder holster. Army cargos were on, bulletproof vest, black fingerless leather gloves. One gun in my hip holster and a bomb device in my cargo pants pocket along with blu tack, a stopwatch, and string. In the other pocket I had some thin wire. Those were my battle tools. Mustang was beside me with Gunner on the other side.

"How you feeling? You good?" Mustang said in a low voice.

"Yeah, I'm real good. Ready to finish this shit," I whispered back to him. In the crevices of my mind I told myself if I got one glance at Wildcard I was pulling the trigger. No matter what. Mustang and Gunner were known as the shooters out of the three of us, but I could pull a gun too, and wasn't a bad shot.

"You and me both. I should have gotten him when I knew where he was at," Mustang growled.

"Don't worry about it. This might be even better."

Hawk stood at the front of the group. "All right, this is it. Follow my lead on directions. If there's any changes, use your radio. We are on Channel 2. Be ready for anything and everything. If I see anything on the road, I'm going to alert you. Don't be complacent and think it will be an easy ride there. We have had guns pulled on us as we ride. Guardians, this is it!"

The chants began as we raised our fists and circled. *"Protect thine own. Protect thine own."*

"Let's ride, Guardians." I mounted my bike and waited my turn in the line. The sound of all our bikes combined created one hell of a buzz. I watched Hawk lead the crew out. Bell was next, then Axle, Havoc, Shadow, Shaggy, Quicks, Mustang, and me. A last-minute change occurred with Gunner in the van along with Dutch and Pop so he could set up his sniper gun. Finn and Red were riding last and would turn off as we got closer to the destination and enter from another angle to cover all bases.

We rode in single file out of the clubhouse and onto the highway. We hit Route 66 smoothly without any interruption. There was a little traffic on the road due to it being close to 7 p.m. but nothing to freak out about. All bikes were in sight, and Hawk was leading well. When he changed lanes to give us clearance, then we changed lanes. The sky made up its mind and turned into a deep ultramarine blue color with heavy clouds, and the temperature dropped considerably and made it freezing on the bike. The wind cut through my jacket, and my teeth started to chatter a little bit as the speed made the wind worse. The road changed to dirt as we turned off toward our destination. I could visualize the warehouse clearly in my mind. I'd checked it out on Google images, and its layout was similar to one that the crew and I had raided. The drop had been changed to be a direct exchange to the gang members we knew about. A late game change had come in from Wildcard requesting it. We were close when my radio stirred.

*Gunner reporting. Snipers in the grass surrounding. Picking off one by one. Shooting has started. Got four in eyesight.*

Hawk picked it up. *Proceed, Gunner.* Every one of us had our radios on and heard the message. I knew Wildcard would have some ace up his sleeve, except he didn't realize that we had an ace up our sleeves as well. I looked out into the fields around the building and could see nothing, but Gunner was in the van for a reason. It was a good call to put him there. He had a sweet pair of night vision goggles and his sniper rifle. He was a bigger gadget guy than me. My heart rate started to increase as we rode into the location address. My breathing was calm; it was just the buzz of what we were about to encounter that had me in a state.

Hawk rode in first and pulled to the right. Bell pulled up and parked next to him, and so on down the line until the Guardians formed a one long barrier. Our headlights shone directly onto the warehouse where a warm amber glow was lighting it up. Five figures were standing on the other side. Not overly tall but each one wearing black and armed. They were wearing balaclavas or purple bandanas. No words were exchanged. Wildcard was expecting 100 thousand dollars. He was about to get 1500. He was lucky he was even getting that much.

Dutch stepped out of the van with a balaclava on and dropped the money in the middle of the dirt. One of the men from the other side spoke. "Is all the money there?"

*Dumb question. We wouldn't tell you if it wasn't...*

Dutch answered. "It's all there. Feel free to check." I tried to look discreetly around the perimeter to pick up any sounds of the men being shot but heard nothing. My finger was sitting on top of my hip. They were outnumbered, so if anything happened, they would be dead. Not smart to approach with only five men. I saw two men move away with the bag and speak in Spanish. I cast my eyes up to the warehouse as all the boys stood next to their bikes. Bell was still on hers.

I saw her beautiful brain working, and my mind knew where she was going. She wanted to storm the warehouse at the back and get Wildcard. I saw the wilderness in her eyes and Axle's eye glittering in the dark as she mouthed something to him. I was still straddling my bike as well. I knew this wasn't it. I knew we weren't walking away like this. I swallowed hard as I saw Dutch make it safely back into the van. We were waiting for a signal. Those five were too close, and nobody wanted to risk getting shot at close range. A coyote sang out somewhere in the hills as we watched the five men retreat and get into the van. One of them held his gun out and pointed it.

"If you try to follow, you will be shot. Sharpshooters are in the bushes. You will be shot. Don't follow."

We stood, knowing what we knew. What a mistake. The men got into the van and drove down back to the lit-up warehouse thirty paces away. Wildcard was inside the building. I knew it. I could feel it.

I pressed the receive button on the radio. "Maverick, Gunner—verdict?"

"All five down, no more spotted. Target Wildcard on the inside. Too many inside to get a clear shot. Make a run, Guardians."

That was the cue. Red pressed the receiver button. "Gunner, how many inside?"

There was a crackling noise that sounded like the wind cutting through the communication. "I sighted eight, including Wildcard. Make a move, otherwise they will. They can see your headlights. I can get the party started and move them if you want."

Red spoke again. "Warning shot only. We want them to scatter and leave. We want Wildcard only. They won't be loyal. They want their cut."

"Okay. I'll give you the go signal," Gunner advised. I heard a shot pierce through the thin sheet metal of the warehouse. Loud voices speaking in Spanish rang out as one of the gang members ran out and rounded to the van's driver's side. Another two had a duffel bag of money under their arm. A shot rang out inside the warehouse. The gunfire pierced the air, and a tragic scream rang out. The van approached, and Hawk yelled out.

"Fire!" Hawk fired at the van first, and it swerved erratically and sharply away from the gunfire. Shots were fired back out of the side window, and Bell raised her gun to target the tires. She missed narrowly. "Dammit!" she screamed as she stepped out to target directly at the back of the vehicle as it sped off. She squeezed her trigger, and I pulled my gun and fired and pierced their back window and she caught the taillight. The rest of the crew were riding down to the warehouse.

I started my engine and rode down to join them. The other members were gathering around a trestle table where a few notes were flying in the wind. Face down at a table in the middle of the warehouse was Wildcard with a pool of crimson blood dripping around him and seeping into the earth.

"Looks like they got to him first," Axle said. "His own crew turned on him." The big guy shook his head. "He should have stuck with us. Rest in peace, Wildcard."

"Rest in peace, Wildcard," I said as we all stood, shocked by the turn of events.

Gunner strolled in, chewing gum. "Well, that was fun."

"Are they dead?"

Gunner made a funny face. "They may not be. I clipped them all, but I tried not to kill them, so they may just be injured."

Axle made a move. "We gotta go. If they are injured and that's it, there's a chance of recovery, and we don't wanna be here when the cops come. Let's roll."

We all made quick exits and mounted our bikes. Hawk held his arm up in the night as the lead, and the same single file of riders followed in line as we kicked up dust and rode out with another successful mission complete. Operation Wildcard. And we weren't the ones to kill him this time.

That's why families should stick together. Now I had one more mission, and that was Operation Stephanie. The one where I got back the love of my life.

# STEPHANIE

"HAVE YOU DECIDED YET? HAVE YOU DECIDED YET?" MELISSA was asking me about my cocktail bar agreement that I was just about ready to sign. She was working with me on one of the quiet nights so I could teach her some new cocktails that I planned to try out in the upcoming weeks. One of them was aptly named the Chocolate Casualty.

"No. I have to go look at the site and make sure it's up to code. I have to do all the stuff first and then I can make a decision about the contract. The short answer is yes, I'm going to do it. The long answer is there are several steps involved."

"I am soooo pumped. It is going to be so awesome." She was more amped up than me about the place. What I saw was a pretty steep learning curve. Not that I minded, but I knew running my own cocktail bar was not going to be a walk in the park or anything.

"That brings some things back to you... what do you want to do?" I asked her as I wet the rim of the martini glass and placed it face down into cinnamon sugar. Melissa copied my steps as I turned the glass upright with a nice rim of sugary goodness.

"I thought about it," she said slowly, looking guilty. "I want to work for you in the cocktail bar. I don't think I can handle the workload of school with the last year of studies coming up. I want to learn how to make all these cool drinks with you." She grinned.

"I thought that might be the case. That means I'm going to have to train someone for here. A new person," I stated.

"Is that an issue for you? I'm sorry. I really did think about it, and I can't."

I was horrified she assumed I was mad about her decision. I was just worried about Justin having two longstanding staff members walking out on him. "No, don't be sorry. I want you to come work for me. I'm worried for Dustin. I don't know how he's going to feel," I explained to her.

"How am I going to feel about what?" His voice boomed from around the corner, and I jumped at the sound.

"Dustin! Stop sneaking around corners like that, sheesh. You scared me," I cried out in an exasperated tone.

"Hey, if you wouldn't keep things from me I wouldn't need to duck around corners," he grumbled.

"Stop it. You're just sulking, but I am needing to tell you that I want to work for Steph when her cocktail bar opens. Eeeep, sorry Dustin." She shrank down, waiting for a barrage of guilt-tripping, but none came.

Dustin groaned. "I figured you would. Steph, I'm sure, will bring me an excellent trained staff member, and all will be forgiven." He placed his heavy hand on my shoulder as he looked at me crazy, squinting one eye.

I stared at my shoulder. "You don't like touching people. This is new for you," I observed with a chuckle.

"Ah, Stephanie, you make my world a very interesting place. That you do. Now if you ladies will excuse me, I have to fix some blown lights so our patrons can see who they're kissing when the lights come on." Both of us giggled. Dustin was a fun guy sometimes.

"Speaking of kissing and making up... have you heard from Maverick?"

My heart stung a little bit as she said his name, and it made me sad to think about him. In hindsight, I'd made another mistake and pushed him away. I shouldn't have given up my love life for my little wayward brother. Now I felt ashamed. I did want to do something about it, I just didn't know what would be the right gesture.

"No, I messed up again. I shouldn't have listened to my brother. He could care less about me. He was willing to pick money and drugs over me. I don't even know what I will do if he turns it around and tries to come back to me."

"Shit. Family huh? They can be the pits. I think you and Maverick belong together, and no matter how silly you look you should always fight for love. Maybe I'm too much of a romantic at heart. I want it to be true. When I see him come into the bar and look at you the way he does, I wish for a man to look at me like that," she sighed as her eyes went dreamy.

"You're not looking very hard. You had that big huge guy from the Guardians come in here and sweet talk you. I know you're single. Did you miss that?"

She blinked her eyes for a few, and then a lightbulb came on. "Oooo that guy. He was really cute and nice too. He's very ripped. I like it."

I gave a wry chuckle. "I knew you were interested! We should get back to these cocktails, though, before the ingredients melt."

"Oh yeah. We completely forgot about them. We can multitask," she replied.

"We want one shot of chocolate Baileys, a quarter cup of fresh coconut cream, one shot of Malibu rum, whipped cream, crushed ice, and chocolate flakes to garnish. So let's shake it up," I said. I watched Melissa measure out the ingredients. "Probably a little more coconut cream. Just a pinch. I haven't fine-tuned the flavors yet, but it feels like it's close. What do you think of it as a drink?" Melissa put her straw in it.

"Hmm. I think this definitely needs to be a chilled drink, it's a bit exotic. The flavors are so different. I like it. Nailed it!" She sucked the contents off the straw and tasted. "We get to drink these, right?"

"Of course! I'm about to get myself a chocolate moustache right now." I put my glass up with hers. "What's the toast?"

"Ahhhh, to finding true love," she cried out.

I put my glass up and clinked lightly. "How did I know you were going to say something like that? Here's to finding true love."

"Some of us have already found it and just don't know how to handle it." She winked at me as she sipped, and I smiled wryly back at her. I didn't have a comeback for that.

Dustin emerged from the dance floor of the bar and looked at us both drinking. "So I'm paying you to drink now? What is this?" he teased as I narrowed my eyes at him. He knew I was coming in early to train Melissa. I grabbed a martini glass, poured out a little portion, and gave it to him.

"Here, drink this and tell me what you think of my latest concoction. It doesn't have the cinnamon sugar ring, but just imagine that it's there."

He held the drink up high and looked at it. He sniffed.

"Smells good, coconut. Lots of it. Hmm." His pinky automatically shot up as he sipped. His eyes went wide. "Oh baby! That's a hit. That's an unsuspecting hit of rum in there. Spicy. I like that. Let's add that to the Steph special list."

I clicked my fingers. "You reminded me, I left out the chili!" Dustin waved his hands like a fan. "You're going to add chili in there as well? I don't know that you need to. It has enough kick to it."

"I'm going to add it and then see what I feel about it," I said to him.

"Okay. Be sure not to burn your mouth... speaking of cocktails, I noticed you haven't come back to me yet about the contract."

"Short answer, yes, but long answer is I want to go check out the site and make sure," I said. "If you give me another two to three weeks on it, I will come back to you with some changes."

He lifted an eyebrow at me. "Changes? I look forward to them then."

"Thanks, Dustin."

The rest of the night was fairly uneventful and painfully slow. The buzz from the cocktail was probably the most enthralling part of the night. We ended up closing the bar early at midnight, as there was only one person in. When I tallied up the tills, it still came in at the same nightly average. Must have been the early patrons that balanced the night out.

As I walked into my house, I realized I liked it better at Maverick's. I liked waking up to his lean body close to mine and listening to his light snore. I liked those little things he did, like making me a cup of coffee and running to Martha's and get me an egg and bacon muffin. I liked that he always left me with a kiss before he went anywhere and that he would send me cute texts through the day. Now all of that was in the past. I went to sleep with my heart a little heavier than yesterday.

The next morning I woke up with the sunrise of Edgewood. Its light was so potent that I couldn't help but wake up. I was up earlier than normal because of the earlier finish last night. I got up yawning hard and shuffled my bare feet to the coffee machine in the kitchen. As soon as I touched it, I thought of Maverick. I thought of how he made my belly ache in laughter and how we stayed up watching movies. It brought a sad smile to my face.

I poured the water in the top of the machine and waited until the coffee sifted through. My phone started ringing, and when I jogged to get it from the bedroom, I looked at the clock. It was 7:30 a.m. Who the hell was ringing me at that time?

When I saw who it was, I wanted to hang it up. *James.* I contemplated letting it ring out, but I overcame that feeling and answered the call. If it turned into the same broken record conversation, then I planned to hang up on him. I was feeling the rage burning through me, and I wanted to give him a piece of my mind.

"James. What do you want?" I didn't mean for it to sound that harsh, but it did.

"Wildcard is dead. He's dead, and now the money's gone. I was doing it for us, and I was going to come back to you with it, I swear." He sounded distressed and delusional.

"Doing it for us, what do you mean? I have a job and I sure as hell don't need you to go and get any funds for me. I didn't ask you for that. Wait. Did you say Wildcard is dead? How do you know that?"

Silence. After a few beats he spoke. "I heard from one of the Vipers. He was shot. I tried to go get my usual supply to sell, and they wouldn't give it to me. They told me that the operation was shut down," he cried.

"Too bad. Now you have to get a real job and stay in Edgewood. Now you have a court case for some dumb shit, and the guy you're supposed to be working for isn't even alive."

"Please. I made a mistake," he pleaded without a single fiber of sincerity in his voice.

"No. I'm not helping you. You need to tell Mom and Dad what you did. All the bullshit you've been lying about," I said. All of the hurt and pain of backing him all these months and trying to reason with him was surfacing now. I wanted revenge in a way, but I knew that wasn't the right thing. I wasn't going to let him just come back into my life after he'd shattered it and put me in danger.

"Okay. I'll tell them. I'm sorry about everything. What I did was fucked up, and I hope that you can forgive me."

"James, I have to go and get off the phone now because I can't deal with this conversation."

"Don't turn your back on me. I'm your little brother." He had some nerve saying that to me. I hung up the call as I heard the coffee machine ping. I jogged to the kitchen and placed my cup under the spout and let the coffee do its thing. I opened the fridge and became depressed when I looked at its contents. It was time to do some grocery shopping. I picked up the milk from the side door and smelled it, looking at the expiration date. Still good. I poured a little bit of it into my coffee and stirred in one spoonful of sugar, letting my teaspoon stir for too long as I daydreamed about Maverick and me traveling together. It would be fun to create adventures with him, not just hear about them from his past.

I realized I was daydreaming and put the spoon in the

sink and sat down on the couch with the sun shining on me. Life really wasn't that bad. I circled back to the conversation I'd just had with my brother. Wildcard was dead. A sense of relief washed over me. No more meth lab bullshit. No more James calling me to pick him up from weird places in the middle of the night. Wildcard's reign of terror on the town of Edgewood was apparently over. I wondered if it were true, and if he was dead, who had killed him. I was halfway through my coffee when the doorbell rang.

If it was James I was going to scream. I did not want to talk to him. Two quick knocks came at the door, and a frown came over my face. There was only one person who I knew would do something like that. Maverick. Butterflies kicked in my stomach and were buzzing. I gripped my coffee mug a little tighter because I didn't want to get my hopes up.

"Who is it?" I called out from behind the door.

"It's your friendly UPS courier. I have a package for you," Maverick called out in a kooky voice. His voice, damn it was so sexy to me. My back was against the door, and I slid down it a little as shivers of hope ran down my spine. *Yes.* I hadn't lost my chance after all. I turned around and opened the door.

Maverick was standing there with a brown paper bag with grease spots on it. I knew what was inside. An egg and bacon sandwich from Martha's. He was holding it one hand, and his face was searching mine with tenderness. "Steph, can I come in? I'm not UPS, but I do have a delivery for you." The sun was highlighting parts of his sandy blond hair, and his smoky gray eyes looked even more captivating than they normally were.

"Sure you can," I coaxed softly. "Come on in."

Maverick stepped into my house, and now things felt like they were truly meant to. He put the brown paper bag down on the counter, and we faced one another in this invisible forcefield. One that magnetized us together. He put his palms up as half of his face lifted to a smile. I put my palms to his and felt his warmth radiate through my hands.

"I missed you so much, Steph." I could tell from the way he said and swallowed the words back that he meant it, and that he had plenty more to say.

"I missed you too. I'm sorry that I said those things to you. I never wanted to break up with you," I gushed out as I felt myself being overwhelmed with emotion.

"I knew you didn't, but I wanted you to be sure. You seemed unsure when we were together and I get it, because of your past." Maverick dropped his eyes as he linked his fingers with mine, and we stood like that with hands clasped together.

"I wasn't unsure. I didn't know what it was to be treated right. I pushed you away, and I was scared for you, for me. I didn't mean to hurt you, and I don't want to be apart from you." I wanted him to know it wasn't all about the circumstance we were in. Some of it was my insecurities. My own fears were blocking me.

Maverick's knees bent, and his head dropped back in relief. "You have no idea what a relief it is to hear you say that."

I put my thumb on his chin and stroked over the stubble affectionately.

"I knew you were in trouble. I could feel it. I get why you did it, and that's why I'm here. We've got too good a thing happening between us. I couldn't just let you go like that. You have to trust me to protect you, though. I'm special ops baby. I'm going to be there if anything happens to you."

"I'm sorry I handled it badly." I leaned into him and kissed his lips gently.

"Mmm. Sweet like you. Missed those lips too. Come on, let's sit down."

He took my hand and led me over to the couch. I snuggled right into him, and he stroked my hair.

"I heard something, and I want to confirm if it's true," I asked.

"Go ahead, ask me anything," he said comfortably.

"I heard that Wildcard is dead. Is that true or false?"

Maverick's expression was plain as he blew out a defeated sigh. "It's completely true. He's dead, and he was killed by one of his own. We ambushed him and we were going to be the ones to put the nail in the coffin, but his own crew ran off with the fake money we supplied them. I told you that Wildcard was trying to extort us. I don't think we would have killed him, to be honest, and the guys were pretty sad about it. When he was at the club, a few of the guys took a liking to him. I think we would have just told him to beat it. I didn't like seeing him dead like I thought I might. The guy just had some misplaced hurt, and now he's dead because of it. Rest in peace, Wildcard."

"Wow. That sounds crazy. I can't believe it." I shook my head as I processed what he'd told me. I was glad that all the crap was over.

"Let's get back to you and me, though. Enough depressing talk," he said in his smooth voice. He reined me in, and I wrapped my arms around his waist and laid my head on his chest. I could hear his heart beating through the fabric of the shirt. I put a hand underneath it to feel his flesh. I was home with him, and there was no place I would rather be.

"Mmm, Steph, you don't know how good it feels to hold you in my arms. I love you so much," he confessed in a husky voice.

"Maverick. I love you too. I *really* love you. I want you to be with me when I open the cocktail bar. I want you to share in my life. I also love it that you bring me egg and bacon sandwiches on the regular. Can you keep that up, please?" I joked. I looked up at him, and he grinned.

"I got plenty of egg and bacon sandwiches that I'm going to bring to you over the years, but right now I think we have some catching up to do, Ms. Bar Owner."

"Did you say over the years?"

"I'm pretty sure I did say that, and I meant it."

Sometimes you get a second chance at love and you just have to take it...

# EPILOGUE

"I can't believe this is happening. I am finally doing this. I'm opening a cocktail bar. Little ole me opening up a bar. This is officially insane." Steph was freaking out a little as we stood inside the doors of her new cocktail lounge bar. She looked amazing in a black pantsuit with this cute little red bowtie and stilettos.

"Believe it, honey. You worked so hard on this. It's been your baby for the last six months. It's spectacular. Very chic, very rock, and all you. I love it, and I love you." I kissed her lightly. I knew she didn't want me smudging off her pink lips. She wiped the excess off my mouth.

It was a nice night in Edgewood, no wind. A Friday night that was perfect for the opening of a cocktail bar in the middle of Edgewood. I made it mandatory that every single Guardian and old lady had to be present at the club to support and have a drink. All of them were out in full support waiting to come in. Everyone was dressed to the nines, and it was exciting to see the family dressed up and with their ladies or single, didn't matter. They were all here and supporting my lady, which was what mattered the most to me. A red ribbon was running from end to end of the cocktail bar doors, and Steph was about to cut it. She had some large pretend scissors with her that she could barely hold. Dustin was here as the investor and looked sharp in a gray pinstripe suit with a black shirt. She turned to Dustin, who was present with his lovely wife, Cassandra.

"Dustin, I could not have done this without you. I can't wait to get this place packed out every Friday."

"What have I done? Now I have competing business. I suck." He grinned.

"No way. No competition. They come here first and get the sophisticated drinks and then I send them around to you for the cheap drinks and the hot bands," she said.

"See. That's why you deserve to run your own bar. Innovation. I'm proud of you, Steph. I'm just the conduit for your success. You helped me get No Name up to speed, and it's thriving thanks to you. I'm paying this shit forward," he said proudly.

"I'm so overwhelmed, look at all these people. I cannot believe it. I hope I have enough staff!" There was a line of eager people waiting to hear about the hottest new cocktail lounge in town. Young people and some older people, a real mix. Steph had a good following in the town, so I expected she would have a good turnout.

I whispered in her ear. "Breathe, baby, it's going to be fine. You have it under control. I'll serve drinks if need be. Could be fun," I said.

She squeezed my hand. "No you won't. You go float around and look handsome."

"Your wish is my command." I bowed, and she giggled.

She was in great spirits, and so was I. The local newspapers were present and were going to take some photos. She was waiting for them to get the right angles so she could cut the ribbon. The mayor was beside her as well, due to a few strings that Chloe pulled.

"Nice to meet you, Stephanie. Chloe has told me wonderful things about you, and I hope this is a successful venture for both you and the community." The mayor seemed like a mayor: conservative and a nice guy. I heard from Havoc that he gave him a hard time in the beginning, but now they got along pretty well. They worked on a lot of home improvement projects together.

"Thank you, Mayor. I'm so happy. This is like one of my wildest dreams to open a cocktail bar. I have lots of tasty drinks for everyone to sample tonight," she said.

"I like the sounds of that, Stephanie. Let's take a few photos, shall we?"

The photos went off, and Stephanie made a small speech. "I want to thank everyone for coming out tonight and taking the time to experience something different in Edgewood. This used to be a well-known cocktail bar back in the 1990s, and I guess it was waiting for the right owner. I want to bring back a little glamor to this town. It's gone through so much with the drug crisis and crime rates skyrocketing. We need someplace safe to go. A place where you can just kick back and sip a nice drink and feel pretty for a night. Well, this is Steph's Bar, and that's what we do here. We leave our troubles at the door. So come on inside, and let's have a ball!" Steph cut the ribbon and beckoned everyone in as the crowd clapped and hooped and hollered. I could see familiar faces from No Name, and it was good to see them supporting Stephanie.

"Great speech, Steph. You are special. You really are."

"Thanks for being the light in my life, Maverick. I love you."

"I love you too. Go mix and mingle with your guests. Do your thing."

I watched her radiantly lighting up the room. The cocktail bar was packed. Every corner and space was filled. Her staff were definitely being kept busy, and she was doing a great job at managing everything. I saw Mustang talking to Melissa, who worked for Steph now at the cocktail bar, and they were hitting it off. I moved through the crowd and chatted with the people I knew and some I didn't. The whole night was a huge success, and it couldn't have gone better. Steph moved in with me and rented out her house. There was nothing better than having her there. We were seamless together, and our love was easy—well, easier than it was at the start. Even her brother showed up. They'd had some rocky patches where they talked and Steph would become triggered by something he would say and they would fall out again. At this time, they were okay. I didn't warm to James immediately. It took me awhile, and I didn't trust him fully, but he was family to Steph, and so I had to respect that. He had a girl with him, which was nice to see. Maybe it would calm him down and stop him from being such a jerk to people.

*The next day at the clubhouse...*

"The tape got out. Wildcard must have given it to one of the Vipers or something. It's surfaced and now the sheriff is out front asking us to come down to the station. We got problems," Hawk said to Axle in the lunchroom as he put his hands over his head.

Axle didn't look one bit disturbed by the news. "He won't convict us. You know why?"

"Why Axle? Tell me why," Hawk asked as he walked up and down the lunchroom. He looked like he was going to explode at any minute.

"Sheriff Malone doesn't like domestic violence. It's his pet peeve. His wife came out of an abusive relationship."

"There's video footage of Axle, did I mention that? How did the tape only come out now?" Hawk asked. He was making me dizzy from his stalking back and forth.

"You're going to wear a hole out in the carpet. Wildcard Willy is dead, so someone would have access to his stuff obviously. Somebody knew to leak it to the police. It must be someone who knew of Wildcard Willy's plans," I said.

"Doesn't matter who. It matters that someone has the tape," Hawk said anxiously.

"Chill out, Hawk," Axle said in a droll tone. "It will blow over."

Hawk was pissed, and I tried to grab him, but he shoved my hand off and walked outside.

"Let him go, Maverick. He'll cool off. He's like that sometimes. Gets hot under his collar. We won't get convicted. You have a crew that is directly responsible for taking out the meth lab trash in this city. Sheriff Malone values that type of loyalty. He will ignore the tape. Nobody is missing Clint expect his parents."

"I guess that's what brought awareness to the case in the first place." I knew a few more reasons Hawk was a little testy. He'd only told me and no one else yet. He planned to ask for Tara's hand in marriage, and this coming up would block or overshadow his proposal if the verdict didn't fall the right way.

"Arghh. Who cares? He was a bitch. He's gone now. Ashes to ashes and all that," Axle stated coldly.

I scoffed at Axle's cold edge. "I see you've got your sword back."

"What do you mean my sword?"

"I mean your edge. You're back to being the enforcer. Zena made you soften up a little, big guy."

"She did, and I'm still soft for her and Bell. Just not others."

On cue, Bell walked in with Brody, Rosemary, Dara, and Tara. "Ah! All the ladies in the house. Haven't seen all of you beauties here for a long time. And to what do we owe the pleasure of this visit?"

Dara with her feistiness spoke first. "No reason in particular. We did want to come down and support. We heard that the sheriff is back on you about Clint." I saw Tara's eyes flicker when the girls said his name.

"Nope. Sheriff Malone would be wise to let that one go," I said.

"He should. He doesn't like DV cases, I know for a fact. He was so helpful with mine I don't see him taking it further."

"Agreed. How are you? How is the salon?" I asked. Dara started to smile and giggle a lot and look back at the girls.

"What is it? Why are you being so coy about things?"

"Maverick," Dara said as she bit her lip, and I knew.

"I swear there is something magical in Edgewood water. You're pregnant, aren't you?"

"Yes," she squealed. "Four and a half months today."

I looked at her, flabbergasted. "But where is it? I can't see anything. You look exactly the same!" I got up off my stool and picked her up in a hug. "So happy for you and Shaggy."

"That bump is there, trust me. Now I have to get bigger pants to fit into, and it's a real bummer. I'm in that transition phase. I wish the basketball would pop out already so I don't feel so frumpy with it." I looked a little harder at her and saw the outline curve of something growing in the belly, but nothing that let me know she was pregnant.

Axle congratulated her next and swept her up in a hug. "Welcome to the club of sleepless nights, dirty diapers, distress, happiness, joy, and limited sex. I will pray for you."

"I don't quite know what to say to that. Thank you?"

"You're welcome. You have a support network here, and you'll do fine," Axle assured her.

"Limited sex? Really babe? Come on, that's not my fault." Bell had no shame in her game as the ladies laughed at Axle. She put her hands out with a *What?* face as I shook my head at her. Axle shook his head too and pointed at Bell.

"See what I have to put up with?"

"Don't you say a word, Maverick!" Bell yelled.

"I won't. This has nothing to do with me, and I plead the fifth." I grinned, and Axle sliced a grin back at me.

"Maverick, where's your bro code ethics? That hurts. You threw me under the bus then. I would have had your back."

"I can't. It's Bell. What do you want me to do? She kicked your ass, remember?"

Bell snickered behind her hand. That was an incident that Axle would never live down. "Why does everyone keep bringing that up? I was in shock, okay?"

"I bet you were, Axle," Bell said as she wiggled her eyebrows at him and blew him a kiss. Axle blew one back at her.

"Maverick, you are not my guy anymore. I expected better from you."

"I'm still here for you, big guy." We goofed with the ladies a little more, and they left. I took a walk to the chop shop and saw Shadow in the back, unpacking stock.

"Hey Shadow. How are you, buddy? I heard you got another show coming up soon?"

"Uh-huh, I do. I can't wait for it. I've been creating a lot lately."

"Good to hear. I love your work. Do you ever get tired of what you're doing here?" Shadow was like clockwork. He was always on time, he knew where every single tool was and who needed what. He had access to the gun warehouses and the safes and was responsible for the alarm systems of the building.

"I was before, but now that I'm running the studio and with the family, I don't mind it being boring. It's balanced things out for me. Ava is thinking of entering a few photography competitions. Her work has been amazing of late."

"You two are such a good match. It's incredible."

"It is. I can't believe myself sometimes. I'm a content man. You should come over with Stephanie for dinner. We can hang out. I know how long you waited to get Stephanie, and now look at you two living together. How is that going for you?"

"We were rocky at first with all the stuff going on around us, but now we are so good. I love it, and I love her."

"It's good, isn't it?"

"Sure is. I like where we're headed. She's all I need."

"You sound like you're ready to put a ring on it. Are you close to that or not rushing?" Shadow inquired.

Steph and I had talked about it. We both knew it was coming and it was hard to make a judgment call like that with absolutes, but to me, I could. Stephanie was the one.

"We've spoken about it and we're still feeling our way through and it's good. Just taking our time with it."

"Hmm, good thing to do. No need to rush. Slow and steady wins the race," Shadow said. He was a classy guy, and

I admired him a hell of a lot. I wanted to ask him about the club and the direction of it. I felt like he would be in the know.

"What do you know about the expansion of the club?"

"I hope they do it. We've done pretty well financially in the last few years, and the club is in a great position. We have the means to expand. I know Scout is on the lookout for a new location too."

"Maybe we should try Santa Fe out? What do you think? Any clubs that you know about over there?"

"I don't know much about Santa Fe, but Shaggy and Dara do. They're both originally from there. I think it could work. It is just what type of work we would do as a club, and if it would be in demand."

"It will be interesting to see what direction Pop wants to take the club in."

"Why? Are you interested in opening a new chapter? If you are, you should talk to Pop."

"Nah. I wouldn't leave. I just got here, and me and my good lady are established. I'm just talking out loud, I guess."

Shadow nodded. "Good to talk out loud sometimes."

"All right, Shadow, I'm going to love you and leave you. I got somewhere I gotta be now."

"Okay, Maverick. Take it easy, and I'll see you soon for dinner. I'm going to hold you to it, brother."

"Please do, Shadow, and give Ava a kiss for me."

"I will."

I headed out and straddled my bike, bound for the Bluewater Complex. I pulled up another ten minutes later and took the elevator to apartment 10C.

Justin and Big Mike opened the door. Big Mike saw me and put his little arms up to the sky.

"Oh my gosh! You're here. You came back to see us. We

missed you." Big Mike was the cutest thing I had ever seen. I wanted to make sure the boys were okay and Grandma. I found out from a call I made to the sheriff that Grandma had agreed to foster the boys until they could be housed together in a good home.

"Yeah I sure did, buddy! I told you I would come and see you. I always keep my promises."

Justin, who was a little more skeptical, stood with one arm hanging down and gripped with his other hand. "Hi. You're here. You should come in."

"Thanks, I appreciate it. I will."

Grandma was sitting in her chair and rocking back and forth. She was clacking two knitting needles together and humming to herself. On her coffee table was two glasses of milk and one half eaten oatmeal cookie.

I held out my hand to her. "Hi, I'm Maverick and I was involved in the mission with you. I wanted to come and check on you and the boys to see that you're okay."

"My name is Bernadine. We are doing just fine." She pressed her lips together and set down her knitting project. She seemed to be a little on the frosty side, and I couldn't tell if that was her demeanor or if she was mad because we'd picked her up for distributing meth to customers. Granted she probably didn't know what she was doing, she was still committing a crime.

"Nice to meet you, Bernadine. I'm sorry we had to meet the way we did. I heard that the sheriff dropped all the charges on you," I said.

"Of course he did. I had no idea that I was selling an illegal substance."

I believed her.

"Hey mister, do you want something to drink?" Justin asked.

"Ah how about a glass of water? It's hot outside. And I wouldn't mind one of these cookies."

"Justin, look inside the cookie tin up there, and you'll find more oatmeal cookies," Bernadine directed.

"Okay." Big Mike was making airplane noises with his toy and running around the apartment, Grandma didn't seem too fazed at all. Justin arrived back with a glass of water and a dish of cookies. I took one and bit into the moist goodness, closing my eyes.

Grandma picked up her knitting again and smiled. "You like them? I bake every Sunday."

"These are amazing. I'm coming here every Sunday if that's the case."

I know she called herself Bernadine, but I called her Grandma. "You would be most welcome. The boys are thriving here. I don't have to tell them too much to do, and they're well behaved. I'm happy to have them and for the company too." Her face was cast over with a wistful smile.

"I'm glad it worked out for all of you."

"Sure did, and if it wasn't for you and all your other friends I wouldn't have Justin and Big Mike with me. Thank you. I was getting rather lonely in this apartment." There was a sadness in her eyes as she spoke.

"Bernadine, any children for you?"

"Yes, one son, but he was killed in a fire eight years ago. He was a firefighter," she said as her eyes glazed over. I knew firsthand you never got over something like that; you just learned to cope with it.

"I'm sorry for your loss. I know what it's like to lose a loved one, but it looks like you have two new loved ones."

"Yes. It does." She went back to humming, and I ate my cookie and left. I hugged the boys and wished them well. Sometimes life has a funny way of working out just right.

Overall, the Guardians were doing pretty well, but Havoc, Shaggy, Mustang, Hawk, and Axle did get called down to the station. They were questioned for a couple of hours, and I thought for sure the club would have to lawyer up, but something changed...

Sheriff Malone said the tape was too scrambled and that he couldn't make out the figures in the video. Axle had been right about the sheriff after all. He let every single one of the Guardians go.

Life was moving forward for every single one of us in the dusty town of Edgewood. I never knew I could thrive in a place like this, but I was, and I loved it.

## BOOK 3: *Mustang*

*Always been a wild one, but maybe it's time to lay down roots...*
They call me Mustang. I'm the wild free-roaming special ops guy coming to save the day.

I got a bad history with women, so when Melissa shows up with her honeycomb locks and endless sparkle, I almost don't know if it's true.

With the missions dying down, it's time for the Guardians to expand into new territory.

Problem is there's an enemy that doesn't want that to happen, and they're threatening my girl.

She's looking for adventure, but she doesn't know what she's in for.

She doesn't know the demons I carry from the past and who will make her a target just for being with me.

*Will Mustang's new enemy get between him and his girl?*
*Will the Guardians be able to withstand the heat and start afresh in a new town?*

**CLICK HERE to buy now**

## LEAVE A REVIEW

Like this book?
Tap here to leave a review now!

Join Hope's newsletter to stay updated with new releases, get access to exclusive bonus content and much more!

Tap here to see all of Hope's books.

Join all the fun in Hope Stone's Readers Group on Facebook.

# ABOUT THE AUTHOR

Hope Stone is an Amazon #1 bestselling author and Top 100 Kindle Select Allstar who loves writing steamy action packed, emotion-filled stories with twists and turns that keep readers guessing. Hope's books revolve around alpha men who love protecting their sexy and sassy heroines.

To keep up with her busy release schedule join Hope Stone's Facebook Readers Group:

**Learn more about all my books here.**

**MAVERICK: A GRITTY MC ROMANCE SERIES**
Book 2 in the Guardians Of Mayhem Series 2
By Hope Stone

living or dead, or places, events or locations is purely coincidental.

*Before You Go*

Please consider leaving an honest review.

Milton Keynes UK
Ingram Content Group UK Ltd.
UKHW020945280823
427620UK00017B/988

9 798223 643197